I0610211

BEYOND THE DARKNESS

THE SHADOW DEMONS SAGA, BOOK 9

SARRA CANNON

DEAD RIVER BOOKS

Copyright © 2018 by Sarra Cannon

All rights reserved.

No part of this book may be reproduced in any form or by any electronic or mechanical means, including information storage and retrieval systems, without written permission from the author, except for the use of brief quotations in a book review.

Cover by Ravven

Get new release updates and exclusive content when you sign up for my mailing list.

❀ Created with Vellum

For Kimberly
I am so blessed to have you for a cousin and so grateful to have
you as a friend. Thank you for always being there for me. I
love you.

INTO THE PAST

HARPER

Atower of flames consumed the building across the street. Smoke billowed through the air around me like dark clouds descending through the darkness.

I clutched the large emerald stone in my hand and stared at the chaos, my heart racing. Breaking.

This couldn't really be happening.

I'd managed to wake myself up from a nightmare only to find myself in a brand new one, even more hopeless than the last.

I didn't want to believe it could be true. I wanted to close my eyes and wake up at Jackson's side, his hand on mine, reassuring me that it was all just one long, terrible dream.

But I knew this was no dream.

It wasn't enough that the emerald priestess had taken me from my friends and repeatedly tried to wipe my memories. It wasn't enough that she'd spent months trying to brainwash me and turn me to her side.

No, she'd also dragged me into the past, the one place no one would ever think to look for me.

The one place where I would be trapped with no hope of escape.

Priestess Evers was the one person with the power to take me home to my family, and I had killed her with my own bare hands.

My heart broke all over again, realizing just how far away I was from the people I loved most.

I stood and took a deep breath, pushing my fear and heartache deep down into my stomach.

I had to figure out how to fix this mess, and I wasn't going to do it by standing on some old lady's front porch with my mouth hanging open.

The first of the firetrucks had already arrived, but the fire still blazed out of control. More sirens wailed in the distance, drawing closer with every passing moment.

The front lawn of the Evers Institute for Troubled Girls was covered in young patients, their white nightgowns billowing around them like ghosts.

These girls were my responsibility now. Just like me, they were all witches who had been stolen from their lives and brought here to the past where they could be held prisoner until the priestess and her daughter, Dr. Evers, were able to turn them into allies or zombies.

As soon as the chaos of the moment died down, the police would start asking questions. Questions I'd better have answers to.

I had to think.

I shook my head, as if shaking off the realization of truth that still held me in its grasp. From the look of the cars, the old television inside the couple's home, and the fact that lobotomies were being performed here without question, I could only guess that we were trapped somewhere in the forties or early fifties.

I had no idea what policies existed back then for girls like us who'd been committed to private institutions, but I couldn't just sit back and let the police handle this. What would they do with all of us once they realized we had no family or home to go back to? No real identity here in this place?

I had to think of something fast.

There was no way to save those who had already been lobotomized or killed, but right now, there was still hope for the eighty or so girls who stood on that lawn. Most of them had no memory of who they truly were, but I was living proof that those memories were not lost forever. They were simply hidden deep inside them.

I took a deep breath, forcing my mind to focus. I had to come up with a plan. I was running out of time, and if I made any mistakes, I could put everyone here in danger of being locked away forever.

Whatever records Dr. Evers had on all of us girls, they were currently turning to ash inside that building. There wouldn't be computers or digital records of any kind this far in the past, so unless she'd had backup files stored somewhere in the priestess's home, there would be no way for me to know who all these girls were or where they truly belonged.

I needed to buy us all some time.

As the first police car rounded the corner, I did the only thing I could think of that might help. I ran down the steps of the couple's home and ducked into the shadows between their house and the one Priestess Evers had called home.

I closed my eyes and pictured the face of the doctor who had told me so many lies and tried to convince me that I'd lost my mind and murdered my own family in a fire just like this one. I took a deep breath and planted my feet firmly on the ground, pushing aside the panic and fatigue that threatened to destroy my focus.

I tapped into the well of power deep inside my core and pulled energy from the earth around me.

My body changed as the power flowed through me. My dress transformed from a loose white nightgown into a pencil skirt and white blouse, Dr. Evers's typical daily uniform. My hair arranged itself into a perfect bun pulled tightly against my head. Even the glasses were perfect, though a glamour this complex would be tough to maintain.

I straightened my shoulders and opened my eyes, nervous as hell, but determined to find a way to make this work.

I quickly hid the emerald stone under the shrubbery beside the priestess's house, whispering a quick shielding spell so that no one would be able to feel its power or see the stone without knowing where to look. Then, I made my way across the street to the cluster of patients and nurses who had survived the fire.

They were all being arranged into straight lines at the edge of the property, out of the way of the fireman who rushed to save what was left of the institute.

Two more police cars arrived on the scene, sirens blaring as all the nearby residents opened their doors and poured into the street to see what was going on.

My heels clicked against the pavement as I started toward the patients who stood just outside the gate of the Evers Institute.

Before I got five steps away, though, a hand clasped my wrist and spun me around.

A cop who appeared to be in his mid-forties met my eyes and yanked me closer. He wore a wrinkled brown suit instead of a police uniform, and judging by the way he gripped my arm, he obviously knew who I was.

Or at least the woman I pretended to be.

I jerked my wrist away and lifted my chin.

"Excuse me, Detective, I need to check on my patients."

"Monica," he said, moving to block me with his bulky frame. "What the hell is going on here?"

I blinked, not understanding the question. He could obviously see the building was on fire. What exactly was he confused about? And just how well did he know Monica Evers?

She hadn't seemed like the type of woman who was on a first-name basis with very many people.

When I didn't answer, he took my wrist again and pulled me further from the group of officers who had gathered there in the street.

"What happened?" he asked in a tense whisper. "Why is this happening now?"

I shook my head, trying all at once to figure out just how much this man knew about the Evers family and what I should say in response.

"Is this really the right time to be talking to me about this?" I asked, mimicking the harsh tone Dr. Evers often got when I wasn't cooperating with her. "We can talk after we've figured out what's happening to the girls and if they're safe."

His eyebrows scrunched together, and he shook his head. "That's exactly why we need to talk about this now," he said.

"Since when have you cared about their safety? And why are they even still alive? Why did you change the plan?"

"The plan?" I asked.

His questions chilled me to the core. What kind of plan did this cop have with Dr. Evers and her mother? Had they planned to kill us all?

"It's too early," he said, running a hand through his dark blond hair. "You're three months early, and the girls have never survived. What the hell am I supposed to do with them all? Where's your mother? We need to figure this out or there are going to be questions."

Three months early? I shook my head. What the hell was he talking about?

I was obviously several steps behind him, but asking questions would only prove I wasn't really Monica Evers. Instead, I decided to take charge, really dedicating myself to this role I had stepped into.

"How dare you question me," I said, narrowing my eyes at him. "Don't ever pull me aside and question my decisions again. I'll let you in on my plan if and when I feel it's appropriate. If you'll excuse me, I have to see to my patients and clean up this mess."

"Monica," he said, stepping in front of me again before I could walk away. "I'm sorry to question you, but I need to know what's going on. How many times have we done this together? Five times? Six? Not once have the two of you made a move like this and not told me about it. Does this mean I can finally go home?"

Six times?

My mouth went so dry, I couldn't force myself to swallow.

I turned to stare at the burning building, chills running along my arms despite the heat coming off the flames.

You're three months early, and the girls have never survived.

His words echoed in my head.

I wanted to sit down.

I kind of wanted to throw up.

There was this ringing in my ears, and my vision blurred. I stumbled backward, but the cop quickly put his arm around my shoulders to steady me.

"I'm fine," I said, pulling away. I didn't want him touching me.

I stepped back to take it all in, catching my first glimpse of a horrifying cycle that must have replayed itself over and over. The girls dressed all in white. The flames rising into the night sky. The detective. A priestess who had the power to manipulate time.

I brought a trembling hand to my lips.

They've done this before.

HER DARK PURPOSES

JACKSON

I stood on the steps of the abandoned Victorian and stared at the ruined hospital across the street.

"What do we do now?" Rend asked. He ran a hand through his thick, dark hair and shrugged. "I'm sorry, man. I really thought this was it."

"Me, too," I said, doing my best to ignore the tightening in my chest.

I'd thought we were coming here to rescue Harper from the emerald priestess. I'd thought we'd finally found her after all this time.

Hell, I had practically felt her in my arms as we passed through the door to the emerald priestess's house.

But she wasn't here. Not now, anyway.

I looked back at the old house. It was apparent from its current condition that no one had lived here for decades. Probably not since the fifties when the hospital burned down.

That meant this house had been a decoy. A sham she'd set

up so that she could run the institute in secret for all those years, torturing innocent witches and trying to turn their minds to her dark purposes.

Staring at it now, I almost felt as though we were right back where we started.

Almost.

I clutched the wooden box in my hands and stared down at the simple H carved into its surface.

More than sixty years ago, Harper must have put this box together and buried it where she knew I would find it tonight. She said to set them free and then come find her, but all I could think about was getting her back.

"What are we waiting for?" Mary Anne asked, pacing back and forth on the porch behind me. "We have a small army here right now. We could go straight to Cypress and release the witches and demons tied to that gate before the Order knows what hit them."

"It's true," Mordecai said. He stepped forward, his long black dreads swinging near his face. "The longer we wait, the more time we give them to gather their forces against us. Remember the sapphire gates? By the time we'd released two or three of them, we had a battle at every single one after that."

Everyone was talking all at once, and my head was spinning with possibilities. In Harper's absence, they were all looking to me as a leader, but we needed more time to put together a plan.

"We have an advantage right now that we didn't have with the sapphire gates," I said. "That buys us some time."

"What?" Rend asked.

I smiled. "We have a dungeon full of emerald gate Primas and their daughters," I said. "We hold the lives of their entire covens in our hands. They won't be able to fight against us with that kind of power. I'm just as anxious as all of you to get started releasing these gates, but I want to go in with a plan. We need to get our core group together at the castle tonight to talk it through. Besides, the ritual only works at three in the afternoon. We've got time."

Mordecai shook his head. "This is a mistake, Jackson," he said. "You know I got your back no matter what, but I think we need to move on this now. Most of the Order probably doesn't even realize another priestess is dead yet."

"We have no idea what the Order knows," I said. "None of us have any experience with time travel. If Harper killed Priestess Evers, she did it back in 1951, and she burned this building down in the process. We have no idea what kind of repercussions that has. It's possible she's drastically changed the timeline, and we don't have enough information about how that changes everything related to it. We have a small window of time here to get this right, and if we make the wrong move, we could put everyone, including Harper, in danger."

"Small being the operative word," Mary Anne said. "If we wait too long to make a move, Mordecai is right. The Order will have an army of witches waiting for us at every single gate we try to free. You know as well as I do that the Order would gladly sacrifice a coven of its own members to protect the overall group. If you want to go back to the castle to talk this through, let's do it now. Who do we need to call together?"

She pulled a small handful of rubies from her pocket. Communication stones. We all used them to talk to each other across long distances and dimensions. Cell phones didn't tend to work in the Shadow World.

"Harper's Sister, Angela, should already be there. Gregory,

too. We'll need to talk to Eloise from Cypress since she's the Prima of an emerald gate and likely to be our first target," I said. "Franki and Rend, of course we want you both there. Mordecai, you should be there but tell Joost and the others to hang back. If we're going to have a productive conversation, we need to keep it somewhat small."

"I'll reach out to Eloise," Mary Anne said. "And I'll let Gregory and Angela know we're on our way and to prepare the war room for us."

"Sounds good," I said. "You guys head back, and I'll meet you there as soon as I can."

"What are you going to do?" Mary Anne asked.

"There are a few things I think we should take care of here before we leave," I said.

Joost and Eric had agreed to stay behind and manage the search of the two properties. Cristo had decided to explore this small Ohio town just to make sure there wasn't a portal or gate here we didn't know about.

They got to work, assigning people to different wings of the hospital and areas of the abandoned house.

"What do I do if the cops show up?" Joost asked. "I have a feeling someone in the neighborhood is going to notice that a bunch of people are searching the old hospital. It's a condemned property."

"Get a few of the more powerful witches together and have them put a glamour on the hospital so that no light shows through the windows. Make it look like no one's here and everything's normal," I said.

"What if someone already saw us out here on the lawn?" he asked, looking around.

I smiled and clapped him on the shoulder. "You're creative. Figure it out."

He laughed and nodded. "Got it. Meet you back at the Southern Kingdom?"

"As soon as the search is over," I said. "Thanks, Joost."

"No problem, man," he said. "I'm sorry we didn't find Harper."

Again, my heart tightened in my chest, and I had to force back the anger and frustration that threatened to take over my emotions. I had to focus on the task at hand, or I was going to lose my mind.

"We're going to find her," I said. "It's just going to take a little more time than we thought."

Joost nodded again. "I'll see you soon," he said.

He hurried off to help direct people to put up a glamour around the hospital and the house. I watched, so grateful for all of the demons and free witches who had been willing to risk their lives to help us here tonight.

I glanced at the condemned hospital one last time, understanding that Harper could be standing in this exact location at this very moment, locked somewhere in the past. She had faced unimaginable horror, but she had fought until the end, overcoming impossible odds to defeat another priestess.

I pulled a worn and faded piece of paper from my pocket and ran my thumb along the drawing. That was still us sitting there in the garden of the castle, watching our son play among the roses. I had seen this future for us, and I still had to believe that whatever trials we faced along the way, we would both survive long enough to see this vision become a reality.

Harper was the strongest, bravest person I knew, and I had to trust that she would be okay.

For her, I would hold on.

For her, I would see this through and find a way to free the witches and demons bound to the emerald gates.

And then, when it was done, I would move heaven and earth to get her back.

WILL THEY REMEMBER?

HARPER

My knees were made of jelly as I walked away from the detective.

This was a new piece of information I hadn't been expecting. And I had never dreamed Priestess Evers would have humans in on her plans here. Or was he human? I dared a glance back at the detective.

How would I be able to tell? I didn't feel demon power coming from him, but that didn't mean he had no powers at all. There were still a lot of things I didn't understand about the hidden world.

But I couldn't worry about him right now. I'd have to deal with him later. Right now, it was taking everything I had just to hold onto this glamour. My power was weak, and I was already feeling sick to my stomach from pushing myself to the limit.

I reached deeper, searching for the well of power within and strengthening my connection to it. I could do this. I had to find a way.

I took a deep breath and stepped forward just as a woman in a white nurse's uniform rushed toward me. I glanced at her and did a double-take as I saw that it was Nurse Melody.

Tears pushed at the corners of my eyes. It couldn't be Nurse Melody. I had watched her die in the surgical room in the basement. She had sacrificed herself to protect me.

At first, I couldn't understand what was happening, but then she grabbed my hand and met my eyes.

"Harper?" she asked in a whisper. "It's me. Brooke."

My shoulders relaxed, and the sadness and exhaustion that lay just under the surface threatened to take over. I was so ready for this day to be over.

"What are we going to do?" I asked. "This is madness."

"I've spoken to the girls who helped us tonight," she said, glancing around to make sure no one was close enough to hear our conversation. "There are only a handful who know the truth about this place and who they really are, but they're going to keep quiet until we figure out a plan. There are just so many of them. I don't know what to do. How are we going to keep them all together?"

"I don't think that's going to be an option," I said. "There won't be enough room for everyone in the house, and even if there was, I doubt the police would let us just take them home. As far as they know, these girls are patients who need medications and constant supervision."

"So, they're going to take them?" she asked. "But where? To the hospital?"

"I'm not sure, but we'll figure this out," I said. "For tonight, I think we have to go along with whatever the police want to do. Once we find a way back home, we'll come back for the girls."

Brooke looked at me, tears shining in her eyes. "I thought that once we escaped, we could just go home, you know? Just walk out and go back to where we came from, but that's not going to happen, is it?"

I shook my head and grabbed her hand. "It's not going to be that easy, but we're going to find a way to get back, Brooke. I swear it," I said. "Let's just get through tonight, and once we've got everyone settled, we'll figure out what we're going to do next."

She nodded and squeezed my hand.

"What year do you think it is?" she asked in a whisper.

"I'm not sure. Late forties?" I said, shaking my head and looking around. "But it makes a lot of sense. It explains the nurse's uniforms. Why no one questioned the tactics being used here. Why there were no sprinkler systems installed or fire alarms in the building. Why the rec room only had old records. I just never put it all together until it was too late."

"I never dreamed any witch could be powerful enough to do something like this," Brooke said. "Do you think she was opening a portal to bring us all here? Do you think it could still be open somewhere?"

"Maybe," I said. "But now that she's dead, I can't imagine it will stay open for very much longer if there is one. We have a lot of work to do, but we need to make sure to hold onto these glamours until we can get back to the house later tonight."

Brooke nodded and wrapped her arms tight around her body. We were in this together, but I could tell from the look in her eyes that she was every bit as scared as I was right now.

I needed to tell her what the detective had said to me, but there were so many people around, I didn't want to risk being overheard. The fire department was finally getting the fire under control, and further down the street, a few large vans had arrived.

"Come on, let's go figure out where they plan to take these girls," I said. "We need to make them think that we'll be contacting their parents, who will be coming to claim them soon."

Brooke followed me over toward where the nurses and paramedics were checking over the girls to make sure there were no major injuries.

"Dr. Evers," one of the nurses said, rushing up to meet me. "Where is your mother? I haven't seen her."

"I'm not sure," I said, glancing toward the building where I knew she had died. "Tell me about the patients. Is everyone accounted for? Is anyone hurt?"

The nurse shifted her weight nervously. "We have two missing patients," she said. "Brooke and Harper. And three of our nurses are missing, too. You don't think they're still inside, do you?"

I touched her arm, and her eyes widened. "I hope they aren't inside, but right now, we need to be grateful that we got as many out as we did," I said.

"Of course, Doctor," she said. She stepped closer and lowered her voice. "There is an official here from the hospital who's been asking questions. He wants to know all the details about our patients. He wants a list of their names and medications so that they can continue to be treated once they're taken to the hospital. What do I tell him? I don't know how to explain the medications. What will happen if the girls don't get their pills for a few days? Will they..."

Her voice drifted off and she glanced around, but I knew what she was trying to ask.

Will they remember?

I could only hope the answer was yes, but I didn't know what would happen. The nurse was right, though, it would be difficult to explain the types of medications these girls had been taking every day for as long as they'd been here. I was just glad they would no longer be filled with that poison.

"All of these patients should have received their nightly dose just a few hours ago," I said. "That should last at least a few days until I can make other arrangements. Make a list of the patients' names for now to give to the official. Let him know that most of the girls were on nothing more than the occasional mild sedative to help them sleep."

"But what if some of them do remember?" she asked, panic in her expression. "We could be arrested. They'll—"

"Stop," I said in a strong voice. "You need to keep yourself together. As far as these officials know, these girls have been brought to this institution because they are mentally unstable. Anything they say will sound insane. No one would ever believe them. You need to stay calm."

She nodded furiously. "Yes, Doctor. I'm sorry."

"Now, get to work on that list, and please make a second list for me. Make sure you know where every girl is being taken," I said.

She lowered her head and rushed away. It was obvious the nurse was afraid of Dr. Evers, which wasn't a surprise. The woman was sadistic, and I had no doubt these nurses were punished if they refused to go along with the torture they were asked to perform here.

The nurse would do as I asked, which meant I would at least have a list of names by the end of the evening that would help me find these girls later.

Exhaustion threatened to pull me under, but I pushed harder, holding onto the glamour for as long as I could. I walked over to the girls and reassured them that everything was going to be okay.

Some of the eyes that sought me out were my new friends. Mary Ellen, Robin, Nora. These girls knew the truth. They knew about magic, and even though I wasn't sure they completely remembered their own powers, I knew they would be my allies in the coming days. Still, there was no way to keep them here with me.

When I had a moment, I pulled those three girls to the side.

"They're going to take you to a nearby hospital," I said. "There's nothing I can do to stop that, but I am going to find a way to get us home. When I do, I'm going to come back for you."

"I don't understand what's happening," Mary Ellen said. "What you did down there in the basement and the other day with the birds. Was that magic? How did you do that?"

I took her hand and squeezed it. "Yes, it was magic. You have the same power inside of you," I said. "Remember how they always told you that you were special?"

She nodded, pushing her hair out of her face in a way that reminded me of Courtney, but her eyes could have been Mary Anne's eyes staring back at me. I swallowed the lump of sadness that formed in my throat.

I missed my friends more than I could ever say.

"You are special, Mary Ellen," I said, giving her a small smile. "Back home where I come from, I have a very good friend who is part of your family. Someday soon, I'm going to introduce you to her, and she's going to show you all the amazing things you can do with your magic."

Mary Ellen smiled back at me, and even though she was afraid, I could tell she trusted me.

"When you get to the hospital, I need you all to keep an eye on the other patients and the nurses," I said. "If anything unexpected happens like someone shows up to take you all away, I need you to find a way to escape and get back here to tell me what's going on. Keep quiet about what you know, but keep your eyes open."

They all nodded, and I knew their lives were now in my hands.

Somehow, I needed to find a way home. For all of us.

THE RITUAL ITEMS

JACKSON

My closest group of friends and allies gathered in the war room of the castle in the Southern Kingdom. In total, there were nine of us here so far.

Mary Anne and Essex sat to my right at the long table. Franki and Rend were beside them. Gregory, the head of the guards here in the domed city, sat directly across from me at the other end of the table.

Angela, Harper's half-sister and the current ruler of the Southern Kingdom in Harper's absence, sat beside Gregory. Then, there was Mordecai, one of Lea's best friends. My sister Illana came next, and beside her, there was an empty chair waiting for Eloise, the Prima of the emerald gate at Cypress.

I set the wooden box on the table in front of me.

Everyone grew quiet, their eyes locked on the box as I withdrew the ritual items Harper had left for us inside.

A dagger. A chalice. A necklace. A ring.

And finally, the large master stone that had once been Priestess Evers' heart.

No one said a word, but I knew what they were all thinking. How soon could we start?

Closing the sapphire gates after the death of Priestess Winter had taken us months. It was a bloody war, and we'd lost a lot of great humans and demons along the way.

We had an advantage right now since we had a dungeon full of emerald coven Primas, but it was still only a matter of time before the other priestesses of the Order realized what we were planning to do. They would no doubt send their armies of witches to make sure we didn't close these gates and free the demons bound to them.

We needed to act fast, but something about this still didn't feel right.

It felt too easy.

"What exactly happened at the emerald priestess's house?" Angela asked, interrupting the silence. She hadn't been able to go with us since she'd been acting as queen in the Southern Kingdom ever since Harper had been taken from us. "Where is she?"

"I think we should wait for Eloise to arrive," I said.

As if on cue, the door to the room burst open and Eloise and her two daughters, Caroline and Meredith, rushed into the room.

"We're here," Eloise said, out of breath. "I'm sorry we're late, but we had trouble getting away from the keepers. They're watching the house so closely, and they've put a block on our demon door. We had to sneak out and travel through a friend's door."

"Were you followed?" Gregory asked, his shoulders tensing.

"I don't think we were followed," she said, taking the empty seat to my left beside Illana. "We were careful."

Caroline and Meredith stood behind their mother, and even though I hadn't expected them to be here, this discussion involved them as much as any of us.

"If everyone is here, let's get started," Angela said. "I want to know what happened to Harper. I thought she'd be coming home with you."

"Yes, this is everyone," I said, but sadness washed over me as I thought of the people who should have been here for a moment like this.

Harper. Lea. Aerden. Zara. Courtney. They all deserved to be here.

"I've sent word to Andros," I said. "He couldn't get away on such short notice, but he's going to meet me here later. He said he had news of his own, so I'll speak with him when he gets here. For now, though, I've called you all here so we can make a decision about what we're going to do with these items."

I motioned toward the emerald ritual items on the table.

"The emerald priestess is dead, and Harper is alive," I said, looking at Angela. "But we didn't find her. Not exactly."

I explained what we had found when we'd gone through the door to the emerald priestess's house. The abandoned mansion. The burned mental hospital. The white rose growing next to the hospital's entrance.

"I knew it couldn't be a coincidence that a white rose would just happen to be growing there, so I dug in that location, and I found this box," I said, tapping my finger on the wood. "It's from Harper."

"I don't understand," Angela said. "Why wouldn't she have just given it to you herself?"

"She left it there for us sometime after that building burned down in 1951," I said. I opened the box and pulled out the newspaper article she had left for me. Illana passed it down to Angela, who stifled a cry. A tear rolled down her cheek. She quickly wiped it away and covered her mouth.

"The reason we were having so much trouble finding Harper is that the emerald priestess had the rare ability of manipulating time," I said. "That's how she was able to completely stop time after the attack on this domed city, leaving everyone on earth frozen for such a long time. Somehow, she must have also used her ability to open a portal into the past. Harper wasn't able to give us all the details in her brief note, but from what I found out when I was searching for her, the emerald priestess was stealing witches from several places, including some of her own emerald gates. Witches she intended to brainwash into believing they were her own daughters."

Everyone in the room was quiet, trying to make sense of this mess.

"It must have been much easier for her to hide them in plain sight inside a hospital in the 50's where shock therapy and lobotomies were normal practice," I said. "I have no idea just how many girls are trapped there, but Harper is one of them. And somehow, she managed to kill Priestess Evers."

Eloise gathered her daughters in her arms, tears streaming down her face.

"I felt a shift in the power," she said. "But I didn't dare hope it could be this."

"I still don't understand what we're waiting for," Mordecai said, standing. "We need to get out there and start setting these gates free."

I waited for the excitement in the room to settle down before I continued.

"I agree with you, but I think we need to stop and think about this for a minute," I said. "I was just as excited as the rest of you at first, but when I started thinking about it, I realized I had more questions. If Harper is truly stuck in 1951, how did she have access to all of these items?"

"Why does it matter how she got them?" Mary Anne asked.

"We know how she got the master stone, but what about the rest of these? The dagger, chalice, and necklace might possibly have been there at the emerald priestess's house in the past, but that doesn't explain the ring."

"What do you mean?" Eloise asked.

"The way the rings work is that they are placed in a secret location of power in the Shadow World. They act as an anchor for the rest of the gates, allowing the Order to open multiple gates all connected to the original gate's power. When we were able to find the sapphire ring and bring it to the human world, we crippled the sapphire gates. They weren't closed, but they were unable to pull new demons through."

I watched as my friends started to understand what I was saying.

"If Harper had gone into the Shadow World herself to retrieve the emerald ring back in 1951, none of the emerald gates would have been working for the past sixty years or so," I said. "It's impossible. And if she'd taken any of these items from the emerald priestess back in 1951, the Order of Shadows would have known about it, which means we would have known. No new gates would have been opened. No new demons pulled through."

"So, where did they come from?" Angela asked.

"That's exactly the question we have to answer," I said. "Until we know for sure how she got them and how it has affected the timeline, it could be dangerous to use them."

"Why couldn't we test them?" Mordecai asked. "We take them to Cypress, tomorrow at three. We try the reversal ritual and see if they work."

"We can't do that," Rend said. "Jackson's right. It's too dangerous. I can't explain it, but this feels wrong somehow."

Rend picked up Harper's note to study it, and then he leaned over and took the newspaper article in his hand. "Evers Institute for Troubled Girls," he whispered.

He looked as though he'd just seen a ghost.

"Are you okay?" I asked.

He closed his eyes and brought a hand to his forehead. "I just got the strangest sensation of déjà vu," he said. "Like there's something important I'm supposed to remember about this place. About Harper. But I can't quite figure it out."

Franki put her hand on his and whispered something in his ear. Rend shook his head and opened his eyes.

"I'm sure it's nothing," he said. "Let's just keep going."

"I still say we should at least try it," Mordecai said. "Yes, it's a risk, but there are thousands of demons out there right now suffering under the control of their witches. Witches die every day, taking their demon with them. We have to do what we can as quickly as we can. Jackson, what would you do if it was Aerden who was still trapped as a slave to these witches? You would be there already, doing everything you could to set him free, no matter the cost."

Mordecai's words hit me hard. He was right.

We had everything we needed right here to free thousands of demons, and each one of them was just as important to someone out there as my brother was to me. How could we sit here and worry about our own lives when we possibly had the ability to set them all free?

I took a deep breath and nodded.

"Okay," I said. "We'll go to Cypress first thing tomorrow morning and set everything up to perform the ritual right at three. But if we're going to do this, we need to spend tonight thinking of every possible attack they could send our way once we start the ritual. Come tomorrow, we need to be ready for anything."

Mordecai drew his hands into fists and slammed them down on the table in celebration. "Hell, yeah, let's do this," he said.

Everyone around the table smiled and started talking with excitement, making plans for tomorrow's ritual, but my eyes drifted to the one person who was not smiling.

Rend stared at the emerald items strewn across the table, his forehead tense with worry.

MY DUTY AND MY HONOR

JACKSON

"Rend, can I talk to you outside for a second?" I asked over the noise that broke out in the war room.

He nodded and slowly stood from his chair. He followed me out into the hallway, and we partially closed the door.

"What is it?" I asked. "What's bothering you?"

He shook his head. "I can't put words to it, but something about this doesn't feel right," he said. "It's that weird feeling like when you have something on the tip of your tongue. It's like I know there's something weird about this whole thing, but for the life of me I can't figure it out. It doesn't make any sense. It feels like I've been here before or that somehow, I knew this was coming."

A chill ran through me.

I knew better than anyone what that felt like. I'd been having visions and dreams of the future for most of my life, but I rarely saw the entire scene. When a vision started forming, I often only had a piece of the scene, and I sometimes spent weeks trying to pull that vision out of my brain and make sense of it.

But as far as I knew, Rend had never had the same ability.

"Have you ever had visions or feelings like this before?" I asked.

"Never," he said. "That's why it's got me so mixed up. Maybe I'm just tired and worried for Harper. I've got this mess with the Brotherhood still hanging over me. It's probably nothing, but..."

He closed his eyes and frowned, but then he shook his head and began to pace the hallway.

"It's not coming," he said. "It's just this really uneasy feeling that something's wrong here."

"Do you think we should go through with this plan, Rend?" I asked. "Because if you tell me to put a stop to it, I'll trust you."

He stopped pacing and glanced at me with worried eyes. "I can't do that," he said. "I can't put the lives of all those demons on the line just for a strange feeling that I have no explanation for. Mordecai's right. We have to do something, Jackson. We have to move quickly."

"Then we go tomorrow," I said, placing a hand on his shoulder. "Get some rest. It's going to be a long day."

He nodded and slipped back inside the room, but before I could follow him in, Gregory stepped into the hallway to join me.

"Do you want me to go with you tomorrow?" he asked. "If you're worried about your safety at the ritual, I can gather a small army of guards to come with us. We can secure the perimeter of the ritual area."

I shook my head. "You should stay here, just in case," I said. "We have no idea how the Order will react to another one of the priestesses being killed. If they attack the city, you need to be here to protect everyone."

"I'll start a few of my men on a regular patrol of the surrounding areas to keep an eye out for any hunter activity," he said. "I promise we'll keep the city safe in your absence."

"Thank you," I said. "I can't tell you how grateful I am that you're here. You were so important to Harper's father, and I know it means a lot to her that you're still here protecting the city."

"It is my duty and my honor," Gregory said.

"I can't imagine how horrible those days were for you after you were captured by the sapphire priestess," I said. "We were all so worried that you had been tortured and killed. When you came home to us, it meant the world to Harper. I think for her, it was like a piece of her father had been returned to us."

Gregory looked down at his feet for a moment.

"Those were hard times for me," he said. "If you guys hadn't killed Priestess Winter, I'm not sure what she would have done to me. I thought my life was over the minute she put me in one of those cages in her dungeon."

He made a strange face, and I regretted bringing it up. He still suffered from some of the injuries he sustained during Priestess Winter's torture of him in those dungeons when she was trying to get information out of him. He had stayed loyal to us throughout it all, though, and had been willing to give his life before he would betray us.

"I didn't mean to remind you of those horrible memories," I said. "I just wanted you to know how much it means to all of us that you're here."

He looked up and met my eyes, then. "You can't imagine what it was like," he said. "My worst fear was that they would put me inside one of their witches, and I would spend the rest of my life locked away inside her body. I couldn't imagine anything worse any demon go could through."

"Me, either," I said.

And as Gregory excused himself to give his commands to the guards, I thought again of my brother, Aerden.

He had spent a hundred years locked inside the body of Peachville's Primas. Then, he'd gone free only to be captured again and thrown into the dungeons of the Northern Kingdom.

I longed for news of him. I hoped he knew how much I missed him and wanted him back here by my side.

I thought of the last time we spoke and all the things still left unsaid between us. The last words he'd said to me were that we should have just let him go and forgotten about him, but I knew he didn't mean that.

And I prayed with all my heart that he knew I still hadn't forgotten him. I never would.

As soon as we set the emerald gates free and found Harper, we would find a way to bring Aerden and Lea home to us again.

THE POWER HIDDEN INSIDE

AERDEN

I stepped back just as Perrick's sword pushed toward me. He barely missed, disrupting his center of balance, and I took advantage of his misstep. I rushed forward, plunging the tip of my ghostly spear straight through his heart.

A guard's whistle sounded, and Perrick shook his head, disappointed.

"Good spar, my friend," he said. "I'm glad we'll be fighting on the same side once we're in the arena."

I placed my hand on his shoulder as the illusion of my spear dissipated into a thin wisp of smoke carried off by the wind. "You're doing well," I said. "Besides, you're much stronger when it comes to the magic."

"Yes, but it's the hand-to-hand I'm worried about," he said. "When we're all close together on the battlefield, it's going to be important."

"We'll help each other," I said. "We'll work together to make sure we win this. I promise."

He smiled, but there was fear behind his expression. We were all afraid of what would happen once we got to the arena, but there was nothing left to do except train and hope.

Hope.

Something I thought I'd lost a century ago. It felt good to have it back now, and even though I was still a prisoner—this time in the very home where I'd grown up—I was determined to prove myself and win my freedom on my own terms.

Another whistle sounded, and I turned to watch two of my other teammates clasp hands. Morway helped Trention to his feet. The old demon met my eyes and shook his head.

It wasn't fair that such a wise, ancient demon who had never been trained to fight a day in his life was being forced to participate in these barbaric games. Just thinking about it made my fists clench tighter at my sides.

The guards had singled him out because of me. A couple dozen demons volunteered to be a part of my team in the games, but Reynar still put Trention into the tournament. I had stood up for the old demon while we were mining together, showing that I had a weakness for the man.

A weakness Reynar was determined to exploit.

Many demons still thought the human witches and the Order of Shadows were our only enemies, but I now understood that cruelty and evil intentions were not solely human traits. We had enemies even here inside the walls of the King's City.

Trention and Morway walked over to join us while other teams continued to spar inside the walls of the training grounds just outside the arena.

"How did it go?" I asked.

Trention sighed. "Like it always goes. I can't keep up."

"You're learning," I said.

"Not fast enough," he said. "The games begin in a few days. I'm a liability to the entire group."

"You're smarter than anyone in this city. You studied battle strategies for centuries as a scholar and teacher in the castle. We're lucky to have you," I said, but he didn't look convinced.

"You are both strong and kind, my friend, but I fear that once we face our first battle, you'll see just how much I'm holding you all back," he said. "Promise me you won't put yourself at risk just to keep me safe. That will only distract you, and I do not want the last moments of my long life to be ones of weakness and regret."

The worry etched on his face made me feel helpless. In some ways, he was right, whether I wanted to admit it or not. I looked up, letting my eyes scan the teams around us. Whichever group we were pitted against in the first round of the games would be a full team of five strong demons, each ready to fight for their lives.

No one else had a demon as old and frail as Trention, but he was my dear friend, and I would protect him with my life if it came to that.

Yes, we were at a disadvantage, but I had beaten worse odds in my lifetime.

"The guards said that no one will die in the games," Rushon, our fifth teammate, said as he approached. "Injuries will be inevitable, sure, but the shamans will be on hand to heal those that fall. We'll survive this even if we don't win, right?"

He didn't sound convinced, and to be honest, I wasn't buying the guards' stories, either.

I didn't doubt there would be shamans on hand to give the

appearance of mercy and healing for the crowds, but once a prisoner was brought to a place where no one was watching, if he was injured badly enough, I had no doubt he would be required to give his life's energy in service to the king.

Anyone who defied that order would be killed, anyway.

At least, that's how I heard it used to go down when the king's great-grandfather ran these games as a yearly event. It wasn't public knowledge back then, either, but I'd heard the rumors when I'd trained with the King's Guard as a shadowling.

The only demon who survived the games was the one demon who won the entire tournament.

As much as I wanted to win, I couldn't bear to watch my friends and teammates die. It wasn't fair.

"Did you see Yuron sparring with his partner?" Rushon asked, throwing a nervous glance toward a towering demon standing at the edge of the crowd. "He's got to be the strongest demon out here in both magic and physical weaponry. I don't see how anyone is going to beat him."

"He's also the most unkind," Trention said. "I've been watching the way he treats his teammates. He's a cruel demon. He doesn't deserve to win."

"Well, unfortunately, this tournament isn't judged on kindness or honor," Perrick said.

I looked over at Yuron, who was currently yelling at his teammates. When he caught me watching him, though, he narrowed his eyes at me and then laughed.

I looked away.

Rushon was right. Out of all the opponents out here so far during our training, Yuron was the one who had caught my eye. Almost everyone out here was stronger in magic than I was right now, but as far as physical weapons, Yuron was my only match.

Unfortunately, when it came down to it, though, physical weapons wouldn't be enough. I had to find a way to unlock my magic before the beginning of the games.

And I was running out of time.

Today's training was nearing the end, anyway, which meant another day lost. The suns were going down, being replaced by the beautiful moons of spring. In the streets beyond the walls of the arena, we could hear the demons laughing and gathering together as they all made their way to the castle for the feast.

Tonight marked the official beginning of the festival being thrown in Lea's honor. A princess returned.

My eyes travelled to the black towers of the castle in the distance. Their pointy tips rose high into the air, and I thought of how I used to look up at those towers as a shadowling in such awe. They were a symbol of strength and power to me then, but now, the sight of them put a bitter taste in my mouth.

My prison here might have been dusty and dirty, but the beauty of the castle didn't make it any less of a prison. Lea was trapped there the same way I was trapped here.

Tonight, she would be paraded around the entire population of the King's City as a trophy. She was their possession, and now that they had her back, they were going to give her away to someone new.

I looked away, anger tightening my fists. Trention caught my eye, and I shook my head. I didn't need him to worry about me any more than he already was. And I didn't need anyone to know my heart belonged to a princess who would never be mine.

Fate was against us, and no matter how much I loved her, I had lost my chance a long time ago.

All I could hope now was that I survived long enough to help set her free from this place.

"One last round," Karn shouted, motioning for us to break off in teams. "And this time, magic only."

He threw a wicked glance my way and smiled. Like every demon on the field of battle, he knew I had no control over my magic.

Three days. If I couldn't find some way to unlock the power hidden inside of me, this arena would become my tomb and my shame.

We raised our fists for one final training round, our bodies dancing as the first sounds of music floated down to us from the castle.

REBEL HEART

LEA

Music filled the court. I stood in the wings, waiting to be introduced and remembering what it had been like as a shadowling, sneaking downstairs to watch one of my father's parties. I used to love the fancy dresses and the music. I used to dream of what it would be like to be queen.

But now, everything around me seemed so fake. An illusion of finery and joy and safety.

It was all a lie.

There could be no true joy here until the Order was defeated, and despite their smiles and laughter, every demon in this room knew they were living on borrowed time.

Including me.

No matter how much Ezrah urged me to play these games for the sake of the kingdom and the Resistance, I could feel a rebellion starting in my heart. I didn't belong here. Not while everyone else was still out there fighting.

There was a pause in the music, and the crowd gathered near the foot of the steps leading up to the throne. My father sat there, his body weakened and withered as he addressed them.

"Demons of the King's City," my father said, his voice echoing through the hall. "For many years, there has been no reason to celebrate within these great walls. But today, I have invited you all here for a grand celebration. My daughter, Princess Lazalea, has returned to us."

He lifted an arm toward where I stood beside the pillar at the entrance, and all eyes shifted toward me. I stepped forward out of the shadows, my long gown sparkling as the jewels caught the light.

The crowd erupted in applause and shouts, and I forced a smile, waving to the crowd.

My mother motioned for me to join them on the steps, and I took my place at my father's side. And even though this was technically where I had always belonged, I'd never felt more like a traitor in my life.

"Her time outside these walls was difficult. She faced many dangers and was attacked and held by our enemies," he said. "But my daughter is strong and her love for all of you kept her going through even the darkest of times. She fought her way back to us, and can now take her rightful place in the kingdom as the future Queen of the North."

More lies.

The king placed his arms around my shoulders, and I stiffened. He'd barely spoken to me, let alone touched me, since I'd returned months ago.

"Friends, let us welcome our princess back to the King's City," he said. "Let us celebrate tonight and over the coming weeks with great banquets, dances, and a return of the King's Games in her honor. Let us show her how much her devotion means to us all."

He leaned over to kiss my forehead, and the stench that came from his mouth almost made me gag. I closed my eyes and didn't dare to breathe again until he'd backed away from me.

I pressed my hands tightly against my dress to keep them from trembling.

The place where he had kissed me burned with fever that spread down the side of my face, as if he'd poisoned me. I shook my head and tried to maintain my composure, but inside, I was frozen in fear.

There was something very unnatural going on inside these walls. I'd suspected it for decades, but I hadn't had a chance to get close enough to my father over the years to see it with my own eyes. Now that I was standing here next to him, though, I could sense the truth of it with my whole being.

Father, what have you done? What has happened to you?

I glanced at him as he spoke to the gathered crowd, but I didn't hear his false words and his lies. Instead, I focused on his features. I noticed the way he'd aged over the years, in a way that demons normally didn't age. He was aging more like a human, decay rapidly taking over his features and clouding his once-clear eyes.

His once-strong body hunched over, and he looked as if a gentle breeze would knock him off his feet. His skin was paper-thin and sagging.

Beside him, my mother still looked as young as ever, none of the decay touching her features. How did she stand there and say nothing about the way he looked? How could she hold onto his arm and not frown at the decay and stench of him?

I shook my head. I didn't understand what was going on between them, but looking at them now, I felt more determined than ever to get to the root of it all.

I'd promised Andros and his guards that I would be a good little princess and do my part to keep everyone I loved safe, but how could they expect me to stand in the presence of some mysterious evil and not notice it? Not do what I could to find the truth?

"Lazelea?"

My mother's stern voice in my ear seemed to wake me out of my own confusion and rage. She slipped behind my father's back and gripped my arm so tightly, it stung.

"Yes?" I asked, blinking.

"Your father asked you to speak," she hissed. "Just as we rehearsed."

I took a deep breath and wrenched my arm from her grasp.

I cleared my throat and looked at the expectant gazes of those in the crowd. Yes, we'd rehearsed a brief speech for me to give to the people, promising them that I was ready to do whatever it would take to honor and serve them the way my father had served them. I was to promise them that I would keep them safe here inside the walls of the city.

But now, seeing the evidence of some rotten magic that was destroying my own father, how could I say those things? How could I promise to protect them when evil had already found its way inside this supposed sanctuary?

I wanted to tell them the truth. I wanted to tell them everything I'd learned about the Order of Shadows and how it was only a matter of time before every demon in the Shadow

World was made a slave to the human witches. But breathing a single word of the truth would only get me thrown back into the dungeons.

Or worse.

Instead, I licked my lips and smiled. My time would come.

"Thank you for your kind words, father," I said, my voice unsteady. I could feel my mother's disapproving and fearful gaze on me. "You'll have to forgive me if I'm still a little bit shaken up by what I've been through. But I'm happy to be home, now. I'm happy to have the opportunity to stand before you once again as your future queen. And I promise you that I will do everything in my power to keep you all safe."

My mother stepped forward. "Enough talk," she said. "We have come here tonight to celebrate the return of our daughter. Let us all dance and feast together and forget hard times."

She nodded toward the musicians, who began a new song. A dance I remembered from my childhood.

The crowd erupted into applause and spread out in the hall, taking their places for an ancient dance of celebration.

When their eyes were no longer on me, my mother grabbed my arm and pulled me back toward the pillar, hiding us from view.

"What do you think you're doing?" she asked. "Trying to get yourself thrown back in the dungeons? You have no idea what I've had to do to gain your freedom and to get the others to trust you again. The sacrifices we've all made..."

Her voice trailed off and she could no longer look me in the eye.

"What sacrifices, mother?" I asked.

She shook her head and placed a hand at her neck, fingering a gold chain that lay across her skin.

"There are things you don't know, Lazalea," she said. "Things I wish none of us had to know or do. Necessary things to keep the demons of this kingdom safe. You must honor those sacrifices."

I swallowed. What exactly what she talking about?

"How can I honor them if I don't even know what they are?" I asked. I wondered what this little speech from her had to do with my father. What had they done?

"This is neither the time nor the place to discuss these things," she said. "Your father and I have worked very hard to put together this celebration for you. Please, at least pretend to enjoy it."

She smoothed her skirts and touched her hair, planting a smile on her face.

"Besides, I have someone very important I want you to meet."

She held her hand out to me, and I reluctantly placed my own in hers. She smiled and pulled me around the pillar, like a dog on a leash.

For a moment, she looked around, raising onto her toes to see over the heads of the guests. Finally, she found whoever it was she was looking for and waved to them. She turned to me and smoothed my braids. She sucked in a nervous breath as she looked me over, briefly touching the spot on my head where my father had kissed me, as if wiping it away.

"My queen," a man's voice said from behind her.

My mother spun around, giggling like a shadowling at the demon who bowed before her. He took her hand and softly kissed her skin.

"You honor me," he said.

"It is you who honors us," she said. "Please, you must meet

my daughter. Lazalea, dear, this is Kael, the demon you shall soon marry."

The demon straightened, his eyes sweeping up from the bottom of my dress to my eyes in a way that told me everything I needed to know about him. He didn't look at me as a man looks at a woman, but rather the way a man looks at a prize he's just won.

His eyes were black as coal, and a smile tugged at the corners of his lips.

"Princess," he said, bowing again, though never quite taking his eyes off of me.

I made no effort to move, but at my mother's harsh glare, I politely offered him my hand.

The kiss he placed on my skin was warm like my father's, though not as feverish. He was a handsome demon. Young and strong. But where had he come from? He seemed to be about my age, but he certainly hadn't grown up here in the city. I would have recognized him.

"It's an honor to meet you," I said, the lie rolling off my tongue.

"Would you join me for a dance?" he asked.

I looked to my mother and she nodded, placing her hand on the small of my back and giving me a little push toward Kael, as if I were still a child.

"Of course," I said through clenched teeth.

I wanted nothing to do with this demon. He was the reason we were all here tonight. The festival and the King's Games had been his idea, and I had no intention of even pretending to enjoy his company.

He could stare at me as his new possession all he wanted,

but if he really thought I would ever agree to marry him, he obviously knew nothing about me.

He led me toward the dance floor, and several of the couples dancing nearby moved to make room for us. A royal couple deserving of our own space, though all eyes were on us.

When he placed his arms around me, my entire body tensed. If the hand currently digging into my hip moved one inch lower, he'd be missing a hand by the end of this dance.

"You are every bit as beautiful as everyone says." His eyes focused on mine.

"I can't say I've heard anyone talking about your appearance," I said, meeting his gaze directly. I wanted him to know he didn't scare me. "I have, however, heard the people speak of how you have become one of my father's most trusted advisors. How exactly did that come to be in such a short period of time? Usually his advisors come from a certain heritage of past council members, but I don't seem to remember you from my time here before I left."

He smiled, not taking his eyes from mine even for a moment as he twirled me around the dance floor.

"You're already suspicious of me," he said, a gleam in his eye. "I like that."

"You do?" I asked.

"It shows you have spirit and want nothing more than to protect your own family and your own heritage," he said. "That will be very important in the decades to come."

He didn't elaborate, and I couldn't shake the feeling that he meant it more as a threat than a compliment.

"Since you didn't grow up here in the castle, where did you grow up?" I asked.

"Is that really so important?" he asked.

"It's important to me."

He shrugged, tightening his grip on me as he turned me again.

"Where I come from is none of your concern," he said. "The only thing that matters is that I've been here for your father when you were not."

I tensed, attempting to pull away, but Kael had a tight grip on me now and wouldn't let me back away even an inch.

"Let's not be enemies, Princess," he said, leaning close to my ear. "After all, we have a lifetime ahead of us. Whether it's a pleasant existence or not is largely up to you."

Again with the shaded threats. I disliked him more with each passing moment.

I certainly had no intention of spending a lifetime at this demon's side.

"What are you trying to say?" I asked. "That if I don't fall in line, you intend to make my life miserable? That's not the most pleasant thing to say to the demon you are hoping to mate with."

"It's more than a simple hope at this point, Princess," he said, tightening his grip on me. "Plans are already being made for our engagement ceremony. Our mating ceremony will take place soon after. This is happening whether you like it or not. I'm simply saying that it's your choice whether to embrace that fact or rebel against it."

"Well, when you put it that way, it sounds delightful," I said through clenched teeth.

Rather than prickling at my anger, Kael laughed.

"I see you haven't quite left your rebel heart behind you in the human world," he said. "That fire and passion will serve us well once it's directed in a more useful way."

"More useful than a war against the Order of Shadows?" I asked, having to be careful not to raise my voice. "More useful than saving thousands of the demons who have been stolen from our lands?"

"Yes," he said, but he didn't offer any explanation of why fighting the Order was such a bad thing in his mind.

Anger pulsed through me, hot and fast.

"Then why are you so anxious to marry me, if you think I'm a traitor?"

He loosened his grip and laughed, throwing his head back.

"I never said I thought you were a traitor, Lea," he said. "Misguided perhaps. Blinded by loyalty to a demon who never loved you. But not a traitor. At least I hope not."

I pulled away from his grasp, wanting nothing more than to punch him in the face. I didn't care who was watching us. He had no right to speak to me that way.

The music ended, and Kael bowed to me.

"Thank you for the dance, Princess," he said. Nothing I'd said to him had managed to wipe that cocky smile from his face. In fact, he seemed amused by my anger, which only pissed me off even more.

He stepped closer to me, and even though I tried to back away, I hadn't moved fast enough. His arm encircled my waist, and he pulled me up against him.

"I so look forward to breaking that spirit of yours," he said. He stepped back and looked into my eyes. "Because I will, Lea. Before this is all over, you'll be even more broken than you were after your betrothed left you behind."

He kissed my cheek, and before I had a chance to respond, he bowed and walked away, disappearing into the crowd surrounding the dancefloor.

I steadied my expression for the sake of the crowd, but Lazalea, the princess had stepped aside. The rebel inside me took control once again, and I smiled.

Let him do his best, but a demon like him could never break me. Kael might know a lot about me, but he obviously had no idea who he was messing with.

RIGHT THERE IN FRONT OF YOU

LEA

I stormed through the crowd, searching for where Kael had gone. If he thought he could threaten me like that here in my own home and just walk away, he had another thing coming.

But before I caught sight of him, I felt a hand on my shoulder.

I twirled around to find Aerden's mother, Tatiana, standing there in front of me.

"Oh, I'm so sorry. I didn't mean to disturb you. Were you heading somewhere? Or do you have a moment to talk?" she asked.

I glanced in the direction Kael had disappeared to and took a deep breath.

Maybe it was good that she had stopped me. If Kael really had as much power as he seemed to think he had around here, confronting him now, in front of everyone, would do nothing but put my life in danger.

"It's not important," I said, turning my full attention to Tatiana. "I always have a moment to talk with you."

She smiled as if she hadn't just recently been talking to her daughter about how to get rid of me.

I glanced around the room and wondered just how many of the demons here were truly glad I had returned? And how many of them were plotting how to break or destroy me?

"Would you like to walk with me for a moment?" she asked, offering her arm to me. "It's a beautiful night out."

I hesitated. She must have wanted to talk about something important if she needed such privacy. Why wait until tonight to seek me out when she could have come to me at any point in the past few weeks here in the castle?

I placed my hand on her arm. "I would love to walk," I said. "Thank you."

She led me through the crowd and out onto the terrace. We walked in silence for a little while before she finally paused near an archway and leaned against the balcony.

"There," she said, pointing into the distance.

I looked out at the city and swallowed as I realized she was pointing toward the arena. From our vantage-point here near the top of the throne room's terrace, we could make out the figures of demons fighting there on the dusty floor of the arena's large battlefield.

"Do you see them?" she asked.

I leaned against the edge of the obsidian bannister, my heart aching. "Is he there?" I asked. "Can you tell?"

"He's there," she said. "They're too far away for me to tell which one is my son, but I know he's there."

She grew quiet, and we watched together as the sparks of spells and magic flew into the air like fireworks.

"Why did you bring me out here?" I asked.

"Because I know you're the only other one here who cares as much as I do that he's down there, preparing to fight for his life."

I needed to hold my tongue and keep my opinions to myself, but I was fairly certain I'd used the last of my willpower up on that dance with Kael.

"Then why didn't you do something to get him out of the dungeons when you had the chance?" I asked. "You and your husband are members of the council. Why didn't you fight to have him set free? He deserves better than this."

She wiped a tear from her face and straightened her shoulders. "He deserves much better than I've been able to give him for most of his life," she said. "But sometimes our choices are not that simple."

I closed my eyes for a brief moment and tried to calm my anger. Saying anything that could have this woman label me as a traitor and have me thrown back in the dungeons would not do me any good right now. I needed to be careful around her, but the rebellious side of me was tired of playing nice.

"I'm sure deciding between your own position in the kingdom and your son's life is quite complicated," I said, keeping as much of the acid out of my tone as I could manage.

She snapped toward me. "Do you really think you're the only one who has made sacrifices to keep him safe?" she asked.

"I know that when he disappeared, you told us to forget about Aerden," I said. "You abandoned him without even trying to bring him home."

"I was trying not to lose both of my sons to the Order, but I lost them anyway. And now my precious daughter is gone, too," she said. "I've lost so much."

"Then why do you stand here watching it continue to happen?" I asked. "Aerden is down there alive. Jackson and Illana are in the Southern Kingdom, fighting for what we all know is right. If you really want to save them all, then fight for them."

She shook her head. "You are still very young and very naive," she said. "You think you understand the sacrifices that have been made. You think you're better than all of us because you left to fight a losing war. You took them both from me, and yet here you stand, ready to take the throne from us, too."

My eyes widened. Had she really just admitted that she wanted the throne for herself?

Was this entire conversation just a trap to get me to admit my loyalty to the Resistance or the Southern Kingdom? Or was she really finally admitting the truth of why she never tried to save her sons?

And how in the hell did she figure that I had taken her sons from her in the first place?

"I had nothing to do with either of your sons leaving this city," I said. "No one knows why Aerden left, and no matter how much I tried to convince Jackson to stay here and find a way to fight without abandoning his kingdom, he was determined to leave. All I did was stand by his side."

Tatiana made a face and turned away. "Don't call him that," she said. "It makes him sound so human."

"He prefers that name now," I said. "Maybe because he feels closer to the friends he's made in the human world than the demons here who betrayed him."

"You speak of things you know nothing about," she said. "I tried to keep them safe, but once they were gone, there was nothing I could do to help them."

"You could have gone after him like we did," I said. "Aerden is alive now because we refused to give up on him. And now you're going to take the second chance you've been given and throw it all away again? I don't understand you."

"Aerden never should have been taken by the Order in the first place," she said, facing me. "I made a great sacrifice to make sure he would be safe. I still don't understand why he was taken. That never should have been possible."

I stepped back, my hand absently fluttering to my chest. I no longer had the diamond key I had worn close to my heart for a century, but I could still imagine its cool metal against my skin.

Tatiana studied my reaction, her eyes widening. She raised a hand to her lips, as if holding back a cry.

"You know, don't you?" she asked. She closed her eyes and leaned against the bannister for support. "Oh my goodness, I can't believe I didn't see it before this moment. He gave it to you, didn't he? He gave you the key? Before he left?"

My heart raced. I had wanted to know the origin of that mysterious key for decades. Even more so after my last fight with the hunter attacking the domed city to the south.

"Where did you get a diamond key, Tatiana?"

"I told him to keep it on him at all times and to never take it off for anything or anyone," she said, still looking into the distance toward the demons sparring in the arena. "I knew he...but I never dreamed he would give it to you. He was the one in danger, not you."

I gasped. "You knew he was going to leave," I said, realizing it for the first time. All this time, I'd thought Aerden's absence from the castle on my engagement day was a surprise to everyone.

Tatiana ran a hand along her own thick braids, smoothing her hair even though not a single one was out of place. "I suspected it for several moons before he left. That's why I gave him that key," she said. "It was never meant for you, and if you hadn't taken it from him, he would have been safe. He would have eventually returned to us. Our lives would be very different if you had never accepted that key, Lazalea."

I closed my eyes and let her words sink in. Were Aerden's years of slavery my fault?

"I didn't know," I said, finally steadying myself enough to look at her. "He said it was an engagement present. He made me promise to never take it off. I had no idea you had given it to him to keep him safe from the Order. How could I have known that?"

Tears shimmered in her eyes. "You couldn't have known," she said. "I just wish it could have been different."

"Where did you get a diamond key, Tatiana?" I asked again.

She hesitated, gripping the stone on the edge of the bannister tighter. For a moment, I thought she would refuse to tell me, but after a long pause, she eventually turned back to me.

"I bought it from a shaman who used to live near the borderlands," she said. "She was not the type of demon I normally would have wanted to have any dealings with. She was rumored to deal in dark magic and items stolen from the witches and hunters of the Order of Shadows."

"Did she tell you where the key came from?"

"She told me she'd stolen it from a hunter who worked for the High Priestess herself," she said. "She said the hunters use keys embedded with a gemstone from each demon gate portal.

That's how they mark a demon to be taken. They mark their chosen demon with a dark kind of magic and lock a piece of their spirit into a small box. Later, when they come back to retrieve the demon, they simply use the key to open the box. The magic summons that demon from their home where they are sent through to the human world and locked inside a witch's body."

My throat went dry. This was information the Resistance struggled for decades to discover. We'd found keys in the lairs of some hunters in the past, but we never knew the purpose of those keys or their small boxes until recently.

"You've known this for all these years and never told anyone?" I asked. "It took the Resistance decades to uncover the truth about how the hunters mark the demons they intend to take. If we had known this information, we could have saved lives, Tatiana."

"We?" she asked, smiling sadly. "You stand here in the gowns of a princess, but you still think of yourself as a member of the Resistance."

"I am both," I said. "All of us should want nothing more than to see the end of the Order of Shadows so that we can bring as many of our demons home as possible."

"When Aerden was taken, I thought that maybe the shaman had lied to me," she said, ignoring my comment. "When I had a chance, I went back to search for her, but she had closed her shop and moved on. I've never seen that shaman again, and I blamed her for my son's disappearance, never dreaming that he had given the key to you all those years ago."

"Did she tell you anything more about the origin of the key?" I asked. "As far as anyone knows, there are no diamond

gates in the human world. We've heard rumors and specula-
tion about diamond covens and gates, but in all our time
searching, we've never once found proof that they exist."

Tatiana shook her head. "She didn't give me any further
information," she said. "She simply told me she'd bought the
key from a demon who claimed to have killed the hunter who
carried it. I foolishly trusted her, and at great cost to myself. I
emptied most of our savings and gave away many of our most
precious family treasures in exchange for that key."

"The key is real," I said. "She didn't lie to you."

Tatiana's eyes widened. "How do you know?"

I swallowed and glanced away. How much should I tell
her? After all, this was a woman I'd recently overheard
discussing my permanent relocation to the dungeons. I
shouldn't trust her.

"Recently, that key saved my life," I said. "The diamond
inside it is real."

"Where is it now?" she asked. "Do you still have it?"

The truth was, I didn't know where my key was now. It
had been inside my bag, along with the diamond amulet I'd
taken from the hunter who attacked the domed city the night
the world was frozen in darkness.

That bag had been taken from me by the guards when
they'd brought us here, but I wasn't sure I wanted to let
Tatiana know that it was possibly still here in the castle.

Besides, Essex had created that bag specifically for me,
making sure that no one else could open it, no matter how hard
they tried. I kept my most important possessions in that bag.

"I lost it," I said, lying.

Tatiana sighed. She looked tired as she turned her gaze
back toward the arena.

"I did try to keep him safe, Lazalea," she said. "And I begged him not to volunteer in these games. He refused to listen to me."

"You went to see him?" I asked, my heart aching. It had been months since I'd seen Aerden, and I missed him so much it hurt.

"A few times," she said. "But, like you, he believes I abandoned him. He hates me. He won't listen to a word I say."

"He doesn't hate you," I said. "He's hurting, and coming back here and being thrown in the dungeons instead of being recognized for the hero he truly is doesn't help."

"I wanted to set him free, but those decisions aren't up to me, anymore," she said. "The council is nothing more than a lie these days. Surely you see that, don't you?"

"What do you mean? The council isn't working together to make decisions for the city?" I asked.

She sighed again, lifting her head as the sparring in the arena came to an end and the prisoners were lined up and taken back through the archway that lead into the cells where they were being kept.

"You are a smart girl, Lazalea, but you see only what's there on the surface," she said. "If you looked deeper, you might start to see things as they truly are, rather than how you imagine them to be. All the answers you seek are right there in front of you. All you have to do is open your eyes. Now, if you'll excuse me, I have to get back to the party. I'm sure it won't be long before our presence is missed."

She started back toward the main ballroom, but I called after her and she turned slightly, her face enveloped in the shadows cast by the large obsidian archways.

"Why did Aerden leave the city?" I asked, a part of me not

quite sure I was ready to hear the answer to the question. "Why did he give me that key when he knew how important it was?"

Tatiana glanced toward the arena one last time. The shadow of a smile played against her lips.

"Maybe you should ask Aerden that question," she said. "Good night, Princess."

She left me standing there, alone in the chilled spring air, afraid that deep down, I already knew the truth.

NOTHING LEFT

HARPER

Hours later, when the sun was close to making its appearance in the eastern sky and the scent of smoke still lingered in the air, Brooke and I made our way back inside the house Priestess Evers had called home.

The local hospital in this small town didn't have enough room for all eighty-three of the girls, so they had been separated and transported to three different facilities in the area. For now, all I had was a handwritten list of their names and the determination to somehow get each one of them home where they belonged.

Did they all come from the same time as Brooke and me? Or had they been captured from different decades and brought here by the priestess? Until their memories were restored to them, we had no real way to know.

I was too exhausted to make sense of all of it tonight. I needed a few hours of rest before I could face the repercussions of everything that had happened.

"How are you feeling?" Brooke asked. "I don't know about you, but at this point, I feel like I could sleep for a week and still not be rested. Do you think it's safe to drop this glamour?"

I closed the door behind us and locked it.

"There are too many windows down here," I said. "And too many unknowns. We have no idea who is working for the Order or watching the house right now. I was really hoping to be able to search the house tonight for any sign of a portal, but I'm so tired, I can barely find the energy to take another step. I think we should both go upstairs, lock ourselves into a room, and get some sleep. We can get up in a few hours and make a plan."

"I like the idea of sleep," Brooke said. "I don't even think I have the energy to jump in the shower and wash the smell of this fire off my body. I just want to pass out and forget this mess for a little while."

We both headed up the stairs and chose a pair of bedrooms next door to each other.

"If you wake up before me, come wake me up, okay?" she asked.

"Same for you," I said. "Get some rest. I'll see you in the morning."

Brooke threw her arms around my neck, and we stood in the hallway for a long time, holding each other. There were no words to express everything we'd been through over the past several months, and we both knew that there was still a long journey ahead of us. And no matter how much she had once seemed like my enemy, I was so grateful to have her here with me now.

As we parted, my knees buckled slightly, and Brooke grabbed my arm.

"Are you okay?" she asked.

I put a hand to my forehead, a sharp pain tearing through me. My glamour flickered, and I suddenly felt sick to my stomach.

"I think I just need to drop this glamour and crawl into bed. My magic is completely spent," I said. "I'll see you in the morning, okay?"

"Okay," she said, frowning. "I'll check on you as soon as I wake up."

I nodded and stepped into the darkness of the nearest bedroom. I closed the door behind me, and let the glamour fall from my body, as if I were releasing a breath I'd been holding for hours.

My shoulders relaxed, and I leaned against the door, just enjoying the release. It had taken everything I had to keep the glamour going throughout the night. Between my mad run through the institute to try to escape Priestess Evers and our fight in the basement, I was drained.

I didn't even bother turning on the overhead light. There was enough light coming through the curtains from a street-lamp outside for me to make my way to the bed. There was a small lamp on the bedside table, and I flipped it on, realizing for the first time that I must have chosen the priestess's bedroom.

I ran my hand along the beautifully embroidered comforter on her canopied bed before I pulled it down and started to climb inside.

Movement on the other side of the room stopped me cold, and chills of terror ran down my spine. I wasn't alone, but the small sitting area on the far side of the large bedroom was drenched in shadows.

I stared into the darkness, feeling that I was looking into the dark moments of my own fate.

"Show yourself," I said.

Another lamp clicked on, and there, sitting in a high-backed chair covered in green velvet, was a woman with dark blonde hair that fell to her waist in delicate waves. Her long, red skirt billowed around her legs and pooled on the wood floor. She wore a pristine white blouse, and there, at her neck, was a gold chain that dipped low against her breasts.

Every muscle in my body tensed. I reached for my power, only to find that there was nothing left.

"Hello, Harper," she said, her crimson lips spreading into a sweet smile.

She absently lifted a hand to touch the pendant hanging from the gold chain. The stone in the center glittered as it caught the light, and I felt the blood drain from my face.

The pendant was a snake made entirely of rubies.

A DEAL WITH THE DEVIL

HARPER

A single moment seemed to stretch out for an eternity, and I could hardly breathe.

I had no doubt the woman sitting in front of me was the ruby priestess herself. But how had she gotten here? And what was she planning to do to me?

Again, I reached out for my power, connecting for a brief moment to the life force of a large oak in the backyard, but I wasn't strong enough to hold onto it. I was powerless. I quickly looked around me to see if there was anything I could use as a weapon, but other than the furniture, the room was bare.

"Calm down, girl," she said. She shook her head and motioned toward a matching chair next to her. "Come, sit down."

My heart raced, and my mind struggled to keep up. I had literally just ripped her sister's heart out less than twenty-four hours ago, yet she seemed completely unconcerned. If anything, she looked amused with her bright blue eyes and light smile.

"I'll stay right here," I said. "Say whatever it is you've come to say."

She sighed and clasped her hands in her lap. "I'm not going to hurt you, I promise. Just sit down so we can have a little chat. I have a lot to say, and I don't have much time. To be honest, neither do you."

"You'll have to forgive me if I don't trust you and your promises," I said.

Amazingly, she laughed.

"I'm simply amazed at your spirit," she said. "I was there for a good deal of my sister's experiments when she first brought you here, and I have never seen anyone come through such torture with this kind of determination and spunk."

Spunk? She was speaking to me as if I were a child who had simply gotten up after scraping my knee.

"What do you want?" I asked.

"I'm impressed by you and what you've accomplished," she said. "None of us believed it was possible to kill even one of us with the power we have gathered and consumed over the years, much less two of us. In our centuries of power, we've never truly been challenged by anyone, and it amuses me that the source of our destruction was a young girl like you."

She genuinely did look amused. Almost giddy.

I struggled to make sense of her reaction. Was she just trying to get me to lower my defenses so she could kill me? Maybe she didn't realize that I currently had no access to my own power.

"I loved my sister, Hazel, dearly. She was by far my favorite sister, but I warned her not to bring you here," she said with a shrug. "Just like everyone else, she underestimated you. She thought she could control you and turn you into one of her precious daughters, but she didn't understand just how strong you are."

The ruby priestess straightened in her chair.

"But like I said, I am not like my sisters," she said. Her eyes were bright and wide as she stared at me. "I think you are an incredible girl. It's so romantic how much you love your demon and how much both of you would sacrifice for each other and for your friends. It's absolutely fascinating to see how much you can accomplish through love and sheer strength of will. These are things my sisters do not understand at all."

I had no idea why she was telling me these things. She admired me? Somehow, I seriously doubted that. What game was she playing here?

"Don't look so confused. I'm trying to pay you a compliment, dear."

"Is that really what you came all this way to tell me?" I asked.

She leaned back in the chair again, pressing her hands together in front of her chest. "You're right. Of course, what was I thinking? We are on limited time here, but I just wanted you to know that I admire what you've been able to do so far," she said. "I've been on the winning side for so long that it's gotten quite boring. Oh, it was a challenge in the beginning to see what we could get away with, how many witches we could recruit to our covens or how many gates we could open successfully. But for decades now, there's been no challenge to what we're doing. Until you came along, of course."

"So, I'm entertaining?" I asked.

"Yes," she said with a wide smile, as if pleased I had finally understood what she'd been trying to tell me. "You've made things interesting again, and it's been quite fun. But as soon as I felt my dear sister Hazel's spirit fade from existence, I knew I would have to find you."

Chills ran up my arms, and I took a step backward. I wasn't sure I would survive a fight with this woman right now, and calling out for Brooke would do nothing but get her killed, too. I eyed the door, knowing that if she attacked, my only hope would be to run.

"I don't want to die. It's as simple as that," she said. "I like being on the winning side, and up until a few months ago, I was. Now, I'm not so sure."

My mouth slid open in shock. Wait a second. Was a priestess of the Order telling me she wanted to switch sides? Had I somehow fallen asleep and slipped into some kind of strange nightmare?

"I need your help, Harper. And, as it turns out, you need me, too. Unless, of course, you want to stay here in 1951. I'm sure you've realized your own mistake by now, am I right?"

I leaned against the side of the bed. I hadn't been mentally prepared for a conversation like this after what I'd been through in the past twenty-four hours.

When I'd realized we were stuck here in the past, I'd been sure that I had just closed off my only chance to get home. But if the portal back home was closed, how was the ruby priestess sitting here in front of me?

In my fear and exhaustion, I hadn't even realized the significance of her presence.

"There's a portal home," I said.

"Yes, indeed there is," she said. "And of the remaining sisters, I'm the only one who knows it still exists. Hazel didn't so much care for our other sisters. None of them understood her obsession with having daughters of her own, but I understood her pain. She was simply doing what she felt she needed to do to be happy. Everyone deserves happiness, so I supported her when she founded the Evers Institute."

It was the second time she'd mentioned something about daughters. What in the world was she talking about?

I shook my head, confused. "Her daughters?" I asked.

The ruby priestess laughed, throwing her head back and clutching a hand to her chest. "You didn't know?" she asked. "What is it you think she was doing here, exactly? Simply torturing girls for the pleasure of it?"

Her eyes were wide, as if that idea was completely outrageous.

"Yes, that's exactly what I thought she was doing here," I said. "That and trying to brainwash us to join her side."

"Oh, Harper, no," she said. "My sister Hazel was infertile. It was the greatest sadness of her life. Daughters are such an important part of what the Order of Shadows is all about, and no magic in existence was able to help Hazel have a daughter of her own. After years of deep depression and anger, she finally decided that if she couldn't have biological daughters, she would simply steal the daughters of other women and make them her own."

I closed my eyes, understanding now why all of us had been brought to this place.

"Whenever she would see a child or a girl she favored, she would bring them here to her little rehabilitation center. She would wipe their memories and torture them until they were broken little things," she said. "Once a young witch was broken down completely, my sister found it very easy to replace her memories with new ones, making her believe that she had been born a true daughter of a priestess."

"And what did she do with the girls she couldn't break?" I asked, thinking of just how close I had come to having an icepick shoved through my brain.

"She had various uses for the girls she couldn't turn into daughters," she said. "Some of them were added to her living doll collection, which you're no doubt familiar with at this point."

I cringed, thinking of the time I had stumbled upon that room of horrors.

"This period in our history is particularly well-suited to this type of rehabilitation," the ruby priestess said. "No one was closely monitoring private mental health facilities the way they are in our current time. And here, if any of her girls escaped, they would have nowhere to go. Of course, Hazel understood better than anyone that it was very dangerous to meddle with the past. Right now, for example, in 1951, all five of us are alive and well. My past self is back home right about now, probably fast asleep in her bed with no idea that I am sitting here with you now."

She crossed her legs and leaned back.

"If I wasn't afraid of causing some kind of catastrophic event, I could go to her now and warn her about you," she said, a secret kind of smile crossing her lips, as if the thought had only just now occurred to her. "I could knock on my own door and say, Magda, in fifty years, go to this small town in Peachville and murder a young girl named Claire before Halloween so she doesn't have a chance to give birth to the woman who will end us all."

She laughed, doubling over in her chair, as if the idea was the most hilarious thing she had ever heard.

It terrified me, though, because she was right. What was to keep any of them from going back in time and killing me before I was even born? I shuddered at the thought.

"As fun as that might be," she said, finally calming enough to speak, "it's simply a terrible idea. Messing with the past is a very dangerous game. For that reason, Hazel always covered her tracks as best she could."

I sat down fully on the bed, no longer strong enough to stand. "She burned the institute down," I said, finally putting the detective words together. "She murdered all the girls she'd been unable to break and burned it to the ground with all of them inside, didn't she?"

"Which is why it's so ironic that she herself was killed the same way," she said. "And yes, she would keep the institute open from 1947 to late 1951, filling it with girls she intended to groom as daughters of her own. When fall of 1951 arrived each time, she would turn some of the girls into hunters. Others she would devour to extend her own life, since she had no true daughters of her own. And when they were all dead, she would burn the institute to the ground. The papers would declare it one of the worst tragedies in the history of the state, and everyone would go about their business. Meanwhile, my sister would destroy her portal and create a new one that led her back to 1947, and she would start all over. Keeping the cycle the same meant very little interference, and since the manipulation of time is such an extremely rare ability, none of us could meddle in her business. Not even our High Priestess."

"How many times?" I asked in a whisper. "How many times did she go through this cycle?"

"Oh, goodness, I can't even imagine," she said. She placed her index finger on her chin and looked up at the ceiling for a minute before finally nodding. "I think this was the tenth."

My mouth went dry at the thought, and my heart ached for all those girls. Hundreds stolen from their lives and tortured. It made me sick.

"She was simply doing what she could to find her own piece of happiness," she said, as if it were a perfectly normal thing to do.

I scoffed, shaking my head.

"What?" she asked. Then, she nodded. "Oh, you don't think we deserve happiness? We're human, too, Harper. Well, as much human as you are."

"Don't compare yourself to me," I said.

She shrugged. "You came to your demon side honestly. I'll admit that much. But in the end, we are both part demon, part human. I know that you think what we've done is horrible, but once upon a time, the five of us were innocent young girls. Just like you," she said. "We wanted to be happy, and we wanted to learn to use our magic to change the world. To help the world."

"Help?"

"Once we realized we were in over our heads, of course, there was no way to stop what we had started," she said. "Not without ending our own lives, and none of us were willing to do that. I know this won't mean much to you from where you stand, but the five of us were every bit as much victims as the rest of the girls who have been pulled into the Order."

I wasn't buying this sob story for one second.

"And the demons you enslave and devour so that you can use their power for your own?" I asked. "What about them?"

"It's so much more complicated than that," she said.

"You're so young. You can't possibly understand what we've all been put through over the centuries since we first were thrown into this life. But I'm not here to try to convince you to forgive the Order of Shadows. I know I won't be able to change your mind about that."

"No, you won't," I said.

"I came here to offer something to you," she said. "But I wanted you to first understand that I have taken a big risk in coming to you like this. Since I was the only sister who knew the portal was still open and where to find it, I knew that this was my chance to get you alone. If my sisters or the High Priestess knew I was here talking to you right now, they would kill me without a second thought."

"I doubt that," I said, shaking my head. "They'd never cripple the ruby gates, no matter how angry you made them."

She laughed at that, her eyes closing and a hand coming to her throat. Her nails were painted blood-red, and a large glittering ruby ring caught the light.

"You know a lot, but you don't know everything," she said. "I can be replaced just as easily as any Prima."

"That's what your sister was trying to do with the sapphire gates the night she kidnapped me," I said. "But she failed."

"My sister was acting in secret, trying to gain more power for herself," she said. "Our High Priestess wasn't exactly happy about that when she found out what my sister was planning to do, I can tell you that. I suspect the High Priestess had her own plans for reopening the sapphire gates until Hazel ruined it all by almost killing the last of Eloisa's bloodline."

"Zara," I whispered.

"She's still alive, though, I've heard," the ruby priestess said. "But that's not what I came here to talk about, either."

"Go on," I said.

"After Eloisa died, the High Priestess put a failsafe in place. A spell that would allow her to replace any of the rest of us much easier should we die," she said. "Since Hazel had no true daughters of her own, it was imperative that we come up with another way to anoint a new priestess without having to kill someone of her direct bloodline. Otherwise, when you killed the emerald priestess, you might have simultaneously killed every witch tied to the emerald gates in a single instant."

The ruby priestess laughed at the thought, but I nearly threw up.

My hand flew to my mouth. Had I really almost killed them all? Eloise and her daughters? The thousands of demons and witches tied to the emerald gates?

"Don't blame yourself, dear," she said, waving a hand in the air as if it were no big deal. "If you didn't know, you didn't do it on purpose. And besides, your precious friends from Cypress are safe. However, it's your demon and the rest of them who are in danger now."

My head snapped up at that.

"Jackson?" I asked, heart racing. "What's happened to him?"

"He's fine. For now," she said. She stood and walked toward me, stopping at the end of the bed and running her hand along the wood of the canopy. "But my sister Hazel knew he was looking for you. He was killing her poor hunters by the dozens. She knew he would eventually stumble on the right information and find this place. Of course, he wouldn't find you there since in the present day, there's nothing here anymore but an abandoned house and a condemned old hospital."

"What did she do to him?" I asked, standing.

"Before she died, she left him a present to find just in case she wasn't there to intercept him herself," she said. "Something so enticing, she knew he wouldn't be able to resist."

"What?"

The ruby priestess walked around the room, touching the things that had once belonged to her sister. She was taking her time in telling me, holding me there at the edge of the cliff.

"Replicating your handwriting and your way of talking wasn't difficult for her after all the work she'd done studying your memories," she said. "It was quite brilliant what she did, actually. Too bad she didn't live to see her trap work so beautifully."

"Tell me," I said through clenched teeth. Perhaps I did still have some power left. I reached for it, finding a spark of energy.

"She made copies of the emerald gate ritual items, put them in a box with a handwritten note from you telling him you were locked in the past, but that you'd managed to kill the emerald priestess and capture her heart," she said, placing her own hand on her chest. "She told him to set the gates free, and that's exactly what he plans to do. Only, instead of releasing the gates, using those items will trigger a trap that will allow my sister, the amethyst priestess, to come through and destroy them all. She gave the tasks to Gladys, of course, because she is the deadliest of us all. At least you can rest easy knowing his death will be swift."

She smiled, and I gathered the rest of the power I had left in my hands. A fiery glow emanated from my hands, but the ruby priestess seemed unconcerned. Her complacence only fueled my anger, and I pushed harder to connect to the tree in the backyard, pulling its power into my body.

"Harper," she said, shaking her head. "You should know better than to try to start something right now. I know what you've been put through. If I wanted to, I could kill you with a glance."

Her eyes flashed red for an instant, and I stepped back.

"If you really are as smart as I think you are, you'll drop that power," she said, the smile gone from her face for the first time since she had appeared. "I have been grateful for the diversion and challenge you've provided, and I would rather continue to play this game. Killing you now would be too easy. If I have to face you, someday, I'd rather do it when you had at least a small chance of survival. Let it go, Harper."

My chest rose and fell with each labored and furious breath. I wished with all my heart that I did have the power to fight her now, but she was right. I was in no shape to start a fight with this woman. Besides, even if I could kill her right now, I'd be giving up my only chance of finding the portal home.

Reluctantly, I let the power drop from my hands and sank down onto the bed.

"Good girl," she said, her smile and cheery tone instantly returned. "Now, I really am running out of time. But before I go, I want to offer you the opportunity to return home. If we go now, you might even have a chance to warn this Jackson of yours before he attempts to use the fake ritual items."

"What do you want?" I asked, knowing we had finally reached the real reason for this unexpected visit.

"I want my sister's heart," she said. "I'm in trouble with the

High Priestess for not telling her about this place. She says I put all of us at risk by keeping it from her, but if I return the master stone to her, I'll be back in her good graces. If you hand it over to me willingly, I will show you the way home right now."

I eyed her. "How do I know the portal home isn't being guarded by your army?" I asked. "I hardly believe you'd just let me go free."

"Oh, I would," she said, walking back around the bed to stand in front of me. "I would take the stone and send you on your way. All you would have to do is agree that even if you destroy the rest of my sisters along the way, you will let me live in peace."

I shook my head. "I don't trust you," I said. "Maybe you're lying about Jackson, too, just to get me to agree to come with you."

"I can assure you I'm not lying about Jackson," she said. "He has the ritual items now in the castle of the Southern Kingdom. I imagine they are already making plans to set the first gate free tomorrow. Cypress? Yes, I am sure they would start there. He's running out of time, and so are you. The portal my sister created will not stay open much longer now that she's gone. This is your only chance, Harper. I can tell you're not carrying the stone with you now, or I would simply take it for myself. I don't have time to search for it, so I'm hoping you'll hand it over."

"You know I can't do that," I said, a piece of my heart breaking as I said the words.

I wanted to keep Jackson safe, but if I gave that master stone to her, they would simply create a new emerald priestess and the witches and demons tied to all of the emerald gates would remain prisoners. I also had these other girls to think about. I couldn't just abandon them.

The ruby priestess drew in a long breath and let it out slowly. She shook her head and clasped her hands together.

"I was so hoping you loved your demon enough to agree to my terms," she said. "But since you do not, I have no choice but to leave you here. Believe me when I say that I will truly miss the challenge you presented to us. Winning this war will be easy now, I'm afraid. Once that portal closes, Harper, there will be no way home for you. Time travel is not something just any witch can do. Are you really sure you want to resign yourself to that fate?"

A tear slid down my cheek, but I brushed it away. I longed for home, but I would not make a deal with the devil herself. I couldn't.

She shrugged and sighed again.

"Well, sadly, I must go. And since I can't have you following me back to the portal..."

She swirled her hands in the air, and red smoke poured from her fingertips, forming ropes that looked like snakes.

Before I could move or reach for my power, a blast of red energy pushed me back onto the bed. The red smoke wound around my legs and my torso, binding my arms to my side. I struggled against them, but they were too strong.

"The more you resist them, the tighter they will grow," she said.

Rope snakes slithered around my throat, red fangs protruding from their gaping mouths.

"As long as you don't try to break free, they're practically harmless and will disappear in about an hour," she said. She leaned closer. "If you do try to get away, though, you'll be introduced to a very particular form of poison that I'm afraid you would never recover from. You'd be dead in minutes."

I stopped struggling, but inside, my heart was breaking. Was I doing the right thing by staying here? How could I make any other choice?

"It has truly been a pleasure, my dear," the ruby priestess said, smiling. She sat on the edge of the bed and stroked my hair, a move that seemed eerily familiar, as if she'd done this once before.

My body shivered at her touch, but I was powerless to move away.

"Before I go, I will make you one last promise," she said, looking into my eyes. "I highly doubt I'll ever see you again, but if, somehow, you do manage, despite all the odds stacked against you, to find your way home and save your friends, I will devote my life to you. I do like being on the winning side, after all, and if you can make it back from this, I will give you all the information you need to take down the rest of the Order of Shadows. I give you my word."

Her snakes were coiled so tightly around my neck, I didn't dare move to respond.

She stood and smoothed her skirt.

"Goodbye, Harper," she said, smiling down at me.

She lifted her palms into the air and a shimmer of red dust seemed to fall on her from out of nowhere. Her body disappeared, but the door of the bedroom opened and closed as she left.

If I could just somehow manage to follow her with my astral projection, I could find the portal. If she'd been telling the truth that these snakes would only last an hour, there was some hope that we could still get to that portal before it closed.

But I had to follow her.

I closed my eyes, praying I still had some power left.

I reached deep inside, connecting to the core of my strength. Beneath the snakes coiling around my body, my skin buzzed with energy. I pushed deeper, seeking out any other source of power I could find. The grass, the animals, the trees. I begged for more.

I stilled my racing heart and focused on separating my spirit from my body. I poured all of my will and strength into this one last wish, but just as I felt my spirit begin to detach, a sharp pain shot through my head.

I cried out and felt the snakes coil tighter around my throat.

My spirit fell back into my body, and the last thing I remembered before passing out was the hissing of a snake in my ear.

AMETHYSTS

JACKSON

I paced the floor of my room late into the night, trying to think of any other possibilities the Order might throw at us tomorrow. We could be facing anything once the ritual began, and right now, I really couldn't afford to lose anyone else. I had to find a way to keep them all safe.

Someone knocked on my door, and I ran to it, knowing no one would disturb me at this hour unless it was important.

Joost stood in the hallway, a worried look on his face.

"Sorry to wake you, but we finished going over everything at the asylum and that house," he said.

"Come in," I said, sweeping my arm forward. "I wasn't sleeping, anyway. What did you find? Anything promising?"

Joost shook his head. He held something in his hand, but it was wrapped in a white cloth, and I couldn't quite tell what it was. My heart tightened.

"What is it?" I asked. Had he found something of Harper's?

He swallowed and handed me the wrapped item. "We didn't find much," he said. "But just before we left, something in the hallway upstairs caught my eye. It was wedged under one of the steps leading up to the third floor, and it was completely covered in dust, like it had been there for a long time."

My stomach knotted as I unwrapped the small items inside the fabric, but what I found inside did not belong to Harper. I had a feeling, though, that it belonged to someone who wanted her dead.

"Oh my God," I said.

I lifted the collar from the fabric and held it up to the light. Dust covered the stones, but there was no mistaking their color.

The entire collar was made of large, square amethysts.

DISAPPEAR

LEA

I returned to the throne room just as my mother announced that it was time for the feast to begin. The crowd slowly made their way to the dining hall, where I was expected to sit at my father's side.

I searched through the mass of demons for the one who might be able to help me right now. I was sure most of the King's Guard was here tonight.

When I finally found him, Ezrah was standing near the head table, guarding the council members who had already been seated.

"I need to talk to you," I whispered.

"Good evening, Princess," he said. He smiled, but behind his eyes was a warning.

I completely ignored it.

"Midnight," I said. "I don't care what you have to do to get away, but I need you to meet me in the south garden."

"Of course your safety is our priority, Princess," he said

loudly as he nodded at a couple walking by. When they were out of ear-shot, he gave me a look of pure frustration. "You're asking this tonight of all nights?"

"Tonight is the best night," I said. "With everything going on, I'm not being guarded by my watchdogs. I can disappear for a while and not be missed."

"Lea—"

"I'm begging you, Ezrah," I said, holding his gaze with my own.

Finally, he gave a subtle nod and looked away.

My shoulders loosened, and I took a deep breath. My mother caught my eye as I turned and waved me over to the table.

"Where have you been, sweetheart?" she asked. "I was looking for you everywhere."

"It seems everyone wants to talk to the long-lost princess tonight," I said with a laugh, ignoring the angry expression on her face. "What's for dinner?"

I sat down at my father's side and for the next several hours, I played the role of the returned and faithful princess. As the hours of eating and dancing ticked by, though, I kept my eyes open, watching the patterns of my parents' movements. I watched Kael make his rounds, talking to everyone. I noticed when he was watching me and when he wasn't.

I noticed every guard who seemed to always be around when I turned to check. I wasn't dumb enough to believe I had freedom tonight just because the handmaidens had not been allowed to attend the opening of the festival. I was certain either Kael or my parents had asked specific guards and servants to keep an eye on me.

And I couldn't have anyone finding out where I disappeared to when the time came.

Shortly before midnight, I saw my opportunity.

Father had fallen asleep on his throne, and Mother was deep in conversation with several ladies I recognized from my childhood. Kael had his back turned to me at the moment, and I knew that wouldn't last long. His eyes seemed to seek me out every few minutes lately.

The guards assigned to watch me would be the hardest to trick, but at this late hour, there was only one guard I had noticed following me. He pretended to look away any time my eyes fell on him, but he was always there, just a few steps away.

A demon stood next to him with a full glass of winterberry wine. I moved closer to the woman, and just as she stepped forward to greet another of her friends, I slipped my foot right in front of hers and stepped away so fast, no one noticed me in the chaos that followed.

The woman's glass flew out of her hands, the crystal shattering on the pure obsidian floors of the main throne room. Wine went everywhere, splashing onto the fine dresses and suits of every demon in a small radius.

The guard turned to help the demon to her feet, and with a quick glance to make sure none of the other players in my secret game of chess had moved, I ran.

As soon as I was out of sight, I shifted and flew through the hallways as fast as I could. There were no guards patrolling the main parts of the castle tonight. The crowd had been contained to the dining room and the throne room, so all of the castle's guards had been stationed there for the evening.

By the time I stepped into the garden, it was a few minutes

after midnight. At first, I saw no sign of Ezrah, and my heart beat faster. What if he couldn't get away? What if he refused to take the risk?

Impatient, I tapped the heel of my shoe against the stones at the base of the fountain. I pressed my lips together, trying to keep my nerves under control, and when footsteps sounded at the garden's entrance, I tensed with a mixture of hope and terror.

Ezrah stepped into the light of the spring moons and shook his head.

"I can't believe you're really here," he said. "Do you understand how dangerous this is? What's this about?"

"I understand exactly how dangerous this is, Ezrah," I said. "But I'm finished with playing it safe."

His eyes flashed with concern.

"Why do I have a feeling you're about to ask me to do something even more dangerous than I could have imagined?"

"Because I am," I said, excitement and hope building inside me. "I need you to take me to see Aerden."

I WILL GIVE YOU MINE

AERDEN

Today's training still wore hard in my muscles, and I lay across my makeshift bed and prayed for sleep.

In the distance, I could still hear the music from the festival. I imagined Lea dressed in a new gown, dancing with the demon she was now promised to. Was she as miserable as I was?

Or was she starting to get used to life in the castle again?

Once upon a time, she had been very happy there, dreaming of her future with Jackson. I could close my eyes and still remember the way her smile would light up an entire room. Even the seasons where six suns were out and shining could not compare to the smile on Lea's face when she was genuinely happy.

I hadn't seen that smile in so long, but I could still see it in my mind. That smile had kept me sane during my century of imprisonment.

But she never smiled like that anymore, and deep down, I knew I was to blame for her sadness.

Footsteps sounded on the steps, and everyone in our small cell sat up from where we were resting. It was late. The guards didn't usually come back to check on us at this hour, so we were all on edge, waiting for the next hammer to drop.

After the training earlier, we were all exhausted. Whoever walked through that door, I prayed they weren't bringing bad news.

To my surprise, though, it wasn't Reynar or any of the regular guards. Instead, Ezrah appeared, his eyes locking with mine the moment he stepped into the cell block.

I stood quickly, walking to the door of the cell I shared with my teammates.

Ezrah made a show of jangling his keys and unlocking the door.

"Aerden, I need to see you outside," he said.

My heart raced. If he'd taken the risk to come all the way down here this late at night, something must have happened. On the outside, I kept my head down and pretended to be a subservient prisoner. I knew that role well, and I was good at it, but inside, I was in a panic.

It seemed to take forever to walk past the other cells and up the stone steps to the arena's holding area.

"What's happened?" I asked as soon as I knew my voice wouldn't be heard by the others. "Is Lea okay?"

"Just follow me," he said sharply. "And keep your voice down."

I wanted to take him by the throat and force him to tell me what was going on. The training and the aches, I could handle.

I could even handle the constant sting of the whip. But I couldn't handle waiting to hear if she was okay.

It took all my willpower to simply do as he'd asked and follow him quietly through the holding area toward the main entrance to the arena's battlefield.

It was mostly dark outside, all the training lights from earlier having been extinguished and the light of the two moons lost in shadows. I opened my mouth to ask why he'd brought me here, but the moment my eyes landed on the woman standing in a patch of moonlight at the center of the battlefield, I lost my voice.

Please, don't let me be dreaming.

The delicate skirts of her dress skimmed the dusty floor as she turned, and our eyes met across the darkness.

I nearly fell to my knees at the sight of her, and for a moment, we both stood still, hardly able to believe this was real.

She broke out into a run, one hand holding up the skirts of her long dress. I ran toward her, and when we met in the center of the battlefield, she fell into my arms.

Everything else vanished in the truth of her embrace. For this moment, there was no pain. No battle. No chains. There was only the feel of her body against mine.

I'd been so afraid I wouldn't see her before the beginning of the games, when we'd have nothing but a distant gaze to connect us to each other. But she was here, her head pressed against my shoulder and her arms tight around my waist.

I lowered my head and brushed my lips against her perfect braids, wishing I could hold her forever, but knowing we might both be killed if we were seen together.

When she finally pulled away, she grabbed my hands.

"Are you okay?" she asked, her eyes sweeping up and down my body. When she noticed the fresh lash-marks across my chest, pain and anger shone in her eyes. She ran a delicate fingertip across one of the wounds, and I shivered at her touch. "Oh, Aerden, what have they done to you?"

"I've been through worse," I said, laughing, but she lifted her eyes to mine and there were tears hovering at the edge of her lashes.

I ran my thumb across her cheekbone to catch the first tear as it fell, and she leaned into me, closing her eyes.

"Don't cry, Lea," I said softly. "We're survivors, you and me."

The light of the silver moon fell across her face, and her beauty in that moment was a gift I would never forget. When she opened her eyes again and looked at me, I knew that this was the woman she was always meant to be. The outward appearance of a true princess, but the eyes and heart of a warrior.

I was grateful her time in the castle had not changed that.

"How did you get here?" I asked. "Please, tell me you didn't put yourself in danger coming to see me like this."

"I had to see you," she said.

"Has something happened?" I asked. "Are you safe?"

"I'm safe for now, but things are shifting, Aerden." She looked away for a moment. "Tonight, I met a demon named Kael. I don't know who he is or where he came from, but some-how, he's managed to gain incredible power here in the city. These games were his idea, Aerden. And..."

Her voice trailed off, and my heart tightened in my chest.

"I already know," I said.

Her eyes snapped to mine. "You do?" she asked, almost breathless.

"Prisoners talk," I said, attempting to laugh it off, but coming up short. "Is he nice, at least?"

She shook her head. "He threatened me," she said. "Not directly, but I felt it. He told me he was going to find a way to break me."

"He obviously doesn't know you," I said. I swallowed back the anger that was boiling inside me. If he dared to hurt her, I would kill him myself. Twice.

She smiled, but I could see that he had shaken her. "I need to figure out where he came from," she said. "And how he got onto the council after only being here for a few years."

"Be careful," I warned. "If he's serious about these threats, he'll be looking for any opportunity to hurt you."

"Let him try," she said.

"You should get out of here, Lea," I said. "Have Ezrah talk to Andros and arrange something during the games, when everyone is distracted."

"I'm not leaving here without you," she said. "Besides, I can't go until I figure out what's really going on with my father. Aerden, he's different. You saw him the day we were brought before him. He's sick, but I think it's more than that. It's like he's cursed or something. Also, something your mother said to me tonight scared me more than anything."

"You spoke to my mother?" I asked. "Don't trust anything she says."

Lea shook her head. "I don't know. I think we've misunderstood her actions," she said. "She told me that the council isn't really making the decisions around here anymore. That's why she couldn't get you out of the dungeons when you returned."

I looked away, not sure I could believe that.

"If the council isn't making the decisions, then who is?"

She raised an eyebrow. "What if it's Kael?" she asked. "Or someone we don't even know about? I'm telling you something terrible is going on here, and I can't help but wonder if it's connected to the Order somehow."

A sick feeling knotted in my stomach. If the Order somehow had control of this city, she had to get out of here. We both did.

"I'm going to find out what's going on," she said. She bit her lower lip, as if she were considering whether or not to say what she was thinking. "Your mother told me about the key, Aerden. Why did you give it to me when you knew it was supposed to keep you safe?"

I avoided her eyes. "You are the future queen," he said. "You were marrying my brother. Your safety was more important than my own."

It was the truth, but not all of it. I couldn't bring myself to tell her the rest.

"She told me she bought it from a shaman in the borderlands," she said. "The shaman told her it was a key used by hunters to pull demons through to the human world."

"But it's a diamond key," I said.

"Exactly. That proves there are diamond gates somewhere, Aerden," she said. "I think there is more to learn here in this city than we ever dreamed. I want to get to the truth of it before we figure out how the hell to get back home."

I shook my head, something bothering me about my mother's story.

"Listen," I said. "If you're going to start looking into this, there's something else you might want to find out about my mother. Do you remember the old scholar who used to run the schools? Trention?"

"I remember him. Why?" she asked.

"He's here in the dungeons with me," I said. "We've been talking a lot, and he told me that he discovered a book inside the castle's library that contained a map of the Shadow World he'd never seen before."

"What's so important about a map?" she asked.

"On the map, there was a third kingdom, Lea. To the east across the Sea of Glass," I said. "A kingdom bigger than the north and south combined."

She laughed. "That's impossible, Aerden. You think we wouldn't know about another kingdom like that? You know the Sea of Glass as well as I do. Once you get far enough out, there's nothing but a wall of darkness at the end of the world. There's no way through it, and there's certainly nothing beyond it."

"Trention said the pages of this book were made of diamond dust," I said. "That has to mean something, right?"

She looked away, trying to make sense of it.

"But there's something else," I said. "He tried to take that book to the council and show it to the king, but my mother intercepted him before the meeting. She promised to show it to the council for him, but the next day, he was arrested and thrown into the dungeons. As far as he knows, she never showed that book to anyone. Why would she want to hide that book, Lea? A book made from diamonds?"

"Do you trust this demon? Trention?"

"With my life," I said.

"Then I'm going to find the answers, Aerden. I won't rest until I figure out what's going on in this city."

"What are you planning to do?" I asked. "If anyone finds out what you're doing...Even coming here to talk to me could put your life in danger, Lea. If they believe you're still loyal to me—"

"I'll always be loyal to you, Aerden," she said, gripping my hand tighter and filling my heart with a strange mix of joy and terror. "You're one of the most important people in my world. Nothing can change that. If I could have, I'd have gotten you out of this mess by now."

"You've already sacrificed enough for me. I can take care of myself," I said. "How are they treating you overall?"

"It's better than life in the dungeons," she said. "Those were not exactly fun times, let me tell you."

She tried to keep her voice light, but my chest tightened at the thought of her alone in those dark dungeons with no one to talk to.

"I shouldn't complain, though," she said. "I mean, just look at you."

She ruffled my hair and stuck her tongue out.

My cheeks warmed. "Awful, huh?"

"Nah, you just look rugged and tough," she said, smiling. But soon, the smile faded from her face, and she shook her head. "Aerden, why are you doing this? These games?"

"It's just something I need to do," I said, hoping she wouldn't try to talk me out of it the way my mother had.

Her eyes searched mine, and I knew if anyone in any world could understand why, it would be Lea.

"You're still that little shadowling near the cliffs, trying to prove himself," she said. "But the truth is, you are the greatest warrior I've ever known."

"Then I'll have no problem winning."

She smiled, and though it was not the sun-bright smiles of our childhood, for now, it was enough.

"Well, from the looks of you, you could use some help with your training."

I suppressed a smile. "Oh, and you think you could teach me something in that dress?" I asked, eyebrow raised.

"I could kick your ass in this dress," she said, laughing. "If I had time, I'd prove it to you."

"I await the day," I said.

Our smiles faded, and the true gravity of the moment fell on both of us. Our time was running out.

"Someday soon," she said, holding my gaze for a long time.

I wanted nothing more than to take her in my arms again and tell her the truth about my feelings. I had waited too long. Lost too many chances already.

But how could I tell her here? Now? When I was still a slave?

"What's going to happen to us, Aerden?" she asked, leaning closer. "There are times when I feel like it's all slipping out of our hands. You're fighting in the games. Harper's gone and no one seems to know where she is or if she's even alive. Jackson's out of his mind looking for her and still trying to keep the Southern Kingdom safe. Brighton Manor is gone. As much as I thought I hated it at the time, I miss our life there."

"Harper is alive, Lea. I can feel her, even though she's distant. And Jackson is strong. We'll all be together again, someday," I said. "We have to believe that, Lea. We've always known that defeating the Order wasn't going to be easy, but at least now we know it's possible. We can't give up. Not now."

"I just wish..."

She paused, looking away. Finally, she sighed and shook

her head. I wondered what it was that she was struggling so hard to say.

"I should go," she said, taking my hand in hers. "Promise me you'll win, Aerden. I can't lose you. Not after everything."

"I promise I will do everything in my power to win," I said. "And when I do, we'll find a way out of here together."

A shadow of a smile crossed her lips. "I like the sound of that," she said.

She threw her arms around me, and I held her close for as long as I could.

"When you walk onto this battlefield in a few days, look for me in the prima cavea," she said, motioning toward the front row in the center of the arena that held two large thrones and a section of tall chairs meant for the council and their families. "When you need strength, look into my eyes, and I will give you mine."

I ran my hand along her face, wishing I could tell her that she had always been my greatest strength and my deepest weakness.

"You should go," I said, breaking my own heart with the words.

She turned and started back toward the north exit.

"Oh," she said, turning when she'd only gotten a few steps away. She met my eyes and smiled. "I have a present for you, but it's a surprise. Keep your eyes open for it, okay?"

I nodded and smiled back at her. "I will," I said. "Goodnight, Lea."

"Goodnight, Aerden," she said, gathering her skirts in her hands and running across the last strips of moonlight before disappearing through the archway.

THE FIRE OF SIX SUNS

LEA

I couldn't sleep.

After leaving Aerden, I spent most of the night tossing and turning in my bed, feeling guilty that he was sleeping on a floor somewhere while I had every comfort in the world.

It was difficult to see him there, dirty and wounded, but deep down, I knew my sleeplessness was about more than that.

I'd originally gone to see him, because I wanted to confront him about the key. To ask him why he'd given it to me when he'd known it was something meant to keep him safe. And I wanted to know exactly why he'd left the castle in the first place.

But seeing him again after our months apart, I realized I was terrified to ask him the truth.

And I'd been nervous as hell to tell him about Kael and the fact that I was expected to marry another demon.

But if Aerden and I were nothing more than friends, why

did I think he would care? I doubted Aerden would want me to marry anyone who didn't have my best interests at heart, but it was more than that. I knew the news would hurt him.

I turned over in my soft bed and brought a pillow to my face so I could scream into it without anyone in the next room hearing me.

What was truly happening between Aerden and me?

In my mind, I was simply going to visit a dear, old friend and make sure he was okay before the games. But in my heart, the moment I had turned to see him standing there, I knew he meant much more to me than any friend.

I could still feel the soft touch of his hand on my face.

When had this happened? During our months at Brighton Manor? Or had there been something between us before, when we were shadowlings?

I'd been told at a very early age that Denaer—who would, of course, someday change his name to Jackson—was to be my future mate. We were promised at birth, and as a dutiful princess, I had never questioned it or thought of wanting someone else. It was simply the way it was meant to be.

And I loved him.

But I loved Aerden, too. The three of us were nearly insep-arable as shadowlings, always adventuring and training together. I cared for them both. The only difference was that Jackson was meant to be more and Aerden was not.

Thinking back to it now, I wasn't sure if that spark of elec-tricity had existed before last night. I couldn't remember ever looking at Aerden and feeling that way before, but there was no denying that it had been there last night when he'd gath-ered me into his arms and pulled me close.

I'd wanted to hold onto him forever. To know what it was like to be kissed by him.

I closed my eyes and screamed into the pillow again.

This couldn't be happening. Maybe the stress of being in the castle and having to pretend to be someone I wasn't was making me think I felt more for him than I really did. It was just the happiness of seeing an old friend, right? Of seeing someone who knew me for the Lea I truly was?

That had to be it.

Of course I cared for Aerden and was happy to see him. I wanted him to be safe, and the way I felt for him was no different than if it had been Mordecai standing there last night, or Joost.

But the moment that thought came to me, I knew it was a lie.

The butterflies that fluttered through me every time I pictured Aerden's eyes on mine was not simply because he was any friend.

It was because he was Aerden.

Dammit.

I couldn't let this happen. As much as I wanted to keep him safe and get us both back to the Southern Kingdom, I simply couldn't allow myself to feel more for him than friendship.

I had tried love once, and look where it had gotten me.

And yes, there was a part of me that hoped Aerden felt the same way when he saw me last night, but once upon a time, I'd believed Jackson loved me, too. The way men fell in and out of love was confusing and hurtful. It couldn't be trusted.

I wouldn't open my heart to anyone like that ever again. I wasn't sure I'd survive it a second time.

Aerden was nothing more than a friend to me. One I cared for very deeply. There would never be anything more to it than that. Period. Thinking there could be more would only distract me, and I couldn't afford that type of distraction right now. I had a lot of things to do before the end of the King's Games.

"Princess?" Presha came into the room and frowned at the pillow pressed to my mouth. "Are you feeling alright?"

I sat up and tossed the pillow aside. "I'm fine," I said. "Is it time to get dressed?"

"Yes, Princess," she said. "There is an early meal in honor of your father this morning in the dining room. He requested your presence, specifically. I believe only members of the council will be present."

I lifted my eyes in surprise. Members of the council only? Was Ezrah's one wish coming true?

The one thing the Resistance seemed to want from me right now was information about the council's meetings. They wanted to know my father's plans. Only, now, I wondered if they were really my father's plans at all.

"That sounds wonderful," I said, standing.

She helped me into the bath and later, into a soft pink dress that whispered across the floor when I walked.

As she and the other girls braided my hair, I asked questions about Kael as innocently as I could.

"What do you know of him?" I asked.

"What would you like to know?" Presha asked.

I shrugged. "Everything, I guess. I'm supposed to be mated to him, after all, and I know almost nothing about him except what he looks like."

One of the handmaidens giggled, and when I glanced at

her, her cheeks were the color of raspberries. She ducked her head, and Presha snapped at her.

"Don't be disrespectful, girl. He is not intended for you."

"It's fine," I said, smiling at the girl. "He is quite handsome, isn't he?"

She blushed again and nodded.

"What else have you heard about him?" I asked. "Do you know where he grew up? Or when he came to the city?"

Presha focused on my braids but didn't seem too suspicious of my questions. She also didn't know much more than I did.

"He's been here for a short time only," she said. "Maybe twenty years or so? I'm not sure where he came from, but he was the talk of the city when he first arrived."

"How so?" I asked.

"The rumor was that he simply walked through the gates one morning and went straight to the castle, demanding a meeting with the king himself," she said. "For a while, some told the story that he almost killed a guard who refused to let him in, but I don't think you should worry about that, Princess. I believe that was nothing more than a rumor."

I seriously doubted that.

"He sounds very confident in himself," I said.

"Oh, yes, he is. In fact, with the king in such poor health, Kael often runs the council meetings, from what I've heard," she said. "He is very well trusted by the king."

I raised an eyebrow at this.

Tatiana had warned me that the council existed in name only these days and that someone else had taken control, but I wasn't certain she meant Kael until just now. If even a hand-maiden realized how much power he'd claimed for himself over the past several years, then it must be known by almost everyone in the city.

They already saw him as the right hand of the king. A marriage to me would only solidify his standing.

How the heck had he managed that in such a short period of time?

"Presha, may I ask you a difficult question?"

She met my eyes in the mirror and nodded. "I can't promise I'll be able to answer it, but you may ask me anything you wish, of course."

"What happened to my father?" I asked. "Why is he in such poor health?"

She and another girl exchanged glances, and at first, no one said a word. Finally, though, Presha cleared her throat and gave me an answer.

"He began to grow weaker shortly after you came to the castle for the last time," Presha said. "Many believe his illness is the result of a broken heart. That's why this festival is so incredibly important. Many demons here in the city are hopeful that your return will restore his health."

Guilt rolled through me in waves. Was that true? Could heartache and regret cause a demon as strong as my father to deteriorate so quickly?

I shook my head. I refused to believe this was all because of a broken heart. I had begged my father to help get Aerden back and to go after Jackson once he disappeared into the human world. He knew I intended to follow them both if he didn't help me, and yet he refused, calling me a traitor.

I knew he wasn't happy to see me go, but he hadn't stopped me back then, and he hadn't done one single thing to help me. Besides, it wasn't like he was truly happy to see me when his guards brought me back here.

No, he had thrown me in the dungeons like a piece of trash.

There had to be more to his illness.

And I wanted to find out the truth, no matter what kind of danger it put me in here in the city.

The problem was, I had no idea where to start. I rarely ever got a chance to get close to my father, and I wasn't sure that asking him about it directly would get me anything more than a trip back to the dungeons below.

My mother acted like nothing was wrong, so I doubted she would tell me anything useful, either. Aerden's mother, Tatiana, had talked to me truthfully more than anyone else here so far, so maybe she was a good one to try to talk to about my father.

Still, I wasn't sure I could trust her, either. For whatever reason, she wanted me labeled a traitor, too, and I couldn't forget that. Maybe last night's conversation was just her way of luring me into a trap where she could prove that I was not as happy to be home as I pretended to be.

Then there was the matter of the book she had taken from Trention.

Other than that, my only ally here in the castle was Ezrah. I was so focused on getting to Aerden last night that I hadn't thought to ask Ezrah about Kael. If I found a chance to see him again without bringing any suspicion to his loyalties, I would ask him, but I was anxious to find out more now. I didn't want to wait.

Patience had never been one of my virtues.

"Are you ready, Princess?" Presha asked. "The king will be waiting."

I studied my appearance in the mirror, once again wishing I could just wear jeans. But there was nothing to be done about it right now. I just had to be a snake in the grass for a little while longer.

Maybe when this tournament was over, Aerden and I would be free to talk without having to sneak around. We could figure out how to escape from the city.

We could go home.

"I'm ready," I said.

"Come with me," she said. "I'll lead you to the dining room."

I rolled my eyes. She said it as if I had no idea where the dining room was in this castle, even though this had been my home much longer than it had been hers.

I followed her through the doorway, but before we could take more than a handful of steps, Kael appeared in the hallway and bowed to me.

"Good morning, Princess." He offered his arm to me and smiled. "May I escort you to the dining hall?"

I wanted to choke that conceited smile off his pretty face, but instead, I smiled and put my hand on his arm.

"It would be my pleasure," I said.

Let him think his threats last night had rattled me. Maybe if he believed I was falling in line, he would open up to me. We were, after all, supposed to be spending the rest of our immortal lives together. If he believed I was on his side, maybe he would begin to trust me enough to let me in on whatever his plans were for this city.

There was no doubt he had come here specifically with the

intention of someday becoming king. And I wanted to know why.

"It's a lovely morning," he said as we walked. "I thought perhaps after the meal this morning, we could take a walk through the gardens together."

"Whatever suits you," I said. "I would like to get to know you better if we're to spend a life as mates."

He raised an eyebrow at that. "It's good to see you warming up to the idea," he said. "If I'm being honest, I thought it would take more time for you to agree to be my queen."

I bit my tongue. I hardly believed he was being honest about anything, but it would no doubt make his ascension to the throne much smoother to have the princess next to him. And I had no doubt that as soon as we were officially mated, my father's life would come to an end.

What would happen to our people then? I found it difficult to believe that a demon who had suggested the return of the King's Games would be a kind and loving king.

The thought made me shudder. If he honestly thought I would simply sit back and allow him to rule this kingdom while I took long walks in the garden, he was delusional.

"If I feel that you're truly committed to going through with this marriage, it will make things much easier on you here in the castle," he said.

"Why is that?" I asked.

"How much freedom have you had so far since you were brought up from the dungeons?"

I glanced over at him, surprised he would bring that up so openly with so many demons walking through these hallways. After last night's speech of lies from my parents, most demons here believed I had come home on my own after a long battle against the Order.

"If you are aware of my time in the dungeons, then you're no doubt also aware of the handmaidens and guards who have been watching my every move since I was freed," I said.

He smiled. An expression I was starting to hate with the fire of six suns.

"Well, what would you say if I told you I was the one responsible for making sure you were brought up here in the first place and given your old room?" he asked. "The council was nervous about giving you much freedom when your loyalties were still in question, so I suggested assigning several handmaidens to guard you and watch over you."

I bristled at this. So, he was openly admitting that he controlled the council.

"Perhaps if I convince the council you are also devoted to our future marriage, they will agree to give you a bit more freedom around here," he said. "Of course, if you break my trust in any way or give me any reason to suspect you are not entirely loyal to me and this kingdom, the consequences could be very uncomfortable for you."

He was resorting to threats, already? Who did this guy think he was?

We walked for a few moments in silence, and we smiled at everyone who passed, as if we were some happy couple taking a casual stroll through the halls of the castle, but as soon as we moved into a more secluded area, he paused and turned to me.

"Do I not get so much as a simple thank you for all that I've already done for you, Lazalea?" he asked.

I stopped, and it took me a second to realize he was being completely serious.

"Thank you?" I said it more as a question, but he seemed to be okay with that.

"You're welcome," he said. He took a few steps forward, but then he turned again, and this time there was cruelty in his eyes. "Except I have one issue I think needs to be addressed between us."

He backed me into a corner, and I glanced around, hoping to see at least a guard or a handmaiden. Anyone who was witnessing this exchange. But there was no one near us.

"Imagine my concern last night after the feast when I wanted to have one final dance with you before the evening was over," he said. "Imagine how it felt to look everywhere and not find the one demon who should be most devoted to me and waiting to see if I would summon her."

"Summon?" I asked, my anger rising despite his threatening tone.

"Yes, summon. You exist here, Princess, because I found it in my best interest to have you here. There is no other reason," he said. "Your mother and father and the other members of the council would have been more than happy to let you rot away in those dungeons for decades. You are only here because I want you here. And yet, when I summoned you, you were nowhere to be found. Why is that?"

I lifted my chin, even though he was much bigger than I was and was obviously trying to get me to shrink down into nothing here in the corner.

"I have no idea," I said. "Maybe you didn't look in the right places. I didn't realize I was expected to be at your beck and call."

"Well, you are," he said. "And I looked everywhere. Where did you disappear to?"

"I didn't go anywhere except my own chambers, and last I knew, there was nothing wrong with going into my own suite of rooms when I was tired," I said.

He sucked in a sharp breath and turned his head, as if I'd slapped him. When his eyes snapped back to mine, they were filled with rage.

"You're lying to me, Lazalea," he said. He grabbed my wrists and lifted them up, pressing them hard against the stone wall behind me. "I cannot express to you how disappointing that is. I was hoping after our little talk last night, you would understand the delicate position you find yourself in, but I can see that I was not being clear enough at the time. So, let me be clear."

He squeezed my wrists so hard, it was all I could do to keep from crying out.

"You're hurting me," I said. "Let me go."

"I will never let you go," he said. "I don't want to hurt you, but this is nothing compared to what I'm fully prepared to do if you don't start treating me with the respect I demand from you. Do you understand?"

"I understand that respect, by definition, is not something that can be demanded. It must be earned," I said.

He released one of my wrists and slapped me hard across the face. My cheek burned, but I kept my head high.

"One of my guards told me that the prisoner who was brought in at the same time as you was called out of his room last night," he said. "He didn't see where the prisoner was taken, but I find it curious that he disappeared around the same time you did. You didn't happen to pay a visit to him last night, did you? Because that would be quite disappointing indeed. A visit to see him now would prove where your loyalties lie, Princess, and I'm afraid that if someone were able to prove you were still loyal to your old way of life that there would be nothing I could do to save you. So, tell me. Where were you last night?"

My heart beat faster, but I kept my mouth shut, afraid that if I dared to open it, I would tell him what I really thought of the way he was treating me. I couldn't get revenge on him or put an end to him from the dungeons, but I vowed right then and there that I would find a way to destroy him.

No one put their hands on me like this. No one who survived, anyway.

"Fine," he said. "You don't have to answer me. I already know the truth. Just know that I'm not about to let the son of a fellow council member go free. I know your history with his brother, Denaer, and as happy as he would be to take his brother's place, I'm sure, your precious Aerden is never going to be given the chance. If you dare to contact him again or attempt to go see him while he is still a prisoner, I will make sure he doesn't survive even the first round of these games. You will watch him die, and you will know that it was your actions that sealed his fate. I will be king, and nothing is going to stand in my way. You can join me, or you can die. Those are your options, Princess."

He released me and straightened his shirt. I rubbed my sore wrists, hoping he would just walk away so I didn't feel tempted to kill him right here and now.

Instead, he smiled and offered his arm to me again, as if he hadn't just threatened my life.

"Now that's out of the way, I hope we can have a pleasant morning together," he said. "Shall we?"

Bitterness coated my tongue as I placed my hand on his arm and followed him the rest of the way to the dining room.

My plan to find out exactly who he was and what he wanted with this kingdom had just escalated to a plan to see him completely destroyed.

No one threatened my friends and lived to regret it.

A MESSAGE

HARPER

Someone pounded on the door to the bedroom, and I opened my eyes to harsh sunlight streaming through the curtains.

"Harper," Brooke shouted.

Something slammed against the door, and I sat up, immediately grabbing my head. For a moment, I couldn't remember where I was, but the instant the memory of last night's visit from the ruby priestess came rushing back, I jumped out of bed and pulled on the heavy wooden door.

It was stuck, no doubt held closed by some magic cast by the witch when she left.

"I'm here," I shouted to Brooke through the door. "I think the door is locked with magic. Hold on."

I placed my palms against the wood and summoned my power. Unlike yesterday, the connection to my magic came easily. I concentrated on a vision of the door opening, and whatever magic held it closed suddenly released.

Brooke rushed into the room, her eyes wide.

"What happened?" she asked. "I've been trying to get into this room for fifteen minutes. I was pounding and screaming like a lunatic. I was terrified something happened to you."

I stepped away from the door and gripped my head again. It felt like my brain was throbbing against my skull.

"Are you sick?" she asked, placing a hand on my shoulder. "What in the world happened?"

"I don't even know where to start," I said, pacing the room. "Did they have Excedrin back in the fifties? Because I need a gallon of it about right now. My head is killing me."

"You're exhausted," she said. "You used way too much magic yesterday, but what happened to the door?"

"When I came into this room last night, the ruby priestess was here waiting for me," I said.

Brooke gasped and brought the back of her fist to her mouth. "Oh my God, Harper, did she attack you?"

"Not exactly," I said, still trying to make sense of everything she had told me. I did my best to explain the conversation to Brooke, but the pain in my head was excruciating. I had taken myself to the limit of my abilities before, but maybe the months of torture had been too hard on my body.

"Come on," Brooke said. "Let's check all the bathrooms and the kitchen for some aspirin or something. Then, we can figure out what we're going to do. At least now we know there's an open portal somewhere. There's still a chance we can go home."

"I don't have time to search this house," I said. "We either need to find this portal and figure out a way to get all the girls out of the hospital so they can come with us, or I need to figure out a way to warn Jackson from here."

"You could leave another message somewhere," she said, pacing alongside me. "Maybe bury another note with a rose at the house in Peachville?"

I shook my head. "The house is gone, remember," I said. "Burned to the ground. Jackson would never go back there now. The ruby priestess said he was already back at the castle in the Southern Kingdom, but I don't have any way to get there. The rose portal by Brighton Lake wasn't put there by my father until much later."

"Where, then?" she asked. "Where else would Jackson go?"

"I thought about Cypress, because that's most likely going to be their first target," I said. "But I still feel like burying a message in the ground at this point is just going to be leaving it all to chance. He might never see it in time, or he might find it way before he's supposed to. I have to figure something out."

"I can't think of anything else we could do," Brooke said. "Short of having someone hand deliver it to him at a specific point in time, I can't imagine how you're going to be sure he received a message like this."

Goosebumps broke out across my arms, and I stopped pacing. "That's it," I said, hope fluttering through my heart. I started rummaging through the drawers, looking for anything I could wear on a road trip. "Brooke, you're a genius."

"I am?" she asked. "Wait, how are you going to find someone in the fifties who would still be able to deliver a message to him without disrupting the timeline? Didn't the ruby priestess warn you about interfering too much with the past?"

I turned to her and smiled. "I'm going to get cleaned up and dressed. Then I'm going to visit a friend. Would you mind going downstairs and seeing if there's any food in this place? I need all the energy I can get right now. It's going to be a long day."

"Of course, I'll do whatever you need," she said. "But I still don't understand. Where are you going?"

I grabbed a dress that looked promising and set it on the counter in the bathroom as I started to undress. I didn't have a second to waste.

"I'm going to Chicago," I said, the buzz of excitement starting to ease the pain in my head.

"To see who?" she asked.

I smiled. "I'm going to see a vampire named Rend."

A WILDCARD

HARPER

Without a cell phone or GPS, I had no idea where I really was or where I needed to go from here. Brooke and I quickly searched the house for an old-school map, but we couldn't find one.

"Where exactly are you going?" Brooke asked.

"Downtown Chicago," I said. "I have no idea when this club was first started, but I'm praying he's there. Rend is my best shot at getting a message to Jackson without messing up the timeline. Also, I'm hoping he might be able to help us with the girls and their memories. He's the most talented alchemist in the world. If anyone can help us, it's Rend."

"Are you sure you can trust him?" Brooke said.

"I would trust him with my life," I said.

At least I would trust the Rend I knew with my life. The Rend of 1951? That was a wildcard for me. I knew he had come by his reputation as a terrifying vampire honestly. I knew that there was a time in the past when any witch who got near him was bound to get her throat ripped out and her blood drained from her body.

I just had to hope that 1950's Rend was the more controlled, non-blood-drinking Rend that I knew and loved from the future.

I'd be lying if I said I wasn't a bit nervous about seeking him out. I had no idea what year he started Venom and what year he'd given up witch's blood as his main source of sustenance.

There was no one else, though.

Most of the people I knew and trusted from my life weren't even born yet, and everyone else would risk altering the future in ways I couldn't begin to predict.

Jackson hadn't come through from the Shadow World yet, so trying to give him the warning myself was not an option. Seeing him now and trying to warn him in person would be too dangerous, anyway.

Lea, Mordecai, and the others definitely weren't in the human world yet, and going to the Shadow World would be way too difficult and dangerous. Without my father's portal through the roses, I wouldn't have a clue how to get there and back safely.

My father.

I stopped cold at the thought of him. It hadn't sunk in until that very moment that he was still alive right now. He was in the Shadow World, but he was alive and strong.

If I could get to him, I could warn him about the battle against the sapphire priestess.

I could save his life.

My heart ached at the thought of all the things I could change. All the deaths I could prevent if I just had the chance.

Was there any version of a future where I could have both my mother and father in my life?

I shook my head. It was impossible to know what messing with the past would do, and as much as it broke my heart that they were both gone, I had to stay focused on saving those who were still alive now.

Rend was my only hope.

"What should I do here in the meantime? Or do you want me to come with you?" Brooke asked. "What if the ruby priestess comes back?"

"I don't want you to come with me. I can't be sure Rend is done with witch's blood at this point in his life, and it's just too dangerous," I said. "But while I'm gone, you could search for the portal home. I can't imagine it's too far from here if the priestess was travelling back and forth all the time."

Brooke nodded. "I hope you're right. If we can just find it before it closes, we'll be saved," she said. "Do you think I should keep up with Melody's appearance?"

"Only when someone from the hospital or the police department comes by," I said. "Otherwise, I think it's probably better to just try to blend in and not bring too much attention to yourself. They know a girl named Brooke apparently died in the fire, but the cops have no idea what you look like."

"Got it," Brooke said. "When do you think you'll be back?"

"I have no idea," I said, sliding into a wool coat I found in the closet. "Only that I'll be back as soon as I possibly can."

"Oh, here. I found this and thought you might need it." She handed me a stack of bills. The cash, mostly five and ten-dollar-bills, looked so different from the money I was used to, but as long as it spent the same way, I was happy to have it. At least ten dollars would go a lot further now than it did in the twenty-first century.

She also reached into her pocket and pulled out a set of keys with an emerald scarab beetle charm dangling from it.

"What's this?" I asked.

"There's a Cadillac parked behind the house. The keys were inside," she said with a laugh. "I guess no one around here is worried about theft these days."

"It's a different world for sure," I said with a nervous laugh.

I was so used to modern conveniences that I had no idea what to expect once I stepped outside the house.

Just before I left, Brooke handed me a small piece of paper with a set of numbers scribbled on it.

"This is the phone number for this house," she said. "Call and give me an update if you can, okay?"

"I'll try," I said.

"Harper, please be careful," she said, taking my hand.

"I will," I said. "I'll be back as soon as I can."

She nodded and held the back door open for me as I stepped out into the cool, April air with a small overnight bag packed with essentials and a change of clothes. The only other thing I brought with me was the emerald master stone, strapped against my thigh, just in case.

I had considered shifting into my demon form to fly to Chicago. It would certainly be much faster, but it would also take a toll on my power. Plus, I didn't need to leave a clear, traceable trail of where I was going.

And magic always left a trail.

So, it was a road-trip for me. With no cell phone or power steering.

Luckily, the Cadillac did have an automatic transmission.

I'd never learned to drive a stick shift, and I really didn't want to start learning now.

I left the house and drove around until I caught sight of a five-and-dime on the corner. I parked on the street and ran inside.

"Do you have a roadmap of the United States?" I asked.

He studied me for a moment. "I have a travelog," he said, pulling a thick booklet from behind the counter. He was an older man with a receding hairline and thick, black glasses. "Where are you headed?"

"Chicago." I placed a five-dollar-bill on the counter.

"Vacation?" he asked, taking his time with the change.

"Something like that," I said with a smile.

He leaned across the counter. "Not all alone, I hope," he said. "A nice young woman shouldn't be on the road by herself."

I stared at him for a moment until I remembered where I was.

"Oh, of course not," I said. "My father asked me to pick up the map before we left."

He smiled at that, obviously relieved that a young woman wasn't heading out onto the dangerous streets all by herself.

I barely turned around before I rolled my eyes. I definitely couldn't get stuck here in this time and place.

I would never survive it.

THE POWER INSIDE MY BLOOD

HARPER

With the help of a local newspaper, I discovered I was trapped in some small town in Ohio. Luckily, that was much closer to Chicago than most places I could have ended up.

The drive over there, though, took a lot longer than I expected. There weren't even any interstates or major highways yet, so I had to take backroads and kept having to pull over to figure out exactly which way to go.

I wasn't exactly proficient at reading maps like this, either. I was so used to just putting an address into my phone and following the instructions called out to me as I drove.

I had to go a lot slower, too, because the last thing I wanted was to get pulled over and asked to present some kind of identification. Sure, magic could help me through anything, but I didn't want to use any if I didn't have to. The less there was to trace where I was headed, the better.

It was dark by the time I pulled through the city limits.

I had been to Chicago before, but the city was nearly unrecognizable. I sat in traffic for a while just staring at the old cars and the way people dressed. Almost every woman who passed by on the sidewalk was wearing a dress that fell well below her knees. Men were dressed in slacks and hats with long wool coats.

I was glad I had chosen a simple green dress for myself. I needed to blend in to the Chicago nightlife as much as possible.

When I saw an opportunity to pull over and park on the side of the road, I took it. I had stopped just about half an hour ago to buy a more detailed map of the city, and I spread it out now across the front of the car, searching for the street closest to Venom's alleyway entrance.

Several men and couples passing by gave me suspicious looks, and a few times, I thought someone was going to knock on my window to see if I needed help, but I did my best to ignore them. I was on a tight timeline here, and I didn't have time to worry about people who were concerned about a woman alone in her car on a dark side street.

I located the street on the map and memorized the turns it would take for me to get there. It wasn't too far away, so instead of taking the car, which someone might be looking for at some point, I got out and started walking.

It was freezing cold here, and the wind whipped my hair back and forth across my face. I pulled my coat tighter around my body, but wished I had something thicker covering my legs. By the time I reached the alley where Venom's entrance was located, it was well past ten in the evening, and I was shivering from head to toe.

I had been to Chicago with Jackson a couple times before

this whole mess started with the emerald priestess. We'd met up with Rend and Franki soon after Rend had repaired the entrance here, and we'd gone on a few double dates in the city.

Still, everything looked so different now. The restaurants weren't the same. Some of the buildings had changed. I kept losing my bearings.

I had to double-check the street signs, but when I was sure I'd found the right alley, I started slowly walking down, hoping to feel the familiar magical pull of Venom's entrance.

It was completely hidden to people who were not magic-users, but everyone who had some type of magic running through their veins felt the call of the place the moment they got close enough. It was how Rend kept it hidden from normal humans.

But the further I walked down the alley, the more I started to panic. I wasn't feeling the pull of the entrance the way I normally did. What if I was too early? What if Rend didn't open this entrance to the club for another several years?

How would I find him?

The entrance to his house in the Hall of Doorways was only accessible from Venom, as far as I knew, which was how he designed his door to work in order to use the Hall without interference from the Order of Shadows.

I still didn't understand how he had managed that partic-ular type of magic, but there was still a lot about Rend I didn't know.

All I knew right now was that I needed to find him. No matter what.

I kept walking down the dark alley, searching for any sign of the familiar doorway to Venom that would usually reveal itself once you got closer, but it never appeared.

Sure that I'd gone too far, I started walking back toward the street. It seemed to be getting colder by the minute, and even though the two tall buildings on either side of the alley kept me shielded from a lot of the wind, I was still freezing my butt off.

If I didn't find him tonight, maybe I could find a hotel close by and try again in the morning. When the sun was out.

Tired and scared, I stopped where I thought the door should be and ran my hand along the rough brick.

"Please," I whispered, leaning my head against the wall. "Rend, where are you?"

Behind me, a growl echoed through the darkness. I turned just in time to see a dark figure materialize out of shadow and run straight for me.

I tried to run or shift, but the man moved so fast, I didn't have a chance. He grabbed my shoulders and spun me around, pinning my back against the rough wall.

His mouth opened wide, fangs extended toward my neck. His dark, red eyes made him nearly unrecognizable.

"Rend, don't," I shouted, pushing against his chest. He was too strong for me to move him even an inch. "Rend, you can't do this. You know me. Stop, please."

He tilted his head slightly, his teeth grazing my skin. The heat of his breath nearly burned me. His hands on my shoulders were feverish, burning through the light coat I wore.

Even though I had met several vampires in my day through Rend and the club, they were mostly very controlled around me. Other than the one night we had helped Rend save Franki, I had never come this close to actually being drained by a blood-thirsty vampire.

Seeing him like this was terrifying.

I didn't want to use my magic on him, because I didn't want to hurt him, but I would do it if I had to.

"Rend, I need you to listen to me," I said as calmly as I could, trying to steady the furious beating of my heart. He seemed to respond to the sound of his name, so I kept repeating it, hoping to get through to him somehow. "Rend, my name is Harper, and I've been looking for you. I have something very important I need your help with."

He growled again and ran his fangs across the skin of my neck, but he didn't draw blood. At least not yet.

I resisted the temptation to reach for my power. I knew that would only send him deeper into his blood-thirst, and if I pushed him over the edge, I would have no choice but to fight him.

It was the power inside my blood, running through my veins, that had him in this state to begin with.

But the fact that he had stopped gave me hope. He pulled back and seemed to study me with his red eyes. Still, his grip on my shoulders never loosened.

I could sense that he was just one moment away from sinking those teeth into my skin. If he got even a taste of my blood, it would all be over for me.

"Rend," I said again, this time more forcefully. "Let me go. I know you're in there, and I know you can hear me. This isn't who you are. Let me go."

He pulled back slightly, his eyes seeming to clear for a moment.

Behind him, footsteps sounded against the pavement. Someone was running toward us. I could only pray it wasn't another vampire. I took a deep breath and prepared to connect to my magic.

"What are you doing?" a woman's voice asked. She stood behind him, and in the darkness, I couldn't see her face, but her voice sounded familiar. "Rend, put her down. Now."

He shook his head and leaned toward me, breathing in the scent of me. Someone grabbed his arm, and he pushed her away. He seemed to barely use any energy, but the motion sent the woman flying across the alley.

She hit the brick wall opposite us and grunted.

"Dammit, Rend, I swear to God, I'm going to kill you if you do that again," she said.

He leaned toward me, inhaling deeply and tightening the grip on my shoulders. He couldn't control himself.

What should I do? I didn't want to start a fight with him. The outcome was too uncertain. If I used my magic, he'd be even more agitated and hungry.

But without magic, I was nothing.

"Rend, please stop," I said again. "I need to talk to you. You're my only hope right now."

His eyes flashed red again, and I could almost feel the hunger rolling off him. I was sure this was it, but when he released me and turned sharply toward the woman behind him, I realized what had caught his attention.

Azure—the head bartender from Venom—stood several feet away with a small dagger pressed to her wrist. Small drops of blood fell to the pavement at her feet.

I had never been happier to see a familiar face, but what the hell was she doing? Trying to get herself killed?

Rend shifted to pure smoke and in an instant, was wrapped around her entire body. When he took human form again, he had her wrist near his mouth.

With faster reflexes than any normal human witch, Azure

kicked Rend in the gut and slammed her dagger into his chest, pressing hard until it was buried in his skin.

I gasped, hardly able to believe my eyes. Was she trying to kill him?

"Don't," I shouted.

But Rend's eyes had cleared, and he stepped back against the brick wall, grasping the hilt of the dagger and wrenching it from his chest. He shook his head and dropped the weapon to the ground.

"Dammit, Azure, was that really necessary?" he asked. "That hurt like hell."

He swayed in place for a moment, confusion in his eyes.

"What did you put on this thing? Poison?"

His eyelids drooped slightly, and he fell to his knees. Just before he passed out, his eyes connected with mine.

"Who are you?" he asked, as if really seeing me for the first time.

He fell face-first onto the pavement, his head hitting the cement with a hard thunk.

Azure stepped over him and picked her dagger off the ground. She wiped it across the leg of her jeans.

"A good question, even if he won't remember asking it," she said, finally turning to me. "It's time you started talking. Who the hell are you? And what are you doing here?"

UNEASY

JACKSON

We gathered at Eloise's house and went through our plan one more time. So far, we hadn't had any contact from the remaining priestesses of the Order. No threats. Nothing. Either they hadn't yet realized their sister was dead, or they were all in hiding again.

Whatever their reason for not coming after us or attempting to get the emerald ritual items back from us before now, I was glad they were leaving us alone.

But I still wanted everyone to be prepared today. We had no idea what might happen when the first gate went free.

"Mordecai, I want you and the rest of the demons to create a tight perimeter around the entrance to the emerald gate," I said. I motioned to a few witches who'd been freed from the sapphire gates. "I'd like three of you to watch the main highways that lead into town. The rest of you stay hidden here in the house in case anyone comes through the demon door upstairs. If you see anything suspicious, call me immediately.

Unless it's just a single witch, don't try to fight them on your own. Just let us know they're coming and let the demons take care of them."

The witches nodded and headed to take to their stations.

"Rend, you and Azure can guard the stairway leading down to the ritual room," I said. "Franki, you stand at the bottom of the steps. If anyone attacks and manages to get through the line of demons, guard that entrance with your lives. We just need enough time to complete the ritual."

He agreed, but I noticed that he still looked uneasy about this whole thing. Maybe he really was just stressed about the Brotherhood of Shadows, but his concern worried me, too. Something was definitely bothering him. He wasn't himself the past couple days.

"We need five witches for the actual ceremony, so Eloise, Caroline, Meredith, Azure, and Mary Anne will all take their places here." I pointed to a crude drawing of the pentagram on the ritual room floor. "Do you guys remember everything you need to do for the ceremony?"

They all nodded, and Eloise and her daughters clasped hands. They were excited, but nervous. As long as we could just get through this ritual, they would be free from the Order forever.

"Essex, you and I will guard the women as they begin the ritual," I said. "These statues lining the room here and here will most likely come to life. When the creatures wake up, I'll freeze them in place. I just need you to send your spear through the soft parts under their shell. Aim for their bellies, and we should be able to take them down quickly."

Essex raised his spear into the air.

"I am being ready," he said.

Mary Anne took his hand and smiled. "We can do this," she said. "We should get moving. We only have about half an hour until three."

I folded my papers and stuffed them in my bag. It was time. We'd been over the plan several times, and I felt like we had all our bases covered. Still, my body was lit up with nerves.

We'd performed this type of ceremony more than a hundred times when we freed the sapphire gates, but this time, there were still so many unknown factors. There were so many lives on the line here, and I knew we needed to do this as quickly as possible.

Still, something had been bothering me last night.

I picked the emerald ring from the table and stared at it.

What I couldn't figure out was how in the world Harper had gotten ahold of this ring. The other ritual items stayed in the human world, but the ring could only be found in the Shadow World.

How had Harper gone into the Shadow World and gotten it on her own?

In her letter, she hadn't explained how she'd gotten any of these items. Sure, it made sense that she had the master stone. That had been the one thing keeping the emerald priestess alive for all these years.

The other items were questionable.

Harper had been with us when we performed all of these rituals to release the sapphire gates. She knew from experience that we didn't need all of the original items from the creation of the first gate. All we needed to release an individual gate were the master stone and ring. Everything else—the chalice, the necklace, and the dagger—came from that gate rather than from the priestess's gate.

So why had she left them all inside that box?

And how had she gotten them? She couldn't have taken them from the emerald priestess of the 1950's or it would have changed the timeline. Without the ring in its place on the Shadow World to act as an anchor, no new gates could have been created and no new demons could have been pulled through.

So the ring had to have been in place until very recently. We knew from asking around that new witches had been initiated in some of the emerald covens right up until the day we discovered these items there in the box.

Without the ring in place, that shouldn't have been possible.

I couldn't wrap my head around it.

I'd mentioned it to Mary Anne this morning, but she told me I was just being nervous about nothing. She said that if Harper left those items for us, she had to have known they were safe.

I had studied her note to me, and there was no doubt it sounded like her. And I had no doubt that she was locked away in the past.

Eloise said she could feel a difference now, so that proved the emerald priestess was truly dead. I was probably worrying for nothing, but as we all made our way out to the ritual room's entrance in the woods at the edge of town, I thought of the collar made of amethysts. Why had it been in the emerald priestess's house? And what did it have to do with Harper?

I couldn't shake the feeling there was still something I was missing.

But what?

THE DOOR

HARPER

I t took a moment for me to find my voice.

Ever since my memories had returned at the hospital, I'd noticed that it was taking my brain some time to catch up with the events around me. I wasn't reacting as quickly as normal, which was bound to get me killed if I wasn't careful.

But I didn't have time to worry about whether my brain had been permanently damaged by the emerald priestess. I needed to come up with a quick answer that would keep Azure from driving that dagger into my heart.

"My name is Harper," I said. "I've known both you and Rend for a long time, but we just haven't met yet. We won't actually meet each other for several decades. I know how crazy that sounds, but I have a story I need to tell you both. I just need you to trust me."

Azure scoffed, her shoulders shaking with laughter. "Trust? I don't trust anyone. Least of all witches dumb enough to walk down this alley in the middle of the night actually looking for the most powerful vampire in town."

"The Rend I know doesn't drink the blood of witches," I said. "I was here looking for the entrance to his club. Venom."

Her eyes flashed with surprise, but she was careful to try to hide it.

"Who sent you here?" she asked, pointing her dagger at me and taking several steps forward. "No one but our closest friends know about Rend's plans for Venom."

"No one sent me," I said, holding my hands up. "I know about Venom because where I'm from, it already exists and has for more than half a century. I could describe it to you down to the last detail. I've been in Rend's home hidden away in the Alps, and I could describe that for you, too. I told you. I know Rend, and I know you, too, Azure."

Her lips opened at the sound of her name. "How do you know all these things?" she asked. "I've never seen you before in my life."

"Yes, you have," I said. "Just not yet. I don't belong here in the fifties. I belong in the twenty-first century, but the emerald priestess of the Order of Shadows brought me here so she could torture me and try to steal my memories. I killed her, and now I'm trapped here. I need your help, and I need Rend's help. I know it sounds crazy, but I'm kind of short on time here. I need you to at least hear me out, and I'd rather we find a safe, warm place to discuss this, if you don't mind."

Azure shook her head. "Twenty-first century, huh? And I'm still alive?" she asked. "And Rend? He's good? He doesn't drink from witches, anymore? At all?"

"Never," I said. "And yes, you're both alive and well. Both working at Venom. In the future, there's an entrance here in this alley. A doorway that appears when someone whose blood contains magic gets close enough to sense it."

"It hasn't been built yet," she said. "The doorway, I mean. But you're right. We were here scoping out this alley as a potential entrance when Rend just took off. He moved so fast, I couldn't stop him. He must have sensed your power. You're a witch from the Order?"

"Not exactly," I said. "I'm half-demon, half-witch. Descendant of a Prima and a demon king."

Her hand fluttered to her mouth. "Holy shit," she said. "No wonder he was so out of control. That's a damn powerful combination. I would venture to say you are the only one who exists."

"I've known others who are half-demon, half-witch," I said, "but no, I've never met another with my exact lineage."

I glanced around the dark alley.

"Don't worry," Azure said. "No one else is going to come running at you from the shadows. The vampires around here know this is Rend's territory, so they steer clear unless they have business with him."

I nodded toward Rend. "Is he going to be okay?" I asked. "I can't believe you actually stabbed him."

She shrugged, as if it wasn't the first time. "He'll have a headache until he can create one of his potions to counteract the poison I used, but he'll be fine," she said. "He just needs to sleep for a little while."

"You're not just going to leave him here, are you?"

"It's tempting after the way he acted just now," she said, laughing. "But no, I'll move him inside. Guess there's no time like the present to make that door. You said in the future it's located somewhere around here?"

I nodded and put my hand on the brick wall. "Close to this point, as far as I can remember," I said.

She shrugged and made a motion for me to move back.

"Make sure he doesn't wake up or anything," she said. "He should be out for a few hours, but you never know. He's even stronger than he looks sometimes."

I stepped back toward where Rend lay on the pavement, his body completely unmoving. Still, I kept an eye on him. I didn't want a replay of that terrifying event.

A dark blue glow emanated from the area in front of me, though, drawing my eye. Azure was consumed with the light, and I could swear I saw the flutter of wings against her back. They were iridescent; translucent and shining.

Since when did Azure have wings? And come to think of it, how was she still just as young and beautiful sixty plus years from now as she was today?

I watched in awe as she crouched near the bottom of the wall and pushed the light into the brick, transforming it with a single touch. She moved slowly up the wall, and a door materialized out of nowhere.

The sheer power radiating from her nearly knocked me to my knees. I had always assumed Azure was a witch. A human. I'd heard someone once say that she had been with Rend since the creation of Venom, and I wondered if he'd created some kind of potion to elongate her life. I never dreamed she was something more, but seeing her now, I had no doubt that Azure was some kind of hybrid, like me.

But a hybrid of what?

When the door was complete, she stepped back, admiring her work. I caught sight of her wings again as the light faded.

When the light was gone, so were the wings.

"How does that look?" she asked, crossing her arms and staring at it with a critical look on her face. "I feel like it's pretty plain. Should I make it fancier, you think?"

"It's perfect," I said, my voice nearly a whisper. "Um, Azure?"

She turned to face me. "Yes?"

"What are you?" I asked. "I always assumed you were a human witch, but—"

She laughed. "I take it you've never seen a fae before?" she asked. "Didn't the wings give it away?"

I smiled, despite the fear and awe flowing through me. "No, I never have," I said. "But I have to admit, that was one of the coolest things I've ever seen. Your wings are breathtaking."

"Thank you," she said, offering me a rare, genuine smile. The Azure I knew didn't smile often, but she wouldn't be the first person in my life who had been hardened by time and heartbreak.

"Come on," she said. "Let's get him inside the club. I'm afraid there isn't much to it yet. It's practically bare at this point. But someday, it's going to be great. A safe haven for everyone like us."

She said it as if it were nothing more than a dream, but I knew better.

"It will be," I said. "I've seen it with my own eyes. It's an amazing place."

Her eyes widened, and she stared at me, as if not quite sure she should believe me.

"Come on, let's get him inside," she said.

I stared at Rend's motionless body and shook my head. I wasn't sure how Azure planned to lift him. He was a giant compared to us, but if I needed to, I could probably lift him with my magic.

Azure beat me to it, though. She simply gathered her magic in her hands and nodded toward the door.

"Open that, will you?" she asked.

I ran over to open the door to Venom, almost laughing as I realized that I was the very first person to ever open this door. Jackson would get a kick out of that when he found out.

Azure's blue light surrounded Rend's body. She lifted him without a thought, throwing his body over her shoulder and carrying him inside.

I laughed and shook my head. This was turning out to be a very interesting adventure.

I followed them through the entrance to Venom and closed the door behind me.

A VERY INTERESTING GIFT

HARPER

The inside of Venom was nothing like it would someday become. Now, it was nothing more than a bare warehouse of a room with a couple long tables in the middle.

Azure dropped Rend on a pile of folded curtains in the corner and met me in the center of the room.

"I don't suppose there's any way to wake him up early, is there?" I asked. "I don't mean to be a pain, but I'm kind of on a tight deadline here."

"Why is that?" she asked, sitting down at the table and pulling over a stack of folders.

"It's a long story."

I sat down next to her, glancing at the contents of the folders as she opened them. It looked like construction plans. Blueprints for Venom.

"We've got some time," she said, glancing at Rend. "And

no, there's no good way to wake him up early. Not without making him angry. Well, angrier."

She smiled as she said it, and I wondered again what their history really was all about.

"Tell me what you're really doing here," she said. "We'll fill him in when he wakes up."

I glanced over at Rend and sighed. This wasn't exactly what I had been hoping for, but at least I was alive. And as far as I knew, Azure was just as likely to be near Jackson right now in the future as Rend was.

"You guys are obviously familiar with the Order of Shadows, right?" I asked.

She gave me a look like I was stupid.

"Okay, then," I muttered. "You're familiar. Well, the emerald priestess kidnapped me and tortured me. She brought me to this hospital here in the past, and she kept me there for months. I didn't remember who I was for the most part, but no matter what she did, I kept having flashbacks and memories of my real life. Anyway, long story short, she couldn't break me, so she tried to lobotomize me."

Azure stopped thumbing through her plans. "She what?"

"She tried to basically put an icepick-shaped instrument through my brain," I said, making a stabbing motion toward my eye.

"I know what it is," she said. "I just can't believe she would do that to you. Why even keep you alive if she hates you that much?"

"I don't know, honestly," I said. "She seemed to have a thing for turning girls into a living doll collection. That or convincing them they were her daughters."

"Good Lord," she said, cringing. "How did you get out of that?"

"I killed her," I said.

Azure laughed and leaned back in her chair. "You killed a priestess of the Order of Shadows?" she asked. "I have to admit, I was starting to believe you there for a second. No one can kill those witches. Besides, one dies, and her oldest daughter takes over. The next priestess is probably already being initiated as we speak."

I sat back in my chair. Oh, right. They didn't yet understand how the Order and its five main priestesses worked.

As far as Azure knew, a new priestess came into power when her mother died. No one back in this time understood that the reigning priestesses were over two hundred years old and living off the power stolen from those they had killed or consumed.

I wasn't sure how much I should tell her. In the end, I needed to be sure that nothing I said or did here in the past would change the future, but I was planning on asking them to forget all of this before I left, anyway.

I decided to err on the side of caution for now. I may have already said too much by telling her a priestess was dead, but I needed for her to believe me.

"I can't tell you everything, but just know that she's dead," I said. "That's part of why I'm here. She was the only one who could get me home. I didn't realize I was stuck in the past until after I'd killed her."

"Well, if you're looking for someone to cast a portal to send you home, you're out of luck," she said. "I can manipulate time and space to some degree, like I did with that doorway, but I don't know anyone powerful enough to open a portal into the future."

"I didn't come for that," I said. "There are two things I need from Rend. One is help creating a potion that will restore the memories of the other girls who were trapped in that hospital with me. Most of them come from the future, like me, and most of them have no idea who they really are."

"How many girls?" Azure asked.

"Eighty or so," I said.

She shook her head, but she didn't speak. I could tell from the expression on her face that she was sad for those girls. And so was I. I wasn't even sure I'd be able to get them all home at this point. The least I could do was try to restore their memories and help them move on.

"Listen," I started, but someone opened a door on the far side of the room and floated in, her wings shimmering behind her. This woman's wings were much brighter than Azure's had been, and I stood when I saw her, amazed at her strange beauty.

"I think I'm finished for the day," the fairy said, stopping as soon as she saw Rend lying on the floor, unconscious. She glanced from him to Azure, and finally, to me. She gave me a very curious look. "Well, what have we here?"

"Sabine, leave her alone," Azure said.

But the fairy didn't look as though she had any intention of leaving me alone. She circled me, as if studying every inch of my body. She ran her pale fingers down my arms, touching the scars the priestess had left.

"You have great love in your life," she said. She placed her hand near my forehead. "May I?"

I had no idea what she was asking, so I looked to Azure, who shrugged.

"I don't understand what you want to do," I said.

Sabine laughed, and the sound seemed to disperse through the room as if it had come from a hundred voices, rather than just one. "I just want to see," she said.

"You might as well let her do it," Azure said. "Otherwise, she'll never leave you alone. But just this one thing, Sabine. Then you go. We have business here."

Sabine smiled at me, her eyes wide and child-like as she asked again. "May I?"

"Okay," I said, my heart racing.

She placed her hand on my head, and my eyes immediately fell closed. Memories passed through my mind like pictures. The fire that killed my step-father. Being brought to Shadowford. My tattoo. It all passed by so quickly, it made me dizzy.

But all of a sudden, the image stopped on Jackson. He sat at the table in my chambers, drawing. I smiled. I'd spent many nights watching him from the balcony as he drew, some of the visions pleasant. Others horrifying.

God, I missed him.

Sabine held me there for a long moment before she pulled away, something sparkling deep in her opal eyes.

"This love of yours," she said. "He sees visions of the future?"

I nodded. "Sometimes."

"A very interesting gift," she said. "Very interesting, indeed."

"Aunt Sabine is very interested in all things relating to time," Azure said.

"Aunt?" I asked, laughing.

"Great-great-aunt," Sabine said, smiling. "But we don't need to get into all of that."

My eyes widened. I wasn't sure how old Azure was since she hadn't seemed to change at all over the decades, but I could only guess that meant Sabine was ancient. I could certainly feel the power radiating from her. She was no hybrid. Sabine was pure fae, and a strong one.

"You're interested in time?" I asked. "Do you know anyone who could open a portal into the future?"

Sabine shook her head. "No, I'm afraid that is not an ability anyone seems to possess, though it would be quite fun to see the future," she said. "If you'll excuse me, I do need to get going. Please give my regards to poor Rend over there when he wakes up."

Sabine blew kisses toward Azure, then closed her palm tightly. When she opened it again, a bright, white light appeared. Sabine threw the light into the air, and a portal opened. It was too bright for me to see where it led, but I could see lush-green grass and red roses growing in the distance.

"Goodbye, Harper," she said, and I was surprised she knew my name. Had she seen it when she'd reached into my mind? "I hope I'll see you again someday. And Azure? You should trust her. In her mind, I have seen more of the future than I ever dreamed."

She giggled and stepped into the portal. A moment later, the light blinked out.

THANK YOU FOR NOT KILLING ME

HARPER

"What was that all about?" I asked when the fairy was gone. "Why did she want to see my memories?"

Azure sighed. "Sabine is complicated," she said. "I gave up trying to figure out why she wants what she wants a long time ago. All I know for sure is that when she decides she wants something, she won't give up until she has it."

"What was she doing here? She mentioned working on the doors?"

"Sabine did a favor for the Order of Shadows almost a century ago, putting a system in place that allows the witches to travel to each other's houses by using these doors," Azure said.

My mouth dropped open. "Wait. Sabine created the Hall of Doorways?"

"Yes. She also created this club as a personal favor to

Rend," Azure said. "He wanted his own door in the Hall, but he didn't want any of the Order to be able to access it. Apparently, she managed to pull that off."

I sat back, laughing. I couldn't believe it. I'd just met the actual person who had created the Hall of Doorways. It was such an extensive network, I'd wondered how a witch had created something like that. I always assumed a group of powerful witches had done it. I'd never suspected a fairy, of all people.

"Anyway, what was it you were saying before Sabine interrupted us?" she asked. "You said there were eight girls you needed potions for?"

"Eighty," I corrected, and Azure whistled. "I had my memories taken from me years ago when I first moved to Peachville and someone helped me restore them with this potion called the Elixir of Kendria. I was hoping—"

"That elixir won't help those girls," Rend said suddenly, sitting up on the other side of the room. He squinted in the light and held his hand to the side of his head. "Azure, did you really have to poison me again? I told you to stop doing that."

She shrugged, a smile playing at her lips. "You were being bad," she said. "You nearly killed this poor girl. If you can't handle yourself around her now, I'll gladly poison you again, so please, behave."

"Sorry for that," he said, standing and walking over to the table. He inhaled and his eyes flashed red for an instant before he regained control. "What are you? I thought I had most of my urges under control, but your scent caught me by surprise."

"Half-Prima, half-demon-king," Azure said, answering for me. "I think you get a pass on this one. Even I kind of want to see what her blood tastes like."

"Thank you for not killing me," I said, trying to ignore Azure's last comment. "I can't tell you how good it is to see you, Rend."

He studied me for a moment. "How do you know me?"

"Azure said you might need to make a potion to counteract whatever she put on that blade," I said. "Get whatever you need to help you feel better. I have a story to tell you, and then I need your help. A lot of lives depend on it. Lives of people we both care very deeply about."

He and Azure shared a look. Azure nodded.

"I think she's telling the truth, Rend. Even Sabine said we should trust her," she said. "What do you need to recover faster?"

"Sabine? She was here?"

"She said she finished with the doors," Azure said. "But let's concentrate on this potion."

"It depends on what you laced that dagger with," he said. "Arsenic?"

"Among other things," she said. "To be honest, it didn't keep you down nearly as long as I thought it would. If we go down to the lab, I can walk you through the ingredients of the poison so you can make an antidote."

Rend rubbed at the place where he'd been stabbed as if it was nothing more to him than a bee sting. He pulled his shirt over his head to study it, and I couldn't help but notice the way Azure's cheeks went pink at the sight of his muscular chest.

I'd always suspected she had a thing for him, but with Franki in his life, it was hard to tell for sure. Poor Azure. From the way she was looking at him, she was obviously in love with him, and I knew from watching Lea what unrequited love could do to a person over time.

It explained why she almost never smiled.

"No offense, but I can't trust you in my lab and my home," Rend said to me. "But I don't know that I can leave you here by yourself, either."

"She's already been to your house," Azure said.

He eyed me, and I nodded.

"Huge mansion in the Alps," I said. "Gigantic stone fireplace. Elevator that leads down to your lab deep inside the mountain. I've seen it."

He shook his head. "Impossible," he said. "Very few people have ever been to my house. I definitely would have remembered bringing you there."

"If you need proof that I've been there before, I can lead you straight to the right door," I said. "I've been there many times."

"I can't believe this," Rend said, almost breathless as he stared at me. It was obvious I was freaking him out just a little bit. "I have no idea how you know about that door or Venom or any of this, but if Azure says she trusts you, then I trust you. Come on. I've got a headache you wouldn't wish on your worst enemy."

I stood and walked over to the entrance to the Hall of Doorways. I looked back, and Rend motioned for me to lead the way.

I walked down the hallway and stopped at the door clearly marked with a cobra ready to strike. I stepped aside for Rend to open the door. He was obviously surprised and confused, but he was also intrigued.

He opened the door, and I walked past him, stepping into the waiting elevator. He shook his head, but rather than doubt

me any further, he stepped inside the elevator and pressed the
button that would take us down to his laboratory deep inside
the mountain.

A MATCHING KEY

LEA

I kept my eyes on Kael every chance I got. He was the key to all of this, but I just needed to know how. And why. What was he hiding?

After the breakfast feast, a guard came up to him and whispered something in his ear that made him frown. Trouble in paradise, perhaps?

When he came back over to where I stood with my mother, he took her hand and kissed it gently. "My queen, I hope you'll forgive me, but there is something I need to attend to before the afternoon's events," he said. He bowed to me as well, but thankfully he didn't try to take my hand. "We'll postpone our walk in the gardens for another time, Princess."

"I can hardly wait," I said, sarcasm dripping from my tone.

He narrowed his eyes at me, and my mother's hand fluttered absently to the gold chain around her neck.

"I'm so happy the two of you seem to be getting along so well," she said.

If only she knew.

Kael made his exit, and I waited only a moment before excusing myself, as well.

"Don't go, sweetheart," Mother said. "I'm so enjoying your company."

"I'm afraid I haven't been feeling well this morning," I said, rubbing my sore wrists. "I'm going to lie down for a while, but I'll see you this evening."

I placed a kiss on her cheek, and turned to leave the room, not giving her another chance to protest. Since Kael had escorted me to the dining hall, there were no other handmaidens or guards to keep an eye on me. I took this rare opportunity and raced through the halls, searching for any sign of where he had run off to.

There was no doubt in my mind he was up to something, and I wanted to know what it was.

Finally, as I turned a corner in the east wing, I caught sight of him just as he opened the door leading down to the dungeons.

Interesting. Was he going to visit a prisoner?

Carefully, I followed him down, shifting to shadows and keeping to the dark places. Down here, there were plenty of corners to hide in.

To my surprise, though, he didn't stop at the first or second level of the dungeons. Instead, he continued down to the third and final dungeon. We were truly in the belly of the castle now, farther down than most people ever dared to go besides the guards who were stationed here on patrol.

He walked to the far end of a deserted cell block and went inside the final, open cell. There was no one down here at all, so why had he come?

My heart raced as I watched him enter the final cell and glance around. I slunk into a particularly dark spot against the wall in the cell opposite him, and I waited to see what he would do.

He removed something from his coat pocket and out of nowhere, a strangely shaped door with odd carvings appeared in the wall. Light seeped out from all around the edges of the doorway.

He slid a key into the center of the door, and a loud clicking sound echoed through the dungeon.

Kael pushed the door open, glanced around one last time, and then stepped inside.

As soon as he was gone from sight, I reformed and ran to the door. Carefully, I pushed, but it wouldn't budge. There was no following him now without a matching key.

But when my eyes settled on the lock embedded in the center of that strange door, I gasped and pulled my hand back as chills broke out along my skin.

The keyhole was surrounded entirely by a row of tiny, sparkling diamonds.

One thought flashed through my mind before I shifted and flew back up to my room.

Somehow, I had to figure out what the hell those guards had done with my bag, because inside, I had a key that just might open that secret door.

THE WAY IT'S MEANT TO HAPPEN

HARPER

Rend's lab looked almost exactly as I remembered it, which was strangely comforting. I'd been surrounded by so many unfamiliar things, it was nice to be in a place that reminded me of home.

As he worked to create the antidote to the poison concoction Azure had put on her dagger, I told them both the story of the emerald priestess and of the people who were waiting on me back home.

"You're telling me that in the future, you've managed to not only kill two priestesses of the Order, but you've also set all of the demons from the sapphire gates free?" he asked.

"Every last one of them," I said. "And we won't stop until every demon and witch is free. But right now, the people who are fighting that war are in danger."

He stared forward for a long moment, as if letting that news sink in.

"If that's true," he said, "why not surprise them now? If

you know how to get to them and how to kill them, we could put together a small group and kill those priestesses right now. They would never know what hit them. Just think how many demons we could save."

I shook my head. "We can't do that, Rend," I said. "Messing with the past in such a huge way could have catastrophic consequences. And besides, if we killed the sapphire priestess now and let all of those demons go, I would most likely never be born. And if I was never born, I wouldn't be here right now. Who knows what would happen to the world if we messed with the timeline in that way?"

Rend slammed a hand against the table and stood.

"I understand what you're saying, but dammit, it makes me feel so helpless," he said. "With the knowledge you have, we could change everything."

"Which is exactly why we can't do it," I said. "Please, you have to understand. There are so many things I wish I could change. In the future, my own mother and father are both dead. You think I wouldn't do everything in my power to bring them back? But any changes made to this timeline could keep us from winning this war. We have to trust that everything is happening the way it's meant to happen."

"Then why risk coming here in the first place?" he asked, stepping toward me. "You're changing the timeline right now by telling me all of this."

"Am I?" I asked, my stomach rolling as my nerves got the best of me. Rend was kind of terrifying in the fifties. "Or was I always meant to be here? I haven't done anything yet that's changed the timeline as far as we know."

Rend took a deep breath and ran his hand through his hair.

"Okay, so tell me what you need me to do," he said.

My shoulders relaxed slightly. I hadn't realized I'd been carrying so much tension, but the lives of most of the people I loved depended on Rend helping, and now that I knew he was at least willing to listen to me, I had hope that it was going to be okay.

"In the future, the emerald priestess left a trap for Jackson," I said. "It's very possible you're a part of the group that will activate that trap and be captured."

"What's the trap?" Azure asked.

I explained what the ruby priestess had told me about the emerald ritual items.

"The moment Jackson uses those items to free a gate, he's going to trigger a portal," I said. "At that point, an army of witches will come through to capture or kill anyone who is there with him, which may very well include both of you."

"But what can we do from here?" Rend asked. "That's decades in the future."

"Yes, but when the time comes, you'll be there," I said. "You're both still alive and close to Jackson. I need you to warn him not to use those ritual items."

Rend shook his head. "This is a lot of information, and while I'm glad to know these things are possible in the future, I'm not sure I can keep this to myself," he said. "Some day in the future, I'm going to meet you. I'm going to meet Jackson. Why not just warn you about the kidnapping when I first meet you? We could save you from the torture you've endured at the priestess's hands."

"No," I said, my voice trembling. It was such a tempting thought, but I couldn't change things too much. "If you do that, it could alter the other events and we might never get close enough to the emerald priestess to kill her. I can't risk that, no matter what danger we're all in right now."

"I can understand that, but what else do you propose?" he asked.

"I have an idea," I said.

They both looked at me and listened as I explained the plan that I hoped would save the people I loved most in this world from certain death.

I'M NOT GIVING UP

HARPER

"And you think this will work?" I asked, eyeing the stack of small bottles Rend was loading into a large leather bag.

It had taken him almost an entire day to create potions for all of the girls we saved from the asylum.

"It's the best memory potion I know how to create," he said. "Much stronger than the Elixir of Kendria. This has worked on some people who had severe memory loss after the types of torture you've described to me, but I've had other instances where it didn't work. It depends on just how deep the priestess's tactics were and how much she used them on each girl."

"And there's nothing we can do for the girls who were lobotomized?" I asked.

He ran a hand through his thick dark hair and sighed. "I've included some strong healing potions for those girls," he said. "It might help to heal the damage that was done to their brains, but I can't promise it will cure them. Give them the healing potion, and if there seems to be some improvement, give them the memory potion. All we can do is hope for the best."

"How do you plan to get them home?" Azure asked.

"I honestly don't know," I said, fear tightening my chest. I was taking this one step at a time. "I'm hoping we can find the portal before it closes and get everyone through. But even if we locate it, I have no idea what we'll find once we go through. There could be an army of witches there waiting for us."

"And if you can't find it?" she asked. "Or if it's closed by the time you do?"

I smiled, holding back tears. "Then we find another way. I'm not giving up, no matter how long it takes."

Azure pulled me into a hug, and it surprised me so much I nearly lost my balance. Azure was so not the hugging type.

"I've never met someone so brave," she said. "If there's one thing I want Venom to become, it's a safe place for witches who have no other home to go to. I want this place to become a home for them where they know they're safe from the Order."

"It will be, Azure," I said. "It will be, because you want it to be."

"If you do find that portal and there's an army of witches defending it, I'll gladly come to help you fight," Rend said. He handed the leather bag to me.

It was so much lighter than I expected it to be, and I smiled, wondering if he'd gotten these bags from the Shadow World. From someone in Essex's family line who knew how to make bags like this.

"I could bring an army to you," he said. "We could help you defeat them. I have a personal stake in the fight against the Order, just as much as you do."

I grabbed his hand.

"I know you lost your sister to the Order," I said. "I know that's why you're here in the human world, and I wish more than anything I could have done something to save her. But there's nothing more you can do to help me in this fight. I need you to be alive. You have a major role to play in the fight that's yet to come. Both of you."

"But—"

"No, listen to me," I said. "I've taken a great risk coming to you now. If you tell anyone the things I've told you or if you do anything to fight back knowing what you now know, it could risk everything we've worked so hard to accomplish."

He nodded, but he still looked determined to fight.

"You have to promise me you'll take those potions as soon as I'm on my way," I said, nodding to the two small vials left on the alchemy table. "I know it's hard when you feel like you could do something now, but you have to trust me. One wrong move and everything could change. I need you to be there to warn Jackson. Please."

Rend sighed and picked up one of the small vials. Inside was a potion that would cause both he and Azure to forget everything about this exchange until some moment in the future when Jackson decided to use the emerald ritual items to free one of the emerald gates. Since we didn't know the exact moment it would happen, it wasn't an exact science.

We just had to pray the trigger would work, and he would remember in time to save them.

"You're asking a lot of me, Harper," he said. "You have no idea how long I've wanted to put an end to the Order of Shadows. Now that we know there's a way to kill them, all I want to do is hunt them down and rip their hearts from their chest. Do you know how many demons will die between now and then, while we wait? Thousands, Harper. Innocent demons, like my sister."

I closed my eyes and took a deep breath.

"I promise you that I am well aware of the innocent people who will lose their lives in the years to come," I said. "People I love with all my heart. People I loved and never even knew, like my own mother. My father. One of my best friends. But if you hunt down the priestesses now, even if you manage to find them and surprise them, you'll change everything. You could put everything we've accomplished so far at risk. You have to see that."

"I do see it, but I don't have to like it," he said, slamming his hand down on the table. "Damn. I want to do more."

"You will," I said. "We all will, but now isn't the right time. You'll take the potions?"

He took a deep breath and finally met my eyes. "I will," he said. "But you better be telling the truth. If you aren't, I'll find you and kill you myself."

I put my hand on his shoulder and smiled. "In a few minutes, you won't even remember you met me," I said. "But someday, you'll remember, and you'll know. I look forward to seeing you again when that moment comes."

"Me, too," he said. "I wish you great power in your battle against the remaining priestesses. I just hope I'm standing there at your side when the final priestess falls."

"And Rend? If we don't... I mean, if I don't make it home... promise me you'll tell Jackson that I loved him until the very end," I said.

"You'll tell him yourself," he said. "Goodbye, Harper."

"Goodbye, Rend," I said. Then I smiled. "See you later."

He nodded and smiled back. "Yeah," he said. "See you later."

Azure hugged me again and walked me to the elevator.

"I'll make sure he takes it," she said once we were headed back up to the top floor.

"Thanks for everything," I said. "I owe you."

"Just tell me one thing." She shifted her weight nervously from one foot to the other. "Are we happy in the future? Rend and I? Are we..."

Her voice trailed off, but I knew what she was asking me, and I couldn't bear to tell her the truth. I wouldn't break her heart by telling her about Franki, but I wouldn't lie to her, either.

"It's hard for anyone to be happy during a war like this," I said. "Even Jackson and I have been through so much heartache, it's hard to say that we're happy."

I thought of the image Jackson had drawn of us sitting on the lawn in the Southern Kingdom, our son playing in the grass. That was the future I held onto throughout all of the torture I'd been forced to endure.

"All I know is that someday, when this war is over and the Order is defeated, we'll all find the happiness we deserve."

She smiled a sad smile, as if understanding that the answer was far more complicated than I could explain during a simple elevator ride.

"I'm counting on you guys," I said.

"We won't let you down, Harper," she said. "Jackson is going to be okay. We'll make sure of it. I know more than most how complicated love can be. Finding the perfect person who loves you back is the most valuable thing in the world. I'm glad you've found that, and I'll fight to make sure that when you get home, he's there to welcome you with open arms."

"Thank you, Azure," I said.

We rode the rest of the way up in silence, thoughts of the decades to come and the uncertain future ahead for all of us.

THE RITUAL

JACKSON

"Is everyone ready?" I asked.

We were all in our places in the underground ritual room. Each of the five witches stood on one point of the pentagram surrounding the large emerald stone embedded into the floor.

I glanced at Essex, and he raised his spear, nodding.

I ran up the steps for a quick look around, just to be sure we were cleared to go through with this. A circle of demons surrounded the clearing in the woods, their collective power buzzing through the air.

Inside the circle, all of Cypress's witches who were old enough to have been given a demon of their own stood hand in hand, anxious expressions on their faces. We were all on edge.

Rend and Azure stood at the top of the steps to the ritual room.

"We're ready," he said. "Let's get this over with."

I nodded. "Okay. Let's do this."

I clapped him on the arm as I descended the steps once again. Franki stood at the bottom of the steps, and she gave me a nervous smile as I passed.

"It's one minute until three," Mary Anne said. She took the chalice from the ritual table behind her in one hand and gripped the necklace in the other.

We all took our places and waited, watching the seconds tick by to the top of the hour.

I closed my eyes and breathed deeply. I gathered my power in my hands, preparing for the battle with the stone creatures as they came to life. Luckily, this gate, like Peachville, was located in the woods, which meant lots of trees for demons to pull our power from. I reached to a nearby tree and consumed its life, drawing the power into myself.

"Here we go," Mary Anne said when there were only seconds remaining.

I opened my eyes and glanced at Eloise. She smiled at me and nodded. She was ready.

As the hour chimed on my phone, Mary Anne lifted her hands and prepared to speak the words that would begin the ritual.

"No! Wait!" Rend shifted and flew down the steps, Azure at his side. Before I realized what was happening, he had taken the ritual items from Mary Anne's hands and put a hand over her mouth.

Not understanding what was going on, Essex pressed the tip of his spear to Rend's throat.

"You will be letting her go," he said. "I do not want to be hurting you, Rend."

"We can't do this," Rend said.

He took his hand off Mary Anne's mouth and stepped

back, away from the spear. He gathered the ritual items in his hand and set them on the stone table.

"You better start explaining yourself," Mary Anne said. "This is our chance. If that clock switches to 3:01, we lose the entire day."

Out of breath, Rend lifted a hand to his head.

"I know how crazy this is going to sound, but just before the ritual began, I had a flash of memory," he said. He looked to me. "Harper. She came to see me."

"When?" I asked, my heart racing.

"In 1951," he said. "In fact, I think I almost killed her."

"You did," Azure said. She glanced at me and shrugged. "It was fine. I stabbed him."

"Wait, what? Why didn't you tell me before now?" I asked. "You've known all this time that she was going to be trapped in the past? How could you have known that and kept it from me all this time? We could have saved her, Rend. What were you thinking?"

"I didn't tell you before, because I couldn't remember it," he said. "I started feeling weird about this whole thing back in the war room when we first started talking about the ritual, but I couldn't quite put my finger on what was bothering me. Standing up there just now, though, I felt nearly ill about it. It wasn't until right before the clock ticked over to three that the memory came back to me."

"To both of us," Azure said. She glanced at Franki with a sad look, but seemed to shrug it off.

"I don't understand," Mary Anne said. "What did Harper say to you when she came to you?"

"She told me that she wasn't the one who left these items for you," he said. "It was the emerald priestess."

Eloise started to cry. "She's not really dead, is she? This has all been some kind of trick. I knew it was too good to be true. We'll never be free of this place."

"She is dead, Eloise," Rend said. "Harper killed her, and she does have the master stone, but the emerald priestess set this trap for us before she died. She set it for us here in the present, just in case Jackson found the institute while he was searching for clues about Harper. She used Harper's memories to replicate her handwriting and her style of speech. Everything."

"What does this mean?" I asked.

"It means these items can't be trusted," he said. "There's a spell connected to them that, when triggered, will open a portal so that the amethyst priestess can bring an army through to destroy us."

My heart nearly stopped. Amethyst? What did all of this have to do with the collar Joost had found?

Mary Anne cursed and slammed her hand down on the ritual table.

"You've got to be kidding me," she said. "So these items aren't even real? What the heck are we supposed to do now?"

"Rend, did she tell you anything else?" I asked. "Does she know how to get back to us?"

He shook his head. "I'm not sure," he said. "When she came to see me, she said there might still be a portal open that would bring her home but that it would be closing soon. She wasn't sure she'd be able to find it in time."

"How does she even know about the trap and these items in the first place?" Mary Anne asked. "I'm guessing the emerald priestess didn't tell her about them before she died. She wouldn't risk us finding out."

Rend hesitated and glanced at me, and I knew whatever he was about to say wouldn't be good news.

"She found out about the items and the portal from the ruby priestess," he said.

I closed my eyes and brought a hand to my head. God, hadn't she been through enough? Now, she had to deal with the ruby priestess on her own, too? I had to find a way to help her.

"Wait, but how is the ruby priestess there with her?" Mary Anne asked.

"The ruby priestess told Harper that the portal her sister created between the past and present was still open," he said. "She tried to make a deal with Harper. If Harper gave her the true emerald master stone, she said she would show her where the portal home was located."

"She didn't do it," I said.

"How could she?" Rend asked. "She didn't trust the ruby priestess, but not only that. She said there were about a hundred other girls there in the asylum with her. They were taken to some hospital after the fire, and Harper couldn't just abandon them."

I shook my head, feeling helpless to do anything about all of this.

Somehow, she had not only managed to kill the emerald priestess, but she'd also had to face the ruby priestess. And, she'd still found a way to survive it long enough to warn us about these items.

But the fact that she wasn't here with us right now meant that she hadn't yet found the portal and figured out how to get home. I knew Harper well enough to know that she would never just leave a hundred girls trapped in the past. Even if it meant never coming home.

"We have to find a way to get her back," I said. "We either need to find that portal ourselves or find someone else who can open one."

"And how exactly are we supposed to do that?" Mary Anne asked. "We don't even know where to start. Mordecai and the others searched everywhere in that town in Ohio and didn't see any sign of a portal. And I've never heard of another witch powerful enough to actually open a portal to the past."

Azure cleared her throat, but looked away when I tried to question her.

"I don't know how, but we have to at least try," I said. "If the portal is still open, we have to put everything we have into finding it before it closes."

"So, we're back to square one," Mary Anne said. "Awesome."

I glanced over at Eloise, who was holding her girls tightly to her. "I'm so sorry, Eloise," I said. "No one here can be as disappointed as you are."

She wiped the tears from her cheeks. "I don't think I'd entirely believed it was going to happen, anyway," she said. "I hoped, of course, but I didn't allow myself to trust it. But I agree with you. We need to find that portal. If Harper has the master stone, we need to put everything we have into bringing her and that stone home."

"Once we have it, we can open the gate, right?" Caroline asked.

"We need the ring, too," I said. "As far as we know, that's still in the Shadow World."

"How do we find it?" Mary Anne asked. "Essex and I can go look for it while you guys are searching for the portal."

"Harper and I got lucky finding the sapphire ring, but I can explain to you how we found it," I said. "Come on, let's get back to the castle and plan our next moves. We can't afford to waste any time."

"What do we do with these items in the meantime?" Rend asked, motioning to the fake emerald ritual items.

I glanced at the items, a plan slowly forming in my mind.

"Bring them with you," I said. "We might be able to use them yet."

AN EXACT REPLICA

AERDEN

When morning came on the day of our first battle,
I woke with one thought on my mind.
Win.

Seeing Lea again had made me even more determined to
put my heart and soul into winning my freedom. There had
been enough dark days in my past where I had wished for
death. Begged for it. But today was not one of those days.

"Are you ready?" Rushon asked as we ate breakfast in our
room. A group of servant girls had appeared a few minutes ago
with trays full of warm food, a rare treat for us prisoners.

I was glad we weren't having to eat with the other teams
today. It was nice to have these moments alone together with
just the five of us. I wasn't sure what would happen to our
team after today's round was over. Would we still be allowed
to share a cell? Or would we be labeled as competitors after
this? And how would they split us into groups of two for the
next round?

The guards hadn't explained what would happen to our fifth member for the second round of the games. Either they all expected that at least one of us wouldn't survive the day, or they had the intention to let someone back out of the games.

I hoped it would be our choice who to take as our partners. These other demons cared for Trention, but I doubted they would put their own lives at risk to keep him safe in the heat of battle.

My hope was that Trention would be excused from the second round after today, and even though he would most likely be condemned to spend the remainder of his life in slavery, at least he would be alive.

"I'm ready," I said. "How are you feeling?"

"Scared, to be honest," Rushon said. "I've been a prisoner of the king for five years now, but I still have a small family here in the city that I would love to see again."

"A mate?" I asked.

He nodded. "And two small shadowlings," he said. "I'm afraid they'll be in the crowd today watching. I don't want them to watch their father die."

I held his gaze. "They won't," I said.

"They said they won't let us die," Perrick said. "I'm still hoping we'll survive even if we lose."

"I wouldn't count on that being true," Trention said. "And even if it is, they'll lock us away and we'll spend the rest of the years we have left mining gemstones. I'm not sure that's a life I care to live anymore."

"Well, I would rather take my chances in the mines than be dead by nightfall," Perrick said.

"None of us are going to die today," I said. "We have a solid strategy. Just remember what weapon you're searching for in the armory and locate it as quickly as possible. They might not give us much time to look around, and each of us having the correct weapons is a key part of our success today."

"I wish they would allow us to watch the other matches of the day," Trention said. "We could gain a lot of good information from that."

I'd been thinking the same thing, but there was no use wishing for things we had no control over at this point. All we could do was wait until our round was called and it was our turn to battle.

Half an hour later, Reynar appeared, telling us it was time to choose our weapons.

"You'll all be paraded in front of the crowds during the opening ceremonies," Reynar said. "After that you'll be escorted back to the ready room where you'll await your turn in combat. I imagine your battle will be swift. Do me a favor and try to at least make it seem like you have a chance. It will make a better performance for the crowds. I was up half the night with anticipation."

The evil guard laughed and sneered at the same time, and I couldn't wait for the chance to prove him wrong.

The five of us walked down to a room I hadn't been in since I was a young demon. My arms broke out in chills as I stepped over the threshold. My father had brought me down here to choose my first real weapon after years of begging him to let me train with more than a stick or a rock.

Back then, I'd been as in awe of the demon steel and obsidian weapons as I was today. The flames of the weapon-smith's workstation pumped heat through the room, and I was surprised to see the master demon working here today.

He looked up as we entered the room, and I noticed a flicker of recognition in his eyes as they travelled over my face. He placed the weapon he'd been working on back into the fire and stood.

Reynar cleared his throat. "You've got five minutes to make your selections," he said. "Each of you can choose up to two weapons and a shield, if you want to use one. The only armor available to you are the helmets along this wall and the chest pieces here along the opposite wall. They will provide some protection, but they'll also slow you down when you shift. Choose wisely, not that I think it will make a difference."

He laughed and stepped out of the room, leaving the door slightly open as he stood guard.

Trention chose a small dagger that he placed in the belt of his pants. We'd decided his best asset was his casting, so it would be best for his hands to be free and his body to be as light as possible to make shifting easy in case he got into a rough spot.

Rushon quickly selected a light buckler and then tested several of the short swords on the rack in front of him, while Perrick went for the heaviest, deadliest morning star he could find. He gripped it in his hand and smiled at me, nodding.

"This has a good weight to it," he said, swinging the chain around a few times. The ball on the end of the chain was covered in large spikes that would do some serious damage if anyone dared to step into its range.

Morway chose a long spear with a deadly point on the end and a smaller rapier that he stuck through a leather sheath strapped to his side.

I searched the room for anything that resembled the axe I'd

loved so much, but as I stepped toward the display of weapons, I realized nothing here would even begin to compare. These were all much smaller and most only had a single-sided blade.

The weaponsmith cleared his throat. I glanced over at him, and he made a subtle nod for me to follow him.

The weaponsmith threw a nervous glance at the guard in the doorway, but Reynar wasn't paying any attention to us. I followed the demon to the back area of his workshop. Most of the weapons back here were deformed or incomplete, but my eyes widened in shock as he lifted a green blanket from the end of the table, revealing an axe that looked like an exact replica of my old one.

"I think what you're looking for might be here," he said, glancing again at the doorway. He lowered his voice and leaned closer. "The princess sends her best wishes for a victorious match today, Sir Aerden."

A lump formed in my throat, and I swallowed it down.

Lea had said she had a surprise for me, but I never expected this. What risks had she taken to make sure I had a weapon I could be proud of in my hand when I faced my first challengers?

"This was exactly what I was looking for," I said, wrapping my hand around the hilt of the axe and lifting it easily. The incredible weight of it made me feel stronger than I had in a century. "Please, tell the princess she has good taste."

The weaponsmith smiled. "She said you'd be able to wield it with one hand, but I told her that was nearly impossible," he said. "I've only ever seen one demon use an axe this heavy with one hand, and he was twice your size. I wish you luck in the games, but something tells me you're going to be just fine."

"Thank you for this," I said.

He nodded toward the door, and I knew he was worried the guard would notice our exchange. I didn't know if Reynar would have the authority to punish the weaponsmith, but I didn't want anything to tie this axe to Lea, so I nodded to the demon and quickly moved back to the rack of weapons, acting as if I had simply found this axe there among the others in a twist of fate.

"Time's up," Reynar said. "Let's go."

He stared at the massive double-headed axe in my hand and although his eyes widened in surprise, he didn't appear to question it. This room was full of every weapon imaginable. There was no reason for him to believe it had been forged for me and me alone.

As we walked toward the ready room, shouts from the crowd roared above us. The battle must have come to an end, which meant it was our turn next.

I clutched the axe tighter, feeling more powerful just for having the weight of it returned to me. God, how I had missed it. There was no other weapon in the world with the same heft and strength of a double-headed axe, and even though this was not the same axe I'd loved before I was captured, it was almost exactly the same. The fact that Lea had taken a risk to make sure I had it meant more to me than I would ever be able to tell her.

When we stepped into the room, though, some of my confidence faded as we caught the eyes of the team we were about to face in the arena.

They stood in a line along the left wall of the room, and we were instructed to stand in a straight line on the opposite side, leaving a small stretch of space between us. None of us spoke, because there was nothing to be said. We were innocents pitted against each other in a gruesome battle for the entertainment of the crowd that roared above us. It was barbaric and unfair, but it was where we had found ourselves.

Sometimes when life gave you no choice in the matter, the only real choice was to accept what you could not control.

And then kick some ass so that later, you could create new choices for yourself.

The losing team must have been carried through another doorway, because the only team that passed through the ready room where we stood waiting was team three. They were battered and bloodied, but they were alive.

They kept their eyes to the ground as they passed us. All except Yuron, the massive demon who posed the worst threat. He looked straight at me and raised his weapon into the air. He laughed and spit blood onto the ground at my feet.

I looked away, knowing that if we managed to win today, we might be facing Yuron next. I wondered what kind of shape the losing team was in and what had happened to them. Were they still alive? Were the healers working now to keep them alive? Or had they been asked to give their energy over to the glory and power of the king?

The only thing I knew for certain was that I would have my answer soon.

Ezrah stepped into the ready room and nodded toward both sides of the aisle. His gaze lingered on me for a moment longer, and I nodded, letting him know I was ready.

"May you fight with honor," he said simply. "Team five, lead the way inside. Team six, follow behind, please. Take your spots in the center of the arena to be presented to the king. The fight doesn't begin until the king commands you to begin."

My hand gripped the axe at my side, and I sent up a prayer to the gods as we followed our opponents into the arena.

Make me strong. Make me quick. Make me victorious.

A FLASH OF PURE SORROW

LEA

I sat in a large throne-like chair beside my mother and waited.

It took everything I had not to act anxious or worried, but inside, I was a complete basket-case. After Kael's threats, I was terrified he would do something to put Aerden in danger today.

I glanced over at Tatiana, who sat behind us as a member of the council. She met my eyes and nodded slightly. She held the same fear in her own eyes, and for a moment, I wondered what secrets the woman was still hiding.

Had she really done so much to help her sons? Had I simply misunderstood her? Or was there more to it she wasn't telling me?

I had tried to get her alone several times over the past few days, but there had never been a good opportunity for us to talk. Did she know I had made a trip out here to visit Aerden?

It was so messed up that we were both supposed to just sit

here and watch Aerden fight to the death. I was nervous as hell.

It wasn't that I didn't believe in Aerden. I knew he was a skilled warrior, and he had a real reason to fight for his life. He wouldn't ever give up. But still, battles like this were unpredictable, and it was obvious he didn't have full control over his magic.

How would that affect him today?

As the two teams on the battlefield finished and the losing team was carried out by shamans, the crowd roared for the winners. Even the winning team was beat up pretty badly, blood streaming down their faces and gashes and burns across their bodies.

Aerden's team had to be next. The last fight of the day.

A pit of acid gurgled in my stomach as I waited for the other teams to be paraded in front of us, but I could feel Kael's eyes on me. He sat there beside my father as if he had already been named King, and I focused my nerves into hating him. As we waited, I daydreamed about all the terrible things I would do to Kael when I got the chance.

Because someday, I would make him pay for what he had done to me.

"Isn't this fun?" Mother asked, turning. "Watching all those strong demons put everything they have into battle is completely exhilarating."

Her voice was full of excitement, and I wanted to place my hand over her mouth and tell her to shut up. This wasn't fun at all. Couldn't she see that those demons were suffering for our entertainment?

I had no doubt that right now, the two teams of demons who had been carried off the field today were being forced to

sacrifice their lives into a stone that would be presented to my
father at the end of the day in his chambers.

It was disgusting, but Mother continued on, obviously not
noticing the daggers I threw at her with my eyes.

"Kael, this was such a wonderful idea," she said. "I
certainly appreciate our safety here inside the city's walls, but
I didn't realize just how much we needed a diversion after
being so sequestered here for the past few decades."

"I'm glad you think so, my queen," he said. "Perhaps we
can make this a yearly event."

"Oh, goodness," she said, faltering a bit for the first time all
morning. I studied her, wondering how much of her excitement was real and what was just an act for Kael's sake?

Why was she trying so hard to make an impression on
him? She was his superior. Why did he seem to matter to her
so much?

"I am not sure I could handle this much excitement
every year, but maybe after the games are over, we can
discuss whether it's a good idea to bring it back another
time."

"Of course," Kael said. He smiled his ugly, confident smile
and looked straight into my eyes. "Look, Princess, the next
teams are entering the arena. This should be a very interesting
battle. The most fun of the day, I hope."

My stomach dropped as I watched the next two teams
enter the battlefield. At first, I didn't see him, and I hoped that
somehow, he had managed to escape or avoid the games
altogether.

But then, my eyes caught sight of him near the back of the
second team. His eyes immediately rose to mine, and despite
the roar of the crowd and the distance that separated us, we

were the only two demons in the entire arena for that one long moment as we sought each other out.

Aerden raised his mighty axe into the air, brandishing it to the eager crowd, and a loud roar rose up. But I knew it was for me, and I brought a hand to my heart. He had gotten the axe. The weaponsmith had stayed true to his word, and I would have to find a way to thank him.

The teams lined up on either side of Ezrah, and once they were all in place, the crowd in the arena grew quiet, waiting.

"King, I present to you our final competitors of the day," Ezrah said. All ten of the demons on the battlefield knelt and lowered their heads toward the king. Toward us. "These warriors honor you today and bring you wishes of a long life."

My father, the king, stood with the help of his scepter and raised a hand into the air.

"May you all fight with honor," he said.

I wanted to stand up and tell him to put a stop to this. Couldn't he see that one of the demons being offered up in his honor was my dearest friend? A son of two of his own council members? Couldn't he see how wrong this was?

But I was helpless to speak against him.

Telling him here, in front of everyone in the city, just what I thought of these games would not put a stop to them. It would only get me thrown in the dungeons, where I would be no help to anyone. Least of all Aerden.

I glanced back at Tatiana again, and she had one hand clutched to her heart and the other pressed to her mouth. She fought back tears, and I wished I could go and sit at her side. At least then, I would have someone to hold hands with and pray for Aerden's victory.

Up here, beside my parents and the demon who had

suggested the games, I had to pretend to be completely unmoved by the whole thing. I could still feel Kael's eyes on me, watching for any sign of misplaced loyalty.

It wasn't my own punishment I was worried about, though. I was terrified that if I showed any signs of despair or worry, Kael would see to it that Aerden was killed during these games.

I had no doubt he had the power and authority to make that happen, and I wasn't about to test him. Not yet.

Ezrah glanced briefly at me, bowed to my father, and left his place between the slaves to disappear through the archway, he lowered the gate, trapping the ten warriors inside. The two teams rose to their feet and took their places across from each other, weapons raised.

The crowd kept their eyes on my father, waiting.

The seconds seemed to stretch out for an eternity, and just before my father lowered his hands to signal the start of the battle, his eyes flickered to mine. In them, I expected to see joy or excitement. Kael might have suggested the games, but my father was the one who had agreed to it, so surely he must have taken some kind of pleasure in this moment.

But instead, there was a flash of pure sorrow and regret. His eyes were an apology, and it rocked me to my core, because it was the first time since I'd returned that he'd actually looked me straight in the eye.

But before I could react or hope that he was about to put a stop to this, he looked away and lowered his hand.

With that, the battle began.

THE BATTLEFIELD

AERDEN

The king lowered his hand, signaling for the battle to begin.

The team facing us immediately began casting, throwing their best magic our way, but the five of us stood still, focused on defense. Flames, acid, and ice crashed against the invisible shields we had each conjured, and I glanced around to make sure that none of their magic had gotten through.

Confused, the opposing team gathered their magic again, this time sending several spells soaring toward us at once. Still, our shields held true, the magic slamming against the invisible barriers and dissipating in a burst of sparks.

The crowd around us roared to life, but I shut them out. Over my years as a slave to the Order, I had gotten very good at shutting out the voices of others. It was a necessity for my own sanity, and it served me well here.

"Stay focused," I shouted to my teammates. "Draw them in."

Several of the demons on the opposing team shifted to smoke and reappeared behind us, gathering new spells in their hands.

"Circle up," I shouted.

My teammates slowly backed toward me and drew into a tight circle, our backs to each other so that our shields were covering every direction.

By the time the other team hurled their spells at us, we were ready. My heart pounded, and I was itching to attack, but we had to stick to the strategy. Wear the other team out as much as possible before we hit them with all we had. Focus on defense until we saw the chance to fight back with great power.

Beside me, Trention gripped his small dagger, his hands trembling. He had never been in a real fight before, and I could sense his fear. But I was here for him. I would not let him fall today.

"Hold strong," I shouted to my team. "Wait for them to come closer. Don't break formation."

We held our circle of shields for several more attacks as the other team threw everything they had at us. But I had instructed my team well. I sent up a silent thank you to all those days in Peachville training at the high school with Zara, Harper, and the others. We'd practiced shielding until it was nauseating, but I had never been more grateful for those boring mornings of training.

I watched carefully as the opposing team crept closer, thinking that if they managed to break through our shields, they would have a chance.

They tried everything they could, giving away the best of their abilities. A couple of the demons on the other team were very talented in different forms of earth and fire magic, but so far, our shields were winning.

"Now?" Rushon shouted.

"Not yet," I shouted back. "Hold."

I lifted my axe, waiting for the perfect moment. The demon focusing on me stepped within my range of attack, and I knew the time had arrived. As much as I loved the safety of our shields, we were never going to win without taking them down.

"Ready?" I shouted, watching carefully for the moment when most of the demons coming for us had expended their most recent spells. When almost all five had gone off, I took a deep breath, drawing every ounce of power into myself. "Now."

At my command, my team shifted into dark smoke and reformed behind each of our targets. Rather than expend our magic, we each attacked with our weapons. I landed a crushing blow to the back of my opponent, a demon I knew only as Asher. He fell to his knees for a moment before he shifted and came back to a standing position several feet away and prepared his next spell.

With my shield down, I was vulnerable. Rather than give him the opportunity to unleash that spell, I shifted quickly and attacked again. He wasn't ready for me, which was exactly what I'd been hoping for.

Most demons were so used to fighting with their magic that they were unprepared for defense against physical weapons. I took him down with a second swift slice of my axe. When he didn't move or make any effort to stand, I shifted and joined Trention, determined to protect him.

The demon fighting my friend had landed a lightning

attack that had burned through Trention's tunic and singed his side, but he was still standing.

"Shift and get out of range," I said to him. "Go. Hit him with your boulder attack."

Trention nodded and shifted, flying out of my field of vision as I lifted my axe against his attacker.

The demon had a similar idea, shifting to fly out of my range, but I wasn't about to let him get away. I threw a glance at my fellow teammates, and when I was sure they were holding their own, I went after the demon who had run.

The demon brought down a lightning storm right there on the battlefield, trying to hit as many of us as he could with a comprehensive attack, but I easily dodged the lightning bolts as I flew toward him. He had already spent so much of his power in the early part of the battle that he couldn't keep it up.

When he saw me take solid form right in front of him, he attempted to shift and run again, but Trention's boulder attack rained large rocks down on all sides of the demon, holding him to his human form. I took advantage of the moment, slicing my axe-blade through the air and cutting off both his arms in a single motion.

He screamed and fell to his knees. I ignored the regret and guilt that threatened to overwhelm me in the moment. I didn't want to hurt anyone, but this was the place where I found myself. It was us or them, and I wasn't planning to lose this battle.

"Aerden," Perrick shouted, and when I turned to him, he was clutching his side. Dark blood spread across his tunic and down his side.

"Shift," I shouted. "Get out of there."

The demon who had attacked him sent a spear made of

pure acid directly toward Perrick, but he managed to shift just before it hit. His sudden move threw the demon off his center, and I shifted quickly, reforming directly behind the demon and aiming straight for his knees.

The axe was heavy and extremely sharp. I had no doubt I could have taken off each of the demons' heads with a single slice, but I wanted to at least give them a chance once the battle was over. I had no intention of killing anyone. I simply wanted to incapacitate them so that we would be declared the winning team.

Whatever happened to them after that was the king's responsibility.

Behind me, the fourth demon attacked before I could move out of the way, and a searing pain stretched out across my back. I wasn't sure exactly what he had hit me with, but it hurt like hell. I tried to shift, but the pain held me to my solid form. I turned on the demon and threw up a shield as fast as I could, deflecting his second attack.

"Trention," I shouted. "Cage him."

Trention nodded and began to cast. Before the demon could prepare a third spell, the ground surrounding him rumbled and a circular wall of solid earth rose from the ground, trapping him inside.

That would hold him for at least a minute or two as he tried to shift and find an open crack through which he could escape.

The five of us on my team all turned to the fifth member of the opposing team. He was fast, shifting before any of us could land a single spell or blow against him.

"Morway, this is your chance," I said.

"He's too fast," Morway shouted. "I can't do it."

"You can," I said. "Focus. Follow him with your eyes. You can do this."

Morway shook his head, but I knew he could do it.

We all stood ready, watching as the demon flew around the battlefield in demon form. I held my axe at the ready, keeping one eye on the wall of earth still surrounding the other opponent.

"Now," Perrick shouted.

Morway shifted, flying toward the demon and tackling him. The second Morway put hands on the demon, he turned to solid form, his body covered in a glowing blue light. Morway had a unique ability in that he could turn energy into a rope of pure light. While shifted, he had wrapped his light around the opposing demon.

Not knowing how long the rope of light would hold, Perrick and I both rushed toward the captured demon, our weapons raised. Within seconds, the demon was down.

I looked away from the blood that poured from our opponents, refusing to let the sight hold me back. We had a job to do out here. I had no choice.

But as I turned, the demon inside the earthen prison broke free and shifted. He soared right for Trention, but Trention was looking at me.

My eyes widened, and I shifted, pushing through the air as fast as I could. I reformed just as the other demon reached Trention. I pushed my friend out of the way and took the blow for myself, the demon's lightning attack slicing through my side.

Before I even realized what I was doing, I focused all of my anger and fear on my axe and the weapon broke out in flames that roared several feet into the air.

I turned in a circle, throwing all of my weight into the action. The demon shifted, trying to get out of the way of my next blow, but I wasn't aiming for him directly. I sunk the heavy blade of my axe into the earth, sending a straight line of giant flames forward toward the demon. The flames engulfed him, and he dropped his demon form, falling onto the dusty floor of the arena, every inch of his body still burning.

I turned, my chest rising and falling with each labored breath. I clutched my bleeding side and for the first time, heard the loud roars of the crowd all around us.

Had we really won?

I glanced around at my teammates as Ezrah raised the gate and stepped onto the battlefield. He nodded at me, and held back a smile.

"Victory for team six," he said, and the crowd went crazy, standing and chanting.

"Aerden. Aerden. Aerden," they shouted. "Victory for the one who returned."

My team gathered around me, and I placed an arm over Trention's shoulders, raising my axe into the air for the crowd.

But it was my princess that caught my gaze and held it. She rose to her feet, cheering. Her eyes met mine across the distance of the battlefield, and I nodded to her, even as the tears began to fall from my own eyes.

The first round of the King's Games was over, and we had won.

WHO SAID WE WERE GOING TO FIGHT HER?

JACKSON

Back at the castle, we spread the emerald ritual items out across the table in the war room. But this time, we knew them for what they were. Fake items meant to trap us.

"I'm sorry I didn't see it earlier," Rend said. He paced the room. "Damn, I almost got all of us kidnapped. Or killed."

"If it hadn't been for you, who knows what might have happened," I said. "Thank God you remembered when you did, or we might be sitting in cages in some dungeon right now. Or worse."

"The key is to figure out where we go from here," Mary Anne said. "We need a new plan."

"I have an idea, but it's risky," I said.

"I'm good with risk, as long as it has the potential to get answers," she said. "Like I said, Essex and I can go to find the emerald ring."

"If it's still there at all," I said. "We have to consider the fact that the other priestesses might have gone after the ring as soon as they realized Priestess Evers was gone."

"It's worth a shot, though," she said.

"I don't want the two of you going alone," I said. "When Harper and I found the ring, there were several hunters guarding it. It's possible the Order increased security on the remaining rings after we stole the sapphire one. We have no idea what to expect, but if we send an army with you, you should be able to handle almost anything they send your way."

She nodded. "I like the idea of an army," she said with a laugh. "It's too bad Andros never showed."

My stomach tightened. Yet another piece of this puzzle that I didn't have answers for. Andros had said he was coming to give me news about Aerden and Lea. Something was happening in the city that he thought I would want to know about, but so far, there'd been no sign of him. Even his communication stones weren't getting through.

"Maybe after you find the ring, you can go look for Andros, too," I said. "I'm anxious to know what's going on in the city."

"We'll do whatever we need to," she said. "But what are you going to do?"

I stared at the ritual items. The idea was crazy, but I didn't know what else to do.

When Harper had disappeared, I spent months foolishly trying to get answers through sheer force. In the end, though, the one thing that had worked was getting the emerald priestess's attention to the point where she had no choice but to seek me out.

Here, we had a direct route to at least one of the other priestesses. If the ruby priestess knew how to find Harper, maybe the others did, too, and if these items opened a portal to any of the others, it could help us. Maybe it was a long shot, but we needed more information.

"What's going through your head?" Rend asked.

"Harper said these items were fake. She told you that she'd heard they were rigged so that if they were ever used, a portal would open up, right?"

"Yeah. She said the amethyst priestess would be ready to send an army of witches through to capture us," he said. "They're completely unusable."

"Not exactly," I said. "What if we use them anyway? What if we force her out of hiding?"

Rend shook his head. "I don't know about that, Jackson. We'd have to put together a huge army just to be prepared for what she might send through," he said. "I don't see how that gets us any closer to our goals right now."

"If the ruby priestess knew where there was a portal back to Harper, maybe the other sisters know about it, too," I said. "We could spend months searching for that portal. We have no idea where it could be, other than the fact that it might be somewhere close to that hospital. But Cristo searched the entire town and couldn't find any sign of it. It could be inside someone's house, hidden deep underground. Hell, it could be permanently glamoured to look like a tree. We have no idea, and the chances of us actually finding it before it closes are slim to none."

"But how is fighting the amethyst priestess and her army going to get us any closer to finding the portal?" Rend asked. "I mean, I'm all for fighting another priestess, but we might be biting off more than we can chew right now."

"Who said we were going to fight her?" I asked. "Right

now, we have an advantage, because we know these items open some kind of portal to one of the Order's hideouts. If we can set it up somehow where we can see them, but they can't see us, maybe we can gather some valuable information about who they are or where they're located. Maybe we can see something that will help us find the portal."

Rend nodded. "I see what you're saying here," he said. "But it's risky. There's almost no way we could hide an entire army from them. They would sense our presence if we bring too many people. But if we only take a handful of people or if you attempt to do this on your own, all it will take is having the right witch there with the right type of ability to see through illusions and it's all over."

"So, we plan for the worst-case scenario," I said. "Any chance you have any potions inside your bag of tricks that can't be detected by any magic?"

Rend brought a hand to his forehead and stood there for a long moment before he nodded. "I might have something that will work," he said. "It's going to take a combination of potions I haven't tried before, but I can use you as my guinea pig. Since you can see through glamours and illusions, I can test it on you before we go."

"How long do you need to get this ready?" I asked, ready to go right now. The sooner we could get to the portal, the more chance we had of actually finding Harper safe and alive.

"I'll go home and get to work on it right away. I should have something to test by midnight or so," he said. "We should plan to trigger the items at three tomorrow afternoon, if we can. Otherwise, they might get suspicious about why we're triggering them at an off time."

"Good point," I said. "I'll hang around here and come up with a plan for how to get away should we be detected."

"Who all is going to go with you?" Mary Anne asked.

"We shouldn't try to take more than a handful of people," Rend said. "I'll go with you. I can bring a bag full of potions that will help us get away if it comes to that."

I nodded. "Then let's just make it the two of us," I said. "Less people to worry about if things go south."

"I'll start putting together an expedition group," Mary Anne said. "In the meantime, I need to know everything about how you and Harper found the sapphire ring."

We had a long afternoon and evening ahead of us, but as I stared at the fake emerald items on the table, I felt hope again for the first time since we'd found the burned building.

Just hang on, Harper. I'm going to find you.

THIS ONE GIFT

HARPER

R ather than lose time driving all the way back to the house in Ohio, Rend let me use his demon door.

Once Azure and I had said goodbye, I walked through the Hall of Doorways, searching for the door with the green scarab beetle etched into its surface, anxious to get back to make sure Brooke was okay.

On my way there, though, the sight of a blue demon door caught my eye, and my heart tightened in my chest.

Peachville.

I stopped in front of the door and stared at it for a very long time. Beyond this door was home. Brighton Manor, long before it had been turned into Shadowford Home For Troubled Girls.

Beyond this door was a family I had never known.

My mother would not have been born yet, but I had spent many long nights talking to Aerden about my family history.

I thought back to our conversations and realized that in 1951, my grandmother would have only just been born a few years ago. If I walked through this door, I might have the chance to see her. It wouldn't be the same as seeing my own mother, but it would likely be my only opportunity to see any member of my family when they were still alive.

I knew it was risky. If anyone saw me, it could somehow alter the timeline in ways that would ruin the future we had built.

Still, how could I let this moment pass? How could I know they were just on the other side of that door and not take this risk? This one chance?

I shook my head and with heavy footsteps, I walked past the door, determined not to put my own future at risk.

But I only got a few steps down the hallway before I turned around and put my hand on the doorknob. I could be careful, and they would never know I was there, right? Walking away would break my heart, and hadn't I suffered enough for one lifetime?

I had earned this. All that torture, being away from Jackson and everyone I loved. Screw the timeline, I deserved to see them. I deserved this one small gift, to make up for all I would still have to do just to find my way home again.

My heart raced. I knew it was wrong, but I couldn't help myself. My entire life, I had longed to know my family.

It was something most people took for granted, and something I had never known. To belong to someone. To look into their face and see yourself. These were things I had never known except those precious months I had spent with my father.

And even then, my father was a demon. In my human form, I looked almost nothing like him at all.

There was simply no chance I was walking away. I had to see them.

I connected to my power and closed my eyes. I took a deep breath and focused on turning to nothing. Air. Invisible.

When I opened my eyes, my body had disappeared.

I turned the knob and stepped inside the pentagram-shaped room on the third floor of Brighton Manor.

I stood there for a few minutes, listening for any sound of voices or movement on the floors below. When I didn't hear anything at all, I nearly convinced myself to turn around. Maybe they weren't even home.

But I had to know.

I opened the narrow door that led to the hidden stairway down to the second floor. I moved carefully, conscious of each footfall. No one could see me, but if I knocked something over or stepped on the wrong step and made a creaking sound, they would most certainly hear me.

I glanced into the bedrooms and smiled. Everything looked so different from the time when I had first been moved here. Instead of a home for girls where each room was set up with an impersonal dorm-room kind of feel, the house had a real lived-in look. Toys on the floor of a bedroom with a white crib and teal wallpaper embroidered with flowers. A brush and makeup strewn across the dressing table I had used for years as my own. Was this my great-grandmother's room now?

I listened at the top of the stairs, and when I didn't hear anything going on downstairs, I tiptoed onto the first step. I knew this place so intimately, I knew exactly which steps creaked and which ones didn't. I took each step with care, skipping the ones that might betray my presence in the house.

When I had made it to the bottom floor, I took my time walking toward the back of the house.

The front sitting room looked almost exactly the way it had when I'd first moved to Shadowford. Stuffy and unused.

One glance in the common room showed that back in the fifties this room was not filled with old, worn couches and ancient computer equipment. Instead, this had been the dining room. A gorgeous mahogany dining table with matching chairs took up most of the space. I stepped inside and ran my fingers across the mahogany china cabinet.

The dishes inside were beautiful bone china, decorated with delicate blue flowers. I wondered what had happened to my family china in the years after my mother died? I had searched every inch of Brighton Manor and had never seen anything like it. It must have been sold or given to another family.

I almost wished I could take a piece of it home with me, just to have a token of this place where I once belonged. But I left it all behind and continued on to the kitchen.

Instead of a long table meant to accommodate a dozen people, there was a smaller, more casual round table made of oak. A wooden high-chair sat at one end, and I could almost picture my great-grandmother feeding her small child there.

But there didn't seem to be anyone home.

Sadness engulfed me, but as I turned around, determined to get upstairs and back to Brooke, the sound of a child's laughter rang out, distant but clear.

I glanced out the window over the sink, and my heart rose into my chest. She was there. My grandmother, Julia. She couldn't have been more than three years old, and she was standing by the fountain, splashing her hands into the water and giggling.

Her hair was exactly the same color as mine. Her eyes were brown, and even though she was just a tiny little thing, she could have been my daughter. I placed a hand over my mouth, watching her in awe as she played.

The garden outside was not the overgrown mess I had found when I first moved to Peachville. Instead, it was flourishing and full of color. It was spring here in Georgia, and the flowers must have all recently bloomed.

A woman emerged from the maze of flowers, and again, I saw so much of myself in her. She couldn't have been much older than I was now. She pulled her gardening gloves off, and she dipped a hand into the fountain, splashing water toward her little girl and laughing.

I gasped, clutching my throat when I saw the sapphire pendant around the woman's neck. It hadn't occurred to me until this moment, but right now, Aerden was trapped inside that woman.

I wished I could send him some kind of message to let him know that someday, he would be free again. Just to give him any hope to hold onto in the dark days yet to come. But I couldn't do anything to help him. Not here.

I watched them for as long as I could, their laughter reaching me through the thin glass. They seemed happy, and I wished more than anything that I could join them, just for a moment. That I could belong to them and convince them to leave the Order. Convince them that there was another way.

Maybe, if things had been different, we could have all fought together.

But in a way, I knew both of these women would someday fight against the Order's evil, because they were a part of me. As long as I still drew breath into my lungs, a piece of them still flowed through my veins, and some part of them had made me who I was today.

I glanced up at the clock ticking above me, and realized I had stood there for way too long. The sun was beginning to set in the distance and soon, they would come inside for dinner. My time was up, but I sent up a thought of gratitude.

Thank you for this moment. This one gift.

I brought a hand to my lips and sent a kiss toward the mother-daughter pair. Then I turned around, made my way back up the stairs and out into the Hall of Doorways.

I had lingered in the past for as long as I cared to stay. Now, it was time to get back to my future.

A NEW KIND OF HOPE

LEA

In the shuffle of the crowd leaving the arena, I searched desperately for Ezrah. While Kael and my father were occupied, I ran through the throngs of demons, begging to see his face among the others.

I nearly cried when he appeared near the east exit.

"What are you doing here?" he asked.

"Thank God I found you," I said, out of breath. "I need something from you, and don't tell me you can't do it or that it's too dangerous. We're beyond dangerous now. This is life and death and the future of our people."

He looked directly into my eyes and nodded. "Tell me what you need," he said.

"My bag," I said. "The one the guards took from me when they first brought us here to the castle. And my bow. I have a feeling I'm going to need it before this whole thing is over."

His face went ghostly white, and he swallowed hard. "I

know where it's being kept," he said. "I think I can get to it, but it won't be easy. What's happened, Lea? Are you in danger?"

"We all are in danger," I said. I glanced around at the demons leaving the arena. "Maybe the entire city. I don't have time to explain, but get me that bag as soon as you can. Whatever it takes, Ezrah. I need something from inside it."

"I'll make up some excuse to come to your chambers tonight," he said. "Something about your safety at tomorrow's battle. Wait for me there."

"Thank you," I said.

"Anything for you, my queen," he said, bowing his head slightly. "Now, go, before anyone from the council sees us talking."

I wanted to hug him. I'd been expecting a fight, but maybe he heard the seriousness in my voice. I had to find out what was hidden behind that door, and as soon as I had the answers I was looking for, I intended to figure out a way to get us all out of here before it was too late.

Watching Aerden go through that battle had nearly killed me. He had won, but there were still two more battles to fight before he would have a chance at his freedom. I wasn't sure I could sit there and watch him go through that again.

I made my way back to my father and the rest of the council, and Kael narrowed his eyes at me, questioning. I simply smiled at him and took my mother's arm, walking with her back toward the castle and not bothering to glance back.

He had his secrets, but not for long. As soon as I had that key, I had a feeling his secrets would come tumbling out of the door he kept hidden in the darkness.

———

LATER THAT NIGHT, I paced the floor of my room, anxious for word from Ezrah. If he couldn't find the bag, or if anyone saw him bringing it to me, Kael would most certainly hear about it.

Ezrah's true identity could not be discovered without ruining everything Andros had set in place here. He was a member of the Resistance, and having him here in the castle had been extremely important over the years since my father closed the city's gates.

But knowing what Kael was hiding in the dungeons was more important. We couldn't afford to play it safe any longer. If the Resistance truly wanted to know what was going on in the council's meeting and who was controlling this kingdom, I was their best hope.

When someone knocked on the door an hour later, I jumped and ran to answer it.

"Let me answer it," Presha said, moving in front of me, as if I'd offended her by trying to do something for myself.

I bit my lip and nodded, watching anxiously as she opened the door to my suite.

"I need to speak with the princess about her security tomorrow," Ezrah said. "Please, give us a moment of privacy and wait outside."

Presha's hand fluttered to her face. "Of course," she said.

She motioned for the other handmaidens to join her in the hallway, and when the door was closed, I nearly tackled Ezrah in a hug.

"You got it?" I asked.

"Just barely," he said, pulling the leather bag from a larger sack he had slung across his back. "One of the other guards came in and asked what I was doing in the king's safe, but I made up some story about needing to retrieve something for the queen. As long as he doesn't ask your mother what I was doing there, I should be in the clear."

I took the bag over to my writing desk and opened it up, checking to make sure that everything was still there. Relieved, I touched the diamond key and closed the bag. I trusted Ezrah, but I didn't want him to know everything until I had more answers.

"Thank you," I said. "And my bow?"

He sighed and removed it from the sack.

I giggled like a teenager and snatched it from him. Holding it felt like coming home again. I held it to me and twirled around.

"What exactly do you plan to do with that?" he asked. "If anyone sees that you have it, I don't know that I'll be able to help you escape the dungeons a second time."

"I'll keep it well hidden until I need it," I said, and when he raised a doubting eyebrow, I smiled. "I promise."

"I know you're only doing what you feel is right, but your position here is as a spy for now," he said. "Not a warrior. The more we can find out about the council's plans, the more we can help the Resistance."

"The council is a sham," I said. "There's more going on here than any of us ever suspected. And I promise that as soon as I have the answers I'm looking for, I will tell you everything. Do you think you can get word to Andros for me?"

He frowned. "It won't be easy," he said. "One of our men is going on patrol tomorrow, though, so if I can get word to him before he leaves, he might be able to send a message to Andros. What do you want me to tell him?"

"Tell him to start making plans to get us the hell out of here," I said. "The sooner the better."

"If you manage to escape, your father will not stop looking for you," he said. "You realize what kind of danger you're putting yourself in even suggesting this?"

"I do," I said. "But we can't stay. We need to be back with our people, fighting the Order. After tomorrow, I hope to have all the answers the Resistance needs to overthrow my father and restore this kingdom. Ezrah, this is everything we've been fighting for. We can't let fear hold us back."

"I'll find a way to get your message to him," he said. "Find me after tomorrow's battle in the arena. I'll wait for you at the same exit if I can. In the meantime, hide those things in a place your nosy handmaidens wouldn't think to look."

"I will," I said. I grabbed the bag and my weapon and walked toward my bedroom. "Give me two minutes, then open the door. And thank you. I owe you."

"You owe me nothing," he said.

I nodded and disappeared into my bedroom, shutting the door. I searched for a place to hide these things. Presha was always going through everything around here, but since she hadn't discovered the axe when I'd had it under my bed, I decided that was the safest place for now.

I slid my bow under the bed, tucking it near the mattress where it wouldn't be seen unless someone was specifically looking for it.

But before I hid the bag, I opened it one more time. I removed the diamond key and tucked it into my bra. I wanted it with me at all times, so that when the opportunity came, I wouldn't have to return to my room to retrieve it.

As I grabbed the key, though, something else glittered inside the bag that nearly made my heart stop. Tears sprang to my eyes, and I reached inside to wrap my hand around the ruby communication stone. I had completely forgotten about it, but this stone was a direct line to Mary Anne and Jackson.

I wanted to use it now, but I heard Presha's voice in the outer room and knew I was out of time. I tucked it into my bra beside the key and quickly stashed the bag under the bed.

A moment later, Presha opened the door to find me standing on the balcony, staring out across the city, my heart racing with a new kind of hope.

IN THE FACE OF DEATH

AERDEN

I lay back on my bed in the cell I shared with my
teammates and closed my eyes.

Visions of blood and the horror in the eyes of the
men I'd defeated flashed through my mind, and I opened my
eyes again.

I couldn't sleep. My side burned like hell, and despite the
assurances of the guards that a shaman would be by to ease our
pain, no one had stepped foot into the prison all evening.

I sat up and paced the room, conflicting feelings running
through me. Guilt. Anger. Pride. Love. Despair.

I told myself that the demons I fought today were volun-
teers, just like me. Demons who would rather face death than
be condemned to a life of slavery in the mines. But was that
really true?

Trention slept just a few feet from where I stood now, and
I knew that he was no volunteer. He was forced into these
games because of me, and though I had done what I had to do

to keep him and the rest of my team safe today, if someone had hurt him, they would have been sentencing an innocent demon to death.

The cell across from us had been occupied by the team that opposed us just last night, but there was no sign of them tonight. I kept hoping the door to the holding area would open and those demons would hobble in, injured but alive. Healed by a team of shamans, just like the guards had promised.

But in my heart, I knew the truth.

Those demons had been taken to some room where they were forced to choose between willingly giving their life in service to the king or having it ripped from them.

I placed a hand on my forehead and fought against these feelings that threatened to overwhelm me.

There were still two battles left to go before I would have any hope of being declared free from the king's dungeons. We had easily won the first fight and had come out of it with nothing more than a few scratches that would heal in time. But how would the next two battles go?

Nothing was guaranteed, and I couldn't afford to let my heart get soft. I didn't want to hurt anyone else, but I wasn't exactly eager to sacrifice my life here, either.

For a century, I had dreamed of my freedom. I had prayed for it for a long time, but as the years went by, I found myself wishing for death more than freedom.

Death simply seemed more achievable.

But there were those who had not given up on me, despite the impossible task before them. They were willing to give everything to save my life and set me free. I would not dishonor them by dying in these games. The only one who could win my freedom this time around was me, and I was grateful for the chance to redeem myself.

Still, I couldn't shake the sorrow and guilt of what I had done.

The door at the end of the cell block opened, and slowly, a set of footsteps approached. I woke my teammates, and by the time Reynar appeared in front of us, the five of us all stood in a row, waiting to hear about tomorrow's battle.

"I can't say I'm happy to see you standing here as a winning team," Reynar said, looking pointedly at me. "But I come tonight tell you that the king has chosen for Aerden and Trention to continue on as partners in tomorrow's battle."

My mouth dropped open. "What about the others?" I asked.

Reynar smiled. "The rest of you will head back to the mines tonight," he said. "Work begins first thing in the morning and continues for the remainder of your pitiful lives."

Rushon gripped the steel bars of the cell. "But we won," he said. "We deserve the chance to fight."

"You deserve nothing but what the king says you deserve," Reynar said. "Be grateful you're alive. I doubt these other two will live to see another moon."

Anger pulsed through me. It wasn't fair. These men had volunteered for the chance to fight, and they had won. We all deserved the chance to keep going. But I knew that arguing with Reynar wasn't going to get me a different result.

Morway slammed his hand against the wall and cursed. "I won't go back there," he said. "I can't."

"Would you rather die tonight in service to the king?" I asked, grabbing his arm. "Go back to the mines. I promise you that if I win my freedom, I will find a way to get you out of there. All of you."

Reynar threw his head back, laughing. "You're a fool if you believe you'd ever have that kind of power," he said. "But since you will most likely die tomorrow, I'll leave you to your foolish dreams. The rest of you, come with me now. You've got to be up bright and early."

Rushon, Perrick, and Morway lined up and left the cell, their heads low and their spirits defeated. When they were gone, I wanted to run my fist through a wall.

What kind of king did this to his own people?

Trention watched as I paced the room, anger radiating from my body.

"Here, sit," he said after a long while, pulling his legs off the side of the bed to give me room to sit. "You're making me dizzy with all this pacing."

"It isn't fair," I said.

"You of all people should know that life is rarely fair," he said.

"I just hate this feeling of complete helplessness. I want to do something to save them. To help them," I said. "Instead, I condemned five men to death today and had to watch my friends get sent back to the dungeons."

"You carry so much on those shoulders of yours," he said. "Did you commission these games? Did you condemn these demons to a life of slavery?"

"No, but—"

"There is nothing else," he said. "We have been put in an impossible position. We must either kill or be killed. That is not our choice, but it's the truth of our situation. Whether you decide to place the responsibility of this horror on your own shoulders is your choice, Aerden. And I thought you of all people would understand that the one thing they can never take from you is your own mind. Your own thoughts. Those are under your control, even when everything else has been taken from you."

I quieted, listening to the wise words of an ancient demon.

"Don't let them have this piece of you," he said. "Master your own mind and you take your power back."

My flesh broke out in chills at his words.

He was right.

He placed a hand on my forehead. "Your thoughts are more powerful than you realize," he said. "Even when things seem hopeless and even when you are forced to watch great injustice performed right in front of you, it is still your choice whether to focus on the pain or whether to steel yourself for battle. You choose to be the victim or the victor. Rule your own mind, Aerden, and stop letting them chip pieces off of you as if you were made of stone."

He moved his hand to my chest, placing his palm above my heart.

"Show them you are made of soul," he said. "Of love. Of strength. Show them you are free because you choose to be free."

A tear rolled down my cheek, and I grabbed my friend's hand. He had been like family to me here in the dungeons, and his words echoed through me as truth.

For him, I would be strong, even in the face of death.

FINDING MY WAY HOME

HARPER

I stepped through the door marked with an emerald scarab beetle. I hadn't gotten a chance to call Brooke to give her an update on how things were going or when I would be home since Rend didn't have a phone at his house in the Alps.

Hell, I wasn't even sure if international calling was a thing in the fifties. I was clueless about how things worked this far back.

But since I didn't know what was going on with her here in the house, I quickly summoned my power and glamoured myself as Dr. Evers once again. Better safe than sorry these days, but I hoped more than anything that I would go downstairs and hear Brooke say that she'd found the portal and was ready to go home.

Instead, I heard Melody's voice at the bottom of the stairs.

"I'm sorry, Detective, Dr. Evers isn't here this evening," she said. "I'm not sure when she'll be home."

I tossed Rend's bag into the bedroom and hurried down, glad I had taken the time upstairs to glamour myself. And so incredibly grateful I had gotten enough rest over the past couple days to have all of my power back. Today, holding the glamour felt as natural and as easy as breathing.

"I'm here, Melody," I said. I didn't want her to send the detective away. Out of everyone I knew about in this timeline, he was the most likely to know where that portal was located. Now that I had the potions for the girls, he was my next objective.

"Oh," she said, turning with wide eyes. "I didn't realize you were home."

"Just got in," I said, smiling.

I opened the door wider, and the detective stormed in.

"Where in the world have you been?" he asked. He glanced at Melody, and then gave me a pointed look.

I took the hint.

"Melody, would you mind making us some coffee?" I asked.

She didn't exactly look eager to leave me alone with this guy, but she nodded and disappeared down the hallway that led to the kitchen.

As soon as she was gone, the cop grabbed my arm and pulled me into the sitting room.

"Where were you, Monica? I've been going out of mind waiting for word about our next moves," he said. "I've been by every half hour since the day after the fire almost. I think this nurse of yours is starting to get suspicious. What is she doing staying here, anyway? Doesn't she have her own apartment?"

"I didn't want to be alone," I said. "Let go of my arm. You're hurting me."

He released me and started pacing the floor behind the sofa.

"I don't understand what's going on. Where is your mother?" He stopped, worry flashing in his eyes. "She didn't leave, did she? If you guys are ready to end this little charade, that's fine, but don't leave me here. You promised me that once this whole thing was over, you would take me home. I don't want to be stuck in this shit decade forever, Monica."

I cleared my throat. What exactly was his role in all this?

"Neither do I," I said. "Trust me on that."

"Then what do we do? How come you didn't kill the girls this time? This whole thing is a huge logistical nightmare," he said. "The hospital's fully expecting that the parents of these poor girls are going to show up to claim them. What do you think is going to happen when no one shows up? They're going to start asking questions, that's what. And I can't afford to have any of this crap leading back to me. You've got your magic to help you do whatever it is you need to do, but if I get locked up, I'm stuck here. I'm ready to go back, Monica. I need to know what the plan is."

Wow, he was really angry and worried. I certainly didn't have any answers for him. I tried to think fast, but nothing was coming to mind except to keep bullshitting him until he said something useful.

"I'm just as in the dark as you are," I said. "I had no idea the fire was going to be set early this time, and I haven't seen my mother since the night of the fire, either."

"She went home, Monica," he said, grabbing my arm again. "What are we going to do if she just left us here? Would she do that? She promised me that if I helped her with this little project of hers for a couple decades, she would set me up for life. In the twenty-first century, though. Not here. I can't live here."

I seriously doubted that the emerald priestess ever had any intention of setting this man up with a sweet life in the present day, but he obviously believed she could be trusted. I had probably saved him from a horrible death when he had outlived his usefulness, but I couldn't exactly tell him that.

"I went looking for my mother, thinking that maybe she had gone to take care of something out of town before the fire," I said. "But I haven't been able to find her. She wouldn't leave us here, though. I know she wouldn't. I'm honestly afraid something has happened to her."

His eyes widened, and he ran a hand through his thinning hair.

"Then we have to go now," he said. "Do you think the portal home would still be there, even if something did happen to her? Monica, I found out that several bodies were discovered in the basement of the hospital yesterday. They were both burned beyond recognition, though. Two girls were unaccounted for, so I assumed it was them down there, but what if one of them was her? What if your mother died in that fire?"

I laughed and shook my head, but I hadn't missed his mention of the portal. Did this guy know where it was located?

"Don't be ridiculous," I said. "You know my mother just as well as I do. Do you think a simple fire would kill her? Come on."

He tilted his head toward me, and I wondered if I had said something wrong. He definitely was giving me a suspicious look.

"Maybe a simple fire wouldn't have been enough," he said. "But if someone figured out what she was doing here? Or if someone she was working with was tired of what she was doing to these girls?"

My mouth went dry. I didn't like the way he was looking at me.

"What exactly are you trying to imply?" I asked, drawing my arms close to hide the fact that my hands were trembling.

"I'm just saying that the past few times we've killed these girls, you simply haven't had the stomach for it," he said. "Last time, you even suggested that you wanted to be replaced with a new doctor. Your mother, of course, would hear nothing of it. You are far too talented at what you do for her to replace you very easily. Besides, you were always her favorite daughter. Everyone knows that."

"I adore my mother," I said, hoping there was enough passion in my voice to make him believe the lie. "I may not have always loved what we were doing here, but I would never have done anything to hurt her."

He turned around and stared into the shadows. "Well, if not you, then maybe someone else," he said. "One of the girls? Maybe one of the ones who was missing from the check?"

I swallowed. I couldn't let him get too close to the truth.

"I'm sure my mother is fine," I said. "The two bodies that were found were most likely those of the two girls who were missing. But you're right that we should check on the portal home. If anything did happen to my mother, we need to make sure the portal is still open. If we have to, we'll go through together and figure out what happened later."

He took a deep breath, but finally nodded.

"We should go together," he said. "I don't want you going through without me and closing it behind you. Besides, the only reason I haven't checked on it yet is because I didn't want you or your mother to find me there and think I'd betrayed you."

I nodded. "Of course," I said. I had no idea where the portal was, but hopefully he knew exactly where to find it. Of course, I couldn't go through with him and leave the girls and Brooke here, but I could figure that out when we got there.

"I need to take care of a couple things down at the station, but as soon as I can get away, I'll come back to pick you up," he said. "We'll go together."

I shook my head. "No, I'll go with you now," I said. "I can't have you heading there without me."

He narrowed his gaze at me. "Now you don't trust me?"

"Right now, I'm not sure I trust anyone," I said. "We go together, and we go now."

"What about this nurse?" he asked. "Should we kill her before we go? She might already know too much."

"She's harmless," I said, my mouth dry. "I'll make up some reason why I need to go down to the station to answer a few questions. She won't think a thing of it. You don't need to worry about her."

"If you're sure, I guess we can leave her alive for now," he said. "Grab whatever you need to grab and let's go. It's already getting dark, and the road to the cabin is hard to find in the dark. I've only been out there once without your mom telling us where to go. I just have to have a simple phone call first."

I swallowed and nodded. "Of course," I said, showing him to the phone. "I'll be right back."

As I walked away, all I could think was this guy better remember how to get to this supposed cabin. This was my best shot at finding my way home, and I wasn't going to let it slip through my fingers.

THIS DIDN'T FEEL RIGHT

HARPER

"Where are you going?" Brooke asked. "What is he doing back here? Does he know something?"

I moved her into the pantry where I hoped he wouldn't be able to overhear our conversation.

"He suspects that maybe something happened to my dear mother," I said in a whisper. "But Brooke, he knows where the portal is. He said something about driving out to the cabin to check on it. I'm going to get him to take me there."

"Oh my God, Harper," she said, putting her hand over her mouth as she realized she'd spoken a bit too loudly. "Do you think this could really be it? What will you do if he wants you to go through with him?"

"I don't know," I said. "I haven't been able to think that far ahead. I'll have to try to convince him to go through without me. I'll give him some excuse about needing to make sure Mother doesn't come back for me. I'll think of something once we get there, but I need to get going before he leaves without me."

"I'll wait here," she said. "Did you find your friend in Chicago?"

I nodded. "And he gave me a bunch of healing and memory potions that should help most of the girls get their memories back," I said, my body buzzing with hope. "I stashed it in my bedroom. See if you can get to Nora, Mary Ellen, and the others who know the truth first. Get them to start glamouring themselves as parents of these patients. There's a list of everyone and which hospital they've been sent to upstairs. We need to restore as many of the girls' memories as possible and get them back here. If the portal is open, we'll have to move quickly."

She grabbed my hands. "I hope this is it," she said. "I'll take care of the girls."

"Okay, I'll be home as soon as I can," I said. "Be safe, and I'll see you soon."

I stepped out of the pantry to find the detective standing at the counter, pouring himself a cup of coffee.

"What were you two ladies doing in the pantry?" he asked, tilting his head to the side. "I could hear you whispering."

"I was instructing Melody on what to do if we don't return this evening," I said. "The girls will have to be taken care of at some point. It will be easier for Melody to gain access to them than anyone else. You know what to do?"

"Yes, Doctor," she said.

"Wonderful," I said. "Are you ready, Detective?"

He narrowed his eyes, as if he didn't quite believe me. My stomach coiled into knots.

I just needed him to take me to this cabin. I could deal with his suspicions later.

"Let's get going," he said. "I can go back and finish my work at the station later tonight if I need to. Should we take your car?"

I paused. How in the world would I explain not having the car anymore?

"I'm having some trouble with it," I said. "Plus, I don't feel up to driving. It's been a long few days."

He nodded. "We'll take mine, then, if you don't mind riding with me."

"Not at all," I said. "Let's go."

"Did you need to pack anything?" he asked. "You know, just in case?"

"No, I have everything I need," I said, thinking of the master stone still strapped to my leg. The only other thing I might need would be a weapon, but I hoped it wouldn't come to that.

"Melody, if I don't return, take care of the girls and destroy any evidence," I said.

"Of course, Doctor," she said. Her eyes reflected my fear and excitement. Could this really be the answer we'd been looking for?

The cop led me out to his police cruiser in front of the house. It was an old black and white Ford of some kind, and compared to the sleek cop cars of the modern day, this thing was positively massive.

He opened the door for me, and I slid in. There were no seat belts, so I folded my hands in my lap and waited for him to cross around the front and get in to drive.

"Do you really think it's still going to be there?" he asked.

"I don't see why it wouldn't," I said, my stomach in knots.

"Monica, we've been through this how many times, now? Six?" he asked. "Your mother is meticulous about setting up the deaths of those girls and making sure the fire happens in the middle of the night when it would be easy to explain how everyone was trapped inside. Why would she change things up now?"

"I don't have answers for you," I said. "I'm just as much in the dark here as you are."

He turned on a road several blocks up, and I kept my eyes forward, memorizing the names of streets. If the portal was there, I would need to be able to get back there alone. I would also have to find a way to transport nearly a hundred girls over there, so I hoped it wasn't too far away.

We rode in silence, and with every turn, I went back through each of the names of the streets, etching them into my brain in the correct order. Right turn on Elm Street. Three blocks down, take a left on Main. About a mile down, turn left on West Turner.

"Are you okay?" he asked. "You seem particularly quiet tonight."

"I'm worried. Aren't you?"

He raised an eyebrow. "You're the one who told me not to be concerned," he said. "I've been suspicious of this whole thing from the minute I heard the institute was on fire. I usually get at least a week's notice to make sure all the paperwork is ready and everything in my life is wrapped up. I like to at least be prepared to stage my own death in the week after the fire."

I did my best not to look surprised. Of course, they had to have some kind of plan for how to explain the disappearances of the detective, the doctor, and the priestess herself. Something that wouldn't cause authorities to look into the matter too deeply.

I was curious what their plan had been each time, but I couldn't exactly ask him. I was supposed to have been through it at least half a dozen times by now.

"As soon as we see the portal, we'll at least have some idea of what's going on," I said.

"And if your mother really was one of those bodies found in the basement of the institute?" he asked. "What's our plan, then? Would that officially mean I can go home for real? My contract completed after all this time?"

Contract? I was dying to find out how a human cop had gotten involved with the priestess.

"That's not my place to say," I said.

"Well, if your mother is gone, then it's you and you alone who holds my contract, Monica," he said. "I think I've more than made up for any mistakes I might have made against your family. You have to know that. I've given you guys everything I possibly could. We're talking about more than twenty years of my life. I haven't seen my sister in a decade. I just want this to be over."

I raised an eyebrow. What the heck had he done to the Evers family to get roped into this gig?

Of course, with the Order you never really knew. It wasn't exactly like they played fair.

Still, he sounded scared, and I doubted Monica Evers would have been very sympathetic. I needed to be careful what I told him, but if the portal was still there, I would probably just tell him to go home. Leave this life behind and forget any of this ever happened.

It would, at least, be one less person to worry about.

After several miles on West Turner, he slowed and turned left on a dirt road that held no street sign. I glanced around in the last of the sun's light and tried to memorize this location. The area was wooded and completely deserted. If I had to guess, I would say we were about ten miles outside the town limits, and so far, I'd only seen one car pass us.

The car bumped and banged down the uneven road, and I held onto the door, just trying to keep myself in the seat. The detective—I still didn't even know his name—took it slowly, but I could tell he was anxious to get wherever we were going.

I held hope in my heart. When the ruby priestess had been to visit me just two days ago, the portal had still been open.

Maybe it would still be open now. I closed my eyes for a moment and sent up a silent prayer. Just let it stay open long enough for me to give these girls their memories back. Then we could all go home.

If, for some reason, Rend didn't give him my warning in time, Jackson would need me. I wasn't sure I would survive it if I failed him now. The portal simply had to be there.

The car slowed as we approached the end of the rough dirt road, but I shook my head. There was no sign of any cabin out here. The sun had set by now, but the headlights shone on thick forest, not a cabin in the woods.

I reached for my power as the cop stopped the car and started to get out. What exactly was he trying to pull here? Was this all just a trap?

I connected to the well of power deep inside me and was grateful, at least, that he had brought me to a place teeming with life. It was early spring, if I had to guess, and even though most of the trees were bare, buds were starting to appear on

some of them. They were dormant, but they were alive, and
their power would come in handy if this came down to a fight.

"Are you coming?" he asked, leaning his head back inside
the car. "We've got a walk ahead of us."

Confused, I got out of the car and looked around.

This didn't feel right. Did the emerald priestess really walk
through these thick woods every single time she wanted to
come back to the institute? Every time I saw her, she'd been
wearing high heels and a dress. I didn't really see her walking
through these woods in those shoes every couple of days.

Then again, the tires on her Cadillac had been covered
in mud.

"It's pretty dark out, already," I said. "Are you sure we
should try to make the walk tonight?"

I was desperate to know if the portal was open, but I was
starting to wonder if I'd managed to walk straight into some
kind of trap. Maybe I should have asked Brooke to come with
me, but as always, I thought I could handle it all myself.

The detective eyed me. "What does darkness matter to
you?" he asked. "Just conjure one of those lights you can make,
and let's get going. We're losing time, here."

"Right," I said, mumbling.

I lifted a trembling hand and conjured an orb of pure
white light. The detective nodded toward the woods, as if he
expected me to lead the way. Only I had no idea where we
were going.

"You lead the way," I said. "I'm not feeling well, and I'm
scared."

"Scared?" he asked, raising an eyebrow and smiling.
"Of what?"

"You've been suggesting to me since the fire that maybe

someone murdered my mother," I said. "Who do you think they would go for next?"

He nodded. "Good point," he said. "Come on. Send that light ahead of me, at least, so I can see where I'm going. The path is always hard to find."

I sent my orb of light in front of him and watched him carefully, sending the light wherever he stepped. The woods were thick out here, and as far as I could tell, there was no real path at all. I stepped over fallen branches, thick underbrush, and vines that grew up from the earth in twisted patterns.

After about ten minutes of walking, I was convinced he'd been lying to me this whole time. I kept a steady eye on his back, waiting for him to turn on me, but he simply kept walking forward, pushing branches out of his way as he went.

"Here it is," he said, motioning to a much more obvious path along the forest floor.

I might not have noticed it if he hadn't pointed it out, but I saw it now. A very small line of cleared trees and underbrush that led straight ahead.

I relaxed slightly.

"Let's move faster," I said.

The detective followed close behind me as I hurried down the path. A few minutes later, the woods opened up into a large clearing. There, in the center, was some kind of structure. I couldn't see it well in the dark. There wasn't much moon to speak of tonight, and there were no lights on inside.

Still, a strange feeling rolled through me. I knew this place.

"We made it," I said.

"Yes, we did," he said. "No thanks to you. It's like you had no idea where it was, Monica."

I brought a nervous hand to my forehead. "It's been a rough few days," I said.

"The Monica Evers I know would never be rattled by these kinds of things," he said. "I've known you what? Twenty-five years? I've never seen you lose your head quite like this."

My mouth went dry. I didn't like his tone of voice.

"How many times has my mother disappeared like this?" I asked, turning to face him. "How many times has the fire happened early?"

He tilted his head and narrowed his eyes. "I don't think that's all it is," he said. "Besides, there's one other thing that's been bothering me. Not once have you called me by my name. Do you even know what my name is?"

I sucked in a breath. "Of course, I know what your name is," I said, lifting my chin and trying to keep up the attitude of the heartless doctor. "Since when are you so paranoid? Maybe mother started the fire early, because she realized you'd outgrown your usefulness."

Instead of looking intimidated, like I'd hoped, he smiled and stepped toward me. "No, it's not that," he said. "You know what I think?"

He took another few steps toward me, and I stepped backward. I gathered my power in my hands, and the energy buzzed through my veins.

"I think the Evers women finally brought someone a little too powerful to their little house of horrors," he said, stepping forward until he was almost touching me. "I think they couldn't torture this girl enough to break her, and she finally got her revenge."

He knows.

"What are you saying?" I asked, using the time to charge

my magic as much as I could. I pulled from the trees around me, drawing as much power into my body as I could handle. "You're not making any sense."

"Oh, I think you understand me perfectly." His eyes widened, the light shining onto his face. "Who are you? Because I'm willing to bet my life that you're not Monica Evers. I'm guessing Monica is one of those bodies in the basement of the asylum. And maybe her mother is the second body. So, who are you?"

My heart raced. What was my best move here? This guy had obviously owed some kind of debt to the Evers women. Maybe if he knew they'd been killed, he would be willing to help me.

Then again, maybe he was fiercely loyal to the priestess and had been playing me all along.

"You need to be careful, Det—"

"No," he shouted, shaking his head. "Not detective. You never called me detective. What's my name? If you're really Monica Evers, you'll know my name. I want to hear it. Prove it to me that you know exactly who I am."

I glanced back toward the cabin in the shadows. I had to be sure no one else was here. If I had to fight one person, I could hold my own. A group would be much harder.

But there was no sign of anyone at the cabin. It looked dead and abandoned.

"Listen, now is not the time to do this," I said. "We need to get inside and see if the portal is still open."

He laughed. "I knew it," he said. "I knew it the night of the fire. Something wasn't quite right about you. Whoever you are, you did a brilliant job with your glamour, but you didn't quite nail the good doctor's attitude. She was a real bitch, you know that? And whoever you really are in there, you just don't have it in you to be as nasty as she was."

I wasn't sure how much longer I could hold him back. He obviously knew the truth, and I couldn't afford to waste another second on this game.

I dropped my glamour and lifted my hands.

His eyes widened, and he stepped back. "Damn. You're just a girl," he said, his voice barely above a whisper. "I don't understand how you defeated them. There's no way someone your age could be powerful enough to take them down."

"See, that's exactly the problem with the Order," I said. "Everyone is always underestimating me. I may be younger, but the Evers women gave me no choice but to fight back. The woman was about to shove an ice pick through my brain. Let's just say they gave me all the motivation I needed."

He laughed and stepped even further away. "Well, let's see how motivated you're feeling tonight," he said.

I glanced around again, this time noticing several shadows moving just inside the treeline. I tensed as five men stepped out of the darkness.

"What's going on?" I asked, taking a step back toward the cabin.

"It's taken me all this time to put together a group of people who were willing to fight against the Order of Shadows and their witches," he said. "But I've had six trips back here to the past to identify the perfect people to help me overthrow the Evers witches."

I looked around, surprised when five women also stepped out of the shadows, magic glowing on their hands.

Shit. What was going on here?

"If you want to fight against the Order, then you're no

enemies of mine," I said. "I've dedicated my entire life to ending the Order. We can work together to bring them down. We just have to find our way back to the present day."

The detective stepped back to join the circle of those who had joined us. The eleven of them stretched out around me, closing me in so that the only escape I had was back toward the cabin. And I had no idea what I'd find in there if I tried to run.

"You don't get it, do you? It's not just the Order we're fighting against," he said. "It's all witches who carry a demon inside of them, and I can feel the demon power running through your veins. You're one of them."

I shook my head. "No," I said. "My father was a demon. I didn't enslave a demon the way the Order does."

"It doesn't matter to me how you came by your demon power," he said. "Demons are an abomination to our world, and we are dedicated to eliminating any witch who has associated herself with these creatures. Besides, we've been looking forward to our first chance to get rid of a witch who had demon power running through her veins. We were hoping to end the priestess and her daughter, but we'll settle for you."

I wanted to scream at them. They obviously didn't understand how witches worked. Every witch here in the human world had some level of demon power running through her veins. That was our source of power. The Order exploited that by enslaving demons to make themselves more powerful, but every witch in this circle who carried her power in her hands now was part demon to some degree.

From the way their eyes focused on me, anger and hatred burning through them, I didn't think logic was going to work right now. Still, I had to try.

"All magic in this world comes from demons," I said.

"Those in your own group who have power get that from a demon and a human mating somewhere in their family line. You are no different from me."

"Lies," one of the witches screamed. "Those are exactly the kinds of lies the Order likes to tell, but it's not true. My power comes from God. It's a gift from heaven. Your power comes from the devil himself. Demons are the devil's minions, and we are committed to killing all demons and witches who have demon power running through their veins."

I stopped cold. Oh my God. I'd heard this before. I knew exactly who these people were, and I couldn't believe this was happening again now, of all times.

"You're the Others," I said, half in awe and half in complete frustration.

How had I gone through all this just to get mixed up once again with this crazy religious sect that wanted to kill all demons? A group of Others had kidnapped Jackson before I even realized he was a demon. They were totally nuts.

The detective raised an eyebrow. "So, you've heard of us," he said. "It took me three trips to gain the trust of their leader and convince enough of them to join me here in this town to fight against the priestess. To be honest, I wasn't sure we'd have enough to take them down, so we were trying to come up with a way to separate them. Luckily, you took care of them for us."

"I helped you, and now it's your turn to help me," I said. "Help me find the portal home, let me and the girls go home to where we belong. We're fighting the Order just like you are, you have to see that. We're on the same side, here."

He shook his head. "No, that's not how it works," he said. "These people all came here to fight, and I'm not about to let a witch with demon blood running through her veins get away, free and clear."

The circle of Others had tightened on me as we talked, and I prepared myself for a fight.

That night at the abandoned hospital when I'd gone to save Jackson, I had fought three of the Others, and I'd nearly died. Jackson had barely survived the whole thing, too, but I would have given anything to have him here at my side right now.

Could I face eleven on my own and survive it?

I shook my head. Man, this really sucked, but the only way home from here was through these people. And I hadn't come this far to be brought down by a group of misguided religious zealots.

"I'll give you one last chance to get out of here and leave me alone," I said. "I don't want to fight you."

"Oh, there's going to be a fight," he said, smiling. He pulled a gun from the belt of his pants and aimed it straight at me. "First, you'll die. Then, we'll go back and kill that nurse at the house. Before the night is over, we'll have killed ourselves two witches, even if it isn't the two we originally meant to kill."

I met his eyes, vowing that I would not let him get to Brooke.

"This whole time, I thought the Others were very different from the Order, but it turns out, you're basically the same," I said, lowering my hands as my power turned to bright flames that surrounded my body. "You murder innocents, worship power above all things, and you always underestimate the ones strong enough to kill you."

At my words, the detective aimed his gun straight at me and fired the first bullet.

A DIM RED LIGHT

JACKSON

I sat straight up in bed, my body covered in sweat.

I'd been dreaming of Harper again. We were back in that abandoned hospital in Peachville, fighting the Others. I hadn't thought about that night in a long time, but for some reason, the dream had rattled me.

I took a deep breath and slid out from under the covers. I poured a glass of water and stood on the balcony, looking out at the garden below. Sleep wouldn't come easy again, so I thought about our plan and shook my head. There were still so many unknowns it made my mind twist into knots.

I seriously hoped that someday, Harper and I would stand here and look out at this kingdom with nothing more to worry about than what to name our son. I longed for peace, but steeled myself for battle.

With a sigh, I turned and saw a dim red light filling the room. I dropped my water, the glass shattering on the tile floor as I lunged for the red stone on the table. My heart raced. This was one of Lea's stones.

I took it in my hand and waved my palm over the top, activating its magic.

"Lea? I'm here," I said.

"Jackson?" Her voice trembled. She was whispering, so I leaned closer to hear her better.

"It's me," I said, keeping my voice low in case she was in danger. "Are you okay? Is Aerden with you?"

"Oh, Jackson. Aerden's fighting in the King's Games. Didn't Andros tell you?" she asked. "Ezrah told me Andros planned to tell you about the games more than a week ago."

"I haven't seen Andros," I said, nearly choking on my own words. I sat down in the chair beside the table. "The King's Games have been outlawed for centuries."

"My father brought them back," she said. "Aerden won the first round, but he fights again in the morning. Jackson, I'm going to do everything I can to get us both out of here before the final round of these games. There's more going on here than we thought. The entire city could be in danger."

"What can I do to help?" I asked. "We'll come to get you."

"I've already sent word to the Resistance," she said. "Just make sure there's room for us at the castle when we get back there. Hopefully, we'll be together again in just a few days."

"There will always be room for both of you here," I said. "Lea, the emerald priestess is dead. We're going to win this war."

"What?" she asked, her voice full of awe. "Is Harper home? Did you find her?"

"Not yet," I said. "It's a long story. I'll pour us some wine and tell you all about it in a couple of days, okay?"

She laughed, but it sounded as though she was crying. "You have no idea how good that sounds to me right about now," she said. "Before I go, there's something else I need to tell you. Just in case we don't make it home."

"Don't talk like that," I said.

"We've found evidence that there's another kingdom, Jackson. Far to the east, beyond the wall of darkness in the Sea of Glass," she said. "The map that was found was made of diamonds. I think it's important."

My hands went numb. Another kingdom? That wasn't possible.

"Lea—"

"Shhhh," she said.

I held my breath, listening.

"What are you doing in here?" a man asked, his voice full of rage.

"Kael, don't," Lea shouted.

I winced at the sound of a hand hitting flesh. Lea screamed, and the stone in my hand went dark.

ONE LAST THREAT

LEA

K ael slapped me hard across the face and threw the
communication stone to the floor. The ruby shattered into a million tiny pieces, and I screamed.

I seriously wanted to kill him for that, but the demon
grabbed my hair at the base of my neck and dragged me over to
the mirror.

"Do you see what you made me do?" he asked, tilting my
head so that I got a good view of the slash now bleeding across
my cheek. "I didn't want things to be like this between us,
Princess, but you've left me no choice. Tell me who you were
talking to, or I will cause you a great deal of pain before the
night is over."

"How dare you come into my chambers uninvited," I said.

"These are my chambers," he said, his lips so close to my
ear, I could feel his breath. "This entire city belongs to me
now. Having you at my side would have made the transition to

king easier for me, but I do not need you, Lazalea. Who were you talking to?"

He gripped my hair tighter, but all I could think about was the bow hidden beneath my bed. I couldn't wait to send an arrow straight through his heart. I smiled at the thought, and he growled, throwing me to the ground.

He lifted a hand to me, and a diamond ring caught my eye. I touched my cheek. That's what must have slashed into me.

"You do need me," I said. "If you didn't, you never would have brought me up from the dungeons. You have power here, but the people don't trust you. They trust the council, but there are those on the council who would not support your rise to the throne. Without me, you have no claim to it. Besides, this festival is in my honor, is it not? What will the people think if I show up at tomorrow's battle with bruises on my skin? Rumors travel fast in this city, Kael. The people would not support you if they thought you abused their princess."

His lips pressed into a tight line. He reared his hand back, but instead of hitting me again, he turned and walked toward the balcony. He stood there for a long moment before coming back. He grabbed my arm and pulled me off of the floor.

"Your usefulness only extends until the day of our wedding," he said. "I will talk to your mother and insist we are so in love, we simply cannot wait any longer. In two days, after the final round of the King's Games, we will be mated. I will solidify my right to the throne, and you will choose to either obey me, or die. I honestly don't care which."

He released me, but before he left the room, he turned around with one last threat.

"I warned you what would happen if you didn't fall in line," he said. "You'll want to pay particular attention to the battle tomorrow, Princess. Your actions here tonight have sealed your poor friend's fate, I'm afraid. Maybe next time, you'll think twice before you betray me."

He slammed the door, and I fell to my knees. I had waited too long to plan our escape, and now, it was too late. Aerden was going to die.

I'LL BE BACK FOR YOU

HARPER

I shifted as the detective's bullet zipped past my head and hit the wall of the cabin behind me.

I'd never been in a fight with guns before, so I had to keep my eyes open. I wasn't sure how many of them had brought guns to this fight, but I caught sight of several daggers in the hands of the other men.

Daggers, I could handle.

I reformed in the woods, my body covered by the dark shadows of the night. I let go of the orb of light I had conjured earlier, and the Others in the clearing were drenched in darkness. Someone else conjured an orb of their own, but it was obvious they had lost sight of me. They scrambled to find me, three witches running into the cabin and two men stepping carefully into the woods.

The rest of them stood in the clearing, turning in circles and looking for any sign of me.

The detective shouted orders at his group, and a couple of

the other men ran to the back of the cabin to search for me there.

I turned my focus to the two men who had come into the woods. They separated and went in two different directions, weapons raised.

I shifted again and kept low to the ground. I flew past the first man's feet and reformed behind him. I sent a rope of white smoke toward him, wrapping my power around his neck before I snapped it.

He silently fell to the ground, his eyes wide open in surprise. I stepped over his dead body and reached down to retrieve the silver dagger in his hand. Just like when I'd fought the Others before, it was a ritual dagger from one of the covens. This time, though, the jewel embedded in its hilt was a ruby. The first I'd ever seen in person. I briefly wondered where he'd come by this ruby dagger, but I didn't have time to think too much of it.

I shifted again and flew after the second man in the woods. He hadn't made it very far, and I repeated the same movements, snapping his neck before he even knew I was there. In his hand, he carried a handgun similar to the one the detective had pointed at me.

Was this guy a cop, too?

I opened the cylinder and counted five bullets. I had zero experience with guns, but the bullets inside were pure silver in color, and I wondered if they were made of demon silver. I would have to be extra careful with the detective and anyone else who carried one of these guns.

I was still part demon, after all, and this type of silver might kill me in an instant.

I dropped the bullets into my hand and threw them into

the woods where they scattered. I was still wearing the dress I'd worn to Rend's, and I wished more than anything I'd been able to find a comfortable pair of jeans at the priestess's house. I had nowhere to keep the gun, and I couldn't afford to have both hands occupied.

I shifted and flew deeper into the woods. When I was far enough away from the cabin, I hid the gun in the underbrush.

Since I didn't really know how to use it, a gun could be more of a liability than a help in a situation like this, but I didn't want anyone else to have it, either.

I glanced back toward where we'd left the car, and for a second, I considered the possibility of just getting back in the car and leaving the Others here. I could get back to Brooke before they could, and we could hide out together until we had a chance to come back out here and look for the portal.

But then we'd be living in fear, always afraid that the Others would find us. I needed to put an end to this tonight.

I turned back toward the cabin and flew through the woods. Two down. Nine to go.

A group of six had come back together in front of the cabin, and I looked around, trying to figure out where the other three had gone. A witch stepped out of the front door of the cabin, and she shook her head.

"She's not in there," she said.

"Robby's dead," someone else shouted as they ran from the woods. "She killed him. I don't see any sign of Logan."

There was still one person unaccounted for, and I flew around the circle of woods that surrounded the clearing until I'd reached the back of the cabin. A single witch stood back there by herself, scanning the woods.

Her hands glowed with a soft amber power.

I took my human form at the edge of the woods and gathered flames into my hands. She turned to look just as I sent a stream of hot fire toward her. She screamed as the flames consumed her, and she managed to send a single spell toward me before she fell to her knees.

The group around front ran back to see what was going on, but I had already shifted and flown high into the trees to watch their reactions.

One of the men screamed and knelt at the witch's side. He slipped out of his coat and used it to extinguish the flames, but it was too late for her. He put a finger to her neck and shook his head.

"Find her," he said. "I'm going to kill her for doing this."

Guilt shot through me. He must have loved that woman, and I hated having to hurt anyone, but I was done playing nice. I had given them a chance to walk away, but they had been determined to kill me.

"She's picking us off one at a time. Pair up," the detective shouted. "No one goes anywhere alone."

Two men and two women paired off and ran into the woods to search for me. The pair of men walked beneath me, never once looking up into the trees. I waited for the rest of the group in the clearing to start walking back to the front of the cabin before flying toward the pair of men.

I couldn't see their hands well enough in the dark to see if they were carrying guns or daggers, but as long as I could surprise them, it wouldn't matter.

I took human form right behind them and brought the silver dagger to the first man's throat. I didn't hesitate, slicing through the skin of his neck.

His partner spun around, gun upraised. He fired, and I

shifted quickly. The bullet grazed my shoulder, and the pain ripped through me like fire through a dry forest. I lost my grip on the dagger and fell to the ground, unable to hold my demon form as blood poured from my wound.

The man fired again, but I rolled to the side.

He cursed and aimed at me again. I took a deep breath and pushed the pain aside. I would deal with this wound later. For now, I had to focus.

I shifted and flew sideways just as a third bullet dug into the ground where I had just been. I needed to get that dagger back, but I wasn't sure where it had landed. I scanned the forest floor but didn't see any sign of it.

Another bullet rang out, and I heard it zip by my ear. That was way too close.

The man was following my white smoke, and for the first time, I wished my heritage was from the Northern Kingdom where my demon form would be black instead of the bright white of my father's people.

I switched directions, flying straight into the air above the tops of the trees. The man below cursed as he lost sight of me, but I could hear his footsteps against the ground as he ran back toward his group.

Once he joined up with them, I would lose my chance to take him down.

My shoulder burned, confirming that the bullets they were using were definitely made of demon steel rather than normal bullets. A second hit might bring me down. I needed to figure out who all had these guns and focus on bringing them down first.

Starting with the jerk who had shot me.

I flew back down toward the ground, pushing myself as

fast as I could go. He had almost made it to the clearing. I wasn't going to catch him in time, so I took human form and threw my hands forward.

I wrapped my telekinetic power around his body and pulled him backwards into the woods. I slammed his back against the tree and held him there as I glanced around, looking for anything I could use as a weapon.

The man struggled against my power, but I held him there as easily as if I had my hands on him. I used my power to lift a small, broken branch off the forest floor. With a single push forward, I sent the sharp-end of the branch straight through his heart and into the tree. I released him, and his head fell to the side as blood poured from his wound.

I turned, wanting to retrieve the gun he'd dropped, but two witches rushed toward the area, their orbs of lights illuminating the man's pierced body. I shifted again and flew up into the trees.

Five down. Six to go.

One witch crouched down and picked up the gun, aiming it into the woods in every direction. Her hand trembled, though, and I could tell she had no idea where I had gone.

"Mark is dead," she shouted, backing up toward the clearing. "What do we do? She's killing everyone."

The detective ran over to her and glanced into the woods. He cringed and shook his head. He ran a hand through his thinning hair.

"It's one witch," he shouted. "How is she doing this?"

"Maybe she's stronger than we thought," the witch said.

"Maybe you guys are incompetent," he shouted. "I want her dead."

The witch looked up, right at me, but she didn't see me in

my demon form. She just shook her head. "I don't know where she went," she said. "How can we kill someone we can't even see?"

"She's been hit," the detective said, running his hand along the ground near the man they'd called Mark. "There's blue blood here. Demon blood. He must have hit her with a bullet. She's injured, so let's draw her in and put an end to her now."

They walked back toward the cabin, and the two witches who had paired up earlier to search the woods joined the rest of the group.

The remaining six put their heads together, and I strained to hear what they were saying, but they were just too far away.

I took the opportunity to fly down toward where I'd lost that dagger. I reformed and got down on my hands and knees in the underbrush and searched for the weapon. I smiled when my hand hit the hilt. I lifted the ruby dagger from the ground and wrapped my fist around it.

Blood ran down my arm, and it wasn't slowing. My vision blurred for a moment, but I shrugged it off. I shifted and flew back into the darkness of the woods. The Others were back at the cabin for now, and I needed a few minutes to deal with this wound before I lost too much blood.

When I was far enough away, I reformed and sat down on the cold dirt beneath me. I ripped the hem of my skirt until I had a long strip of cloth. I tied it just above the wound and used my magic to tighten the knot. I winced against the pain, but tightened it further.

The flow of blue blood slowed a little, and I stood up, dagger in hand.

If the group was going to stick together from here on out, I needed a plan.

I shifted and flew into the trees, trying to get a good look at where they were gathering now. From my vantage point in the trees, the six remaining Others stood just in front of the cabin, as if they were guarding it for dear life. Hope rose inside me. Did that mean the portal was truly there inside that cabin? Why else would they be so determined to keep me from getting inside?

I made my way back down to the forest floor. If I couldn't separate them, I could at least make them extremely uncomfortable.

I gave thanks to the Cypress demon who had given me the power to control the weather as I planted my feet far apart and reached deep into the earth, drawing more magic into myself. I knew this spell would take a great deal of my power, but if my plan worked out, I wouldn't need to hold on much longer.

I circled my hands in front of my body, and the wind picked up around me, blowing my hair across my face and causing the trees to sway. The group near the cabin looked up just as large raindrops began to fall. A couple of them ran onto the porch of the cabin to get out of the rain, but they wouldn't be safe there.

I increased the motion of my hands, pouring my magic into the storm. Leaves, branches, and debris blew into the clearing. The witches in the group gathered together, and I realized quickly they were casting a shielding spell that covered the small group still standing in the clearing.

While the heavy rain beat down and the wind whipped around them, the group huddled together inside a bubble of protection.

Crap.

I hadn't planned on this. I placed my palm downward,

sending my power deeper into the earth. When I felt my power charge up, I flipped my palm up and reached into the sky, pulling down a strong bolt of lightning that hit the ground at the witches' feet. The group scattered away from the scorched earth, and I took the opportunity to focus on the detective as he ran toward the steps of the cabin.

I reached toward him with my magic and yanked him backwards, into the woods. A witch screamed and ran after him. She grabbed his hand and tried to pull him back into the clearing, but my magic was too strong for her.

I pulled the detective deeper into the woods, and the witch holding onto him stumbled, losing her grip and falling to her knees.

Before he could make a move to shoot at me, I wrapped my power around his handgun and pulled it from his hands. The weapon hit the ground with a thud, and I pushed the detective back against a tree.

He struggled hard against my magic, but without his gun, he was powerless.

I sent a stream of white ropes toward the tree, wrapping them around his body a hundred times. He was trapped, but I wasn't ready to kill him just yet. I wanted to know where this portal was, and if I managed to survive this attack and the portal wasn't here, this detective could still prove useful to me.

I approached him, and he attempted to talk, but the ropes that covered his face kept him from speaking.

I placed a hand on his head and ran it all the way down his body, turning him into the color of air, glamouring him to look like the wind. Like nothing.

"I'll be back for you," I said as I shifted and flew across the ground to retrieve his gun.

The witch who had run after him had apparently changed her mind about trying to save his life. She ran back toward the group at the cabin, the wind still whipping at her clothes and her hair as she ran.

I gathered the wind in my hands and focused it at her legs. She fell and started crawling toward her friends. I was just about to send my magical ropes toward her when the gleam of a gun's barrel caught my eye.

The witch who had gotten the gun from the woods earlier aimed it straight at me, but her hands were trembling so hard, I had just enough time to shift and fly out of the way before she fired.

I was tired and bleeding, and between the weather, the glamour, and holding that detective to the tree, I was running out of power faster than I could replenish it. I needed to put an end to this.

Rather than fly back toward the trees where I knew I would be safe, I flew straight toward the witch on the cabin porch. She fired the gun, but I dodged it easily.

I flew around the witch's body, reforming just as I grabbed her arm and placed the dagger against her throat. I pulled her backward, away from the others so that my back could be against the wooden slats of the cabin's wall.

"Drop the gun," I shouted over the rain pounding against the roof.

She lowered her hand, but instead of dropping the gun, she tossed it to the man who stood near the steps. He caught it and immediately aimed toward us.

I sliced the throat of the witch in front of me and shifted to smoke. I focused, knowing this was the moment of do or die.

I knocked the gun from the man's hand and plunged the

dagger into his chest. His eyes widened for a moment before the life drained from his face.

Heat on my back caused me to shift again, barely avoiding a ball of flames that slammed into the dead man as he fell across the steps.

I made quick work of the three remaining witches, using my power to push them backward into the storm before I shifted and plunged my dagger into their chests, one at a time.

When the last witch fell, her blood soaking the front of her shirt, I closed my eyes and lifted my face to the sky in gratitude, letting the rain wash their blood from my skin.

THE PERFECT SHAPE OF A PORTAL

HARPER

I wiped the edge of the dagger against my dress and stepped into the woods.

I released the glamour on the detective, but I didn't release him from the ropes of my power.

"What am I going to find in that house?" I asked, removing the white smoke ropes that held his mouth closed. "Is the portal there? Or am I going to find another trap waiting for me?"

He gulped the air, his face red.

"What have you done?" he screamed. "Those people had families."

"I have a family, too, but you were more than willing to kill me," I said. "I gave you the chance to walk away. You chose to fight. Now, tell me what's inside that house."

He closed his eyes, as if he couldn't stand the sight of me.

"The portal is in the house," he said. "Or at least it always was before. If you really did kill the priestess, it might have already closed. I haven't been back to check."

"What other traps have you set for me?" I asked, bringing my dagger up so he could see it.

He swallowed and stared at the dagger.

"No traps," he said. "But you can only get to the portal beneath the house if you carry a bracelet or stone from the emerald priestess. She didn't give me one, so I can't take you down there. She wanted to make sure I couldn't go down there without her. I was going to be trapped here regardless, and so will you."

"I'll get in," I said.

"Who are you?" he asked. "I've never seen someone move so fast."

"My name is Harper. And you were right about Priestess Evers. She brought me thinking she could break me, only I refused to be broken," I said. "But you were wrong about the demons. They aren't creatures. They aren't the devil's minions. They're incredible beings of great power, but they are people just like we are. They aren't evil, Detective."

He laughed, even as a tear rolled down his cheek.

"James," he said. "My name is James."

"I would say it's nice to meet you, James, but it's been a real bitch," I said. "I've been through enough the past few months without your group trying to kill me, too."

"And yet you're still here," he said. His eyes met mine. "Are you going to kill me?"

"Not yet," I said. "I'll be back."

I used my rope magic to cover his mouth again, and I walked back to the cabin.

I conjured a bright light to illuminate my path, and as I

approached the small cabin in the woods, I was again struck by how familiar it seemed. It was almost as if I had been here before, but I couldn't quite place it.

Goosebumps rose on my arms as I walked up the steps, avoiding the dead body of the man I'd killed just a few minutes earlier.

Had I climbed these steps once before?

I shook off the eerie feeling of familiarity and sent my light into the front room of the cabin. There wasn't much to this place at all. At least not on the surface. It looked as if there was nothing here beyond a single room with a long counter running along one wall. No kitchen. No furniture. No electricity, even.

But the detective—James—had said the portal was underneath the house.

I pulled the strip of fabric off my leg and took the emerald master stone in my left hand. This had to be better than any key.

I walked around the inside of the small cabin in the woods, holding the emerald in front of me and praying for a miracle. On the first pass, nothing seemed to happen, but the second time I stepped into the center of the room, I noticed a slight sheen on the floor in the shape of a square.

I squatted and ran my hand along the floor boards. The wood shimmered and faded away, revealing a narrow staircase that led into the basement of the house.

It was that moment when I finally realized how I knew this place. I had dreamed of it before the emerald priestess first attacked my father's city.

In my dreams, there had been a cage here, a strand of emeralds wrapped around a white rose lying inside. Illana's attempt to warn me after she was captured. This had to be the right place.

I stood, heart beating faster, and walked down the steps, my orb of light leading the way. I gathered my power in my hands, ready for anyone or anything that might attack as I descended the stairs. But nothing emerged from the shadows.

I sent the orb around the room, desperately searching for any sign of the portal or a doorway to another room. It just had to be here. I needed for it to be here.

On the left side of the room, a strange set of markings on the wall caught my eye. I directed my orb to the spot, and as I stood there, staring at the strange oval shape burned into the wood, tears flowed from my eyes.

There was no mistaking the perfect shape of a portal. I'd seen enough in my short years to know exactly what it should look like.

But as I placed my hands on the wood, I knew that I had gotten here too late.

The portal home had already closed.

SO CLOSE NOW

JACKSON

"This is the place," I said, motioning to the burned skeleton of the house we'd all once called home. "We'll do it here."

"Are you sure?" Rend asked. "Why here?"

"It just feels right," I said. "Poetic that this is the place we lure them to. This is where it all began for us, and this is where we'll make our next move to bring this whole thing to an end. Besides, I know this place like the back of my hand. I lived here for decades. If we run into trouble, I know all the hiding places in the area. It will give us the upper hand if things go south."

"They won't," Rend said, holding up two large vials filled with a thick silver liquid. "I worked on this all night, and I tested it several times with Azure and Franki. There's no way the Order is going to be able to detect our presence after we take these potions."

"What if one of the witches with them can see through illusions?" I asked.

He shook his head and smiled. "Not even then," he said. "If you couldn't see them earlier when we tested it, no witch will be able to, either. Besides, this isn't an illusion potion. It's not even an invisibility potion."

"Then what is it?" I asked, taking one of the vials in my hands and turning it upside down. The mixture inside was so thick, it moved slowly toward the cork. "How does it work?"

"It's a complete displacement potion," he said. "I based it off a transmutation spell I've been working on for years. It won't make us invisible or glamour us in any way. It will literally make us disappear completely. We'll be here, but we also won't be here in our current form. A witch could walk straight through us and never feel us or sense our presence."

I stared at him, mouth open. "I don't totally understand what you just said about trans-whatever, but if it makes us impossible to detect, I'm glad you're smart enough to know what it does."

Rend laughed. "Let's just say it will rearrange our matter for about an hour," he said. "Our consciousness will be here, but our bodies will be spread into a billion tiny particles in the air around the area."

I swallowed and stared at the potion again. "And you're sure that after the hour is up, we'll come back to normal, right?"

He raised an eyebrow. "Probably."

But when I gave him a frightened look, he smiled and shook his head.

"I'm just messing with you, Jackson," he said. "We tested it on Azure's cat first. Then both Azure and Franki drank the potion. Everyone, including the cat, came back just fine. But we only have an hour. If, for whatever reason, the encounter with whoever comes out of that portal lasts longer than that, we're screwed."

"Can't we just leave the area?" I asked.

He shook his head. "Nope. Once we take the potions, we will basically be frozen in place for that entire hour. I didn't have enough time to try to think of another solution," he said. "I'm good at what I do, but I'm not capable of miracles."

"That's just going to have to be good enough."

I glanced around the area. We needed to find the perfect place to be when we took the potions. The portal would most likely open wherever the fake ritual items were triggered, so that meant we would only have a few seconds to start the ritual, get where we wanted to go, and take the potion before a witch stepped through looking for us.

Brighton Manor had been reduced to a pile of ash and rubble. All of the second and third floors were completely gone. All that remained were pieces of the foundation and the skeleton of charred boards on the front porch.

The house that had belonged to Ella Mae, my fake mother during those years when I'd been kept here in Peachville, still stood. So did the shed behind Brighton Manor.

The garden Zara had worked so hard to restore to its former glory was once again nothing more than a tangled mess of dead vines with an empty stone fountain in the center.

I pushed back feelings of regret and worry. After hearing Lea's voice last night, I missed my family more than ever. I just prayed Andros got to them in time. If I didn't hear from him soon, we would all go after them ourselves.

"We trigger the items here," I said, standing in the place

beside the rubble where I had stood when I first saw Harper. Her room had been just above here on the second floor, and I'd passed by just as she had stood at the window, staring down. I pointed to Ella Mae's house. "As soon as we trigger them, we shift and fly to the roof of that house. It's close enough that we should still be able to hear what they're saying. But if anything goes wrong, we'll be close to the woods and have a barrier between us and the witches. They'll have to run around the house to follow us."

"Okay, so we start the ritual right at three. As soon as the items are triggered, we fly up to the roof of the house and down the potions," Rend said. "Then we watch."

I nodded and glanced around the area one last time. It was almost three, and even though I was ready for the next step, I hoped that whatever we found out here would help me find Harper.

Staring at the remains of Brighton Manor, though, my heart ached for us to all be together again. I had to believe the time would come. Andros was strong, and I knew the warriors of the Resistance Army were capable of getting into the King's City with the help of their people hiding on the inside.

I just had to believe that he would bring Aerden and Lea home soon. Meanwhile, I had to focus on bringing Harper home. The sooner the better, and if we hadn't heard word from Andros by then, we'd go to the King's City together. We were so close now. We just had to keep fighting.

"You ready?" Rend asked. "It's one minute to three."

I nodded and set the ritual items on the ground by the burned house. We didn't need a pentagram or a ritual room to trigger these items. Since they were fake, the Order couldn't possibly have tied them to any one coven or portal. No, they would have set them to trigger in the most logical way. With spell words.

My heart raced as I knelt by the emerald items. I watched Rend's face as he watched the time on his watch. After a long moment, his eyes met mine and he nodded.

We each took the corks off our potions. I placed my other hand on the fake ritual items and spoke the first words of the original initiation ritual, only backwards.

"Cognatus ab adnexus."

A light appeared inside the emerald master stone, and I quickly shifted, flying by Rend's side until we each took human form there on the roof of the house where I used to live. We lifted the potions to our mouths and drank the thick liquid down.

Our bodies disappeared just as a bright portal opened just above the fake master stone and an army of witches spilled out, hands and weapons raised in attack.

IT WAS TOO LATE

JACKSON

Witches covered the grass beside the remains of Brighton Manor, spreading out into the garden and the area behind the house.

"Where are they?" one witch shouted. "They should be here."

A tall witch dressed in jeans and a black turtleneck stepped through the portal. In her hand, she carried a ritual dagger, and around her neck, she wore a pendant that looked almost identical to Harper's mother's necklace. Identical except that the stone embedded into the silver was an amethyst, not a sapphire.

A Prima.

They had sent a Prima here to capture us, and if I had to guess, I would say most of the witches spread across the grounds of Brighton Manor now were part of her coven.

"Spread out," she shouted. "They have to be here somewhere. Someone activated these items. Find them."

The witches scattered, walking through the rubble, checking the shed, and running into the house. Several witches ran into the woods and others searched the tangled mess of the old garden.

The Prima gathered a ball of amethyst energy into her hands and closed her eyes. When the light had grown quite large, she tapped it in the center, and the energy spread out in concentric circles across the area.

She waited, watching everything, a confident expression on her face. But when the light had dissipated, she frowned and set her lips into a thin, tight line.

She recreated the spell, making the light twice as big this time. She threw the light into the air and tapped it again, sending more concentric circles across the area. This time, the light passed straight through me. I felt a distant chill, but I was disconnected from it, as if it were happening to someone else.

The witch frowned again and turned in a circle, staring back at the burned house.

"Check the basement," she said. "Most Prima houses have basements. See if there's one here where they're hiding. Where's the ritual room in this town? Find it and report back to me. Is this an active coven town? If it is, I want the Prima brought to me immediately. She might be working with the demons."

A small group of witches bowed to the Prima and began searching through the rubble for any stairs leading down to a basement. They wouldn't find anything in this home. Peachville's home had never had a basement. Only a third floor, like all Prima homes. And that was now gone.

Another group bowed and ran into the woods in search of the coven's ritual room. If they did manage to find it, they would find nothing more there than another pile of rubble with a broken sapphire stone.

Rend and I watched from our perch on top of the house as the witches searched everywhere. Various locating spells went off, but Rend had done his job well. None of their magic could find us.

The Prima grew more and more frustrated as witches returned to her with bad news. She shouted at the top of her lungs for someone to bring her better news.

But instead of moving, everyone standing in front of her turned their eyes to the portal and quickly fell to one knee.

"What are you doing?" the Prima shouted. "I said to keep looking. Get up."

"They are simply kneeling out of respect, Alina," a voice said from the portal's entrance. I couldn't quite see the woman from my spot on the roof, but I could feel the fear that rippled through the area.

"Priestess, forgive me," the Prima—Alina—said. She turned and knelt with her head bowed. "I didn't know you would be here today."

"I didn't want to miss the torture of the demons and witches responsible for the deaths of two of my sisters," the woman said.

She stepped out of the light of the portal, and a chill went through me.

The woman was dressed in black leather from head to toe. Her long black hair was pulled back into a long ponytail that fell down to her waist Around her neck, a collar made of pure amethysts sparkled in the sunlight. An amethyst panther pendant hung from the collar.

The amethyst priestess.

BEYOND THE DARKNESS 257

In all our research, we'd never been able to find out much about the priestess standing in front of me. Now, we knew her spirit animal, and we knew what she looked like. But that collar gave me chills. It was almost exactly like the one Joost had found at the abandoned house. All except for the panther pendant.

"Where are the traitors?" she asked, glancing around. "Bring them to me."

Alina kept her head bowed, and as she spoke, her voice trembled. "We haven't been able to locate them, Priestess," she said. "When we came through the portal, they were already gone."

The priestess seemed to take in her surroundings for the first time, and a fiery look flashed in her eyes.

"Where are we?" she asked. "This isn't an emerald portal."

She bent over and took the fake master stone in her hands. She crushed it in her fist, and tiny emerald particles fell to the ground as dust at her feet.

"Someone triggered these items," she said. "They can't be far, and I want them found."

"We've looked everywhere, Priestess," a witch near the back said, lifting her head. "They aren't here."

The priestess lifted a finger toward the woman, and she went very still for a moment before falling to the ground. I hadn't seen any magic pass from the priestess to the woman, but she was motionless on the ground. Had the priestess killed her with a single look?

A gasp went through the group of witches, and the amethyst priestess raised a hand to smooth her already-perfect hair.

"Does anyone else care to speak against me?" she asked,

her eyes surveying the group. "I didn't think so. Now, get up and find them."

For a moment, no one moved, but then, all at once, the witches stood and started going back over the rubble, the garden, and the buildings.

"What happened here?" the priestess asked as Alina stood. "Why are we at this place?"

"I don't know," Alina said. "The portal opened as soon as the items were triggered, and we came through immediately, ready to take the demons and witches prisoner and bring them back to your dungeons. But when we came through, there was no sign of them."

The priestess looked around, studying the burned house. She bent down and took a handful of ash from the pile. She brought it to her nose and breathed in, her eyes closed.

When she dropped the ash, she stood and drew her hand into a tight fist.

"We're in Peachville," she said. "This house was burned by emerald fire, one of my sister Hazel's favorite destruction spells. They brought us here to prove a point."

"What point?" Alina asked. "I don't understand."

The priestess's eyes scanned the entire area. "That they think they're more powerful than we are," she said. "That they knew about the trap my sister set for them. They knew we were coming before they triggered the spell that opened the portal."

"But why would they do that?" she asked. "Why would they trigger the items and just leave? Why wouldn't they stay and fight?"

"Because, you fool, they think we're going to give them some kind of clue," she said. She raised her voice, and I knew it was fully for my benefit. The priestess wasn't dumb. She knew we were listening, even if she couldn't see us. "I know you're watching, so listen very closely. You may have managed to save yourself this time, but your precious Harper is on her own. At first, I was content just leaving her in the past. The portal that my sister created has closed. Your Harper has no way home."

I listened, unsure whether I should believe a word this priestess was saying. How could she be sure the portal was closed? She could be lying. Harper could still have a way home.

I refused to believe it was too late.

"Since you've found it necessary to try to make me look like a fool, however, I am going to show you what it means to mess with me," she said. "I am going to be the one to finally teach you what it feels like to lose someone you love with all your heart. You have taken two of my sisters. Now, I'm going to take Harper from you."

I couldn't move or feel my body in the normal way, but in some distant, disconnected way, I felt my muscles tense. I wished we hadn't taken these potions. I wished we could fly down there and fight.

The priestess turned on her heel and walked over to one of the witches standing near the garden.

"It's time," she said. "Summon the fairy."

The woman—a younger woman with nearly white-blonde hair and bright blue eyes—shook her head. "I can't do that," she said. "She'll be furious with me if I summon her like this."

The priestess slapped the woman across the face, leaving a bright red mark that the woman ran her hand across as tears spilled across her cheeks.

"Don't make me ask you again," the priestess said. "I can make you hurt a lot more than this, and you know it."

The woman fell to her knees, trembling.

She pulled something from her pocket and held it tightly in her palm. "I'm begging you, Priestess Black. Please at least tell her you commanded me to do this," she said.

The priestess pointed a finger at the woman, and for a moment, I held my breath, waiting for the woman to fall to the ground like the other woman had done. But the girl simply closed her eyes and lifted the gemstone she held in her hand up into the air.

"Sabine. Sister. I call to you," she said. She turned her palm downward and pressed the gemstone into the ground. "I summon you to this place."

The stone erupted in a bright, white light, and both the priestess and the woman stepped away from the light.

The woman who had held the gemstone ran into the ruined garden, hiding her face behind a dead dogwood tree. As she ran, I could swear I caught sight of a pair of iridescent wings twitching across her back, but when she stepped behind the tree and out of the sunlight, the wings seemed to disappear.

Movement caught my eye at the edge of the bright light, and I turned my focus to the small woman stepping out of the new portal.

SHE SEES ME

JACKSON

L ong, white hair fell to her waist, and she wore a gown that appeared to be made entirely of dark green vines. She was barefoot and had a wildness about her. Shimmering iridescent wings fluttered behind her as she stepped forward, her eyes narrowed toward the amethyst priestess.

Unlike the hiding woman, there was no mistaking this woman's wings. I knew there were fae who walked this earth, but I had never seen one who radiated such raw power.

"What is the meaning of this?" she asked, her voice a strangely dissonant mixture of tinkling bells and pure rage. "Why have you summoned me from my home?"

The amethyst priestess bowed her head low. "Forgive me, Sabine," she said. "But you do owe me a favor, do you not? And you of all people understand what it means to owe someone a favor."

Sabine walked around the priestess, her eyes taking in the

surroundings. When she looked up toward the roof where Rend and I stood, I could have sworn her eyes met mine directly. A slow smile tickled the edge of her mouth, and she spun around to face the priestess.

"What is this favor you ask of me?" she asked. "Let's get on with it, as you know I don't like to be away from my home for long."

"Of course," Priestess Black said, lifting her head. "You have no doubt heard of my sister's death?"

"Eloisa?" Sabine asked. "Such a tragedy. She was a powerful witch."

"No," the priestess said. "My sister, Hazel, has also been murdered by the same witch."

Sabine turned her back to the priestess, a smile definitely playing at her lips as she glanced directly at me. "Oh my goodness," she said. "I had no idea. You must be utterly distraught."

The priestess cleared her throat. "We are furious," she said. "My sister, misguided as she was, used her time manipulation talents to open a portal into the past where she could take a handful of girls in order to rehabilitate them."

"A handful?" Sabine said, narrowing her gaze as she turned back to the amethyst priestess. "From what I have heard, it was a lot more than a handful, Gladys."

"Well, let's not get into numbers here," the priestess said. "The point is that Hazel kidnapped Harper, the same girl who murdered Eloisa. She took her to the institute she'd set up in the 1950's and attempted to destroy the girl's mind."

"Quite the risky move," Sabine said, shaking her head. She stepped over toward a cluster of vines at the edge of the garden and placed her hand on them. A line of bright green flowed through the vines as they came back to life. Beneath them, tulips in half a dozen different colors grew up from the ground.

She glanced up at me again and nodded.

She sees me.

Not only did Sabine somehow know I was here, she could see me clearly. And she was trying to send me a message. The way she'd touched those flowers reminded me so much of Zara that it made my heart hurt. But Zara was not fae. She couldn't have been. She was the daughter of the sapphire priestess. A witch who was purely human.

And Zara had only had wings when she'd shifted into the form of a blue butterfly. Wings, yes, but not the same fae wings that Sabine had.

What was she trying to tell me?

"My sister's stupid quest to turn witches into her brain-washed daughters is not my concern right now," Priestess Black said. "Harper, however, is of grave concern to all of us."

"Oh?" Sabine asked, tilting her head. "How is that? I thought you said the poor girl was trapped in the past."

"Exactly," Priestess Black said. "She's in the past where she's capable of altering the timeline. Her actions there could have devastating results for us all."

"But they don't," Sabine said simply.

"What do you mean?" Priestess Black asked. "How could you possibly know that?"

"Because you're still standing here," Sabine said, smiling as she touched another set of vines and the right half of the garden burst into bloom. "If Harper had somehow altered the timeline or caused some sort of catastrophic change in events, you would most certainly know it."

Priestess Black shifted her weight. "It's possible she hasn't done anything yet to change the timeline. That doesn't mean that she won't."

Sabine laughed, and the sound rang out like windchimes. "Silly, Gladys. That's not how time travel works," she said. "But I didn't come here to explain these things to you. Tell me what this favor is, and let me be on my way."

"I want Harper dead," she said, her voice tense.

"So kill her," Sabine said with a shrug. "What do I have to do with any of this?"

"The portal back to the past has closed," Priestess Black said. "I need for you to open it again."

Sabine sighed. "Is that all?" she asked. "You pulled me from my home for such a trivial task?"

She threw a nasty glance toward the woman hiding behind the tree.

"Marta, you should be ashamed of yourself," she said, bending down to retrieve the stone the woman had used to summon her. Sabine tossed it into the air, and as it caught the light, I realized it was an opal, multicolored and shimmering like the fairy's wings. "You may be distant family, but that doesn't mean I will forgive you for this. You owe me now, girl."

Marta clapped a hand over her mouth and slid down the tree, her entire body trembling. I wondered what it meant to owe a favor to this fairy. Obviously, it wasn't always a bucket of rainbows, or Marta wouldn't be acting like she was about to throw up.

"Can you do it or not?" Priestess Black asked.

"Of course I can," Sabine said, waving her hand in the air. She passed beside the priestess and looked straight up at me as she spoke. "For me, opening a portal into the past is child's play. It takes almost nothing. I won't be able to reopen an older portal, but I know where the girl is. I can open a portal straight to the house where she's living in the past."

Even though my body was separated into billions of tiny particles, I could feel my own heart beating a million miles a minute.

"So, will you do it?" the priestess asked, tapping her boot against the hard ground.

"Are you certain this is how you would choose to spend your one favor?" Sabine asked. "Because after this, I will owe the Order nothing. I want to be sure that's absolutely clear. I don't care if the Hall of Doorways itself is destroyed. After this, I will do nothing to help you again."

"Yes, I'm certain," Priestess Black said. "I wouldn't have summoned you here if I wasn't sure."

Sabine shrugged. "Okay, so let's get started."

Priestess Black grabbed the fairy's arm, but immediately stepped away when Sabine gave her a look of pure death, her eyes turning instantly black as coal.

"I'm sorry," Priestess Black said, bowing her head again. "I forgot myself for a moment. I don't want you to cast the portal here. If you would, please accompany me back to my dungeons. We'll open the portal there, and I will send five of my best assassins through to the find the girl. I imagine she'll be dead by nightfall."

"Don't forget yourself again," Sabine said. "Put your hands on me one more time, and the Order will lose another priestess, I assure you."

"Of course," Priestess Black said. "I apologize."

Sabine lifted her chin. "I will go with you to your dungeons," she said. "But after this, any debts I had to the Order are paid."

"Agreed," the priestess said. "Follow me. I'm anxious to get started. The sooner the girl is dead, the sooner we can turn our focus to rebuilding what we've lost."

The priestess motioned for her witches to go through the portal ahead of her. Sabine appeared to wait patiently as the crowd cleared out, each witch disappearing through the portal in turn.

She turned her attention toward me once again.

"What are you looking at?" Priestess Black asked when she was the only witch left at Brighton Manor. She squinted up at us, holding a hand to block the sun.

"Nothing," Sabine said. "Come. Let's get this over with so I can go home."

The priestess nodded and walked with Sabine toward the portal. In seconds, they crossed over the portal's barrier, and the light disappeared entirely, leaving Brighton Manor just as we had found it.

Everything was the same, except for the flourishing garden near the fountain.

THE DEMON INSIDE HER

HARPER

I emerged from the cabin in the woods as the light of another day rose on the horizon. The storm I'd started had long since calmed, but the ground was still soaked, and so were my clothes.

I needed to do something about these bodies. I couldn't very well have the police or some random hunter stumbling across this scene and tying it back to me. The last thing I needed was to get locked up here and have to find a way to break free and disappear.

My exhaustion was bone-deep, and I just wanted to lie down on the grass and go to sleep for twelve hours. But there was still work to be done. Even if the portal was closed, I refused to give up hope. Even if it took ten years, Brooke and I would find someone else who could manipulate time. We would find someone who could send us home.

In the end, I decided to bury the bodies in the basement of the cabin. It was the safest place I could think of, and with the portal now closed, no one should be coming through here any time soon.

It took time to lift each of the bodies up with my tele-kinetic power and float them down the steps and into the base-ment. I piled the ten of them up in one corner, trying not to look at their faces as I dropped them there and turned to leave.

But there was still one more person to deal with.

I trudged through the woods to find the detective sleeping against the tree. I laughed. How the heck could he sleep tied to a tree like this? He was still breathing, so I knew he wasn't dead, but he was completely out cold.

I clapped my hands twice, and he didn't even move.

I thought about just putting an end to him right now. He had, after all, been the leader of this group. If I left him alive, there was a good chance he would come after me again. I had no idea how many of the Others lived in the area, but if they had planned to face the emerald priestess or her daughter, surely they would have brought everyone at once.

I knew I was taking a risk in keeping him alive, but since he was the only one besides the nurses who knew the truth about the emerald priestess, I hoped he would still have some useful-ness. Besides, I might need help getting in to see the girls so I could give them the memory potions Rend had made for them.

I just had to hope that last night's events would help convince him to leave me the hell alone.

"Detective," I said loudly. "James."

He stirred, a string of drool coming from his mouth.

He swallowed and opened his eyes slowly. Then, he quickly became alert, snapping his eyes to mine.

"What happened?" he asked. "What time is it?"

I glanced up at the sun coming through the trees. "I'm not

sure what time it is," I said. "Still somewhat early if you're worried about making it to work on time."

He shook his head. "That's the least of my worries right now," he said. "The portal?"

"It's closed," I said. "We got here too late."

He slumped against the ropes that still tied him to the tree.

"What are you going to do now? Are you going to kill me?"

"I should probably put this dagger through your heart for what you did last night," I said. "But I'm hoping you can still help me. If you agree not to attack me again or get any of the Others to come after me, I promise you that if you help me free the girls from the hospital and find a way home, I'll let you come back home with me."

"I'll do whatever you ask," he said. "I swear it."

"I don't trust easily, but right now, I really want to believe you, James. I'll tell you right now that if you so much as think about betraying me again, I'll kill you without hesitation."

"I won't," he said. "Not after what you did last night. Those were our best people across five states. The leaders of the Others won't be happy when they find out what happened, though. They'll be expecting a report this morning."

"Then you'll give them one," I said. "Do they know you were trying to kill me? Or did they still believe you were going to be fighting the emerald priestess and the doctor?"

"The doctor," he said. "They knew about the fire and that the priestess was nowhere to be found, but I told them we would take care of the doctor."

"Okay, good. So tell them the good doctor is dead," I said. "That won't be a lie, so you should be able to convince them relatively easily."

"What do I say about the rest of the group, though?

They're going to notice when none of them check in or show up at home today."

"Stall for time," I said. "Tell them the doctor is dead, but you have suspicions that the priestess is still alive and in hiding. Say that the group agreed to stick around until you find her."

"Okay," he said. "That should buy a few days at best, though. If none of the others check in with their group leaders, someone is bound to come looking for them."

"Then we need to make sure we're long gone by then," I said. "I'm going to let you go now, okay? You don't breathe a word of what happened here to anyone, you understand?"

"I won't," he said. "I want to go home just as badly as you do."

I shook my head. "You know, it's entirely possible that portal was open when we first got here last night. If you hadn't wasted my time by trying to kill me, we might have been able to go home."

"Would you have, though?" he asked. "Would you have left those girls here?"

I sighed. "No. I wouldn't have left them here," I said.

"I didn't think so," he said. "The way you talk about them, it's like you feel responsible for them, even though you weren't the one who brought them here. If you hadn't been here, though, most of those girls would have been dead in a few months, anyway."

"Thanks in part to you," I said. "Why were you working for the emerald priestess, anyway? What did she have on you?"

"Let me go," James said. "I'll tell you on the drive home. It's a long story."

I released the ropes that surrounded him, and he stepped

away from the tree and stretched. His face twisted in pain as he moved his body around and worked out all the kinks from being in one position for so long.

I half expected him to pull out a second gun and try to come after me, but he didn't. He simply walked back down the path through the woods and out to his car.

I followed behind him and listened as he started telling his story.

"When I first met the emerald priestess, I was only twenty-years-old," he said. "I had just been admitted into the police academy. My mother was a single parent, and I still lived at home with her and my younger sister, Amanda."

We reached the police cruiser and climbed inside. He fished his keys out of his pocket and started the car up. He backed down the rough path slowly as he spoke.

"Amanda was only thirteen when she was recruited to join the local cheerleading team."

I groaned. I had a feeling I knew exactly where this was going.

James laughed, but there was no joy in the sound. "I see you already know what the local cheerleaders were up to," he said. "But I had no idea what was really going on at that school. I thought cheerleading was a stupid waste of time for someone as smart as Amanda, but I didn't think it was dangerous by any means."

"When did you find out the truth?" I asked.

"About six months after she first joined the squad, our mother got sick," he said. "Cancer. It was bad, and it spread fast. I tried to be there for her as much as I could, but I had a rough schedule back then, and I knew we would need my income to get by since Mom had to stop working. Amanda wanted to drop out of school for a semester to help out at home, and even though I hated the idea of her missing some of her work, I didn't see much choice. We couldn't afford a full-time nurse at the time, and there was just no way for me to be home every day."

"But the cheerleading coach wouldn't let her quit," I said, a clear picture coming to me.

"They were ridiculous about the whole thing," he said. By now, we had reached West Turner and had started back toward town. "Amanda came home crying saying the coach had threatened her. She said that if Amanda dropped out now, she would see to it Mom didn't live out the week."

I shook my head. The Order had to be destroyed. How many lives had they ruined over the years? How many people had they killed or terrorized in the name of power?

"I was furious, of course, but Amanda begged me not to say anything to the coach. She said I would only make it worse, but I wouldn't listen," he said. "To be fair, I had no idea the coach was really a witch, and even though Amanda knew something of the truth by then, she must have been too scared to tell me."

"What did you do?"

"I went straight up to the school and confronted the cheerleading coach. I wore my uniform up there and every-thing, hoping to intimidate her and show her that I meant business," he said. "She was a relatively small woman, but she had fire running through her veins. She tore me a new one, insisting that I was out of line and that if I didn't back down and allow Amanda to continue on at school, she would personally see to it that I never joined the police force. I refused to back down, thinking this woman couldn't possibly have the power to have me kicked out of the academy. I was a model recruit. Top of my class. I thought I was invincible back then."

"You kept pushing her?" I asked.

He nodded. "I threatened to report her to the principal for harassment. She threatened my mother again, though, saying she would personally make sure my mother died a horrible death before the week was over unless I allowed Amanda to stay on the team," he said. "I lost my temper."

"What happened?" I asked. When I glanced over at him, there were tears at the edge of his lower lashes.

"She got up in my face, screaming at me, and I just snapped," he said. "I pushed her. I shouldn't have done it, but I was a real hot-head back then. When she threatened my mother, I couldn't take it anymore. I pushed her backward, and she hit the white-board. I went to apologize, but she got this crazy look in her eyes. She lifted her hands into the air, and they were covered in green flames. I freaked out. I pulled my gun and shot her twice in the head."

"Oh my God," I said, raising a hand to my mouth. "You killed her?"

"I didn't mean to, but I'd never seen anything like it," he said. "I had no idea magic was real, but as soon as I saw those flames, I knew she was going to kill me. I had no choice."

I sighed, thinking how many times it had come to this choice. Most of us pushed to the edge were forced to become killers. When it was kill or be killed, what choice did any of us have?

"What did you do after that?" I asked.

"I ran. It was after-hours, but there were still a few people there at the school, so I knew someone had to have seen me. They must have heard the gunshots," he said. "I drove home as fast as I could, threw a bunch of clothes into a bag, and started putting together a plan. I called a friend who had moved to New York City after graduation and asked him if I could crash on his couch for a while. I still remember the heartache on my mother's face when I told her I had to leave. I couldn't tell her why, because I figured the less she knew, the better, so I lied and told her I couldn't handle the pressure of the academy. I told her I needed to get away for a while."

"What about Amanda?" I asked. "What did you tell her?"

"I told her the same thing, but Amanda knew better. She knew I'd gone to see her coach, and by then, she knew her coach was part of the Order of Shadows," he said. "Of course, at such a young age, she didn't know about the demons or the true nature of the Order, but she'd gotten a taste of the power they held. She knew something had happened between me and her coach. She begged to come with me. She said we should all pack up and get the hell out of there, but I told her to stay put and to deny anything if the police came looking for me."

I took a deep breath. I could feel his tension and pain as he talked me through these memories.

"In the end, none of it mattered, anyway," he said. "I never even made it out the door before Priestess Evers found me. She came into my home, murdered our mother right there in front of us. She forced Amanda to take some kind of potion that wiped her memories and put her into a deep sleep. Then, once she'd forced me into her car, she made me an offer I couldn't refuse."

I nodded, putting together the remaining pieces of the puzzle.

"Help her here at the institute, keeping the government out of her business, in return for the life of your sister," I said.

"Yes," he said. He ran a hand across his face, wiping away the tears that had fallen. "Apparently the guy she'd been using to help her out with the local police had gotten tired of the job. She killed him in the previous fire, so she needed a new cop. My lucky day, huh?"

"Did she at least stay true to her promise?" I asked.

"In a way," he said with a shrug. "Amanda's alive, but she no longer knows who I am. I've even spoken to her a few times, hoping that somewhere deep inside, she'll recognize me, but she never does."

"She's one of the priestess's daughters?" I asked.

He nodded. "One of the lucky ones, if there is such a thing in a situation like this," he said. "Priestess Evers put her in charge of an emerald gate coven in North Dakota. She's got two daughters of her own now, too."

"She's a Prima?" I asked, surprised.

"She is," he said. "But you can understand why I've come to hate the Order as much as I do. And the demons are part of it. I want them all to pay for what they've done. Not just to me, but all of these girls and the families they've ruined over the years."

"You're wrong about the demons. They're victims just as much as your sister."

He shook his head. "No, that's a lie," he said. "The demons come here at the bidding of the Order to possess these witches and make them stronger, but their spirit turns these once-innocent girls into evil witches, just like the priestess. I've seen it with my own eyes. Once my sister was taken over by a demon, she changed."

"And who told you that about the demons? The Others? Priestess Evers? Do you really think those are credible sources?" I asked. "I've been in the same position as your sister. They tried to make me a Prima, too. They wanted to force me to take my mother's place as leader of a sapphire coven in Georgia, and I saw what they do to the demons when a recruit goes through her final initiation. James, it's not like you say. The demons don't come here at the request of the Order, they are forced here by horrible creatures called hunters. These hunters scour the Shadow World where the demons live in relative peace, and when they find a demon who is powerful or vulnerable in some way, they kidnap them and force them into the body of a witch. They're slaves to a witch's power."

"That can't be true," he said. "My sister. The things I've seen her do."

I touched his arm, forcing him to look at me.

"That isn't her anymore," I said. "She's been brainwashed and taught to be the way she is by the woman she believes is her true mother. Priestess Evers. She's not the Amanda you once knew, anymore."

He could no longer contain the tears that fell in streams down his face. He pulled over to the side of the road at the edge of town, and turned his face away from me as he sobbed.

I had never seen a man his size cry so hard, but I knew the pain he was feeling. Losing people you loved more than life to the Order of Shadows was unbearable, so it made sense that he had sought out the Others. He wanted revenge, but killing innocent demons wasn't the answer.

"James," I said, placing my hand on his shoulder. "What if I told you I might be able to help Amanda?"

His body shook with the force of his sobs, but he turned to me, wiping his face.

"What do you mean? How?" he asked.

I hesitated, scared to trust him. Everything he'd told me could be a complete lie just to get me on his side. But in my gut, I knew his story was true. His tears were genuine. I'd bet my life on it.

I explained the potions to him, leaving out where I'd gotten them or where they were now.

"If they work to restore the memories of these girls and you help me get them home, I promise you that I'll get one of these potions to your sister," I said. "More than that, there's a way to free her from the demon inside her."

He shook his head. "No, it's impossible," he said.

"Another lie told to you by the Order," I said. "But I've freed thousands of demons over the past year. When I killed the sapphire priestess, we were able to set every witch and demon connected to those gates free. Now that I have the heart of Priestess Evers, I can free the emerald gates, too. I wouldn't lie to you about something like this, but you have to trust me."

His sobs subsided, and he gripped the steering wheel harder, glancing in the rearview mirror as a couple of cars passed us.

"Okay," he said. "I would do anything to save Amanda and her girls. Just tell me where to start."

I took my hand from his shoulder and nodded toward town.

"Start by taking me back to the Evers house," I said. "We have a lot of girls to visit today."

THE LAST BREATH

AERDEN

The crowd roared as I stepped onto the battlefield for the second round of the tournament. I lifted my axe into the air, and the massive crowd in the arena roared louder, chanting my name.

I glanced up at the prima cavea, and met Lea's eyes, just as I had before our last battle. She nodded to me, but even though she sat up straight and looked calm on the outside, I knew her well enough to see the signs of worry in her eyes.

She looked scared, and I wondered if something new had happened since we last spoke. Had she discovered anything new about her father?

I was dying to talk to her again, but I knew our time would come. I simply had to focus on winning this second round. After that, only one final round would stand between me and freedom.

Our opponents followed us onto the battlefield, and the crowd in the arena booed as Yuron raised a giant sword into the air. I had heard talk in the cells after the first round about Yuron and his team. They played dirty.

But the beast was going down today, if I had anything to do with it.

I glanced back at him and smiled as he sneered at me.

"You ready to meet your ancestors?" he shouted over the noise in the arena.

"No, but I'm sure yours will be disappointed to have to see your ugly face again," I shouted back.

"That's enough," Ezrah said, holding his hands up. "You'll get your opportunity to fight in a minute, but for now, show respect for your king. Kneel."

Trention and I bent one knee to the ground and lowered our heads toward the king. Yuron and his partner, Sylar, followed suit soon after.

"My king, I present to you today's challengers," Ezrah said, magic amplifying his voice so that he could be heard over the shouts of the spectators. "They fight today in your honor."

Ezrah bowed his head as the king stood, his scepter raised into the air above his head.

"May your weapons be swift and your magic powerful," the king said.

I waited, muscles tense as I reached for my magic. I had somehow managed to cast during the first battle, and even though it was only a portion of my old power, it had been there for me when I'd needed it.

I prayed for it to reappear today. Yuron was one of the strongest competitors, and I couldn't help but feel it was no accident that we had been pitted against each other today. I had assumed he would be there to face me in the finale, but now I wondered if someone close to the king wanted me to fall today.

My eyes fell on the face of the demon they called Kael, and my hatred for him intensified as he grinned.

I couldn't wait to wipe that smile off his pretty face.

At my side, Trention trembled. I reached a hand out to steady him.

"Faith, my friend," I said. "This day will be ours. I will not let you fall. Just stick to the plan. Let me do the rest."

"I trust you," he said, but his voice betrayed his fear.

I prayed for strength and gripped my axe tighter in my hand, my eyes glued to the king's upraised scepter.

"May you fight with honor," he said, and with one swift motion, he lowered the scepter.

Trention and I both shifted at the same time, dodging Yuron's first spell. True to our plan, Trention stayed in demon form, racing around the oval battlefield, moving as fast as his power would carry him. As long as he stayed in motion while I brought Yuron's partner down, he would be safe. Then, together, we would bring Yuron down to end the battle.

I focused on Sylar, watching as he turned in circles, trying to get a good reading on Trention's location. It wouldn't take him long to sync up with Trention's pace and fire a deadly spell toward my friend, so I had to hit him hard and fast before he got the chance to cast.

Unfortunately, Yuron stood at his partner's back, not giving me any room to hit Sylar from the back. I would have to face him head-on.

I waited until the demon seemed to get a lock on Trention's location. He gathered his power into his hands, forming a large boulder out of thin air. He raised his hand to throw it toward Trention's smoky form, and I rushed forward, blocking the boulder with a magical shield and lifting my axe into the air.

I brought the heavy axe down, but Sylar shifted just before the blade reached his head. Yuron spun around, and with a motion too fast for my eyes to see, he grabbed my axe just beneath the powerful double-edged blade and ripped it from my hand. He threw it to the side and thrust his sword forward, barely missing me as I shifted and flew to recover my axe.

I reached for my weapon, but a powerful wind blew it just out of my reach, and when I searched for the source of the wind, Sylar smiled from across the arena.

I searched for Yuron, and my heart tightened as I saw him shift and fly after Trention.

I had to get to him before he reached my friend. I conjured a wide shield to guard me from the wind roaring across the battlefield. I couldn't shift and hold the shield at the same time, so I held the magic in front of me with one hand as I turned and raced toward my axe, finally gripping it in my palm.

As soon as I had a hold on it, I shifted and chased after Yuron, but I'd let my shield drop too soon.

A boulder the size of a truck slammed into me, forcing me back into my human form. My body screamed out in pain, but I pushed it way down. I could hurt later. For now, I needed to save my friend.

I picked up the large boulder with my free hand and tossed it back toward Sylar. Wide-eyed, he tried to shift, but the boulder landed on top of him, crushing him beneath its weight.

I knew it wouldn't take him long to work free, but all I needed was a few seconds.

I was too far away from Yuron to take him out with my axe

from here, so I took a deep breath and summoned my power. To my surprise, flames formed along my arms. I watched the two demons flying around the arena, and focused in on Yuron's form.

I counted to sync up with his pace, and when I was sure I had it right, I sent a ripple of flames across the arena floor. As Yuron passed over the small flames, I raised my hand, commanding the fire to rise.

Yuron dropped to the arena floor, but the flames didn't stop him. He stood and sucked in a deep breath. When he exhaled, the fire around him went out like the light of a birthday candle at a child's party.

Trention reformed at my side.

"They're much stronger than I expected," he said. "I'm not sure the original plan is going to work."

"Fly in a more erratic pattern," I said. "Don't let them pace you."

"I can fight them at your side," Trention said.

"No," I shouted. "I can do this. Just go."

Trention shifted again just as Yuron sent a ripple of earth toward us that opened the ground like a chasm straight down the center of the arena floor.

I shifted and moved out of the way just as the earth split around me.

Yuron set his sights on Trention as his partner finally freed himself from the heavy boulder and flew toward me.

I hoped Trention could hold Yuron off for at least a few minutes while I dealt with Sylar once and for all.

Sylar reformed just out of my reach, and I lifted my axe into the air. I intended to shift and come up behind him before he had a chance to react, but Sylar opened his palm and threw something on the ground at my feet.

Glass broke and before I could shift, a cloud of black smoke surrounded me, paralyzing me.

I struggled against it, realizing too late what had happened. Sylar had brought that vial into the arena with him. He was cheating, but no one moved to stop the fight.

Slowly, Sylar turned toward Trention with a smile on his face.

"He's all yours, Yuron," Sylar shouted. "End him."

No.

I struggled to shout the words, but I had no control over my voice. I was as frozen and helpless as I had been for all those years while the witches of Peachville searched for their missing Prima.

I begged for justice. For help from the gods. Anything.

But no help came.

I watched in horror as the two demons converged on my friend, an ancient demon who had no place in these games. He belonged in the castle's library, surrounded by books for the rest of his days.

When they had Trention cornered, Yuron reached into his pocket and took out a second vial.

Please. This can't be happening. Trention, get out of there.

But it was too late.

The vial cracked open beneath Trention's shadow form, and he fell to the ground, forced into solid form. Paralyzed, he stared upward toward the sky as Yuron plunged his sword into Trention's chest.

Something inside me broke open, and a fiery rage flowed through me.

The potion that held me captive seemed to melt away, and a black liquid slid down my skin.

Yuron raised his sword again as his partner laughed and cheered, but I raised my axe and shifted, flying through the arena faster than I'd ever flown before.

With a single, mighty swing, I sliced the heads off both demons standing over my friend.

The crowd roared, but I fell to my knees and gathered Trention in my arms.

"Hold strong, my friend," I whispered as I cradled his bloody body against my own. "The shamans will come. Hold on."

The magic holding Trention prisoner melted from his skin, and he drew a deep breath and clutched my arm.

He looked into my eyes, a tear rolling down his face and falling into the dirt beneath us.

"I will not give my life to a king who is not worthy," he said. "But I will gladly give what's left of my power to a great warrior."

"No," I shouted, rocking him back and forth. I pressed my hand against his wound, willing my healing powers to come. I didn't have nearly the talent my brother had, but I did have some. I could still save him. "I won't let you die, Trention."

"I died the minute they locked me away in those dungeons," he said. "My greatest fear was spending the last moments of my life feeling nothing but weakness and regret. Because of you, my friend, I can die with honor. With purpose."

My heart broke as I recognized the resolve in the old demon's eyes.

"I can't lose you, too," I said. I focused all my power toward healing him, but even as I felt the magic begin to flow from my hands, I knew it wouldn't be enough to save him. "You have to hold on."

Trention shuddered and closed his eyes against the pain that rocked his fragile form.

He put his hand on mine and pushed it away, breaking the healing magic that was keeping him alive.

"Promise me something," he said. He opened his eyes again and stared up at me, determination in his gaze.

"Anything, I swear it," I said.

"Promise me that when you win this tournament, you will tell the princess how you truly feel," he said. "Promise me that together, you'll put an end to the Order of Shadows and restore this kingdom to its former glory. Free our people, and then claim the happiness you deserve. You've earned it, Aerden."

"How did you know?" I asked. I had never told him of my love for Lea.

But he simply smiled at me. "Your love for her shines brighter than any I've ever known," he said. "It's time she learned the truth."

"I will tell her, I promise."

Trention's body shook with another tremor of pain, and he groaned.

Guards and shamans rushed toward us, but I lifted my hand, warning them to keep their distance. I had no true power to command them, but they obeyed me, standing several feet away.

"Follow your heart," he said, lifting a hand to my chest. "It knows the way."

"Trention—"

"I am honored to give my life to further yours," he said. He took a deep breath, even though it pained him. When he spoke again, his voice was strong and clear. "I choose this moment with pride, knowing your life is a worthy one."

I held him tighter as he spoke the words of a demon preparing to pass into the Afterworld. I wanted to tell him not to do this. That I wasn't worthy of such a sacrifice. But I would not take this moment from him. He had lived a long and worthy life, and he had the right to choose his own death.

I would not take that away only to see him forced to give his life to a king who had abandoned him.

"You honor me," I said, holding my head high, though my heart was breaking. "With what's left of my life, I promise to honor this gift and these promises I have made. I will miss you, my friend."

Trention's eyes closed as his energy left his body and flowed into mine.

"You will make a great king someday," he whispered.

As the last breath crossed his lips, a dark mist lifted from him and hovered in the air above his form. It shimmered with a great light and then disappeared as Trention's spirit passed from this world to the next.

I WILL KILL YOU MYSELF

LEA

On the battlefield below, Aerden released his friend and stood, ignoring the roars of the crowd as he picked up his axe and slowly walked to the archway that would take him back to his cell below.

I stood, my body shaking with rage and sorrow. Aerden was alive, but this was no victory.

"They cheated," I said, turning to my parents. "They could have killed him, and you just watched it happen. Why didn't you intervene?"

My father stood, his eyes meeting mine for a brief moment. In them, I thought I saw heartache and sorrow that matched my own, but it was gone just as quickly as it had appeared.

"I saw no such thing," he said. "It was a fair fight, if over a bit too soon for my taste."

He turned and began walking back up the steps that led to a private walkway back to the castle.

I started after him, but my mother put her hand on my shoulder, holding me back.

"If you know what's good for you, you'll let this go, Lazalea," she warned, her voice tense. "Go back to your chambers and rest for a while. Perhaps you're simply not feeling well after all this excitement."

Tears rolled down my face, and I did nothing to stop them.

"Rest and let it go?" I asked. "You saw what happened down there. Hasn't Aerden been through enough, Mother?"

"And he won, did he not?" she asked. "How could it be unfair if he still emerged the victor?"

"They murdered his friend, and if Aerden hadn't broken free of whatever potion that demon threw at his feet, he would have died right alongside him," I shouted.

My mother shook her head and touched the gold chain around her neck. "I'm afraid the princess isn't feeling like herself today," she said, motioning for a pair of guards to join us. "Please, take my daughter back to her room where she can rest and think about how she should address her parents with respect, rather than accusations."

"Mother—"

"Take her, now," she commanded.

The guards each took hold of one of my arms and dragged me up the steps. I struggled to break free, but their grip on me only tightened.

As we passed Kael, he held up a hand and the guards stopped for a moment.

"You see what happens when you disobey me, Princess?" he whispered into my ear. "Your precious Aerden survived today, despite my best efforts. Perhaps I will have to find a worthier opponent for tomorrow's battle."

"I'm through with your threats," I said. "Attempt to harm him again, and I will kill you myself."

Kael laughed. "I'd like to see you try," he said.

He waved his hand, and the guards pulled me forward, up the steps and down the long walkway back to the castle. When we reached my room, they threw me inside and locked the doors, instructing Presha to keep a close eye on me.

"Are you okay?" Presha asked, rushing to my side.

I slammed my fist into the wall. "No, I'm very far from okay," I said. I straightened, staring at the blood that trickled free from a wound on my finger.

"Should I call for the shaman?" Presha asked, staring at my wound.

A chill passed through me. The shaman, Lisette.

She'd once told me that I'd helped to free her daughter from the sapphire gates. She'd said she owed me her life. I could only hope she still felt that way, because what I was about to ask of her would certainly get her killed if anyone found out.

"Yes, I would like to see the shaman, please. Can you call for her? I'm not feeling well at all, and I need for her to look at this wound."

"Of course," Presha said. She instructed one of the other girls to find the shaman, while she wrapped a strip of cloth around my hand.

When she arrived, I asked Presha to step outside. The handmaiden frowned.

"I was told to keep an eye on you," she said.

"And where do you think I'll go if you're standing right outside the door?" I asked. "I need my rest, and I'll never be able to relax with you hovering over me. When Lisette leaves, you can come back inside and watch over me as I sleep."

"I promise to watch over her in your absence," Lisette said, bowing slightly.

Presha frowned again, but she nodded. "I'll wait just outside your door," she said. "Please call for me if you need anything."

"Thank you," I said. I waited until she had ushered the other handmaidens out of the room and shut the door behind her. Then, as Lisette began to prepare a concoction of herbs meant to make me sleep, I put my hand on hers. "You once told me you would do anything you could to help me. Can I trust you to help me now?"

She paused in her work and nodded, glancing briefly at the closed door.

"Of course," she whispered. "Anything you need, Princess."

"Good," I said. "I need you to give me something I can put in the drinks of my handmaidens to make them sleep heavily through the night."

She nodded. "I can do that, easily," she said. "But for what purpose?"

"I can't tell you," I said, afraid to put her in any more danger than I already was. "But there's one other thing I need from you, if you can manage it."

"Anything," she said.

I thought of the sorrowful look in my father's eyes when he had first looked at me earlier. It wasn't the first time I thought I'd seen a glimpse of the man he'd once been, and I wanted to get to the truth, once and for all.

"Can you create a potion that will suspend any magic in the area for a brief period of time?" I asked.

Her eyes widened. "A protection spell?" she asked.

"Something like that," I said. "I want a potion that will keep any magic from being cast inside a small area, no larger than this room, for at least fifteen minutes. Can you do it?"

She sat back, and brought a hand to her cheek.

"It's not the type of magic I'm usually asked to cast, but I know of a spell that can be contained in a potion, as you ask," she said. "At most, it will give you twelve or thirteen minutes of time. I'm afraid that's the most I can offer."

"And inside this space, can you place a sound barrier where no one outside the area can hear what's happening inside?" I asked.

"That's a bit more complicated," she said. "I'll have to combine several potions to make it work."

"But you can do it?" I asked, hope rising in my heart.

"I think so," she said.

"How long will it take you to create such a potion?" I asked.

She shook her head and looked off into the distance. "If I start working on it now, I might have it ready by tomorrow afternoon," she said.

The hope fell to the pit of my stomach. Tomorrow would be too late. The final round of the King's Games was scheduled to begin just after the morning feast, and I intended to be long gone by then.

"I need it tonight," I said. "Lisette, I'm begging you. If there's any way you can get that potion to me tonight, it will give me a chance to save someone's life. Please."

She met my eyes and gripped my hand. "For years, I believed my youngest daughter was lost to me," she said. "I mourned her as if she had died, but when word came that she was alive and free, living in the human world as a waitress at some club, it was as if my own life had been returned to me. I owe you everything, Princess."

I smiled. "A club?" I asked. "It's not called Venom, is it?"

"Yes," she said, her eyes widening in surprise. "How did you know?"

"It's run by a good friend of mine," I said. "What's her name?"

"Melisandre," she said. "The demon who brought word of her said she goes by Melissa now."

"Melissa," I repeated. "I promise you that if I ever make it back there, I will let her know that you are here, and you are safe."

Lisette threw her arms around me. "Thank you, Princess," she said. "I would love to see her more than anything, but I'm not allowed to leave the King's City. A guard offered to smuggle her in to join me here, but I told him to let her be. She's safer there than here."

I wanted to ask her why she would say that, since most demons felt that the King's City was the safest place in the Shadow World, but I didn't have time for a long conversation. I needed her to get to work on that potion as soon as possible.

"So, you'll help me?" I asked.

"I will," she said. She got to work mixing herbs together until there were four small piles on her tray. "Sprinkle these into the drinks of each of your handmaidens. This will send them into a deep sleep, and they will not awaken until morning."

"Thank you," I said, clutching her hand.

"I'll need to return to my workshop in order to mix the other potion," she said. "But as soon as I can, I'll return to you here in your room and deliver it myself."

"I appreciate this more than you can ever know," I said.

"It is my pleasure to help," she said. "But I must go now. The potion will take hours and my full concentration if I'm to finish on time."

She gathered up her bags of herbs and nodded to the piles still lying on the tray.

"Put those in the drinks before I leave," she said. "It's likely to be your only chance, since I'm certain the handmaidens will return as soon as I cross that threshold."

I stood and did exactly as she said, sprinkling the herbs into each of the handmaidens' goblets. It was common for them to drink winterberry wine late into the night as they gossiped about the events of the day. No doubt they had already heard rumors about the battle in the arena and would return to the room to discuss it at length when Lisette left my side.

When the herbs had dissolved into the wine, I hurried back to my bed and climbed under the covers. I nodded to Lisette, and she bowed toward me as she opened the door and greeted the handmaidens on the other side.

I closed my eyes as the women entered the room, pretending to be fast asleep.

I waited as the girls discussed my reaction to the games and went over the death of the former scholar in today's tournament. I listened, biting my tongue to keep from saying a word as they spoke about Aerden and the death of his friend.

After a short time, though, their voices grew sleepy.

Minutes later, they were all fast asleep, slumped over in their chairs with the last drops of their wine spilling onto the floor.

I sat up in bed and started thinking through my plan.

I would speak to my father tonight in private, or I would die trying.

But first, I needed to know what secrets Kael hid behind that door in the dungeon.

IT ALWAYS COMES BACK TO HAUNT YOU

JACKSON

When our hour was up, Rend and I reappeared there on top of the old house.

The shifting unsettled me, and I fell to my knees, my head spinning as my body reformed itself. Rend sat down next to me, his hand tight against his forehead.

We sat in silence for a few minutes as we got used to being back in our own bodies.

"How are you feeling?" he asked.

"Weird," I said.

"At least you didn't throw up," he said with a laugh. "Franki tossed her cookies when she reformed, and she was only disconnected from her body for twenty minutes."

"That's super comforting, thanks," I said.

We both laughed and stood.

"So, what now?" Rend asked. "We obviously found out

some new things about the amethyst priestess, but I think we just made her mad."

"I'm not thinking about the amethyst priestess right now," I said. I flew down to the garden and ran my hand along the green vines and flowers. "I want to know more about this fairy. Sabine."

Rend shuddered and shook his head. "Trust me, friend. You don't want to mess with Sabine," he said. "She's lovely on the outside, but she's rotten on the inside."

"I think she could see us standing there," I said. "I thought you said no one would be able to detect us with this potion?"

"I said no witch's magic would be able to detect us," he said. "Sabine is no witch."

"She's obviously fae," I said. "But she's not like any fae I've ever seen before."

"No, she's far more powerful," Rend said. "She's the daughter of the fae who rules the Summer Court, and she's very dangerous. We need to focus on how to stop the amethyst priestess from getting to Harper. Did you see the pendant she wore around her collar?"

"A panther?"

"That's what I thought it was, too. If we can find a door with a panther on it—"

"We'll be no closer to finding Harper than we are now," I said. "Without some kind of trinket or gemstone, we won't be able to get through the amethyst priestess's door."

"We have to at least try," Rend said. "You heard her. She's planning to send deadly assassins after Harper. We have no idea what her situation is back there."

"You said she was fine when she came to see you, right? No injuries?" I asked.

"Other than some scars on her arms, she seemed fine," Rend said. "But her power was low. She depleted everything she had when she killed the emerald priestess."

"That's just a matter of a good night's rest," I said. "But you're right that we need to focus on how to get back to her."

I ran my hand along the tulips again.

"And I know exactly how to get there," I said.

Rend drew in a shaky breath and stared at me. "I know what you're thinking, but I have to warn you. Sabine is not as she seems," he said. "Even if you manage to find her, she never does anything for free or out of the goodness of her heart. She's not going to open a portal for you just because she sees how much you love Harper. She'll demand some type of payment, Jackson, and with Sabine, nothing is ever easy."

"You talk about her like you know her," I said.

"I do." He ran a hand through his hair. "She's the one who helped me create Venom. Sabine has a similar power to the emerald priestess in that she can manipulate time, but her power is a thousand times stronger than Priestess Evers."

"Wait. She created Venom?" I asked.

"In order for Venom to be a safe haven for all creatures to meet, I needed it to exist outside of the normal bounds of time and space," he said. "I needed for there to be entrances to the club all around the world, making it accessible to everyone, no matter whether they were in France or the United States."

"I thought you said she was dangerous, but you obviously survived working with Sabine," I said. "How bad can it be?"

"Yeah, but I didn't go to Sabine asking her for a favor," he said. "Sabine owed me for something I'd helped her with a long time ago. I'd saved her from a vampire, and I gave her a place to stay while she healed. She owed me, and creating Venom was her repaying me."

"Still, I have to try, Rend. I have to get back to Harper somehow," I said. "This fairy can make a portal for me. You heard her. She said it took almost no power for her to make a portal into the past. She was looking at me when she said it. I think she wants to help me."

"Jackson, Sabine never wants to help anyone just for the sake of helping," he said. "If she's willing to help you, then she must want something from you."

"She doesn't even know me," I said. "What could she possibly want from me?"

Rend shook his head. "She doesn't know you, Jackson, but she's met Harper."

I stopped dead in my tracks. "What? You didn't tell me this before. When did she meet Harper?"

"At Venom," Rend said. "When she came looking for me in 1951, I was just getting Venom started. Sabine was there the day Harper showed up. She was completing the Paris door when Harper walked into Venom. I was passed out cold when they met, but she was there."

"Why didn't you tell Harper about Sabine?" I asked. "Maybe she could have opened a portal home for her. She could have walked straight through, Rend."

He shook his head. "That's not how her magic works," he said. "She can manipulate time and space, but there are limits to her power. She can open a portal into the past, but she can't open portals into the future. She wouldn't have been able to help Harper even if I'd asked her to."

"Dammit," I shouted, kicking at the fountain with my boot. "I have to get to her, no matter what it takes, Rend. You have to see that. No matter what this fairy wants from me, I'll give it to her. I don't care."

"You say that now, but Sabine, she's tricky," he said, gripping my shoulder. "Sometimes what she gets you to agree to can be heartbreaking. Life changing in the worst ways. You may not even fully understand what you're agreeing to until it's too late."

"I'm done arguing about it," I said, pulling my arm away. "She said she would cast the portal for the Order and go home. Do you know where she lives? That's all I need to know."

"Jackson—"

"No," I said. "My mind is made up, Rend. You're either going to help me or you better get out of my way."

Rend sighed. "You're the most stubborn demon I ever met in my life."

"You can't tell me you wouldn't do the same thing if it was Franki," I said.

Rend looked me straight in the eye. "I understand. I really do," he said. "But I joined the Brotherhood of Darkness thinking they could help me save my sister. I foolishly let them turn me into this abomination, twisting my true demon power into something evil and unbearable. And in the end, she still died in my arms, Jackson. Making deals with the devil never turns out the way you want it to. In the end, it always comes back to haunt you."

I turned away from him, not wanting to see the pain in his eyes.

Yes, he had made a bad deal with a group of vampires. He had trusted them when he shouldn't have, but he had still managed to do something incredible with his life. He'd made a deal with the devil and survived it.

I had to believe I would, too.

"I don't have a choice, Rend. It's the only way to bring her home. I have to try."

Rend moved to stand beside me, and we stared at the garden together, the weight of the moment weighing heavy on both of us.

"I don't know where to find her," he said. "But I know someone who does."

"Who?" I asked.

"How fast do you think you can get to New Orleans?"

THE SWAMP OF NIGHTMARES

JACKSON

"Get back to the castle," I told Rend. "Check on Mary Anne and Essex. If they've recovered the emerald ring, reach out to me through the communication stones. And let me know if there's any word from Andros about my brother."

With any luck, we'd all be back together by morning.

"I will," he said. "Jackson, please be careful."

"I promise," I said. "Hopefully next time you see me, Harper will be standing at my side."

Rend nodded and backed away as I prepared to shift.

It took only a few hours to get to New Orleans, and by the time I pulled up to the old Victorian mansion marked with the numbers 1912, the sun was just starting to set. I landed on the back steps of the house and took a deep breath.

I hadn't been here in years, but I knew I could count on the demon inside to help me. He was an old friend, and I trusted him with my life.

I knocked on the door, my heart pounding.

Please, let him be home.

He answered quickly, and his face broke out in a smile as he pushed the door open to welcome me inside.

"To what do I owe this honor, old friend?" he asked, holding his hand out to me.

"Hello, John," I said, clasping his hand and meeting his eyes. "I'm sorry to show up like this unannounced, but I need a favor."

"Anything for you," he said. He offered me a cup of coffee, but I shook my head, my heart racing at the thought of what I was about to do.

John Pierce was an ancient demon. He'd come to the human world a century before me, and he knew this area of the country better than anyone.

"I need your help," I said. "I need you to take me to see Sabine."

The cup in his hand crashed to the floor, and a girl came running in from the next room.

"John? Is everything o—"

She stopped mid-step, her eyes locked on my face. She wore a glamour that had turned her hair brown and her features plain, but I could see through it to the real woman beneath the trick. Her blonde hair hung in curls around her face, and her blue eyes lit up in surprise.

"Hello, Allison," I said, a slight smile touching my lips. I was glad to see she was alive and well.

She touched her hair. "How did you know it was me?" she asked.

"He can see through glamours," John said. "It's one of his many talents. Not the least of which is knowing how to scare the crap out of me. What do you mean you need me to take you to see Sabine? No one goes there willingly, Jackson."

"I have to go," I said. "As soon as possible. I need her help."

"She won't help you," he said. He waved his hand over the broken cup and it rose into the air, piecing itself back together as if it were brand new. "Not without a price."

"At this point, I'll pay anything she asks if she can help me get to Harper."

He shook his head. "She's a trickster," he said. "She plays the long game, Jackson, and if she does agree to help you, she'll ask way too much in payment. It's not worth it."

I looked from him to Allison, easily seeing how much they cared for each other. I had known this demon a very long time. Long enough to know that whatever he felt for her was different this time. He truly cared for her. Loved her, maybe.

"What if someone took Allison away from you?" I asked. "What if you knew she had been tortured beyond what anyone should have to endure? If you knew that at this very moment, assassins were being sent to seek her out and kill her? Would you risk a trip to see Sabine?"

Allison sat down at the large oak table that took up most of the kitchen. "Oh God, Harper," she said. "You still haven't found her?"

I shook my head. "I know where she is, but I can't get to her without Sabine's help, so unless you know someone else who can open a portal into the past, I'm out of options."

Allison sighed, and a tear rolled down her cheek. John went to sit at her side, running his hand along her back.

Allison had been in Harper's class at Peachville High School, and even though Allison had not openly joined our fight against the Order back then, she had been smart enough to get away from Peachville when the gate was closed. She'd been on the run from the Order ever since.

Most of the recruits from the sapphire gates had been rounded up a few months ago by the emerald priestess and killed in a mass-sacrifice so Priestess Evers could cast the spell that had kept the entire world frozen in time. Allison was lucky to be alive, and from the way he was looking at her now, I was sure John understood the kind of fear I was currently facing.

"John," I said. "Please."

He whispered something in Allison's ear and she nodded. She took his face in her hands and kissed his lips softly. "Be safe," she said.

"Where's the fun in that?" he said, laughing.

She sighed and stood up, making her way over to me and wrapping her arms around me. It was so unexpected, I stiffened before finally hugging her back.

Allison and I had never known each other very well, but she obviously cared about Harper, and that made her a friend to me.

"Be careful," she said.

She touched John's arm tenderly as she passed by him, and then she walked out of the room. A few seconds later, I heard her footsteps on the stairs.

John stood up and grabbed a set of keys off the kitchen counter.

"You're crazy to do this, you know," he said. He glanced toward the hallway. "But you're right. If it was Allison who was missing, and I felt I had nowhere else to turn, I'd pay whatever price the fairy asked just for a chance to get her back."

"Thank you," I said.

"We'll see if you're still thanking me in a few days," he said.

I followed him out to his car, and he drove me far outside the city limits of New Orleans. I watched the landscape change from concrete and skyscrapers to wetlands and deserted backroads.

Two hours later, he pulled down an overgrown path and stopped just shy of a thick forest. The trees here were covered in dark green vines that wrapped around them like blankets, their roots were drenched in swampy water.

"We have to walk from here," he said. He laughed and studied his shoes that I was sure cost more than my entire closet combined. "I should have changed clothes first."

We travelled a rough pathway through the trees, standing on solid ground at first. As we got deeper in though, we had to trudge through water as deep as our knees with nothing but the moon to guide our way through the dark swamp.

"Should I be worried about getting my leg chomped off by an alligator?" I asked, stepping carefully.

John laughed. "Not here," he said. "The gators don't dare come this close to the Swamp of Nightmares."

"What?" I asked, a chill running through me.

"That's where Sabine lives," he said. "Nice name, huh?"

I definitely didn't like the sound of any place with nightmare in the name, and I wondered exactly what I was getting myself into. There was no turning back now, though.

About two miles into our walk, a shimmering light appeared in the distance.

"This is as far as I go," John said. "Just follow the light."

I nodded, my heart racing as I stared at the entrance to the

Swamp of Nightmares. "Thank you for bringing me here. I owe you one."

"I'll wait for you as long as I can," he said. "And Jackson?"

"Yes?"

"Whatever you see in there, it isn't real," he said. "She'll try to get into your head and find your worst nightmares. She'll do everything she can to break you open and tear you apart. Don't let her win."

"I won't," I said, shivering as a strange wind blew through the cypress trees.

"Good luck, my friend."

I nodded and turned toward the shimmering light, walking slowly toward the unknown. From what John had told me on the drive over here, many people—demon and human alike—had come to this swamp, seeking Sabine's help in desperate times. Most of them never found their way out.

I had no idea what I would face once I passed through the light, but I knew that I was willing to face anything for the hope of finding Harper before she was lost to me forever.

As I stepped closer to the entrance, its sparkling rays within my reach, I turned to look at John Pierce. He raised a hand, and I waved back, then stepped through the portal into the Swamp of Nightmares.

HOW HEROES WERE MADE

AERDEN

My heart was shattered, and even though I could feel my friend's spirit and power inside of me, I couldn't believe he was really gone. I replayed our battle in my head a thousand times, each time trying to figure out how it could have gone differently, and each time still seeing him there, bleeding to death in my arms.

Potions were strictly forbidden in the games. Competitors could use their own magical abilities, but any enhancements were supposed to be an immediate disqualification.

And yet, no one had stepped forward to stop what the other team had done.

In my mind, that could only mean one thing. Someone in power had set us up on purpose.

I closed my eyes, seeing Kael's smug smile so clearly that I felt I could reach out and strangle him now with my bare hands.

I had no doubt that I was the real target in today's battle.

My two opponents thought they had more time to murder Trention and then come back for me. It was supposed to be torture on two levels. Make me watch my dear friend die first, and then end my life, too.

Something inside me had been strong enough to break free of whatever magic that potion contained, but it was too late. By the time I reached him, Trention was already dying, and deep in my heart, I knew he was right. Even if the shamans had taken him away to a healing room, he would have then been asked to give his spirit in service to the king.

How had we gotten to this point? How had this great kingdom turned into such a horrible, hopeless place?

I let my head fall into my hands as I sat at the edge of Trention's bed. I was such a fool.

This whole time, I had believed there was still honor in fighting for my freedom. I had believed that if I was just strong enough to win and to prove myself out there on the battlefield, that I would be rewarded with freedom.

Now, I could see the truth.

I was never meant to survive these games.

Tomorrow's finale would be set up so that there would be no chance of me winning. Whether my opponent would have potions or some other trick up his sleeve wasn't the point. Whoever was truly running these games wanted me dead, and no matter what I did, they were never going to set me free.

Maybe their plan was that even if I managed to win for the benefit of the crowd, they would still usher me into some room where I would be forced to lay down my life for a king who clearly wasn't himself these days.

But no matter how many times I went through the possibilities for tomorrow's fight, I couldn't figure out how to escape it.

I had volunteered for these games, and in doing so, I had signed my own death warrant.

Short of fighting almost the entire king's guard to try to get out of the city before they killed me, I couldn't think of a single solution.

I had been stupid to believe they would ever let me go.

Deep in the darkness of my cell, I knelt at the side of my bed and prayed for strength to face the day to come.

Everything I had been through, everything I had overcome, was all down to this final battle. All this time, I had convinced myself that it was freedom I was after. Freedom that I wanted more than anything.

I wanted to be free from these chains. Free from the voices that still echoed in my head after a century of slavery. I wanted to be free to use my own power and to seek my own happiness.

But what I'd come to realize in the hours since Trention's death was that freedom was not something to be given by another. It was not something granted to you simply because the chains that had held you were removed.

Because even after I'd been released from the sapphire gate that had held me for so long, a part of me had still been a slave to that pain. I had allowed myself to relive it every night for months. I had allowed the memories of my past to trap my power inside of me. To dull my own magic.

In the end, freedom was a choice.

Choosing to be free didn't mean that the pain would go away. It wouldn't loosen the physical chains around my hands and ankles.

It meant that no matter what I had been through and no matter what situation I had yet to face, I would be free to make my own choices. To be the demon I knew I needed to be.

My original master had not been the Order of Shadows. It had been fear itself.

Fear drove me from this castle, and I had been its slave, refusing to stand up and open my heart to the one person I loved more than life itself.

My pain was of my own making, and as difficult as it was, it was time I faced the truth. I had blamed others for far too long. I had been a coward.

But tomorrow, I would stand as a hero.

Win or lose, I would stand on that battlefield without fear.

I would be free, because I chose to be free.

I sent up a prayer to the spirit of my dear friend, thanking him for his sacrifice. I said a prayer for my brother, that he may someday understand that I pushed him away because letting him in would mean having to face something I wasn't yet ready to face. I hoped that wherever he was, he knew that I loved him.

I said a prayer for Harper, thanking her for saving my life. For not giving up on me, even when her own life was on the line.

Finally, I said a prayer for Lea. For myself. The one thing that kept me from moving forward in my life was the mistake I'd made a hundred years ago in choosing to leave rather than tell her my truth. I prayed for the chance to right that wrong before I died.

When the guards came for me, I would be ready. I had laid all my fears before the gods, and now there was nothing left but to fight.

THE ASHES OF OUR HOPES AND DREAMS

LEA

By the time Lisette returned with the potion, I had changed into my old clothes. My human clothes. I strapped my bow and the bag to my back and thanked her for the potion.

"What are you going to do?" she asked. "I'm worried for you."

"I'm going to get answers," I said. "Don't breathe a word to anyone about what you've seen tonight or what you've done. I'm trusting you, Lisette."

"I won't, Princess," she said. "If anyone knew, I would already be dead."

"Lisette, I know you've already done so much, but I need to ask one more favor of you," I said.

She nodded. "I will help you, Princess."

"There is a guard named Ezrah," I said. "Do you know him?"

"I know his face, yes."

"I need you to find him for me. Tell him we leave tonight," I said. "Tell him to meet me in the south garden in four hours. Can you do that?"

"I will find him," she said.

I said goodbye to her, and stepped out onto my balcony. I had no idea what truth I would find in the dungeons and in my father's eyes tonight, but I prayed this was a risk worth taking.

I had spent the years after Jackson slipped away from me doubting my own intuition. Feeling that I must have been a fool to believe he loved me. But over the past few months here in the castle, I'd started to connect to that intuition again, trusting that the things I knew to be true were real.

I had been wrong about Jackson, but maybe it was as simple as a tragic change of heart. Losing his brother had changed him in ways neither of us could have predicted. I could no longer use that loss as a shield to guard my own heart.

Pain was inevitable, but if we could somehow learn to rise from the ashes of our hopes and dreams once they burned to the ground, maybe we could also learn to rebuild.

To dream again.

I gripped the potion in my hand and took a leap of faith, jumping from the balcony and shifting into smoke. I soared through the night, finding my way to the east wing of the castle. I stuck to the shadows like darkness itself.

Carefully, I made my way down to the lower dungeons, thankful to find it still empty.

I walked to the back of the hall and stepped into the final cell, my heart beating wildly. I removed the key from my bra, and with trembling fingers, I placed it into the lock.

For a moment, I hoped it wouldn't work. Maybe Tatiana

had been telling me the truth about the shaman. Maybe this key was not a match at all.

But the lock clicked open and something shifted in my heart.

Tatiana had lied.

But she had given this key to Aerden long before Kael ever arrived in this city. Had she found it? Stolen it? Or did she have something to do with Kael's presence here?

I couldn't wrap my head around it. Kael was her enemy. Besides me, he was the only person blocking her and her husband from taking the throne when my father died. I didn't think she would be working with Kael, but something tied them together. I just couldn't figure out what.

I swallowed and opened the door, making sure to remove the key before I shut the door behind me.

Inside, it was dark and cold. I was certain my magic wouldn't work here, since we were so close to the dungeons, but when I reached for my power, I was surprised to find it waiting for me. I conjured a small light and looked around, realizing I was in an ante-chamber of some sort.

The ceilings were several stories high, and in front of me, an enormous door had been carved into the stone. More of the strange markings from the previous door were etching into this one, but there was no place to insert a key. Nervous, I stepped forward and ran my hand along the symbol of a crown etched into the surface.

My heart raced as the giant door swung open. I shifted to shadow, scared that someone inside might discover me here. I waited in the darkness, fear flowing through me, but no one came searching for intruders.

After a moment, I finally reformed and stepped into the

room. The ceilings were massive here, too, reminding me of the Underground where the Resistance Army lived. Had this place been created by trolls in some ancient day? The stonework was the same, and it was possible the carvings on the door matched those of the Underground, but I couldn't be sure.

It was so dark, however, that I could only see a few feet in front of me. I pushed my light deeper into the room, knowing I was close to secrets I was never meant to learn. But nothing had prepared me for this.

My eyes widened, and the air around me grew so cold, I was frozen to the spot, my body shivering.

I shook my head, not wanting to believe this could be true. Andros had come to me back at Brighton Manor with rumors, but I never dreamed it could have gone this far.

I suddenly understood the sheer massiveness of the door. The sleeping creatures entombed here were easily three or four times my own height, and each of their chests spanned at least fifteen feet wide.

Stone Guardians. Rows of them so far back in the darkness, I couldn't even begin to count. Hundreds, maybe.

Andros had said there might be one Stone Guardian here in the city, and that had terrified us, but this? It was unimaginable.

I was too shocked to even cry out or run away. I could only stand and stare.

When I finally found my voice, it came out as a whisper. A plea. A curse.

"My God, Father, what have you done?"

HEARTS

LEA

W hen I'd recovered from my shock enough to feel confident on my feet, I walked around the massive room, studying the Stone Guardians and trying to understand why they were here. And why they were sleeping.

Their bodies were made of light stone, almost like alabaster or marble. They had joints similar to humans in their knees and arms and shoulders. Their heads were massive, and though their eyes seemed to be open, they didn't seem to move or see at all.

I sent my light toward one near the front, and explored every inch of the creature, noticing that in the center of the guardian's chest was an indentation where its heart should be. Was that why they were sleeping?

I continued to explore, thinking through the legends and stories I'd heard about the guardians. Some legends said that before the Stone Guardians first appeared in this land, we were much like humans. Except for our ability to shift, we had no magic at all.

But during the first Stone War, when the guardians fell, their decaying bodies turned to gemstones. Over time, the magic inside these stones seeped into our land and our magic was born. The stories said that each guardian had a colored gemstone for a heart, and when its body, decayed, a massive crater of that same gemstone appeared.

I had seen these craters before, of course, but I always thought those stories were myths. I'd never truly believed in the existence of Stone Guardians, and the stories about them were so varied, it was hard to know what was real and what was simply made up over time.

During the Age of Stone, the guardians came again, this time starting a war that nearly wiped out demonkind. Those were the stories that kept shadowlings up at night.

If the people of this city knew there were a hundred sleeping guardians beneath the castle, they would never sleep again.

Still, it didn't make sense that they were here. Stone Guardians were not supposed to be easily controlled, but these were arranged like soldiers. The rows were perfectly formed, as if these creatures had been created on some assembly line and placed here on purpose.

I studied each of them, searching for one with a diamond heart. When Andros came to me, just before the attack on the domed city, he'd said the rumors were that a Stone Guardian with a diamond heart had been seen here. But none of these guardians had a diamond for a heart.

None of them had any heart at all.

Looking for more answers, I finally reached the back of the

chamber. Here, I found a set of five equally large doors. Each door had a stone embedded in its center.

Sapphire. Emerald. Ruby. Citrine. Amethyst. The five stones of the Order of Shadows.

There was no door with a diamond stone in its center, and I wondered why.

I stepped forward and placed my hand on the sapphire stone, jumping back as a loud clicking sound filled the chamber. The door swung open, and I pushed my light inside, terrified of what I might find.

The room beyond was lined with large sapphire stones of all shapes and sizes. In the center of the room was a long work bench with smoother, rounder stones being shaped. The new shape perfectly matched the indentation on each guardian's chest.

Hearts.

I closed my eyes and leaned back against the wall, my entire body trembling in fear.

The prisoners had been mining stones so that Kael could create new hearts for his army of guardians.

The only question that remained was why?

THE WARRIOR YOU WERE BORN TO BE

LEA

An hour later, when I had gotten all the information I could from the chamber hidden in the dungeons, I made my way to the one person I hoped would have some answers.

I had come here many times as a shadowling, seeking comfort in my father's wise words, and as I landed on the balcony of his private room, I prayed for one last chance to speak to the demon I'd admired so much back then.

I prayed I wasn't making a huge mistake. On the outside, it appeared my father was my enemy, but there had been several times lately when he'd looked at me in such a way that I could have sworn I saw his sadness. Regret. It was as if the man I once knew was trapped inside his own body.

But if I was wrong about him, and he was truly my enemy, I would be killed by morning.

All I needed was a few minutes with him. I prayed my intuition was guiding me down the right path.

With silent footsteps, I walked into my father's private chambers where he lay sleeping in the center of his large bed. I stood at the foot of the stone platform in the middle of the room and slowly uncorked the potion Lisette had given me.

I poured the murky brown liquid onto the floor and watched in awe as a dome rose up around us, locking my father and me inside.

"Father," I said, placing my hand on the bed at his side. "Father, please wake up. I need to talk to you, and I don't have much time."

I held my breath as he stirred, opening his eyes wide at the sight of me.

"Lea, what are you doing here?" he asked, and I nearly cried at the sound of his nickname for me. He hadn't called me that once since I'd come home. Not until now. "It's too dangerous for you to be here. Go, before someone hears you."

I shook my head and reached for his hands, recognizing the man I had once loved still there behind his eyes.

"We're safe for now," I said. "I don't have time to explain everything, but I've encased us in a protection spell. No one can hear us, and no magic can reach us inside this room."

He glanced at the diamond scepter lying against the edge of the bed and let out a breath of relief.

He gathered me into his arms and held me so tightly, I thought he might crack a rib.

"Dear girl, how I've missed you," he said.

His tears fell onto my skin, and I hugged him back.

"I've missed you, too, Father," I said. I pulled away, wiping tears from my own eyes. There was no time for tears now.

Thirteen minutes would pass by in a blink if I let it. "I need you to tell me the truth. What happened after I left? What happened to you? Why don't you fight it?"

He shook his head. "I'm so sorry, Lea," he said. "But I'm afraid the time for fighting has come to an end. I no longer have the power to stand against the Order the way I should have all those years ago when you begged me to join you. You have to believe me when I say that I truly thought I was doing what was best for our people at the time. I believed the Order would take what they wanted and leave us alone. We are immortal, after all. I thought we could outlast them. I never dreamed they would destroy our lands the way they have."

"But why didn't you fight after you saw what was possible?" I asked. "I don't understand what's happened to your power, Father. You should be stronger than ever."

His face crumpled as more tears flowed from his eyes.

"I was only trying to protect you," he said.

"Protect me?" I asked, clutching his hands. I remembered Tatiana's words to me the first night of the King's Festival. She'd spoken to me of sacrifices beyond my understanding, and I realized I was about to hear the truth from my own father's lips. "Please, tell me. What have you done, Father?"

He shook his head. "After you left, Kael came to the city gates, demanding to speak with me. He said he had news of the princess, so I allowed him to pass into the city and meet with me in the throne room. He told me you had followed Jackson into the human world. I had already suspected as much, but I knew you were a fighter. I thought you could hold your own."

"What else did he tell you?" I asked, chills running through me like waves.

"He said that the High Priestess herself had taken notice of you," he said, finally glancing up to look in my eyes. "He said that unless I agreed to her terms, she would capture you and use you to open a new portal in the human world. He said that you would become a slave to the Order, and that I would never see you again."

I lowered my head, the truth of his words finally starting to sink in.

"Tell me you didn't make a deal with the High Priestess," I said, glancing again at the scepter with its large diamond embedded in the top.

"I felt as though I had no choice," he said. "You are the future of this kingdom, Lea. At the time, I had no idea it was even possible to free a demon who had been captured by the Order. If I refused to agree to their terms, it would be like condemning my own daughter to death. I couldn't let that happen."

"So, you condemned the entire kingdom," I said. "You condemned yourself, instead."

"The High Priestess demanded a piece of my power," he said. "A large piece of my power. Kael placed a curse on me, allowing him to drain my power whenever he wants. He was placed here as watchdog for the priestess, keeping your mother and me in line with her diamonds that are constantly watching us. In return for this piece of me, she agreed to keep her hunters away from you. She also agreed to let me continue to rule this kingdom, even if only in appearance. The demons who lived here in the King's City would be spared, as well, as long as I agreed not to interfere with her hunters outside these gates."

"All those demons," I said, my heart breaking. This was all

my fault. Thousands had been taken just to save my life. "Father, how could you agree to such a thing?"

He lifted a hand to my face. His lip trembled for a moment before he spoke again. "How could I refuse her?" he asked. "You did what you thought was right in following Denaer, giving up your place and duty here at my side to save Aerden and bring him home, no matter the cost. Have I not done the same thing?"

I shook my head. "This is different," I said. "You had an entire army at your command. You could have refused her offer and joined us in the fight. You could have stood by my side in the human world and helped me bring them down."

"By the time Kael had worked his way into this castle, the choice had already been taken from me," he said. "If I had refused him, he would have taken you and destroyed this city with an army of hunters. Yes, I made a mistake not joining you in the human world when I had the chance, but when Kael arrived, it was too late for me."

I fought for the words I needed to say, feeling the seconds tick by and turn into minutes. I was running out of time.

"How do I fix this?" I asked. "If I kill Kael, will that restore your power?"

"I don't know," he said. "But Kael is much stronger than you can imagine. He not only has the greater half of my power flowing through him. He also has taken every soul stone and sacrifice given to me over the past twenty-five years for himself. You are strong, my daughter, but taking him on in a fight by yourself would be a death sentence."

"I would rather die than see you like this," I said. "But I do understand Kael's power. He's manipulating the games, Father. He sees Aerden as a threat, and he's determined to have him killed. Those potions today? I know you saw them. Those demons cheated. They could have killed Aerden if he hadn't broken free at the last minute. I'm not sure he'll be so lucky in tomorrow's fight. But there's something else, Father. Something I have just now seen with my own eyes. Did you know Kael has an entire army of Stone Guardians beneath the dungeons of this castle?"

Father shook his head, the truth evident in the flash of fear in his eyes. "That can't be true," he said. "The Stone Guardians have been extinct for centuries."

"No, Father. He has at least a hundred hidden below the castle," I said. "That's why the prisoners have been mining sapphires for months in the secret deposits at the edge of the city. I think Kael has slaves working down there to create sapphire hearts for each of the guardians. I think he intends to awaken them soon and destroy this city. He has to be stopped before he gets the chance."

"It doesn't make any sense," he said, bringing a hand to his forehead. "Everything I've ever heard about the Stone Guardians proves that they battled themselves into extinction almost a thousand years ago. It doesn't make sense that you could simply give them a new heart and awaken them in this way. There has to be another explanation."

"Could they have been conjured?" I asked. "Their appearance and magic replicated, somehow?"

My father nodded. "Yes. If a demon had the right magic, they could recreate the appearance and strength of a Stone Guardian," he said. "But for what purpose? What could he be planning to do with them?"

"We're running out of time to figure this out," I said. "The spell that is holding the magic at bay will run out in less than two minutes. I'm not sure when I'll have the chance to speak with you again."

"My smart girl, thinking of such a potion," he said, smiling. "You always were a clever little thing. When the magic returns to my scepter, Kael will again be able to see and hear everything that goes on around me. He watches me like a hawk, punishing me if I step out of line. He tells me what to say, how to act, and what to do at every moment. He is the true ruler of the King's City these days, only no one knows the truth except your mother and I, and we are both helpless to speak against him. If either of us so much as hints at what he's done to me, the diamond in that scepter will drain the rest of my power instantly. Your mother wears a similar diamond around her neck. We are prisoners in our own kingdom, no different from you or Aerden."

I closed my eyes, realizing why my father had only been communicating with me through the odd glance at just the right time, when Kael wasn't watching. It also explained why my mother had been so eager to please Kael and to see me obey him. I'd known he was powerful here in the city, but I had never imagined to what extent he had stolen that power for himself.

"I can't ever step more than a few feet away from that damned thing, or I am hit with an excruciating pain that takes weeks to recover from," Father said, motioning to the scepter. "When he gave it to me, he cast some sort of binding spell on it, linking it to me for the rest of my life. I tested it in the early days, and I lived to regret it."

"Tell me what I can do," I said.

"You can live," he said, brushing my hair from my face. "Find a way to get out of this city, and take Aerden with you.

Go tonight, if you can. Go far away and don't look back. Continue your work with the Resistance, and once you've put an end to the High Priestess herself, come home and put a dagger through Kael's heart."

He smiled, and I threw my arms around him.

"I will," I said. "I hate to leave you again, but I will do everything I can to be home soon."

"That's my girl," he said, stroking my hair the way he did all those years ago, comforting me when I'd had a nightmare. "I love you more than anything in this world. I'm so proud of all you've accomplished, Lea.I hope you know that."

"Proud?" I asked, pulling away so I could look in his eyes. "How can you be proud of me when I'm the one who was responsible for the death and kidnapping of so many of our people?"

"Don't put that guilt on yourself," he said. "You were simply following your heart and doing what you felt was right. You were brave, even in the face of unimaginable horror. I am the one who has failed our people, Lea, but I am powerless to make things right, no matter how much I want to. It's up to you now to save as many as you can. Return home when the Order is through, and I will pass the kingdom onto you, so that you may be the queen and ruler they deserve."

"I'm so sorry, Father," I said.

"Don't be sorry." He smiled as he wiped a tear from my cheek. "Be fierce. Be the warrior you were born to be."

I nodded, wishing for just a little more time with him, but knowing that only a handful of seconds remained.

"I love you," I said.

"I love you too, my sweet, strong Lazalea," he said. "You

are the last hope of our kingdom now. Go quickly, so that you may live to fight another day."

I stood, my heart racing as the barrier that surrounded us began to fade.

We were out of time.

"Goodbye, Father," I said, squeezing his hand one last time before I darted toward the balcony. Before I passed through the barrier, though, my father called my name one last time, and I turned to him. "Yes?"

"I will see you again, my daughter, in this world or the next."

"In this world or the next," I repeated softly.

The barrier shimmered and faded from sight. I turned, great sadness in my heart, jumped from the balcony, and flew into the darkness toward the south garden to meet Ezrah.

SOMETHING GREATER THAN ME

HARPER

J ames pulled up to the Evers house just after dawn.

"Get cleaned up and meet me back here in a few hours," I said. "I'm hoping my friend Brooke has already rescued a few of the girls, but I may need your help to get the rest of them back here."

"Brooke?" he asked. Then, recognition settled in his eyes. "Melody."

"Yes, I said. If you can, arrange for Monica Evers and her nurse, Melody, to visit each of the hospitals. We'll prepare the proper paperwork to have them discharged from the hospital, so they can come home with us."

"They'll never agree to let you bring a hundred girls here to this house," he said.

"They won't know that's what we intend to do," I said. "We'll make it appear as if the girls' parents will be picking them up. Evers Institute was a private facility, after all. None of these girls were every officially committed to any type of state hospital or mandatory facility. As long as we make it look like their parents intend to take them home, I don't think it will be a problem."

He shook his head and glanced up at the house. "But how will you keep them all here?" he asked. "It's a big house, but feeding everyone and making sure you have enough beds is going to be a nightmare."

"Once their memories are restored, I'll let the girls decide what they want to do," I said. "They were brought here against their will, and right now, I can't promise them a trip back to the present day. We may have to face the fact that we're all stuck here, at least for a while. If they want to stay with me, maybe we can find a place to rebuild and start our lives over."

"But what about the danger of disrupting the timeline?" he asked. Stress formed wrinkles on his forehead. "If you just restore their memories and let them go and do whatever they want to do, they could change everything. We may get home to the present and find out that nothing is at all what we thought it was."

I thought about his words for a long time as I sat staring up at the house. He made a good point. What if any of these girls decided they wanted revenge for what happened to them? The emerald priestess might be dead in the present day, but there was still another version of her here in the 50's, living her life and making plans for this horrible place. Hundreds, if not thousands, of girls would die here in the years to come, and right now, there was something we could do about it if we had no choice but to stay.

It was a powerful temptation to try to change the things we knew were yet to come, but at what cost? We could save hundreds, but if that meant the Order itself would be free to continue enslaving demons and witches for their own evil purposes, what would we really accomplish here?

Yet, how could I free these girls and expect them to sit back and let it all happen? If I ended up stuck here for the rest of my life, how would I live with myself knowing all the things happening around me that I could have changed?

I took a deep breath to calm my racing mind.

For the past several years, ever since I was brought to Peachville and told that it was my last chance to make something of my life, I'd been fighting. Through it all, I had somehow found the strength to believe that I would survive and that we would win this war.

And somehow, I had. Even in the darkest of times, when hope had seemed to abandon me, I believed that I would make it through.

I had no idea what the future would bring. I had no idea if I would find my way home. But even now, with the portal closed and no way out, I knew in the deepest part of myself, that it was going to be okay. My job wasn't to know how it would work out. My job was simply to trust.

"I don't have all the answers for you," I said. "I don't know how this ends. What I do know is that I will always continue to do what I know is right. And restoring the memories of these girls is the right thing to do, James. Beyond that, it's up to something greater than me."

James gave me a strange look. "How can you say that after everything you've been through? How can you even know what the right thing is? I thought for sure that joining the Others was the right thing to do. That killing you was right. But now..."

"The difference, I think, is that I've learned to let my heart guide me. This war against the Order is not about revenge for me. It's not even about justice. Not really," I said. "I want to put an end to the Order because as long as they exist, the people I love most are in danger. You want to save your sister? Fight for her. Don't fight for revenge. Fight for love."

His lip trembled, and he looked away.

"Do you really think we can save her?"

I touched his hand. "I know we can try," I said. "Let's save these girls, first. Then we can find our way home, James. We can free the emerald gates and restore your sister's true memories. One step at a time. We can do this as long as we believe we can."

He nodded. "Somehow, I believe in you. As crazy as it sounds."

"Come back in a couple hours?" I asked.

"I'll be here," he said.

I opened the door of the police cruiser and stepped into the cool spring air. I was exhausted, scared, and the future was uncertain, but in my heart, there was still the whisper of hope.

AMETHYST COLLARS

HARPER

I let myself into the house and called out for Brooke.

"I'm home," I shouted.

She came rushing down the steps, but stopped in the middle, her eyes widening.

"What the hell happened to you?" she asked. "Oh my God, Harper, have you been shot? And why is your blood blue?"

I glanced at my shoulder, laughing. I had honestly almost forgotten about that.

"They shot me with demon steel," I said. "Have you ever heard of the Others?"

She shook her head. "Who are they?"

"Come upstairs with me and let's look for peroxide or something while I tell you all about them," I said.

I explained about my first encounter with the Others after I had first gotten to Peachville. I told her how they had been the ones to kill Morgyn Baker the night of our Homecoming dance, but that their original target had been Jackson. I explained how the Others believe magic comes from God and that demons and any witch who hosts a demon are tainted with evil.

"Wait, so this cop was part of the Others?" she asked. She held up a bottle of peroxide she'd found in the medicine cabinet of Doctor Evers' bedroom. "Hold on, this is going to hurt. A lot."

I winced as she poured the liquid on my wound. When the pain had subsided enough for me to take a break, I continued with my story.

"Yes, much to my extreme disappointment," I said through clenched teeth. "I had to fight them just to get a chance to check on the portal."

Brooke poured more of the peroxide on my wound.

"I take it the portal was closed?" she asked, not meeting my gaze straight on as she screwed the cap back on the bottle.

"Closed," I said. "I'm sorry. If I hadn't taken all that time to go find Rend, we might have been able to get there before it was too late."

"Maybe, but then what? We just leave all the girls here while we go back?" she asked, shaking her head. "We couldn't do that."

"I know," I said.

"Wait a second," Brooke said, pointing toward the front of the house. "But wasn't that the cop who just brought you home?"

"Yeah," I said. "It's a long story, but basically he's going to help us now. I hope."

"Do you really think we can trust him? I mean, what if he

comes back with more of those people?" she asked. "Maybe we should take the girls and find someplace to hide for a while. At least until this stuff with the Others blows over?"

"I think we can trust him," I said. "He thought he was doing the right thing, and I hope I convinced him to look at it another way. Plus, now that the portal has closed, we're probably his only chance of ever getting home. He's really just a victim in all this as much as we are."

"He helped them kill all those girls," she said.

"To keep his sister and himself alive," I said. "He had no choice. Not any good ones, anyway."

"Well, I have to say I wouldn't have been so forgiving if it was me," she said. "But if you trust him, I'm willing to go with it."

"He'll be back in a few hours to take us by the hospitals so we can start releasing the girls," I said. "Were you able to get to any of them while I was gone?"

She smiled. "I found Mary Ellen and Nora first," she said. "I pretended to be their mothers and had them discharged from the hospital. The potions worked beautifully to restore their missing memories and their magic. Now, the two of them have been going around and doing the same thing, having the girls discharged one at a time."

I sat back, hardly believing we were finally making progress. "How are they going to explain the truth to them? It's bound to be a bit disorienting."

"They're taking it one girl at a time," she said. "As long as every girl that's awakened agrees to help, I think we'll have them all back here by the afternoon. At least I hope. But then what?"

"I don't know," I said. "Maybe then we get everyone

together and start thinking about where we could go to hide out in safety while we look for another way home."

Something thumped on the floor above our heads. Brooke and I both stood up at the same time.

"What was that?" she asked.

"Shhh," I said in a whisper, holding up my hand.

I strained to listen, keeping my body as still as possible. I didn't even breathe.

Several faint footsteps followed the sound, and I jumped up quickly, grabbing Brooke's hand.

"Someone's in the house," I said. "We have to hide."

We ran out of the bathroom and searched for any good place to hide, but I quickly realized how futile that would be. Whoever was here had magically appeared on the secret third floor of this house.

They had to be witches, which meant magic. Hiding in a closet or under the bed would do us no good. Even an invisibility illusion wasn't going to work against a group of talented witches.

"You need to get out of here," I said, taking her hand and practically dragging her to the window. "Do you still remember how to levitate?"

"Magic 101," she said. "But I'm not going anywhere without you."

"Whoever is here in this house, they're here for me," I said. "No matter where I go, they're going to follow me, Brooke. I'm not going to put you or the girls in that kind of danger. This is my fight, but if I don't make it out of here, you have to promise me you'll save as many as you can. Find a safe place to hide."

"Where?" she asked, tears shining in her eyes as she clutched the bag to her chest.

My eyes widened as an idea occurred to me. "Chicago," I said. "Find Rend and Azure. The entrance to their club is in an alley just off Hubbard Street. You'll feel the pull of the door when you get close. He'll take you in and keep you safe from the Order. If I make it out of here, I'll come there to find you. Now, go."

There was movement just outside the bedroom door now. I could feel them. Definitely witches. Powerful ones.

"I'm sorry, Harper," she said. "I don't want to leave you."

"The girls are all that matter now," I said. "Go. Please."

She nodded and wiped a tear from her cheek. She pushed the window open and flew safely down to the ground. With one final look, she started running.

Behind me, the door to the bedroom opened, and when I turned, ready to fight, Five witches, dressed all in black with amethyst collars around their necks, rushed into the room.

I gathered my power in my hands, but I was a second too late.

A bright light exploded behind my eyes as the first of their spells slammed into my body. I fell to my knees, half-blind. I couldn't move my arms. I struggled to reach out for my magic, but I had lost the connection.

With cat-like grace, one of the witches walked toward me, a black rope in her hands.

"Hello, Harper," she said. She wrapped the rope around me several times, and when she was done, she leaned toward me and whispered, "Priestess Black will be so happy to meet you. She's been looking forward to this for a very long time."

She put her hand on my head, pushing some kind of dark magic through me that tasted like bile on the back of my tongue.

"Now, sleep," she whispered.

And I did.

BEYOND THE DARKNESS

JACKSON

I trudged through the swamp, knee-high in murky water for half a mile before something strange appeared in the distance. A black tower rose high above the trees. Its surface gleamed in the sun, reminding me of the towers of the King's City.

I attempted to shift so that I could reach it faster, but my magic didn't seem to work here. I ran, wondering if the fairy, Sabine, lived there in the tower.

When I reached it, a door appeared at the base of the tower, but when I reached for the doorknob, the entire door solidified and disappeared. Confused, I walked around the tower, searching for another way inside.

On the far side of the tower, instead of a door, a single open window appeared on the second floor, just out of my reach. I took several steps back and made a running start, jumping as high as I could and planting my hands on the window ledge. Using all my strength, I pulled myself up, my shoes sliding against the smooth, slick surface of the tower's outer wall.

Once inside the first room, I stared in awe. This was an exact replica of the room I'd slept in as a shadowling. I turned to glance out the window, but instead of a swamp stretching into the distance, I saw the King's City, exactly as it was when I was young.

When I turned again, my mother was sitting in a chair beside my bed. "Mom?" I asked, but she didn't look up or seem to notice me there at all.

She clutched something in her hand, and when I stepped closer, I noticed it was a locket. The locket I had given Lea when we were first engaged. The locket I later gave to Harper.

I looked down at my wrist, but the broken necklace I kept with me at all times was gone.

"Mom, what are you doing here?" I asked, kneeling in front of her.

"You just had to go after him, didn't you?" she asked. "I tried so hard to keep our family together and safe, but look what you did. You wasted your life trying to save him, and now he's gone, anyway. You're both gone. And for what?"

She lifted the locket to her cheek and began to rock back and forth, tears flowing from her eyes.

"Aerden?" I asked. "What are you talking about? He's safe in the King's City, and I'm right here. You're the one who abandoned us."

She looked up then, her eyes glazed over with sorrow.

"No," she said. "You're wrong. No one is ever safe here in the King's City. Aerden is dead. He fell in the King's Games, and you weren't there to help him. You should have been there, Denaer."

My stomach knotted. This wasn't real. It couldn't be.

"Andros is on his way to rescue Aerden and Lea," I said. "They're safe."

She shook her head. "You're so foolish," she said. "Do you really think the king would allow those traitors into his kingdom? Andros was captured, and Aerden is dead. Everything you fought for has been for nothing, can't you see that?"

"I refuse to believe that," I said, but the fear had already worked its way into my heart. "This isn't real."

I closed my eyes, remembering John's warning to me.

Don't believe anything you see in there.

"You're not real."

When I opened my eyes, I was kneeling in water up to my waist. I tried to stand, but vines had wound their way around my ankles and legs. I reached for the dagger I'd brought with me, but it was gone.

In a panic, I checked my wrist. Harper's locket was gone, too. I was sure I'd worn it into the swamp. I hadn't taken it off since the day she was taken from me.

I plunged my hands into the water, frantically searching for it. I must have dropped it during the hallucination. But the necklace was gone.

I ripped at the vines holding me down, but they were strong and thick, pulling me deeper into the swamp. The more I struggled, the tighter they seemed to become.

I willed myself to calm down, taking several deep, controlled breaths. Slowly, the vines loosened, and I was able to free myself and walk over to higher ground a few feet away.

I glanced around, trying to decide which direction to walk. At this point, I was so turned around, I couldn't even be sure which way I'd come in from.

But at least now, I'd had a pretty good taste of what this Swamp of Nightmares was all about. Illusions. Fears. The more trapped in an illusion I became, the deeper the swamp would pull me in. The more I struggled against it, the tighter it would hold me.

All I needed to do was to keep my head, refuse to believe anything I saw or heard was real. I just needed to stay calm and keep moving forward. I could do this. Easy.

With a deep breath, I picked a direction and started walking again.

I couldn't be sure how much time passed before something glittered in the distance. The sun didn't seem to move across the sky here, so it was almost as if time itself had ceased to exist. For a moment, I considered walking in the opposite direction of the glittering object. If I avoided the nightmare altogether, maybe I would eventually find my way to the fairy's hideout.

But when I turned around, the glittering object appeared in front of me again.

I shook my head and turned left, deciding to take my chances in this direction.

Several feet ahead, though, the same glittering object appeared in the distance. There was no avoiding it. Whatever it was, I would have to face it to move forward.

Carefully, I stepped toward it, squinting to make it out so that I could mentally prepare myself for whatever new torture awaited.

But nothing could have prepared me for what I saw when I crossed over the next piece of solid land.

I closed my eyes against it, determined not to look at it again.

"This isn't real," I said loudly. "Show yourself, Sabine. Your tricks won't work on me."

"Jackson, please help me," Lea said. It sounded so much like her, I couldn't help but open my eyes, just to be sure.

A gleaming arrow embedded with a row of diamonds protruded from her chest as she lay on the ground, her blood soaking into the ground beneath her.

She reached her hand out to me and attempted to sit up, but a flash of pain caused her to wince and lay back. "Please, don't abandon me again," she said. "Not when I need you most."

"I won't," I said, but as I moved to kneel at her side, I remembered the illusion and held my ground. "This isn't really you. I can't help you."

She clutched the diamond arrow and attempted to pull it from her chest, but she screamed at the pain, the sound echoing in my heart a thousand times.

"Stop," I shouted, squeezing my eyes shut and placing my hands over my ears. But when she spoke again, I could still hear her. As if her voice was inside my head.

"I really loved you, you know that?" she asked. "Look at this mess we've gotten ourselves into, though, huh? Did you ever think it would come to this? I left everything behind to follow you, thinking that someday you would love me again. But look at us. I'm dying, Jackson, and you won't even look at me. What kind of person have you become that you would abandon your closest friends to the darkness? It's like I don't even know you anymore."

In the back of my mind, I knew this wasn't real, but something in her words felt true. I had abandoned her. When the hunters had attacked the domed city and it had been a choice between Lea and Harper, I had left Lea there in the woods to save someone else. What kind of person did that make me?

I had to explain myself. To make things right.

"I'm sorry," I said. "I never meant to hurt you. You have to believe me, Lea."

I opened my eyes, only to realize that Lea was gone, and I was once again deep in the water, vines circling me up to my waist this time. I could feel them writhing across my skin, tightening and pulling me deeper.

Frustrated, I tugged at the vines, trying to calmly loosen them, but only getting myself more entangled as one of the vines wrapped around my wrist.

Calm. Stay calm.

I took several deep breaths and released the anxiety Lea's vision had caused. Yes, I had hurt her, but I had every right to follow my own heart. Deep down, I think she understood that.

I had carried the guilt of betraying Lea with me for so long, it had become a part of me, but as the vines began to loosen, I realized that in order to move forward with my life, I would have to start forgiving myself for the mistakes I had made. I was not perfect. I would never be perfect, and that was okay.

The vines released me, and I stood, my body drenched from the chest down.

A slight breeze blew across the top of the water, and I shivered as I searched for higher ground. There was nothing here, though, but trees whose roots descended into the murky water and seemed to go on forever in the darkness below.

I could only hope that meant I was getting closer.

It sounded so simple. Just don't get involved. Don't interact. But it was different to see and hear my friends and family like that. To know that at least part of what they were saying was true. These were things I needed to answer for, and I felt compelled to validate my choices.

But this second illusion was that much more dangerous. Next time, the water would be nearly up to my neck at this rate. What would happen if I found myself underwater and couldn't get free?

As an answer to my question, I tripped over something in the deep water and stumbled forward, my hand grasping for a nearby tree to steady myself. I glanced back, only to see the outlines of several bodies bobbing just under the surface of the water, their eyes and mouths open as if in shock. Vines wrapped around them, holding them there for all eternity.

Were they still trapped inside their nightmares? Living their fears over and over? Or had these people found some type of rest here in the swamp?

I wasn't sure I wanted to know the answer.

THIS WAS NOT MY FUTURE

JACKSON

I walked for what felt like hours before another nightmare began chasing me.

Exhausted, I reminded myself to stay strong. Keep my head. I could do this.

Only, when I turned the next corner, I came face-to-face with something unexpected. Not a nightmare. A dream come true. The one thing I wanted more than anything else.

"Harper," I whispered.

I wasn't prepared for how hard it would hit me to see her again. It had been so long since I'd held her in my arms or heard her voice. But there she was. She wore a crown on her head and a dress that sparkled when she turned.

The swamp around us disappeared and was replaced with a garden full of white roses.

"There you are," she said. "I've been looking for you every-where. Where did you run off to?"

I couldn't move. I wanted nothing more than to run to her,

pull her into my arms, and never let go. But I knew that I couldn't. Not yet.

Instead, I turned away, my heart breaking.

I forced my legs to move, each step taking me further from her. And I was doing it, until I heard the laughter of a small child.

"Daddy," he said. "Don't leave us."

I couldn't help myself. I turned around to find a boy in Harper's arms. He was small, no older than two or three at most. When he smiled, his silver eyes gleamed with joy. He reached his arms out to me.

"Why don't you take him for a minute," Harper said.

"I can't," I whispered.

She stepped toward me, even more beautiful than I remembered, if that was possible.

"Don't be silly," she said. "Just hold him for a few minutes. He's missed you so much. We both have."

She looked at me so expectantly, and for a moment, I fantasized about staying here in this dream forever. No more fighting. No more struggle. This was the future we had held onto for so long, and it was right here within my grasp.

But some distant part of me understood that if I took that child in my arms, he would never be real.

"I love you," I said. "But I have to go now."

I started to turn again when a shadow crossed behind her. My heart tightened, and I reached again for the dagger that wasn't there.

The shadow moved closer, and the sky suddenly turned dark.

"What is it?" she asked, bouncing the child on her hip. "Jackson, what's gotten into you?"

I wanted to warn her to move. To turn around. I couldn't bear to see her swallowed up by the darkness. Not again.

But this was not my future. This was merely a manifestation of my greatest fears.

I didn't want the illusion. I wanted the real thing.

I watched as the shadow approached them, threatening to swallow them whole, but instead of going to them, I closed my eyes and thought of the real Harper. The person I loved and would give my life for, if it ever came to that.

"Please," I said. "I need your help. No more nightmares. No more tricks."

Laughter seemed to crawl out of the darkness, surrounding me on all sides, and when I opened my eyes, I was again transported to a new place. The swamp was gone. The garden. Harper and our child. All of it gone.

Instead, I stood on a floating piece of earth covered in thick, lush grass, sky surrounding me on all sides. I turned in a circle, searching for the sound of the laughter.

Sabine appeared before me, sitting cross-legged on a cloud of pure white. She was dressed in a gown made of red roses and wore a matching crown on her head.

I wasn't sure whether to bow to her or cuss her out for what she'd put me through.

I decided the bow was a better choice, especially since I'd come here to ask for her help.

I got down on one knee and lowered my head. "Thank you for seeing me."

"It's been my pleasure," she said. "I've always had such a fascination with the fears and desires of others. Yours have proven to be quite enjoyable."

I wasn't sure how to respond to that, so I kept my mouth shut.

"Please, stand," she said. "For a moment there, I wasn't sure you'd be able to resist that last illusion. You'd be surprised how many don't even make it through the first."

I straightened, looking her in the eyes for the first time. Her eyes were as iridescent as her wings, like opals.

"I was hoping you would come," she said. "You want me to help you get back to Harper?"

"Yes," I said. "Please."

I wanted to ask her why she'd helped the amethyst priestess at all if she'd also planned on helping me. Was this all just a big game to her? An amusement? Did she even care about the outcome? Or did she just find pleasure in putting the pieces in play and watching how it would all end up?

"I met her, you know," she said, picking at one of the roses on her dress. "I can see why you care so deeply for her. I can't say I've ever felt that way about anyone."

"Rend told me," I said.

"I can tell a lot about a person just by touching them," she said. "It's one of my many gifts. For example, with a single touch, I could see the torture she'd endured at the hands of the emerald priestess. Nasty stuff."

I winced. I didn't want to know about the things she'd endured. I knew enough of that already. I just wanted to bring her home.

"I could also see her connection to you," Sabine said. She glanced up from her roses to look at me. "And in that connection, I could see your gifts."

My stomach knotted. So, we had come to talk terms.

"What is it you want from me?" I asked.

"It's a rare ability to be able to see the future," she said casually. "One I have often coveted for myself. There are many things I can do with time and space, but when it comes to the future, I'm completely blind. I've tried, you know, but I can never see it for myself."

I swallowed, my throat suddenly very dry.

"You want me to show you a vision of the future?" I asked, trying to figure out exactly what she was asking of me. "It doesn't always work like that, I'm afraid. The visions come to me on their own. I don't control them. I'm not a psychic or anything. And I rarely see visions of things that don't affect me directly. I'm not sure what use that would be to you."

She laughed again, the sound like windchimes floating through the air.

"No, Jackson," she said. "I don't want some drawing of my future."

I sighed in relief. I wasn't sure how I was going to be able to force a vision of her. I'd never done something like that before.

"What I want," she said, "is your power to see the future."

I shook my head, not quite comprehending.

"My power?"

"Yes, your ability," she said. "I want to take it from you so that it will be mine to control and use however I see fit."

I felt sick to my stomach. She wanted to take my ability away? What would that mean for me?

"I didn't know that powers could be transferred from one person to another," I said.

"Oh, yes," she said. "It's one power most of the Summer Court have access to. I couldn't take it from you without your permission, of course. Not without breaking the rules, anyway.

But you can give it to me as a gift. And in return, I can open a portal to the past."

"How would that work?" I asked. "I would never have visions again?"

"No, the ability would be gone from you forever," she said. "And, of course, any visions you've already had would no longer be guaranteed."

My eyes widened, and I stepped backward, my hand on my pocket.

Sabine raised an eyebrow and smiled. "May I see?"

She stretched a hand out to me, expectantly.

Not this. I can't.

Slowly, I reached into my pocket and withdrew the worn piece of paper I had carried with me for months. It was nearly falling apart now, the pencil markings slightly faded.

With a trembling hand, I held it out to her.

Like a giddy child, Sabine unfolded the paper and studied it.

"Oh, my," she said. "This is quite the choice for you, isn't it?"

"What do you mean?" I asked.

"If you walk away from me, refusing to give me what I ask, this future is still guaranteed to you," she said. "Your visions always come true eventually, right?"

I nodded. "Sometimes they're different from what I've drawn," I said. "Or rather, I should say, sometimes I interpret the images wrong. It isn't always as it seems."

"But it's always true," she said. "So, if you leave without my help, someday, the two of you will sit in this garden as King and Queen, your child playing in the grass like one big happy family."

She placed a finger to her cheek.

"On the other hand, without my help, Harper may never get home," she said. "She's trapped in the past now with no portal back except through the dungeon of the amethyst priestess. That's if Priestess Black allows her to live at all. So, what do you do? Do you walk away and trust that you've interpreted this vision correctly? Or do you risk it all for the chance to save her yourself?"

She handed the drawing back to me, and I ran my thumb along the image.

How many times in the past few months had I looked to this drawing for hope? How many nights had I stayed awake, dreaming of this future?

Giving it up seemed impossible.

But at the same time, what if Sabine was right? What if I had misinterpreted this vision all along? What if, like my nightmare here in the swamp, there were shadows surrounding us even there?

I had always imagined this would be our life once the Order was defeated. I thought it was promised to us.

But what if I was wrong? What if we were only guaranteed this one happy moment before it all disappeared?

Was I willing to give up the guarantee of that one moment in time?

But then I thought of the assassins hunting her down. Torturing her. Even if I managed to save her in some other way, what more would she have to endure just so I could hold onto a moment I didn't even fully understand?

My entire life, my visions had been a part of me. When the rest of my magic had been taken from me by the Order and placed in the statue, these visions were the one thing I still had that were mine. To part with them would be like giving up a piece of myself.

I folded the paper again and handed it back to Sabine, my decision made.

"Are you certain?" she asked. "There's no going back once the transfer is complete."

"I'm certain," I said.

I didn't need a piece of paper to tell me that Harper and I were meant to be together. That we were meant to live a happy life beyond the darkness of the Order's tyranny.

All I needed was her.

Sabine climbed down from her cloud and placed a hand on my forehead. My eyes closed as she whispered words in a tongue I didn't recognize. Something tugged inside me, pulling and stretching as it flowed up from my core. It didn't hurt. Not exactly. But it pained me to lose something I had held so dear.

When the transfer was complete, Sabine stepped away and nodded.

"Thank you for this gift," she said. "Once the portal is opened, you will have twenty-four hours to return before it disappears."

"The amethyst priestess has a head start on me by nearly a day," I said. "What happens if they've already taken her?"

Sabine smiled. "To make it interesting, I'll send you back to almost the same exact moment I sent them," she said.

"Almost?" I asked.

"It wouldn't be as interesting if I didn't give them a tiny head start," she said. "Let us see if love truly does conquer all."

My heart raced, but I would not complain. She was giving me a chance, and that would have to be enough.

"I wish you strength and good fortune on your journey,"

she said. "You have a good heart, Jackson. I hope we meet again someday."

She stepped back and removed a single rose from her dress. She held it in her hand and whispered into it. When she set it down on the grass at my feet, a light shone forth, rising into the sky before feathering out to form a perfect oval made of shimmering light.

"Your twenty-four hours starts now," she said.

I nodded and stepped through the portal, determined not to come back until Harper was at my side once again.

THE DREAM SLIPPED AWAY

LEA

I raced down the steps of the arena's prison, Ezrah's keys jingling in my hands.

Aerden lay sleeping on a small bed in the farthest cell, some restless dream tensing his features. He opened his eyes as the cell door swung open, and I rushed into his arms.

"What's going on?" he asked, holding me tight against him.

"We're leaving," I said. "Ezrah's getting your axe. He'll be waiting for us in the arena. Andros is on his way here right now with half the Resistance Army."

He shook his head. "Please, tell me I'm not still dreaming."

I smiled. "You're not dreaming," I said. "Let's go."

I grabbed his hand, and together, we raced through the long hallway of the cell block and up through the ready room to the arena's beyond.

But the moment we stepped onto the battlefield, I stopped cold, the smile wiped off my face in an instant and replaced with a gasp of horror.

Kael stood in the center of the dusty floor, a large sword in his hand. At least twenty guards stood behind him, one of them holding Ezrah in a set of thick chains. Another was holding Aerden's axe.

"I warned you, Princess," Kael said. "Betray me again, and I would make you watch everyone you ever loved die before your eyes. Why don't we start with him?"

He pointed his sword toward Aerden, but I stepped in front of him, my head held high.

"I know who you are," I said. "You're nothing but a thief. A lapdog for the High Priestess, sent here to do her dirty work and hold my father prisoner. Let us go, or you will die here tonight. I promise you that."

The guards behind Kael backed away from him slightly, their eyes full of questions. Beside me, Aerden's mouth hung open in shock.

"See? Deep down, even your guards know the truth about you," I said. "No one rises to power this quickly without some kind of deception. You and your priestess preyed on my father's love for me and for his people, twisting it and manipulating him. You stole his power, and you made me doubt him. But I know the truth now. After tonight, the entire city will know what you are. Do you think they'll still want you for their king?"

Kael's eyes flashed with a strange white light, and he turned on his own guards.

"Do not believe her lies," he said. "Seize them. They are both traitors to the crown, condemned to death by the council."

But the guards made no move toward us.

"Do you really think they would trust you over their own princess?" Aerden asked.

"Was I talking to you?" Kael asked, pointing his sword toward Aerden again. "You will speak when spoken to, prisoner."

"I am no prisoner," he said, stepping forward, his eyes seeking out those of King's Guard. Without their strength, Kael would never be able to defeat us. "I am Aerden, Son of Walther. I am The One Who Returned. I spent a hundred years as a slave to the Order of Shadows, and I returned to this city only to be labeled a traitor and forced to fight here in the games. Those of you who were here for the tournament this morning saw the true nature of the demon who stands before you, claiming to be your future king. He commissioned these games so he could watch me die. When I won the first round, he slipped illegal potions to my opponents. Is this a demon you would call your king? Or will you believe the princess's words and see him for the traitor he is?"

Some of the guards lowered their weapons, their eyes wide with fear and confusion.

"When I trained to become a member of the King's Guard as a shadowling, it was a title given with honor," he said. "Only the truest, most fearless warriors won the right to protect this kingdom. I know you are honorable men with strong hearts. I know you hear our words and recognize their truth."

"Enough," Kael shouted. "I command you to take these traitors into the dungeons. If you do not obey this command, I will have each of you beheaded. If you have families in this city, I will seek them out and parade them through the streets so that everyone can see their shame. I will have them thrown from the gates of the city where they will no longer be under the protection of their king."

I put a hand on my bow, bringing it down by my side. If I could just convince the guards of his treason, I could take my shot.

"This man is no king," I said. "He rules with threats, just like the Order of Shadows. He is the one who should be put in chains."

Two of the guards near the front exchanged looks, but no one moved.

Kael turned on us, his eyes again flashing with that strange white light. I had never seen a demon's eyes do that before, and it chilled me to the core.

"Fine, if I can't trust my guards, I will seize them myself," he said.

"Don't move," a woman's voice said, stopping Kael in his tracks.

I looked toward the prima cavea to see my mother and father standing near the thrones, the light of two moons shining on them.

"Mother?"

She looked at me, an apology in her eyes as she ripped the golden chain from her neck and threw it into the dust below.

"Guards, as your king, I command you to seize this demon and have him brought to the lower level of the castle's dungeons until he can be brought to trial for these accusations," my father said.

Kael's face wrinkled in horror. His chest rose and fell with heavy, labored breaths.

"You?" he asked. "After everything I have done? This is how you reward me?"

The king did not respond. His eyes turned to the guards, and they raced forward, chains in hand.

Kael gripped his sword tighter in his hand, an angry roar sounding deep in his chest. His eyes exploded with light, and the ground at his feet rumbled.

I grabbed Aerden's hand and stepped back as the demon's body transformed.

Terrified, I shouted to my parents. "Run! Get back to the castle. Now."

Kael's hands solidified into pure stone that traveled up his arms and neck, down his torso and legs. He expanded, rising into the air like a mountain. His clothes ripped from his body, and there, standing before me, was the Stone Guardian Andros had warned us about, a towering creature with stones for eyes and a glittering diamond for a heart.

THOSE UNSPOKEN WORDS

AERDEN

With a single sweep of his hand, the Stone Guardian took out half a dozen guards, their bodies crushed and motionless on the field of battle.

"Get your axe," Lea shouted to me.

"I won't leave your side," I said.

She conjured a set of three arrows and let them fly toward the guardian. The arrows seemed to bounce off its hard skin, and she cursed.

"Aerden, if you don't get that axe right now, we'll both die," she said. "I'll keep this thing distracted."

There was no arguing with her when she spoke in that tone, and despite our current situation, I realized how much I had missed seeing Lea, the warrior. I thought of all our training sessions in the woods late at night back at Brighton Manor, before everything went to hell. This would be just like old times, only with a much more terrifying opponent.

As she conjured another set of arrows, I shifted and flew toward the place where my axe had fallen in the chaos. The guards were doing their best to fight, but several more had fallen to the guardian's blows. I searched for any sign of Ezrah, but I didn't see him anywhere. With him bound in chains that prevented him from casting magic, he was useless to us anyway. I only hoped he had made it out of here safely.

I wrapped my hand around the hilt of my axe and shifted just as the Stone Guardian's foot stomped down on where I had just been standing.

When I reformed at Lea's side, I shook my head. "Yeah, great job keeping it distracted," I said. "That thing almost crushed me."

"So, pay more attention next time," she said, the flush of battle on her cheeks. "My arrows aren't hurting it. Not even my armor-piercing spell seems to make a dent."

"Watch and learn," I said, raising my axe in the air.

I shifted to smoke and flew around the guardian's back, reforming just as I let the heavy axe swing. I aimed for the back of its knee, sure that a strong swing would at least do some damage to the creature.

Instead, the blade hit stone and reverberated back toward me, flying out of my grip and out of reach.

The guardian reached back with one mighty hand and swiped me to the side. Pain exploded behind my eyes as I flew across the field and slammed into the wall of the arena.

"Aerden," Lea shouted.

I raised my thumb to let her know I was okay, but I was going to need a second to regroup. This creature was far more powerful than I could have imagined. If our weapons were doing nothing against it, the only option we had was to try our magic.

The last of the guards still standing screamed as the Stone Guardian lowered its foot onto the demon's back. I stared in awe. These were the best fighters in the kingdom. Heroes. And they had been crushed in minutes.

Across the field, Lea flew out of the guardian's reach and reformed near me, a stack of six flaming arrows nocked and ready to fly. "I'm going for that diamond," she shouted. "If we can damage that, maybe he will fall."

She let go, and the arrows all soared straight toward the creature's heart. He managed to deflect three of them with his hand, but the other three met their mark. Still, the arrows seemed to do no damage.

"Shit," she said. "What do we do?"

The guardian ran toward us. Each footstep shook the floor of the arena like an earthquake.

"Run," I said.

We both shifted and flew in opposite directions. Thanks to the guardian's massive size, he was too slow to reach us in time, but how long could we keep this up? We couldn't simply shift and run every time it headed toward us. Eventually, we would have to figure out a way to hurt him if we ever had any hope of winning this fight.

When I reformed on the other side of the arena, I summoned my magic, surprised to find it strong and flowing through me as if I had never lost my connection to it. My hands exploded into flames that rose high against the night sky.

I inhaled, drawing the power deep into myself before thrusting my hands toward the ground. A line of flames travelled over the floor of the arena toward the Stone Guardian.

When the fire reached him, I stood, lifting my hands high into the air. The flames roared to life, consuming his body.

The Stone Guardian stepped out of the fire, soot darkening its alabaster skin, but there was no sign of a wound.

The creature smiled, taunting me.

He raised his hands into the air and slammed them down, hard and fast. The ground split in two, the earthquake knocking me off my feet and nearly sending me into a deep chasm that formed in the center of the battlefield. I pulled myself up, and reached for my axe.

Maybe this would crack that stone in its heart.

"Pelt him with arrows," I shouted toward Lea on the other side of the chasm.

"It won't do any good," she said. "They're totally useless against him."

"It will keep him busy for a second," I shouted. "Just don't hit me."

She nodded and took a deep breath, nocking her first arrow and letting it fly toward the guardian.

He lifted his hands in defense and started running toward her, all his attention on Lea for the moment. I took my chance, shifting and flying through the air toward the beast. I kept my eye on the diamond in its chest, and when I got close enough, I spun three times to build momentum and reformed during the final spin, putting all of my strength behind the attack.

The blade of my mighty axe chipped a tiny piece off the guardian's heart, and the creature wailed, slamming its shoulder into my side. I fell to the ground, pain rolling through me in wave after wave.

My vision blurred, and for a moment, I was terrified I

might lose consciousness, but somehow, I managed to fight it, shifting just as the guardian brought his foot down.

I reformed near the wall, holding onto it to steady myself. The guardian reached down and scooped a chunk of earth from the arena floor and threw it at me before I had time to shift, knocking me back down.

My ears rang, and I struggled to stay present. My stomach rolled and tightened, but I tried to stand. Instead, I took one small step and fell to the ground in a heap of pain.

I had to get up. Lea couldn't fight this thing on her own.

I blinked, watching as the Stone Guardian placed its fingers end-to-end, a bright light forming between them like a globe. I forced myself to stand. The buzz of the guardian's energy made my teeth rattle, and I squinted against the light.

I reached for my magic, focusing on creating a shield around my body, but before the guardian unleashed its spell, he smiled and turned, hurling it toward Lea.

Time slowed as the spell flew through the air. I saw every chance I'd ever had to tell her how I felt pass before my eyes. Every day we trained out on the Black Cliffs, the sun on our faces, our hearts open to the wild possibilities of an endless future.

Every breath of every moment leading up to the days of her engagement, when she would be promised to another.

The endless nights at Brighton Manor as we trained, two broken souls searching for something to live for.

That night by the fire, my hands in her hair as it fell around her face, the truth a whisper on my lips.

I stretched my hands toward her now, the thought of losing her tearing down the walls of fear I'd hid behind for more than a century. All those unspoken words burst from my heart, ripping me open as I screamed her name.

Her eyes widened as a being made of pure, golden light formed before her, its hand reaching out to crush the guardian's spell. The being stepped forward at my command, towering over the battlefield with the strength and brilliance of a thousand stars.

It grabbed the Stone Guardian by the throat and slammed it onto the ground, pinning it down. I took my axe in my hand, walked over to the creature who had threatened the one woman I would ever love, and with a single, swift movement, I broke its diamond heart into a million pieces.

When I looked at Lea, she fell to her knees, her eyes locked on that light.

My truth.

My deepest secret.

My greatest love.

She finally knew.

I DIDN'T KNOW MY OWN HEART

LEA

Tears rolled down my cheeks as my knees hit the ground.

How had I been so blind?

All this time, I'd been chasing that one moment in the veil when that locket opened and the most brilliant light I'd ever seen spilled forth like a dream. It was the happiest moment of my life, but it was a moment I never truly understood until now.

Sobs shook my body as I cried for all those years of heartache. Misunderstanding. All those nights spent wondering how such true love could disappear in an instant.

But it was right here in front of me the whole time.

Aerden stood like a giant on the chest of the Stone Guardian, the light of his love dissipating at his side.

He came to me, a question in his eyes. But I had questions of my own.

He knelt in front of me, his heart at my feet.

"Why didn't you tell me?" I asked. "Do you know how hard this has been for me all these years?"

His bottom lip trembled as his eyes filled with tears. "I know," he said. "I was a fool. I was afraid."

"How long?" I asked. "How long have you felt this way?"

"For as long as I have lived," he said.

I closed my eyes, trying to make sense of the hurricane in my heart.

"The locket?" I asked.

"I knew I couldn't have you, but I wanted you to know how dearly you were loved," he said. "I wanted you to understand the depth of it. All I wanted was for you to be happy."

I sat back, placing a hand on my chest, as if the locket were still there after all this time. "That locket was my greatest joy, and my darkest pain," I said, looking into his eyes. "I don't know what to do."

He placed his hands on my face, and I reached up to hold his wrists, uncertain if I wanted to pull him closer or push him away.

"Forgive me," he said. "I made a terrible mistake. One we have both paid for over the past hundred years. I can't change what I did, but I promise I will spend the rest of my life making it up to you. Please, forgive me."

My eyes searched his, desperate for answers. For understanding. I didn't know my own heart. I had spent so many years loving Jackson. Cursing him for showing me his love and then taking it away.

That light had made me love him, but it had never been his to give in the first place.

Where could we go from here? How could I possibly

forgive Aerden for those years of unyielding, life-shattering pain? Those years of doubting everything, including myself?

Yet, how could I deny the truth pounding through my heart at the touch of his skin on mine?

I could not walk away from this moment, letting him believe he was alone.

"Those years after you left changed me," I said. "My pain changed me. I can't simply forget all of that and go back to that shadowling who danced in the sunlight and laughed without a worry in her heart. If that's the girl you fell in love with—"

"I love you," he said, his hands buried in my hair. "Not some distant idea of who you used to be. I love everything about you, and even if there is no hope that you could ever feel the same way, I will never stop loving you the way I do right now."

I kissed him, then, my heart overruling my mind and my doubts. My questions disappeared as my arms found their way around his neck, pulling him closer, tasting his lips for the first time.

The emotion that poured from me as my heart finally opened to the truth terrified me, but there would be time for fear later. Right now, I wanted to feel his hands on me. His heart pounding against my own.

Two warriors, fresh from battle, getting their first glimpse of home.

THE ONLY THING THAT'S REAL

HARPER

I dreamed of home, but I woke to the pain of being dragged down the hallway to my death.

I struggled against the ropes that bound my arms and legs, but the witch standing over me laughed.

"You'll only tire yourself out, dear," she said. "Those ropes are unbreakable, sealed with a magic so dark, you'll never break free."

I closed my eyes and begged for my magic to come. Nothing was unbreakable. There had to be a way.

But whatever magic held me also blocked my power. I tried to think of another way, twisting my arms to try to reach the bindings.

The witch brought a boot down on my temple, nearly knocking me unconscious again.

Just a few more steps, and we would reach the staircase leading up to the third floor. No doubt they had found another way to conjure a portal, and once they took me through, I would be in the hands of the amethyst priestess.

Judging from the power and strength of her assassins, she would not be an easy witch to kill. After last night's battle against the Others, I wasn't sure I would have the strength, anyway.

All I needed was to find a way out of this rope. Without my power, I was helpless against them.

But just as we reached the bottom of the narrow staircase, a bright light appeared below us on the first floor. I couldn't see what was happening from where I lay against the cold hardwood floor. Had Brooke come back for me?

"Go see who that is," the witch dragging me shouted. One of the other witches nodded and ran down the steps to investigate. "Whoever it is, kill them quickly. We don't have much time. The fairy only gave us an hour."

Fairy?

I thought of Azure and the strange woman I'd met at the club that day. What did they have to do with this? Had the fairy opened this portal for them? Had she betrayed me?

Azure would never do such a thing, but there had definitely been something strange about the other one. Sabine. The way she had looked at me, as if she knew a secret she couldn't wait to tell.

Sounds of a struggle down below made the witches stop cold. They turned toward the steps just as someone appeared.

Tears blinded my vision, and I blinked several times, sure that I must be dreaming.

Jackson stood at the top of the steps, an amethyst collar clutched in one hand. His eyes met mine, and one side of his mouth curled into a half-smile that made my heart race.

He threw the collar to the floor and lifted his hand to form a shield against the magic the witches threw at him. The spell exploded in a burst of light, its energy dissipating well before it reached him.

He wasted no time firing back, conjuring spears made of pure, blue ice. The first one sliced through the neck of the witch behind me, and she fell to the floor like a ragdoll.

His second spear was aimed directly at me. I lowered my head as the pointed tip slashed through the black ropes, freeing me from its trap. I quickly reached for my magic and shifted just as the witch who'd been dragging me slammed the tip of her dagger into the floor, missing me by millimeters.

I reformed several feet behind her down the hallway and held out my hand, summoning her dagger toward me. The witch lost her grip on the weapon and immediately reached for her power. Bright violet light exploded from her hands, but I knew that trick.

I closed my eyes against the light and shifted again to smoke, flying toward her and reforming just in time to drive the tip of her own dagger through her heart from behind. I lifted my foot and pushed her forward. The wound in her back made a sucking sound as her body slid off the blade and fell to the floor.

Movement out of the corner of my eye made me turn, just in time to see one of the two remaining witches lunge toward me, purple flames covering her hands.

Jackson placed his palm on the floor and blue ice quickly travelled from his hand to the witch, crawling up her leg and torso until she was encased in it. I focused all of my power on her, lifting my hands into the air, commanding her body to rise off the floor. With one strong gesture, I threw her off the balcony, where she shattered on the hard floor below.

The final witch standing between us ran toward the stairs in a desperate attempt to call for help from whoever waited above, but Jackson covered the doorway in a sheet of ice, blocking her exit.

She backed away from the door, glancing toward the balcony as if she were trying to decide whether to jump or fight.

I didn't give her time to choose.

Without hesitation, I spun once, driving the dagger into the side of her neck.

The final witch fell in a heap on the floor, and I nearly fell to my knees in disbelief. Joy. Exhaustion.

Tears flowed down my cheeks as Jackson ran to me, pulling me into his arms and lifting my feet off the ground. He covered me in kisses, and I held tight to him, hardly able to believe he was here.

"Is this real?" I asked, taking his head in my hands as he looked at me.

"This is the only thing that's real," he said.

I kissed him, drunk on happiness as his lips met mine. We had months to make up for. Decades. I clung to him like life itself, one touch of his lips healing me from the inside out. Every touch of his hands baptizing me with love.

I wanted to laugh and cry all at the same time. I wanted to tell him everything, and I wanted to say nothing so that our lips would never have to part again.

His hands dug into my hair and pulled me closer, only nothing was close enough.

I could have stayed in that moment forever, but the sound

of the front door opening pulled us apart. I reached for the dagger on the floor, and Jackson's hands turned to ice.

"Harper?"

I leaned over the balcony to find Brooke standing in the foyer, a small army of girls from the institute standing in the doorway and on the porch outside. Some of them held spells hovering in the air above their hands, as if they had come here looking for a fight.

"Brooke?" Jackson asked. "Is that you?"

She laughed and threw her hands into the air, spinning around like a schoolgirl. "You found us," she said. "But how?"

"It's a long story," he said, putting his arm around me and pulling me closer. "One I'd rather tell from a different decade, if you don't mind."

Brooke smiled as Mary Ellen stepped forward and took her hand.

"I don't mind that one bit," she said.

Jackson and I descended the stairs together, and Brooke ran forward, pulling us both into a giant hug.

"Are the girls..."

"Healed," Brooke said, taking my hand. "Harper, even the ones who were lobotomized. Rend's potions were a miracle. You have to thank him for me."

I smiled. "As soon as we get home, you can thank him yourself. But how did you get to everyone so quickly?" I asked. "You couldn't have been gone for more than half an hour."

"By the time I got to the hospital, almost everyone had been discharged," she said. "Each time a girl was awakened, she took a potion and helped to awaken someone else. There are only a handful of girls still coming. I saw James at the hospital, and he said he'd bring them as soon as he could."

I sighed, releasing the tension and worry I'd been holding inside for so long.

We sent the girls through first, and waited until James arrived with the rest. I checked them off on the list the nurse had given me, making sure we didn't leave anyone behind. Jackson kept his eye on the portal on the third floor, keeping the room filled with ice so that no one else could get through.

Later, when the final girl had been sent through the portal back to the present, Jackson kissed my forehead, and I snuggled closer to him, breathing in the scent of him.

"Take me home," I whispered.

And together, we walked out of the darkest place I'd ever known and stepped through a portal made of pure light.

TO HELL AND BACK

HARPER

I could only imagine what it must have looked like when a hundred people walked out of the swamp that day. The look on John Pierce's face said it all. Shock. Victory. Courage.

With his help, we arranged transportation home for each of the girls who felt they still had a home to go to. The others were offered a home with us in the domed city.

Nora, Mary Ellen, Brooke, Robin, and ten others chose to stay and fight beside us against the Order. We rented the largest van we could find and made the journey back to Peachville where we walked out to the lake and disappeared through the portal made of white roses. A tribute to a mother, I would never know.

Mary Anne welcomed me home by nearly tackling me in the garden the moment I stepped into the Shadow World. We held onto each other as if I'd been gone for years instead of months.

When we parted, she smiled and pressed something into my hand.

A ring. The missing piece of the puzzle to free the emerald gates, at last.

I untied the strip of cloth on my thigh and held up the master stone, the one thing that made all the other struggles disappear. The one thing that made it all worth it.

My sister, Angela, ran from the castle and threw her arms around me, spinning me around like a little girl.

"I missed you so much," she said, planting a kiss on my forehead.

"I missed you, too."

When I turned, I noticed a demon standing in the shadows, watching. He smiled at me, and I took off at a run, throwing my arms around his neck.

"Thank you, Rend," I said.

"We did it together," he said. "I missed you while you were gone."

"I would say I missed you, too, but I just saw you a couple of days ago," I said.

"It's been a bit longer for me, but I've been meaning to apologize for that thing in the alley," he said. "You know, with the fangs."

I threw my head back and laughed, the sound almost foreign to my ears, but welcome to my heart. I shoved him playfully. "Yeah, you owe me one," I said. "Or actually, I owe Azure. Is she here?"

"She's inside," he said. "Come on, we've got a surprise waiting for you."

Once I'd said hello to everyone, we settled down to a huge feast at the castle. Ryder, the young shadowling we'd once saved from poverty in the borderlands sat on my lap the entire time, telling me stories about the city and giggling with happiness as he opened gifts the citizens of the domed city had brought for me.

I was overjoyed to see everyone, but Jackson kept catching my eye, and I knew exactly what he was thinking. We needed time alone together. To talk. To heal. To just be.

When the feast was over and most of the villagers had returned to their homes, Jackson and I linked arms and headed toward the stairs that led up to my chambers.

"We have so much to talk about," he said.

I placed a finger over his lips, and he ran his hands down my arms, caressing the scars that marked my journey to hell and back.

"No talking tonight," I said.

Jackson gathered me into his arms and carried me over the threshold, as if we were newlyweds coming back from a wedding rather than warriors coming back from the darkness.

He locked the door behind him and carried me to bed.

THE PROMISE OF PEACE

HARPER

When we finally emerged from our little cocoon, I was eager to explore the domed city and find out everything that had happened while I was away.

I also couldn't wait to get to Cypress for the ritual today. Eloise and her daughters would soon be free. It was finally coming together. Hopefully, Lea and Aerden would be home soon, too, and we could all celebrate the death of another priestess and the joy of coming home.

As I walked down the stairs, though, I heard someone shouting from the streets. I moved faster, afraid of another attack so soon. We deserved some peace, and I wasn't sure my heart could take more bad news.

"What is it?" Gregory asked, his voice ringing out through the throne room.

A guard came rushing up the steps of the castle, out of breath and wide-eyed with terror and confusion.

"What happened?" I asked.

Jackson ran to my side, the same fear of bad news reflected in his eyes.

"Someone's at the front gate of the dome," the young guard said. His mouth fell open, as if he couldn't believe what he was about to say. "A woman in a red dress. She claims to be the ruby priestess. That can't be true, can it?"

Gregory's face drained of color. "Is she alone?" he asked.

"Yes, she's all by herself, saying she wants to talk to Harper."

"Why would she be here?" Jackson asked, stepping in front of me. Always my protector.

I placed a hand on his arm. "I think I know," I said, surprise and confusion stirring in my heart. "I honestly didn't think she'd honor her promise."

"Promise?" Jackson asked, running after me as I walked down the steps and through the middle of the city toward the front gate. "What's going on?"

"When she came to see me at Priestess Evers' house the night of the fire, she told me that if I somehow managed to make it home alive, she would surrender herself to me," I said. "I never in a million years thought she meant it."

"Wait," Jackson said, taking my arm and pulling me back. "We can't trust her, Harper. She could be coming here to attack us."

"What can she do to us here?" I asked, motioning to the dome above our heads. "She's alone. As long as the dome is intact, no human witch can cast here in the city. Her magic will be useless."

"I still don't like the idea of inviting her in," he said. "This is a priestess we're talking about."

"She warned me about the trap her sister set for you," I said. "You wouldn't be standing here if it wasn't for her. She was telling me the truth then. Maybe we should listen to what she has to say. I think she's scared they're really going to lose this war. If she's willing to switch sides, she could give us valuable information. The location of the other priestesses. The identity of the High Priestess herself. This entire thing could be over in a matter of weeks with her help. We have to at least talk to her."

Jackson ran a nervous hand through his hair and sighed.

"Okay, but we put her in the dungeons," he said. "We have a guard stationed with her at all times. We bind her hands so that she can't cast. We take every precaution."

I nodded. "This could be a real turning point for us, Jackson," I said, walking faster now that the woman in red was visible in the distance.

"I hope you're right," he mumbled.

When we reached her, the ruby priestess began to clap. She shook her head and smiled at me.

"Bravo, dear girl," she said. "I knew the moment I first laid eyes on you that you were special. I never dreamed you'd really find your way home once that portal closed, but I made a promise to you that night that I intend to honor."

"How do I know I can trust you?" I asked.

She shrugged. "How do we ever really know we can trust anyone?"

"That's not an answer," Jackson said.

Gregory joined us at the gate, his face still white as a sheet. This wasn't the first priestess he'd encountered, and I was sure he didn't exactly have fond memories of his torture at the hands of Priestess Winter.

"If you'll give me the chance, I will prove my loyalty," the priestess said. "I know that it will take time, but like I said, I never like to be on the losing side. I'd like to figure out a way to survive this war, and I'm not going to do it as your enemy."

"You'll have to live in the dungeons if you want to stay here," Jackson said. "It won't be comfortable for you after the life of luxury I'm sure you're accustomed to back home."

"I'm sure I'll manage," she said with a shrug. "Your dungeons are bound to be much nicer than the ones my sister Gladys would put me in if she found out I'd come here."

Jackson looked at me, and I nodded.

Yes, we were taking a huge risk by bringing her into the city, but as long as we got her safely locked away in the dungeons, she would be powerless to make a move. She was, after all, trusting us not to rip her heart out for the sake of freeing the ruby gates. She'd come alone, bearing gifts that we simply couldn't afford to refuse.

"Follow me, then," I said, inviting her into the city.

The three of us escorted her up to the castle and then down several flights of stairs to the dungeons below. I was surprised to find so many of them full of witches. I raised a curious eye toward Jackson, and he shrugged.

"We have a lot to talk about," he said. "Let's take her to the lower dungeon. There's no one else down there."

The lower dungeons were hardly ever used, but they were just as secure. I couldn't imagine she would be comfortable here, but maybe once she'd truly proven herself, we could figure out something better. A set of rooms with a special lock on the door or a barrier spell, maybe.

But first, she'd have to give us enough information to make it worth the risk.

I motioned for Gregory to open the first cell, and he nodded, taking out a set of keys and placing one in the lock. These cells were made of a special, imbued form of demon steel my father had commissioned from a powerful demon who was a genius at traps and prisons.

We'd imprisoned hunters and witches down here for years with no incidents, and I knew that once the priestess was safely locked inside, she was harmless.

When the door was open, the ruby priestess walked inside without hesitation. She ran her hand along the steel as she walked to the back of the cell and sat down on a wooden stool, the sole piece of furniture in the entire room.

Gregory shut the door of the cell, and I let out of sigh of relief.

I didn't fully understand it, but if her presence here helped us end the Order, I didn't need to understand it. If she didn't prove useful in the next few days, or if she showed any signs of betraying us, we could have her killed.

"If you'll excuse me, we have something else we need to do," I said, anxious to get to Cypress. "We'll be back tonight to talk through the terms of our agreement. Do any of your sisters know where you are?"

"I certainly hope not," she said with a smile, smoothing out her skirt. "To be honest, I'm hoping I can give you whatever information will help you win this war while still keeping me alive, and then I can be on my way before anyone realizes I'm gone."

"We'll be back soon," I said.

"Don't let her out of your sight," Jackson said to Gregory. "If you have to leave, make sure to send another guard to take your place immediately. And don't open that cell under any circumstances."

"Yes, sir," Gregory said.

Jackson placed his hand on Gregory's arm. "I'm counting on you."

We made our way back up the stairs toward the portal of roses, our hearts full and the promise of peace on the horizon.

EPILOGUE

GREGORY

Silently, I followed Harper and Jackson through the castle, careful to stay far enough back that they wouldn't see me.

I watched from around the corner as they disappeared through the rose portal. I closed my eyes and pressed my head against the cool, smooth stone of the archway.

I didn't want to do this.

I let my hand fall on the hilt of the sword at my side. I still had a choice, didn't I?

But was death really a choice?

I pretended to be brave, rushing into battle when adrenaline was high, but here, in the light of day, I saw myself as I truly was.

A coward of the worst kind.

A traitor.

Death was a choice for the honorable, but I had faced death once, and I hadn't liked the look of it.

Now, it was time to pay for the gift of my life.

Slowly, I made my way back down to the dungeons, taking my time to draw out the inevitable, still hoping I might be brave enough to make a different choice. But I was who I was, and my choice had been made a long time ago in a dungeon much like this one.

"There you are," the ruby priestess said, her voice purring with confidence. "I was wondering when you'd return. Have they gone?"

I lowered my head, hating myself.

"Yes. I don't think they'll be coming home any time soon," I said.

"And everyone else in the castle has joined them for this ritual?" she asked.

I nodded. The castle was deserted.

"Good," she said, resting her arms on the bars of her cell. "I knew when I saved you from the dungeon at Winterhaven that your loyalty would come to good use someday. Now, be a good boy, Gregory, and let me out of this cage. It's damp in here, and I've never liked damp places."

My hand trembled as I reached for my keys. One last chance to refuse her. To make another choice.

But I had made a deal with the devil that day when she'd found me hanging there in one of Priestess Winters' cages, my life nearly depleted. It seemed almost harmless at the time. A single favor in return for an entire lifetime.

I'd convinced myself I'd never see her again. It had felt like an empty promise, something so ethereal and distant compared to the imminence of death.

Once freed, the ruby priestess had cast a spell on me, binding me to my promise. If she asked me for this favor and I refused, my greatest fear would come true. I would be locked away in the body of a witch, forever.

One small favor.

I never dreamed it would turn out to be this. To betray my queen and the memory of her father, whom I had served loyally for a lifetime.

But still, I was not ready to die.

I slid the key into the lock and turned, opening the door.

"My debt is paid," I said.

Magda Thorn, the ruby priestess of the Order of Shadows, stepped out of the cell and patted me on the shoulder. She smiled and lifted a hand to touch the ruby snake pendant hanging from a chain around her neck.

"We'll see about that, dear," she said, sending a ripple of fear and instant regret through my soul.

As she walked up the steps to the main part of the castle, I slid down the bars of the cell until I hit the floor. I lowered my head into my hands, and with the soul of a coward, I began to cry.

ABOUT THE AUTHOR

Sarra Cannon is the author of several series featuring young adult and college-aged characters, including the bestselling Shadow Demons Saga. Her novels often stem from her own experiences growing up in the small town of Hawkinsville, Georgia, where she learned that being popular always comes at a price and relationships are rarely as simple as they seem.

Sarra recently celebrated eight years in indie publishing and has sold over half a million copies of her books. She currently lives in Charleston, South Carolina with her programmer husband and adorable redheaded son.

Love Sarra's books? Join Sarra's Mailing List to be notified of new releases and giveaways!

Also, please come hang out with me in my Facebook Fan Group: Sarra Cannon's Coven. We have a lot of fun in there, and I often share exclusive short stories and teasers in the group. Join now.

Want more? Get insider information on my writing process, inspiration, and what it's like to be an author with weekly videos on my YouTube channel.

Connect With Sarra Online:
www.sarracannon.com

www.ingramcontent.com/pod-product-compliance
Lightning Source LLC
Chambersburg PA
CBHW051937240626
47153CB00005B/1532